UNCOMMON LANDS

P.K. TYLER   TOM O'BRIEN   RALPH WALKER

BEY DECKARD   KENNETH ROBBINS

MICHAEL K. SCHAEFER   ROSLYN CAY

CHRISTOPHER GODSOE   SHEBAT LEGION

DANIEL ARTHUR SMITH   JEREMY RODDEN

E.E. GIORGI   MICHAEL J.P. WHITMER

BRENT MESKE   TAUSHA JOHNSON   LEVI JACOBS

JON ETTER   ASHLEIGH GAUCH

Edited by
JESSICA WEST

Edited by
P.K. TYLER

STORY SUMMARIES

The Creaser by Tom O'Brien: Sea levels have risen around the world and with it new ways of living have to be found. In drowned London, a scavenger known only as The Diver has found the scent of magic by the coast and she means to make it hers.

Gators in Kansas and Other Hazards of Modern Farming by Ralph Walker: Sal has been working the farm for years to earn his stake, but rising water and invasive species threaten to take it all away.

Rakka Surprise by Bey Deckard: It was a simple task, a bit of diplomacy, on a new world for some blue bloods of the Polyverse Coalition. Unfortunately, Captain Drayan failed to read the fine print, the bits that put his sensory system into freefall. Good thing he had Sitik the Rakka, his first mate, to sort it all out. Except, that sorting led to more fine print and a Rakka surprise to end all surprises.

The Crater by Kenneth Robbins:: In the waning year of the American Civil War, the Union army outside Petersburg, VA, digs an impressive tunnel under the Confederate fortifications. They fill it with tons of explosives and detonate it. The chaos and confusion is immense. A Union officer sends an unnamed Private into the "crater" to assess the extent of the damage. The Private enters the smoke and haze. On the other side, he is transported to Hiroshima, Japan, on August 6, 1945, and what he witnesses confuses him. He must report back. He rushes through the mist toward the Union lines, but fails to share what he has seen.

Galileo's Dog by Karen Gemma Brewer: Two companions arrive on the Red Planet and set about their work like man and dog. Solar-powered Rover must slumber at nightfall, while his master toils on through the dark under battery power.

Exhibit D by Michael K. Schaefer: When Dale goes to sleep in a prison cell, he doesn't expect to wake up on top of an incredibly tall stone pillar. And he isn't alone: the pillar is just one of countless similar ones scattered across a long valley, and on many of them are other prisoners. Nobody knows how they got onto those pillars, why they are held there, and who is responsible for their unexpected relocation. It looks like Dale will have to spend the rest of his life in this strange place, when one day a man arrives and tells him of a way out he has never even dreamed of...

Ecumenical Outpost 732 by P.K. Tyler: Making friends is hard, especially when you live on a space station at the very end of the known universe. T'se's life is filled with questions, from what will happen to her in the future and who are the strange people who live on the prison planet covered in red dust out her window?

The Pillars of Theonasa by Roslyn Cay: The King of the Wind Demons ponders the phenomenon destroying his city.

The Rite by Christopher Godsoe: Nyla wakes up on her 18th birthday prepared to make the hardest choice of her life. Being an intelligent, well-educated young woman, she has spent plenty of time thinking about what she wants and has a plan. But even the best laid plans often go awry.

Silicon Oar by Shebat Legion: An entity struggles with the perception of illusion and memory.

Carcerem–A Spectral Worlds Story by Daniel Arthur Smith: There are worlds around us that we cannot see...and some we cannot escape. In the future, parallel planes of existence and their inhabitants have become known to humanity. These are the Spectral Worlds. Blitz's adventure occurs in the Prison Plane Carcerem, a gray shadow of the Alpha Plane's Nor East Meg, a mega-city of towering ziggurat structures. For most, a trip to Carcerem is one-way, but his custom-fitted cybernetics and reputation from the Spectral Wars have made him a candidate for an offer he cannot refuse.

Look for more adventures from Blitz in the Spectral Worlds series.

Somewhere I Belong by Jeremy Rodden: Toonopolis is a cartoon city that is home to the thoughts and ideas of all sentient beings in the universe. Angel comes into existence in the Tooniverse in a place she thinks is Toonopolis but quickly realizes she appeared in Ao, the adult section of the Tooniverse, instead. Follow her journey to right this wrong through such fantastical sections of Ao as Penisville and Hentaitown. Even if it means disobeying tahe will of her creator, Angel will find somewhere she belongs.

A Trap in Eshwar by E.E. Giorgi: After defecting his troops and leaking secret war plans to the enemy, Hyleesh escapes to the perfect hide-out: a ghost city at the bottom of the Tadhun Basin, one of the valleys on planet Eshwar that are completely submersed in toxic fog. He's pretty certain nobody can ever find him there until he receives a cryptic message: *I want to meet you.*

Dreamsolution by Michael J.P. Whitmer: Jesse discovers a mysterious website named Dreamsolution. Accepting a bargain without knowing what he has agreed to, Jesse embarks on dream-quest to save his fiancé, Heather, from her nightmares.

ConseQuent by Brent Meske: Somewhere in space and time, a civilization of poor, peaceful farmers live out their simple existences on floating rocks, where trade and news come in at times from the skyships and their skysailor crews. Yet one amongst them is an outsider, observing silently from the fringes. Who is this Watcher, and what designs does he have for the simple folk of the Vall?

Dragomir by Tausha Johnson: Dragomir has been warned to

avoid certain parts of the forest. The woods are full of wild beasts and monsters. But when he takes his sheep to feed then finds himself lost, Dragomir meets age old beliefs and superstition in the land beyond the forest.

The Last Immaculate by Levi Jacobs: On a simulated tropical island, accurate to the atomic level, people are being used as test subjects for genetic experiments in cancer research. Mei, angry about this treatment (including the deletion of her parents), plans to escape to the physical world with her boyfriend Oliver's help. Oliver, an administrator in the real world, is desperately in love with her, and trying to get her out before the island is restarted and all its inhabitants erased. Mei, meanwhile, gets embroiled in a plot to threaten the real world using altered DNA, and together they must find a solution that doesn't end in his world sick and hers erased, before the power struggle plays out.

Anderson's Necessaries by Jon Etter: Anderson's Necessaries, a five-and-dime store in the tiny town of Meadowbrook, has a habit of having everything the residents of the town need. However, when proprietor Earl "Andy" Anderson tries to find chalk for new schoolteacher Ruth Thatcher, the store knows what both of them really need.

No Small Favors by Anne Skinner: What would you sacrifice to have everything you could ever want? After Lucy Jones receives an invitation to the Room, she learns exactly what her limit is.

Walker Between the Worlds by Ashleigh Gauch: When

Shephard Mercer breaks the greatest law found in Haida shamanism and uses his powers for his own personal gain, his love Aria pays the price. Now he must go through live burial and a series of trials in the World Between to earn her soul back and prove himself worthy enough to return to the world of the living.

THE CREASER

BY TOM O'BRIEN

"So you swam London, Lady?" the broken tooth girl asked. Around us, the hum of the wind jinny faded and part of me started counting.

I did, I told her. "Every street that's under water in The City. All of Westminster. As far east as Canary Wharf. I dived from the dome of Saint Paul's the day after Tilbury dam broke. Found more scrap there than I ever did before or since."

Some of that was nearly true. I dived from the dome about a month after the dam burst and caught nothing but diarrhoea. But why spoil a little girl's illusion of the big city?

The lights of the eel house guttered off. Ten seconds. Always good to know.

"Lady, why would anyone come from London to Battery?" the girl asked from the gravy scented darkness.

Good question. But not one I was going to give a straight answer to. Many reasons. I had been politely asked to leave. If asked was ordered. If ordered was a threat.

With not much more than the diving board on my back, it had taken me the best part of a week to get to Battery. I hitched a battle barge from Chelsea, bodyguard to a grain merchant going back to

Wessex to pick up another load. The barge half full of scrap computers to make the journey pay, the other half stowaways he pretended not to know about.

Then I swam some, on a whim, to keep lean. That got me to the raised rail at Woking, which got me close to Winchester 'til a storm came up and the solar went down. After that, a 'borrowed' boat and a few more miles on the board, all the way to this nowhere on the edge of nowhere else.

As the lights spluttered back to life, I could see the real answer to the girl's question standing just past her shoulder. Well, I say standing but the crone who had just taken my bait had a spine like a hook. Her eyes had darted to the piece of paper under my pint glass. She couldn't help it if she tried. To a Creaser, paper is gold. And I can smell gold.

I swallowed a smile. I'd found my myth. There are some people who don't believe in magic. I'm not one of them. I hadn't travelled nearly 100 nauts on the back of a rumour of magic. I had travelled 100 nauts for the cold wet fact of magic.

A Creaser can fold something; paper, leather, cloth, whatever, with something else inside. A stone or a pea, a fly or a nail. Anything. And when they open it up, something else is in there. Like gold or a pearl.

I wouldn't have believed it if I hadn't seen it more than once. That's how it is. Something's impossible. Then it's done. Not impossible anymore.

People cope. They find what they need, where they need. England is a land of rice and fishes and I know it wasn't always that way. You grow what you can grow. Eat what you can catch. And make money out of creased paper if you can.

I hushed the kid away. Normally a mouth like that is worth giving chat to. They say more than they know, however smart they are, but I couldn't be distracted. She sulked as she went and tried to steal the dregs of my pint but I never took my eyes off my meal ticket, even while I cuffed the brat. The crone paid for her supplies in metal and cracked pearls. More proof than I needed.

I finished my drink, strapped on my board, and left before she did. If she took the sheet, I would make her use it to make my first nugget.

***

UNDER THE FISHEYE MOON, I sat on the pier, looking out at a grumpy sea.

Battery was the highest point for miles around. One of the few above water. North and South of it was nothing. East much the same, maybe some cropping. West, past the needles, nothing at all.

Not a lot made sense, since I hadn't seen the crone come in. But she didn't live here, I knew that. I would see her leave and follow her. If she wasn't wearing her home, she might be living in it or on it. A Creaser could be rich but they had to be careful, more than most. Careful of people like me, truth be told, but careful of those who wouldn't mind reviving witch drowning, too.

My days watching and waiting had told me a few things. Firstly, this town was a dump. In the evenings I played dice with the locals and won enough to eat the next day but not so much to be interesting. They fished, they drank, they mated and died, mostly in that order. Hard to tell what they lived on, harder again to tell why.

One night they argued about where we lost first to the melt. Norwich. Hull, Bristol? No one could remember but all agreed it was only when the melt started to nibble at London that anyone paid real attention. Too late, of course. The Thames Barrier was locked 'til it burst. By then the emergency dam at Tilbury was nearly built. Turns out the sea isn't impressed by nearly and blew it out of the way one November Wednesday. After that it was high ground or no ground.

So now the pumps were running twenty four seven and the government had relocated to Birmingham, as far from water as their dry little arses would carry them.

***

I WATCHED my Creaser haul her bag of provisions to a coracle dragged up against the sea wall, popping on the lively waves. She moved so slowly, with her slicker billowing, I had to fight the urge to go help her. She was no quicker getting into the little boat but finally, she was afloat, supplies covered in the slicker that was now a tarp.

I gave her a head start. I'd dropped my board to the water while I waited, toggle tied to my ankle. As I wondered what direction she'd take, the board tugged at me like a seal pup, eager to go. I slid on without making a ripple.

The Creaser was faster over water than land, surprisingly good with a paddle. But no match for me.

I paddled low and slow, down by the needles. By the time I saw where we were going, we were on top of it. The fins of rock that hid the old lighthouse were too thin to stand a man, never mind a house.

Crafty as a conger, my Creaser.

I lay still on the water while she pushed her tiny boat around the lamphouse, but as soon as she was out of sight, I hand paddled in. There must be a door of some sort and I couldn't afford to be too far behind.

My board rasped against the top apron of the lighthouse, but I wasn't worried about the sound. The crashing sea made more than enough noise to cover me. That and the fact I didn't care if she knew I was there or not.

She had led me to her nest. If this was where she lived, this was where she kept her homemade loot. This place would be out of sight on most tides, and left alone on any other. Just another freak construction from before the melt. The world was as flooded with them as with water.

I was ready for the catch. Not the kill. I would rinse a purse full of gold out of her before I brought her back to Shooter's Hill. There, she'd clear more than a few debts for me, whether I milked her dry myself or sold her on.

Up close, the glass was patterned in circles that must once have focussed the light in beams. Now they served to distort my view of the Creaser through the glass, a twisted silhouette against the white of a battering wave.

She was gone by the time I circled round but I saw the door. A whole circle of glass on a latch. I was growing more and more fond of the old dear. We were going to be great friends. I opened it and stepped inside. When it closed behind me, the silence was disorientating. I could see the waves roar outside even while I heard my breathing rasp.

The silence didn't last. It was replaced by the distinct thrum of a jinny down below. Must have been welcoming momma home. I ignored it.

I needed to find where she went. There had to be an opening somewhere, a trap door. She must have gone down into the lighthouse somehow. The huge lamp that would have filled this space was gone, but it had left no ruts behind, just a smooth floor. I knelt, running my hands over it. Touch often finds what the eye misses.

The noise of the jinny was drowned by a scream of gears. Much closer. Up here, not down below. I was beginning to not like that tune. Something else had changed. The glass walls were moving.

I don't know how long that took to register. Not long, but as soon as it did I darted back to the circular door I had come in through. It wasn't there anymore. The clip had slid behind another layer of glass and was sliding further.

The distorting circle over circle showed me two moons. What silly game was this? I threw my shoulder against the inches-thick glass but did nothing more than bounce off it.

The glass walls were already just two arm's length apart and closing. All right, old lady. Let's dance. I jumped to grab the top of a moving wall, to climb out of this trap.

Too high. Should have brought my board in. Vaulted up. I'd done it before. But my board was outside.

My body had an idea before I even thought of it. Let them get closer together. Then brace myself against each side to climb up. All I needed was a finger grip to haul myself up and out.

I crouched, my back against one moving wall of glass, waiting for the other to be close enough for me to push back against, shoving myself up.

Then I saw them. Outside. The Creaser and the broken tooth girl. The child was wrapped in the tarp from the coracle.

Gears tumbled in my brain. The girl here. How? Under the tarp, in the boat all along. Helping to row maybe. But why were they outside? Stupid bloody question. Inside was a cage. They had trapped me.

My thighs burned as I pushed back against the glass but it was too slick. I couldn't get any traction. I pushed and slid.

My mind pushed and slid, too. I hadn't followed them. They had lured me here.

Why? To kill me? Hardly worth the risk.

All the time, I climbed and slipped while the walls closed in like a kaleidoscope around me. One layer slid over another all around me, enfolding me. That thought snagged in my head. The word. Folding. Creasing. While I should have been trying to think of a way out, I was mesmerised by that thought. She was folding me. Scaled up. Glass instead of paper, person instead of pea.

My inaction made no difference. There was no left or right I could move to. The glass frames above and below touched at an narrow angle. The same to either side. I was neatly packaged and the package was getting smaller. I had to think of something but my lungs were being compressed now as the walls squeezed against my ribs. I had to turn my head to one side just to breathe. I had to think of something.

The last thing I saw was the Creaser and the girl, huddled together while the sea danced around them.

"SHE WASN'T A NICE LADY, GRAMMA," the broken toothed girl said, her hand on a lever the same height as her. "She hit me."

"I know girl. But everyone has some good in them. Now push that spike and let's if we can't find it."

The girl leaned into the lever and pushed it back into position with all her weight, releasing the brake on the gears.

She watched with wide eyes as the glass puzzle in front and above them opened like a fisherman's net dropping its catch.

The diver who jumped from the dome of St Paul's, who swam drowned London from west to east, glistened in the fisheyed moonlight. She made her final plunge, from atop an underwater lighthouse, through the opened floor of the lamphouse, to the granite floor at the base. Only thirty feet below did she lose her form, a splash of diamonds when she hit the ground.

About the Author

Tom O'Brien is an Irishman living in London. He's been published in numerous places across the web and has stories printed in the Blood & Bourbon, Blink-Ink and DEFY! Anthologies.

GATORS IN KANSAS AND OTHER HAZARDS OF MODERN FARMING

BY RALPH WALKER

I UNTIE ANOTHER BALE, pulling the loose end tight and stitching it into the soil with the pogo. *Ker-chunk, Ker-chunk, Ker-chunk.* The sound is dull underwater, but the tool kicks just the same.

A window pops up inside my snorkel hood. Little Sal's wails invade my ears.

"Salvatore, I need your help. You have to talk to Lucy." Gabriella rocks the baby on her hip. She is in her blue chevron dress, the one she likes to wear to mass.

"I'm working," I say.

"You have to talk to her now. She isn't listening to me." Gaby has her 'take no prisoners' look.

I march forward, unrolling the bale of seeded sponge. Every few steps, I secure the edge from floating to the surface with another stitch of the pogo. "Is it that important?"

Gabriella doesn't answer. "Lucy! Your father wants to talk to you."

Little Sal wails louder as mother and daughter argue in the background. On the projection, I see Charity pull a chocolate milk from the fridge. Steam wafts off something simmering on the stove. I wish

I could smell it, but it is better I can't. There are at least thirty bales left today, more tomorrow.

Lucinda comes into view. Her hair is combed straight, thick and brown around her face. Green eyeshadow, dark eyeliner, cherry lipstick; she has dressed her face for a nightclub but it is the middle of the afternoon and Lucy is only fourteen.

She looks at her shoes, but smiles up at me. "Hi Papa."

"Hi Lucy." I don't need to scold her yet. I'll give her excuse a fair shake. "What're you doing?"

"Um. I'm just meeting some friends. We're going over to Chantelle's house..." She pulls a lock of hair straight while she talks. The lie is so obvious I didn't bother to listen to the rest. She knows better.

Overhead, loops of hoses bleed bubbles of air. They dance in green water around the square shadow of the float. I pull two hoses down and tuck them under the membrane securing them in place. *Ker-chunk, Ker-chunk, Ker-chunk.*

Lucy moves around the kitchen as she talks in the handheld. The counter is covered with ingredients; turtle beans, plantains, and chilies. My mouth waters. I cut her off mid-sentence. "What's your mother making?"

"Um. I don't know. Red bean soup?"

"Sopa de Frijoles?" I ask.

Her eyes roll. "Yes Papa."

"Do you know how to make it yet?"

"No."

Of course she doesn't. She doesn't appreciate her own heritage, her own language, her own food. "Well I want you to make it for me when I come home, just like Mama."

"Do I have to?"

I've had enough. "Lucinda. No more makeup until you know how to make that dish. Go wash your face and help your mother."

She lets her head fall in defeat. "Papa?"

"Yes Lucy?"

"When are we coming to the States?" The question is innocent, but sharp.

"Soon Lucy. Don't lie to your mother or me again."

She purses her lips and hands the screen back to Gabriella.

The seed carpet puffs up from end to end. Tiny pearls of gas appear around edges, growing until they jettison to the surface.

Gabriella has calmed the baby. "I'm sorry I bothered you. I didn't think you'd be working."

"I'm always working."

"Salvatore, its Sunday."

"I know." I didn't actually know. The days of the week don't matter; only the planting, the tending, the harvesting, the drying, the selling. It is the second day of planting for cowpeas, day eleven for tending the giant blue lentils, third day of harvesting the berries in the bog. The cycles are short, but that only means we have more to do.

We've got a good thing going, Nora and Cliff and me. Between the three of us we can handle all seven hectares. We've only lost one crop in the last twenty four cycles. A few varieties had small yields and the carp liked to nibble at the leafy greens, but we like to eat the carp so that seems fair.

She puts the baby in his playpen and moves to the corner of the kitchen, away from the rest of the kids. "Salvatore?"

"Yeah?"

"I talked to Sergio. The coyote can take us all across together."

"All five of you? It will cost too much. Besides, Little Sal is too small for the trip."

"We can make it. You've done it enough times. We need to leave soon. The peninsula is too crowded. Honduras isn't the same. Besides, with your stake, I know we can help."

The sweat goes cold between my wetsuit and my back. My stake. That lie has gotten out of hand. It wasn't mine. This is their land, their water, their seed. It is only my sweat.

"Wait until the start of the next year. The kids won't be any help until they can swim."

"You can't swim Sal," she says.

The weights around my ankles feel heavier with her words. They pull me down.

"Gabby I need to keep working. At this rate I'll never make it to mass." I grin trying to lighten the mood.

"You aren't going to mass." She purses her lips, just like Lucy. "We need to be together. My bed is cold"

"So is mine."

"We can make it across," she says.

"No. I'll be home as soon as we finish the season. We'll all come back together. No coyotes, just us."

"I don't want to wait. We need you Salvatore."

"I know. I need you too. Teach the kids to swim."

We each murmur our love for the other and the window blinks out, leaving me alone in the green water field.

I lean against the pogo and look up to the surface. My snorkel rises to the black silhouette of a floating donut. Out across the muddy bottom another twenty nine bales of seed carpet wait for me to unwind them. A walleye investigates the closest one.

I finish the next three rows quickly, laying them side by side. Inflated, the blankets look like a puffy coat. Soon enough, sprouts will puncture through.

The fourth bale rolled into a low, a few yards from where I need it. I stab the pogo in the muck and walk downhill carefully. It's easy to twist an ankle in the loose drift soil in the lows. A few sunnies scatter. I lean over and right the bale, pulling it towards me.

A spit of green water hits my cheek. Startled, I check my hood. The seal is tight around the rough edges of my face. I look up. My snorkel tube rises like a chimney up to the surface, almost perfectly vertical. It isn't taut when I stand, but there isn't enough slack for me to touch my toes. I shouldn't be this deep.

The grease pencil field chart strapped to my arm shows an average of eight feet of standing water here. Even in the low it shouldn't be more than nine, at most ten. I have enough tube to work in at least eleven feet of depth without a worry, but I'm pulling my float underwater when I bend over. Something is wrong.

No reason to panic, yet. I tap the radio control on my arm.

"Cliff? Nora?"

No response. It is probably nothing. It hasn't rained in a while. Maybe my chart is wrong, but three feet of depth is a lot to be off by. Either way, I'm not drowning. I re-pressurize the hood and clear the water from my chin.

My pogo lays in the muck. I turn my head as I bend over, watching the snorkel tube pull taut. Another sputter hits my face as I pick up the tool. This time I expected it, but something is definitely wrong.

"Nora. Cliff. Are either of you on radio?" I ask again.

"Yeah Sal. Sorry," Nora's voice crackles through.

"Something's wrong with my chart. The water depth in the cowpea wedge is off."

"Should be eight, maybe nine feet," she says. "You said you'd be fine in water over your head."

"I am fine. My chart says eight feet, but it is more, at least eleven."

"The bog feels deep today too. I'll check." She keeps the radio line open. "Three nine at bog marker one. Plus fourteen. Sal, maybe you should come out."

Plus fourteen. We check the depths each week with painted yardsticks, binoculars and a notebook. We aren't super scientific about it, but fourteen inches above high water when it hasn't rained is something new.

"I'm coming in." I finish securing the bale I had opened and start for the closest jetty. A ladder of bent rebar pokes out from a pile of broken precast. Cliff had scavenged the structure of the abandoned parking garage four years ago. He and I pushed the cracked concrete further and further into the water to slow the currents, protecting the crops.

Breaking the surface, I release the seal and push my hood up. It is a perfect day. The sky is clear and still. The sun is warm. I sit on the flat top and drag up my snorkel tube, float, and pogo. Six concrete fingers reach out from the spit of dry land. A thin wire fence ties the tips together, our weak attempt to keep more invasive species at bay. A pair of yellow box turtles drift outside the fence. A gator follows just beyond. Every year there have been more; more turtles, more carp, and more gators. I guess they moved to Kansas in search of abundance, just like me.

The drying house rests on stilts where the jetties come together. A prism of color shows through the clear plastic tubes on the south wall and roof. Nora carries a pallet of freshly picked berries up the stairs. I leave my gear at the base of the jetty and follow.

"Why is the water so high?" I ask.

"Flash floods," she says, not looking up, just working.

"No clouds here."

She points to a digital weather map on the wall. The readout was all charts and numbers I don't really understand. "Upstream. Barton and Rice counties. They've each had more than three inches of rain today. River authority released the Ninnescah."

"Nice of them to tell us. Is this the high water?"

"No." Nora won't look at me.

"How high?"

"They don't know. It could be four, maybe five more feet. I called Angie. She thinks the Arkansas will wash out."

High water might not be a problem, but a strong current or a shock of temperature or acidity—our crops can't weather that.

"How long do we have?"

"Today, probably sometime tomorrow. Not much more than that."

"Is Cliff harvesting already?"

"No! I can't even get him on the radio. He turns it off when he is plowing..." She stopped herself before she rolled into a rant about his need to 'concentrate'. Nora and I both know he just wants some time alone.

"Why didn't you get him?" I ask.

"I have to pull the berries. It's the only way we'll bridge if the

Arkansas really does wash out." She pushes another full rack under the drying tubes.

Nora and Cliff have invested everything in this farm. They've been trying to grow the things the Agra-Corps have given up on: artisan, heirloom, hand-farmed, organic seed, and aqua-temperate. The labels don't make the work any easier but they drive the prices up. Real crops, in real soil, by real people. Callouses on our hands prove it. Together we grow beautiful, authentic crops the way things used to be grow, almost.

Nora keeps sorting and racking. The berries are small, but even small cran-blues are unusually profitable. A flood will definitely wipe them out.

"Do you need help with those?" I ask.

"No. I'll harvest what I can."

"What about the lentils? I can start them?"

"They aren't mature."

"Even small runts should sell for a few dollars. It's better than letting them drown."

Her lip quivers. "If the river spills over..." She stops herself looking out to the furthest wedge. "Cliff built this house."

I look out in the same direction. Each of the five wedges spread out from the land, shallow to deep. The pools of water are each a different color; browns, greens, tans fading towards the fence. They muddle together in the flow. The bog is shallow and black. Normally leaves and vines poke up through the surface, but now it's just ripples. The other wedges are dotted with rafts and pontoons keeping the compressors and solar panels afloat.

Cliff's float moves steadily in a straight line across the furthest wedge. In the shallows the water is a tan, but behind his float a plume of liquid rust water flows. Gulls and geese investigate from above.

He doesn't even know. His whole farm, his whole livelihood, is going to drown in a rainless flood, and he doesn't even know.

"Why is he plowing?"

"The field was fallow. We were getting it ready."

"For what? This season's almost over."

Nora looks at my face. Her eyes are wet. "You've taught us both so much. He wants you to have your own wedge, your own stake. We both do."

A stake? I stand there with my mouth open. She didn't really say that. We've been at this together for six years, since the beginning. I don't know what to say.

"If you want it." She turns away again.

I am dumbfounded. "Of course, I—" None of this matters if the Arkansas River washes it all away.

It was like she read my mind. "We were going to tell you at the end of the season. Cliff wanted to get it ready so you could plant early. You earned it, but I guess that doesn't matter now."

"I'll get Cliff. We need the plow motor to run the harvester." I don't know what else to say. I run down the stairs and grab an extra length of snorkel hose.

"Sal," she calls after.

"Yeah?"

"Be careful, it's deep."

I add the hose to the breathing kit as I jog. Nora's words ring in my head, but I have to ignore them. I put them in a box and lock them away. The promise of land doesn't exist. My float drags on the ground. I pull the hood back on. The radio channel is open. Nora is calling out for Cliff every few minutes.

A pair of pontoons support the farm's only machine engine less than one hundred yards away. Cliff's orange float bobs in front of the raft, moving away from me.

With three quick steps, I jump out from the jetty, throwing my float wide. Instinctively I hold my breath. The water is immediately over my head, cold as I sink to the bottom. I reach out in all directions. My feet dig into the ground. My eyes adjust to the cloudy water. My mask is secure. My hood is sealed. My snorkel tube rises to the surface. My float is upright. I breathe.

"I'm in the water Nora."

"Okay. Are you okay?"

The gator's mouth snaps shut.

"Mierda!" I yelped, with water in my mouth. The tips of two fingers don't make it out.

I push off the gator's back, staying behind him. My snorkel is tangled. I pull the hood off, and jump, breaking the surface.

I gulp for air, flailing.

Sinking down, I compressed my body and jump again towards the shallows.

Cliff is ahead, struggling to swim. The gator circles around for another attack.

My feet find bottom. I run-bob-jump trying to get to shore as fast as I can.

Even with a broken knee Cliff is faster than me in the water. He pulls away into the shallows. I keep my bloody hand overhead like a torch breaking the surface.

Another ten yards and my face is above water. Nora has hooked an arm around Cliff and is pulling him out. I don't see the gator. I don't see the jetties. All I can see was green water.

Nora has gotten Cliff to the steps of the dry house. I emerge from the wedge, climbing the steep slope to what should be dry ground. My gear, discarded but attached, drags behind. My hand throbs. The damn beast has taken two knuckles. A small price compared to what the flood will take from Nora and Cliff.

"Sal!? Are you okay?" Nora calls out.

I catch my breath and look at my hand. "Better than Cliff."

He leans up on an elbow and gives me a thumbs up. Nora splashes towards me, pogo in hand.

"I'm not doing any more planting today."

"Move!" she yells.

The pogo cocked like a shotgun. *Ker-chunk, Ker-chunk, Ker-chunk.*

The gator had drifted behind me. She impales it in the side and hops back from its hissing open jaws. The beast retreats to the depths.

Together, we help Cliff up to the dry house.

NORA BANDAGES our wounds while we watch the water rise.

The gator fence is already gone. The jetties disappear next, submerged protectors of our soil. One by one the floats break loose and drift away.

We stay in the dry house, warming under the solar tubes and eating berries. Nora shows me the wedge they want to give me. With it all underwater, it is impossible to separate what is mine from what is theirs. Cliff draws up a deed, nothing really legal but something more than a handshake and a promise. We have worked together for six years with less.

After sunset, I call Gabriella.

The vid-phone rings and rings. She finally picks up. Her hands are soapy and her sleeves are rolled up.

"Hello Sal. What's wrong?" I never call twice in one day.

"Nothing. Nothing is wrong." I smile wide, probably goofy, keeping my bandaged hand out of the frame. I'm not sure what I want to say. "Gabriella. It doesn't matter."

"What doesn't matter?"

"We had a flood."

"Oh. Has it been raining?"

"No Gabriella. There hasn't been rain for days, but my whole stake washed away."

Her brow furrows. "What are you talking about Sal? How is there a flood without rain?"

I let my thoughts loose. "The sunny days are just as hard as the rainy ones. The water comes when you don't expect. It's the worst when we are trying to harvest. The water isn't all that warm, but the algae bloom faster and the carp get a little bolder and the smell of sulfur blossoms just enough to turn my stomach, but not enough to kill my appetite..." I am babbling, grinning from ear to ear. "Gaby, *my stake* washed away."

Her eyes narrow. "Your stake?" She crossed her arms.

"Yes. No! Not just my stake, this is our stake! Free and clear. It washed away, but it doesn't matter. It doesn't matter if we plant cowpeas or soybeans. It doesn't matter what the coyotes charge. It doesn't matter if the gator fence comes down!"

"Salvatore, have you been drinking?" She hasn't seen me like this, not in a long time. Maybe it was the loss of blood or the nip of painkillers, but the euphoria doesn't fade.

"I earned our stake today. The Arkansas River might wash it away, but it is still ours. No one can take that, not even the gators."

Gabriella shifts her feet. Her hands drop. Her lip stiffens. "Our stake? Today?" I don't care that she caught the lie. In her heart, she has probably known all along. I nod. My grin pulls wider across my face.

Her eyes follow the grin, softening. Her hand covers her mouth and she burps out a giggle. "Really?"

"Yes. Really. Come. Come today. This is our stake. We'll do this together. Pay the coyote. Pack the kids. It doesn't matter if they can swim or not."

About the Author

Ralph Walker is an architect and writer in New Jersey. His work, both built and on the page, explores our rapidly changing environment. A graduate of Syracuse University, Ralph has been practicing architecture on both coasts for 20 years. His science fiction has been featured in Into The Ruins and previously received an Honorable Mention from the Writers of the Future contest. He is currently working on his debut novel. He can be found on twitter at @RW_Igloo and his website ralphwalkerauthor.com

RAKKA SURPRISE

BY BEY DECKARD

Easing back on the thrust, I squinted at the landing zone far below me on the planet surface. Something weird was going on. If I turned my head one way, the black square seemed to rise up into the air. If I turned it the other way, misty purple auras emanated from the landing zone, blurring its edges. What the hell? I grimaced and tapped on the navpad to make sure I wasn't coming in on a weird angle. The gravity on Beto was supposed to be just a touch below Standard and I'd just shut off my ship's imperfect Standard plus-two. Could be that I was having a gravity-lurch and getting my horizon wrong—but, then again, I had twenty *ots* of flying rust buckets under my belt and I hadn't lurched since I was a rookie. Didn't hurt to get a second opinion, though.

"Hey, Lala... how do I look?"

"Like a man in need of a shave," the ship quipped back in her mellifluous Grao accent. "But if you're talking entry, you're looking just fine, Drayan... though, we'd be wheels-down faster if you'd let me take the controls."

"I've got it," I muttered. I flicked on the landing fog lights to get a better view, but that did nothing for the wobbling, ill-defined target, and I considered letting Lala land herself, despite her penchant for dropping like a rock with little regard for the tender meat sitting inside her metal guts—a wrenched neck was nothing compared to becoming a smear on an alien world.

Suddenly the cabin was filled with a high-pitched whine and I winced in pain, shaking my head as I controlled the ship's descent.

"What the hell is that noise?"

"What noise?" asked Lala. "I'm not picking up anything."

"Are you sure?"

"Of course I'm sure, Drayan. My sensors don't detect any noise besides the usual. Maybe you can describe it?"

"Like—" I ground my teeth, tears forming in my eyes from the agony building in my skull "—like a whistle. Or hissing. Or... someone screaming." I realized the sound was different in each ear and it was drilling right into the center of my brain. "You're telling me you can't hear anything?"

"Maybe you're having some kind of mental breakdown." Lala sounded smug. "Maybe you're dying."

"Maybe your sensors aren't worth shit."

"Maybe you're the *grepslat* who can't afford to upgrade me."

Ignoring the insult, I just rasped, "Lala, just tell Sitik I need him here *now*."

"Aye aye, Captain."

A few seconds later, the huge shaggy form of my first mate appeared at the hatch.

"Sitik. Tell me you can hear this."

"Neg, Dray. I gen no whachoo mean, *doudou*," the Rakka replied in his deep, gravelly voice, staring at me quizzically with his forward facing eye. "You right-a, Dray?"

"No, I'm not all right," I replied through clenched teeth. My vision was blurring and overlapping, just like I'd had too much to drink. Maybe Lala was right. Maybe I *was* dying. "I can't see... and... and *shit*, strap in, Sitik. I'm going to let Lala take over."

"*Kep shekep!*" Sitik swore as he thunked down into the seat next to me, snapping the restraints over his furry bulk. "Lala missama'am, you care wichoo crew, yea-oh?"

"Of course, honey," Lala replied. "Drayan?"

"Go for it," I gasped, giving her control. Then I leaned over, puked on the decking next to my feet, and passed out.

THE FIRST TIME I woke up it was only long enough to see that we had landed and were still in one piece and that Sitik was staring down at me. I convulsed, puked again, then promptly lost consciousness.

THE SECOND TIME, I waited before peeling my eyes open. It seemed like the screaming in my ears had dulled a bit. If it wasn't just in my head, that meant either I was getting used to it, or I was losing my hearing. However, I could clearly hear Sitik and Lala discussing my condition in rapid Outer-ring pidgin and I was amazed to hear concern in the ship's voice—she claimed to dislike me about as much as she loved the big Rakka.

Slowly I opened my eyes and instantly regretted it. My first impression was of being inside a big, reflective soap bubble while simultaneously swirling around in a lake of burning potassium. The worse part, however, was that my left eye couldn't agree with what my right eye was seeing, so I clamped my eyelids down tight and retreated to the stability of darkness.

"Hey-a Dray," Sitik said softly, and I could feel him settling down next to me on the cold metal surface. We were still in the ship, but from the amount of space around me, I figured I was lying on the floor of the cargo bay.

"Sitik, what the hell is going on?"

"I gen you Earthing part no gon' good wit Beto, yea-oh?"

I put my hands over my face, massaging around my eyes—I was still incredibly nauseous so I didn't dare move more than that—and tried to recall the minimal amount I'd read about Beto. It was the fourth planet from the orange dwarf star Chyron, had a passably breathable atmosphere, no plant life to speak of but had nutrient rich "sap springs" that sustained life, and the sentient beings were friendly but somewhat curt... then, with a sinking feeling, I remembered the part about atmospheric wave-length and interspace distortions. I'd figured they were things that would affect the ship, not *me*.

"*Shekep*," I said, my throat raw. "That'll teach me to ignore the fine print." It had seemed like such an easy job. Pick up a little metal box from Vedescendart IX and deliver it to the leaders of Beto as a peace offering and make a short speech. I hadn't figured on puking up my guts and passing out in the process. How was I going to complete the job if I couldn't even open my eyes?

"Wasso?"

"Nothing. Hey, how come this isn't affecting you?" I asked, cracking one of my eyes open a slit.

Through the violent haze, I saw Sitik swivel both eyes to face me, the convex black facets reflecting the light in various sharp colors.

"Whachoo see, Dray?"

I tried my best to describe the overlapping, brain-numbingly bright imagery I was being bombarded with and how it felt like my eyes were seeing completely different things.

My first mate shook his head and gave the dry double-cough noise he used to indicate laughter, then rotated his eyes on different axes, pointing to his left one with a clawed finger. "No so primi, Earthing."

"My eyes aren't primitive," I said, smiling despite the pain I was in. But Sitik was right. Rakka had uncoupled, non-stereoscopic vision—each compound eye operated and collected data independently, thanks to the Rakka's dual brain system. It also made sense that he wasn't getting the same aural effect since he didn't have inner ears. Folks liked to blame Rakkarian resistance to "proper" spoken language on their perceived feeble-mindedness, but in truth they relied entirely on an embedded prosthetic to translate sound-waves for them in a way that was compatible with most species. It's not that they were deaf, per se—I liked to compare it to a two-dimensional being having to learn to communicate in three dimensions. Granted, that didn't really explain why most Rakka tended to adopt a similar sort of pidgin. A small part of me thought they were all fucking with us.

"Crap... what am I going to do? How am I going to deliver that box if I can't even stand? And it's not like I can have you deliver it for me, can I?"

Sitik's right eye swiveled away. I knew that probably hurt his feelings a bit but he knew I was right; unfortunately, most people didn't see Rakka the way I did, including the people who provided my paycheck.

"Mayya you gon be getcha used to? Big-li'l time?"

"I don't know," I said and swallowed against my nausea. "I don't think this is something I can get used to, no matter how long."

Sitik made a *chik-chik-chik* sound with the cartilage disks in his throat, something that usually signaled anxiety, and I reached my hand out.

"Come on, help me sit up. Maybe I can do this with your help." It couldn't hurt to try—we really needed the money if I was going to keep Lala running, not to mention I didn't need another failure on my record.

"Yea-oh," Sitik said, taking my wrist. The pad on his palm was rubbery and cool in contrast to the warm gray fur on his fingers and thumbs. "Easy, Dray." He slowly dragged me up to a sitting position. However, it caused my world to whip around me like I was a spinning toy top and it was instant lights-out for me.

Again.

When I came to the next time, I found a cloth tied around my eyes and the world swaying beneath me as I was held in a warm, furry embrace. It took me a sec to realize that Sitik was carrying me cradled in his arms like a baby. I was feeling better, the high pitch whine had nearly disappeared, and the material blocked out all the light, but I was still weak and disoriented.

Sitik must have noticed me waking up because he gave his dry-cough laugh and said, "Jus-a me, Dray." He chuckled again. "Hey, big bad Rakka *banga* gonna see you troo, *doudou*."

"Yeah, great. Thanks," I muttered. The landing zone was a good hike from the citadel where I was supposed to present the peace offering to the ruling powers of Beto, but with Sitik's long stride, we'd be there in no time. But how was I going to stand on my two feet without Sitik's support, let alone actually communicate in a way that didn't embarrass me or the High Vedescians?

Great, my first experience with an interspace planet was going *real* well. I took a deep breath, trying to quell the rest of my nausea, and noticed then that there was a pleasant scent following us. At first I thought it was environmental, but as I turned my head, I realized it was coming from Sitik's fur. This close, the big Rakka smelled like something familiar. I frowned, trying to think of what it reminded me of when I got a flash of my grandmother standing in her homey kitchen on Enceladus—an old memory from when I was a kid. A really good memory.

Salted caramel. That's what Sitik smelled like. I'd never noticed it before. I wondered if it was a natural smell or if he perfumed himself like us humans liked to. I lay there pondering, rocked gently by the Rakka's smooth gait. There was a lot I didn't know about my first mate. Hell, I only knew Sitik was male because of the time we got stopped at the Gellex border. An authoritarian and xenophobic independent state, Gellex was downright zealous about security. The border guards had simply been following standard protocol when confronted with an un-sexed Rakka. They'd pinned him down to the floor and pulled out his genital sack in front of everyone when he refused to say if he was male or female—the Rakka are *extremely* private about what sex they are.

Back then, I hadn't had much experience with Rakka and I'd only hired Sitik on the cheap to take care of cargo after my rotator cuff injury. Rakkas didn't seem all that bright to me—I could barely understand their mangled speech—and I hadn't been planning on keeping him on for that long.

However, when I saw how rattled he was after being manhandled and put on display by the Gellexian guards, I started to give him some other odd jobs around the ship. It began out of guilt for not having done anything during his ordeal, but was I impressed when he showed a real knack for navigation and could convince Lala to do things that I normally had to bribe her for. So, less than three *cycs* later, I made him my first mate. The title doesn't mean much in a crew of two, but I feel like he deserves it.

"You right-a, Dray? You don' be too chat-see."

"I'm okay," I replied. "Really though... thank you. This is helping."

"Gaw," was all he said, and I heard the *chik-chik-chik* come from his throat.

I quietly breathed in his salted caramel scent, a bunch of questions drifting through my mind. Like, how Sitik sometimes called himself a *banga*—was he just kidding around? Bangas were members of the antiestablishment gangs that caused no end of trouble for the Polyverse Coalition. I knew there were Rakka among their number, but had Sitik really been one of them? He seemed so easy going. And why was he so loyal to me? Was it because of the title? Because I paid him well?

Was he *happy*?

I think the empty stomach and the assault on my senses was making me a touch dippy. Laughing to myself, I shifted to get more comfortable and when my hand landed on his forearm I left it there. His fur was much softer than I'd imagined, probably due to the fine secondary hairs, and I wondered idly if he liked being brushed...

Chuckling quietly to myself, I drifted on my loopy thoughts.

Obviously, the Betoans were sympathetic to my plight because they immediately offered me the chance to recuperate a bit before I

presented myself to their leaders. The Betoans were tall, reedy creatures with a single eye and no other facial features to speak of, but I
got a sense of their curiosity and excitement as they helped Sitik to
settle me into the spherical room. They were one of the newest
members of the Polyverse Coalition and as such hadn't yet been
exposed to many "aliens" before—I wondered how often they *would*
get foreign visitors, given that their world would be so uncomfortable for the vast majority of species. It certainly could be a while
before they got as jaded to "otherness" as the rest of us.

Lying on the soft gel floor of the room we'd been given, my right
eye covered with a makeshift patch, I followed the shifting curves of
the window above my head with the other eye until I felt I could
make sense of my surroundings. On the whole, I was feeling better,
and with my stereo vision turned off, I was sure that I'd be able to
present the peace offering, no problem. Or at least, I was sure I
wasn't going to just puke and pass out again.

"Dray? You good, *doudou?*" Sitik was stretched out on his back
beside me, his hands clasped over his furry belly, one eye turned my
way. Rakka had three fingers and two thumbs on each hand, tipped
with blunt blue-black claws, and he twiddled his thumbs in a
mesmerizing, complex way.

"I'm going to be fine, Sitik," I replied. "The eyepatch was a good
idea. Thanks."

Sitik just nodded, swiveling his eye back to the ceiling.

I studied his noseless, bulbous-eyed profile in silence, wondering
if he was considered handsome for a Rakka. Sitik's eye slowly
rotated back to focus on me and I saw myself reflected in multiple
facets.

"Wasso think, Dray?" His words were clipped, even for a Rakka,
and I thought he sounded tense.

"You know.... you take good care of me." I shrugged as best as I
could, considering the way I was lying on my side.

"Yea-oh. You dem big boss ..." Sitik gave his dry-cough laugh.

"But, are you happy working for me?"

Sitik's thumb gymnastics stopped. "Whachoo do if this Rakka neg?"

"I'd ask how I could make you happier and then do it."

Nodding slowly, Sitik went back to staring at the ceiling and twiddling. "See-oh, thatta my happy there, *doudou*. S'all dumplings."

"Okay, so you *do* like working for me. I'm glad. I was just making sure." I sat up slowly, keeping my eye focused on a single spot so the world didn't start doing flips again. Hesitantly, I reached out and placed my hand on what passed for his shoulder. This time, Sitik turned his whole head so he could stare at me with both eyes. "I appreciate you, Sitik."

I felt my face get a bit warm. I wasn't exactly sure where this urge to share had come from and I was probably making the both of us uncomfortable, judging by the *chik-chik-chik* noise coming from him, but it was suddenly very important to me that he knew how much I valued and trusted him.

"I'm serious," I continued, petting his soft, furry shoulder. "I don't know what I would have done without you today, buddy."

"Dems true dat, yea-oh," Sitik replied with a cough-laugh. His fanged mouth stretched out in the semblance of a human grin and it was hilariously terrifying to behold. Then he placed his hand on top of mine to stop it. "You ah... you gon' wan no be... ah..." Sitik pushed my hand off his shoulder, and I noticed that he was breathing rapidly. Grayish lumps had appeared through his fur along the side of his neck and for a second I thought he was having some kind of allergic reaction.

"Sitik? You okay? What's going on?"

Another laugh came from the big Rakka and he shook his head from side to side, touching the swellings on his throat.

"Jus' fine, *doudou*. Don' be mind no *kep shekep* Rakka trasha."

"But what is—"

"Hey-oh, done chat-see, right?" He sounded downright embarrassed so I decided not to press him any further. I didn't know what I had said to make him act so odd.

"I'm sorry. Okay?"

"Mm."

"I think I'm all right to stand. Can I get your help?"

"Course, Dray." Sitik got to his feet, then hauled me to mine and steadied me while I found my balance in the lower gravity. When I felt like I was ready, I touched the glowing block on the wall opposite. A beautiful, polyphonic chime echoed throughout the chamber. Almost immediately two Betoans slid through the wall, staring at me expectantly with their huge, single eyes.

"I'm ready," I said.

THE HANDING over of the peace offering had gone well enough, if a bit awkwardly on the part of our hosts. The Betoans had no idea what to do with the carved rock inside the box—turns out that gift giving wasn't part of their culture at all so they were at a loss as to how to act. They left me standing in the center of the room with my eyepatch and vertigo while they huddled together in a tight knot to discuss an appropriate reply. Sitik turned an eye towards me, and I saw unmistakable amusement in its segmented depths. The swellings on his neck were still visible but didn't seem to be bothering him. I inched closer, and surreptitiously sniffed. Sitik's salted-caramel scent was tied up with such pleasant memories that it lessened my discomfort quite a bit just to be near him.

The Betoans must have come to some agreement because they quickly retook their places around the semi-circular table I was facing. I found them a rather interesting species and wondered if the fact that they moved in pairs and nictated at the same time had to do with cultural convention or something physiological. Smiling, I gave them a shallow bow and waited for them to either present me with some token of their own or send me on my merry way. I was tired of seeing the world through a hazy, wobbly, too bright lens and was looking forward to the comforting deep black of space.

"We would like to thank the Vedescians for the curious cast-off they were motivated to leave behind on our planet," droned the translation matrix as two Betoans chittered, seeming to finish each other's sentences. I winced inwardly at their choice of words, already rewriting their response in my head. "As a moderate reaction to this event we would like to invite Captain Delor Drayan and his mate Sitik to partake in shared nutrients before departing."

I shared a glance with Sitik. I couldn't refuse, could I? Keeping my impatience in check, I bowed again.

"I would be honored, Your Excellencies. However, our physiology may not be compatible with the delicacies you are offering."

"Have you no sustenance aboard your vessel?" the Betoans asked through the translation matrix. Even without inflection, I could tell they were astounded it hadn't occurred to me to bring my own food.

"Err... yes. I do. I um—" I turned to Sitik. He had much longer legs and was more used to the lower gravity than I was. Nipping back to the ship for some grub would take less time if he did it. "Could you please go get something we can eat? Um. Maybe some of the uh... *treb* mix?" The mix barely passed as a snack, but I didn't know if my stomach could even handle that much—plus, it would take less time to eat.

"You betcha, Cap-ty," Sitik answered. Then he let out a cough-laugh. "Back in li'l time, *doudou*, dontcha fret." He'd obviously picked up on my feelings about being left alone with the Betoans.

"Thanks."

I watched him lope away, then stood awkwardly trying to think of something to say. I wished I had a chair to sit on or even just an invitation to sit on the ground. Time stretched on, oppressively filled with silence, as we waited for Sitik to return. Some smaller Betoans arrived, their skin a lighter orange than the ruling class, bringing bowls of steaming... something. The smell of rotting fish would have been more appetizing.

"Your mate has been spotted on the return," the Betoans closest to me said reassuringly, flicking their ocular membranes in unison.

"First Mate," I corrected them with a smile.

"Oh, you have many mates then?" asked another pair of Betoans.

I burped quietly into my hand. The smell of their food was making me feel ill again. "Ah... no, just the one. And it's not *mate* mate. It's First Mate... he's second in command of my ship."

The Betoans turned to each other to confer, and when they faced me again, they asked, "Why does he call you a mate-term?"

"A mate-term?" I was confused and dizzy. I really needed to sit ASAP. "Oh, you mean '*doudou*'? I don't know what that means, honestly. I think it's just a Rakka thing."

"Rakka's have no native language. The word conveys a similar meaning in seven hundred thirty-nine languages in the database sent by the Polyverse Coalition, including one language from your home planet. The equivalent in your English is 'sweetheart'."

"Oh." I tried breathing without using my nose but the horrible food smell was coating the back of my throat. "That's... um. I don't think that's what he means."

The Betoans chittered again, and something told me they found my reaction confusing.

"But he is in rut. And you display attraction. Do you plan on making him your mate?"

"He's in *what*?"

Again the Betoans conferred with each other before replying through the matrix. "He is showing signs of high sexual desire. Rakka display desire and availability through hormones and enlarged scent glands."

"They do?" I asked, thinking about the gray lumps on Sitik's neck. "How... how do you know this?"

"All known species are within the database sent by the Polyverse Coalition. Perhaps you should peruse it as well?"

"Uh... yeah. I, uh..." The smell mixed with the visual shenanigans and the low gravity finally got the best of me and I keeled over backwards, my eyes rolled back in my head. However, just before I hit the ground, I felt a pair of strong, furry arms rescue me.

I SAT HUNCHED over the instrument panel, nursing the headache to end all headaches while calculating the jump vectors to reach Vedescendart IX by the shortest route. I felt heavy and weird and uncomfortable because the ship's gravity module was acting up again and it felt more like Standard plus-three rather than our usual plus-two.

Also, I was still mulling over what the Betoans had said about Sitik.

"Hey Lala," I said quietly. "Do you we have a species catalogue on board?"

"Of course we do. Why wouldn't we?" she replied. If she had eyes, she would have definitely rolled them.

Gritting my teeth, I shook my head. "One of these days I'm going to get you wiped."

"Oh, I'm shaking in my boots... you've been threatening that for how long?"

"Or, better yet, I'm going to trade you in for a real ship's computer. None of this recycled corpseware business."

"Where are you going to get the money, honey? You going to start peddling your pud on the side? From what I've seen in the shower, that's not going to get you much..."

I smacked the control panel and then laughed. "Stay out of my shower, you pervert."

Lala responded by lighting up the LEDs on her console so they made the outline of a dick and I shook my head. Sobering a moment later, I asked, "Um... speaking of that sort of thing... I think Sitik might be in some kind of sexual heat thing."

"He is."

"You knew this?"

"Sure. He's a healthy male Rakka in his sexual prime. It happens every two-point-eight *cycs* like clockwork. This is the first time you've noticed it?"

"I guess. I think he might have... feelings for me though. I don't know what I should do about that. I mean, are we even compatible?"

"Why do you think he has feelings for you?" All the teasing had gone from Lala's tone; she honestly seemed interested.

"Turns out he calls me 'sweetheart'," I muttered, locking in the coordinates for the first jump. I wondered where Sitik was in the ship, and thought about asking Lala, but I figured she would go back to teasing me.

"No, he doesn't."

"Yes, he does. The Betoans told me that's what *doudou* means."

"*Doudou* means 'friend' on Pellos Prime. You know... where Sitik was born?"

"Oh." I actually had no idea he was born there. What was that I was feeling? Jealousy over the fact that my ship knew more about my first mate than I did? Maybe a smidge of disappointment about the *doudou* thing? Ridiculous.

"Right," I replied gruffly, fiddling with controls that didn't need fiddling with. "I knew that. Forget I said anything. Just a misunderstanding."

Something about the way Lala stayed silent, just twinkling her lights, made me frown. It wasn't like her not to get in some sort of insult when she had the chance.

"What is it?" I asked.

"Wellll..." Lala said quietly. "I never said he *didn't* have feelings for you."

"He told you that?"

"Told Lala wasso, Dray?" Sitik said, climbing through the hatch to join me in the cockpit.

"Oh uh... about how you were born on Pellos Prime."

"Ooh... smoooth," Lala said, and Sitik swiveled a curious eye towards the camera mounted on the dash.

"Yea-oh. Been born 'n biggen in dem Rakka camp," he said, settling into his seat. Sitik fixed one eye on me and stretched his mouth in the facsimile of a smile. "Wasso? You chat-see 'bout em Rakka trasha?"

"I don't think you give yourself enough credit, big guy," I said, trying to sound like my normal self. "I don't think Rakka are trash and you know that."

"Hm," Sitik conceded and I heard his cartilage disks go *chik-chik.*

His sweet-salty scent wafted towards me and I wondered if it was part of his hormonal mating season thing and how I could have possibly missed it before. Maybe having my senses put through the ringer had done something to make me more sensitive. Maybe it was just that I was more aware of him since he'd carried me so gently in his arms. I scratched the back of my neck, feeling flushed.

"You good, *doudou*?"

"Yeah, I'm fine. I've just got a, um... logistics problem on my mind."

I heard Lala snicker quietly, and I surreptitiously turned off the main cockpit speaker. If she had something to say, she could use the panel. She hated text, though—her spelling was horrendous.

"Hey, Sitik?"

"Yea-oh, Dray? Whatchoo say?"

"I was wondering if, when we get to the moon port at Vedescendart IX, you'd join me for some Lascarran brandy... or something."

Sitik just stared at me with both eyes, not saying anything. I busied myself straightening out the gimbal on the dash, trying to act nonchalant. Finally, I looked over at him.

"No?"

"I would love to join you, Delor," Sitik replied, his English still accented but clear as day. Then he gave me another of his horrifying grins and reverted to Outer-ring pidgin. "You betcha Cap-ty."

"Well, damn," was all I could muster. I watched him finish the sequence, correcting one of my calculations as he went, and I wondered what other surprises lay in store for me with the big Rakka. He sat back in his seat and hooked his thumbs into the harness, his eyes focused on the stars beyond the viewport. I thought he looked smug.

"So Lala said *doudou* means 'friend'," I said, pulling the navpad closer. I glanced over at Sitik and saw that he had turned an eye towards me. "Does it?"

"Neg," he replied in a quiet voice, staring at me intently. "Neg, *doudou.*"

About the Author

Canadian indie author Bey Deckard writes stories that aren't quite romance and aren't quite erotica, and they jump from genre to genre, but they're all character driven and he likes to think they're interesting. These days, if Bey's not writing or working on graphics, you'll find him posting pics of his best buddy and constant canine companion Murphy, cooking up some tasty vegetarian eats, hanging out on Facebook, or sitting back to watch a movie.

THE CRATER

BY KENNETH ROBBINS

THIS IS what they did to while away the hours that hot and empty summer of 1864: they dug a gopher hole two hundred and fifty yards long, ten feet wide, and high enough for the tallest man to walk through without dipping his head. They dumped the hard displaced Virginia clay in the swamps spread out like festering sores behind them.

When the tunnel was long enough, they stood back from it and gave it the admiration reserved usually for the most beautiful of women. This lasted perhaps half an hour, if that long. Then they grew bored once again. The Private, whose blue pants and white shirt were the color of the earth from so much digging, wondered what the blasted thing was for. He asked but nobody seemed to know.

Sure, they had dug it and they had welcomed the reprieve from camp boredom such work had given them. But now that the task was finished, they were filled with curiosity. What use did the higher ups, those who had ordered it dug in the first place, have for a tunnel that burrowed directly toward and beneath the enemy fortifications? Maybe the tunnel served no purpose. Maybe the digging of it was the only use it had.

Then again, nobody knew. The train that pulled in from Maryland had a load that needed hauling, the higher ups told them. So, they left their digging and hiked the mile or so to the depot, hundreds of them, triple file and swearing at the heat and the biting mosquitoes. At the waiting train, each was given a wooden barrel that weighed fifty pounds or more, all barrels the same, and told to tote the things back to the tunnel.

What's in these casks, they wanted to know. And the higher ups said it didn't matter, did it, since they had to be toted anyway. But, the higher ups said, with more sincerity in their tone than usual, "Whatever you do, don't none of you drop your load. Else you'll know it from here to yesterday and back."

Men, hundreds of them who had once been soldiers when the war had given them something to do besides sit around and wait and dig holes in the ground, were transformed into pack mules, at least for this trip to the depot and back.

Stack them barrels atop each other, they were told, down as deep in the hole as you can go. The men, like ants, worked well into the cool of the night, and when they were finished, they looked with pride on what they had done. But what they had done, nobody had any idea. Dug a hole in the earth, filled in a swamp with dirt, packed maybe three hundred barrels of unknown substance as tight as they could get them in the far end of the hole. This man's army done gone all queer, somebody whispered in the Private's ear, and both of them had laughed as if it was some sort of joke.

"Now we'll see something," said one of the higher ups, a Colonel who wiped at the cold sweat running through the dirt on his brow. "We'll all of us see something like we never seen before."

Though nobody told them what, for sure, they had dug the hole for, the men understood, or so it seemed, and the boredom they called waiting turned into an exciting time. "Gonna be something, that's for damn sure." On this they all agreed.

A couple of men, who hauled artillery from battlefield to battlefield in the days when battlefields were still a possibility, took a long spool of rope that looked an awful lot like fuse into the hole, and when they came out an hour or so later, the spool was empty and they held the tail end of the rope in their hands. "Ready when you are," they said to the Colonel who nodded that he understood. The men could tell, the artillery fellows were eager to put a match to the rope they held.

But the Colonel had to wait for someone even more higher up than him to give the go ahead to striking the match. So there they stood, for the better part of a week, waiting, waiting with excitement inching toward mania with each passing day.

Finally the orders came down. Number one, get the men on their toes and ready to move forward and deliver the enemy one final fatal blow. Number two, don't let anybody stand too near one end of the tunnel or the other. Number three, hold off on the match until the higher ups get there themselves. This was going to be an event none of them wanted to miss. They were on their way. Don't get antsy. Patience is a virtue.

So many blue-garbed men gathered in one place for so long attracted the enemy's attention. Several in their gray rags glared at them from atop their earthworks which had proven time and time again to be untakeable by assault. Too much abatis. Too much open ground. Too many torpedoes buried in the open field. Too many rifles with fine honing pointed over the top of the earthworks for them to do much more than stare at the enemy's handiwork. But now, the gathering around one spot and especially with so much brass on display, attracted too much attention. The Colonel, sitting astride his brown mare with sweat darkening her hide and the back of his collar, said to twelve or so sharpshooters with old fashioned buffalo guns in their arms, "Take out the sumbitches." And the rattatat of musket fire sent most of the men looking for a place to hide.

The higher ups, two Major Generals, three Brigadiers, two dozen Colonels, and a whole train load of majors, captains, and lieutenants, arrived in time for the thickest exchange of small arm fire any of them had witnessed in over a month. The fun of war had returned, and all of them seemed to welcome it. Whatever the ruckus was about, it wasn't boring any longer.

The sun had just ducked out of sight beyond the trees in the West. Perfect time to do the thing.

The top Major General, the highest up of the higher ups, a squat little man who needed a shave, nodded his approval. "Good thinking," he remarked, engaging the enemy and getting them clustered like that. The Colonel nodded the compliment aside. "Just doing my duty as I see fit," he said.

Okay, the top Major General said, looking first at the mouth of the tunnel and then at the enemy's earthworks two hundred and fifty yards away. "Okay, let's do her." And he took cover behind a copse of scrub oak trees along with the rest of the higher ups. The Colonel turned to the artillery man who still stood there, fuse in hand, and gave him the nod everybody had been waiting so long to see.

The match was lit.

The fuse took on its own life.

The hiss of the burning fuse disappeared down the long dark hole in the earth.

"Sort of like flushing out rats," mused the Private who watched all this with recognition in his eye. Pour some kerosene down a rat hole then hit it with a match. Gets them every time. Then you stand on the ready for the rats, usually with fur all ablaze, to come pouring out of the hole, and you pop them off with your musket until there's no ammunition left. That's when you use your hoe or garden rake or anything that's at hand, anything for swinging and crushing blows.

It seemed to the Private that the fuse was taking an awful long time to flush their rats. "You don't suppose the damn things gone out, do you?"

The Major General must have had the same thought. His head appeared from behind the stand of scrub oak. He gestured to the Colonel, any time now. Sun'll be gone in a few minutes and they won't be able to see a damned thing. Already the edge of night was turning the woods behind the men into a series of scattered camp fires. And over there behind the enemy line the small arms fire had stopped, the enemy going to their supper more than likely. But then, as the higher ups had informed them earlier, "Don't get antsy. It's on its way. Patience is a virtue."

The Private thought the world was coming to an end. The earth leapt like a wounded animal, first this way, then that, before it became still again. The fireball that burst from the bowels of mother earth was like the sun rising all over again, throwing a strange white light into the early evening twilight and packing the heat of a thousand cannons spending fire without pause for days on end. A shower of earth and wood and burning air fell all over and around them. The Private slapped at flakes of something that burned as it tried to ignite his blue tunic. Whatever it was that flamed carried with it a rancid smell; then he realized it was probably a fragment of the enemy or the enemy's supper. The copse of wood where the Major General hid caught fire and the bevy of higher ups doused the blaze with water and earth. Then the wind came, swirling in this direction and that, bringing more dust and fumes to where they stood. As quick as it came, the wind was gone, leaving a hush over the scene.

And then all of them turned to the tunnel and where it had led. There, where the enemy earthworks had been only a moment before, was a crater fifty feet deep, maybe more, two hundred feet wide, a massive gaping hole in the middle of the enemy fortifications, illuminated by fires of all sizes. And in the crater, there was no life. None at all. No sound. Nothing.

All of them, the men, the Colonel, the higher ups, and especially the Private, gazed at the sight with silent and prayerful awe. "My God," the Private whispered, "what on earth have we done?"

A STRANGE SORT of twilight hung over the field, giving the trees, the men, the higher ups, and the crater a gray and ghostly pallor. It was a bit scary, standing in total silence, waiting for the order to charge, an order that did not come. Instead, the higher ups resolutely stood there, too, in awe like everybody else.

Where's the damn enemy, everybody wanted to know. It was the quiet of death like a battlefield three days after the armies have both withdrawn.

"You don't reckon we done killed them all," somebody whispered to nobody in particular.

The Colonel, from underneath a magnolia tree, having been tossed to the ground by his terrified mare, pointed to the Private with his sticky cigar and said, "You--good soldier, go see what it is we did to them poor folk, and be quick about it." The cigar was now pointing toward the crater where a dark and heavy haze filled the hole.

The Private took a deep breath. His body hadn't quit shaking from the power of the detonation, and now it was his job to go check the thing out? "By myself?" he asked, a near plea in his voice.

"Do you see me pointing at anybody else?" the Colonel said. "And don't dawdle."

The Private strode toward the low hanging haze and the raw scar in the earth's crust. The further he went into the crater, the quieter it became. He noticed through the thin soles of his worn and laceless boots that he was stepping on more than earth. There were pieces of clothing, fragments of skin, slabs of flesh, and several coconuts lying around. Coconuts? He picked the fruit from the ground. Where in heaven's name had the enemy come to get their hands on coconuts? But wait. Coconuts don't have eyes--and when smashed like this one was they don't bleed. He dropped the thing and lost his dinner in the freshly turned earth, then straightened himself and moved deeper into the dark, low-hanging cloud of smoke and mist.

He could hear the earth crunching under his boots, like he was walking on brittle gravel or maybe broken glass. He could smell death around him, the ugly smell of animal fat being fried in an ought tub with no grease to lessen the searing. And heat, as if the furnace of hell had found a vent in the middle of the crater.

He stepped through the cloud of smoke and felt something enormously strange. All around him, the world was different, and the land, and the ruins of a city all about him. He felt the hot mid-day sun. He felt a surge of heat through his body as if he might give way to exhaustion. But he had no time for that. He had to seek out the enemy, ascertain his condition, and quickly report to his Colonel who was probably even now beginning to lose patience. Remember, he wanted to tell his Colonel, patience is a Virtue.

Strange. The crater had become the entire landscape. He turned in a circle. Everywhere, as far as he could see, was rubble. Smoke rose here and there from fires that still burned. From them came the acrid stench of death. There a collapsed building that had burned to ash, leaving only the melted remains of roofing tiles. Strangest looking tiles the Private had ever seen. They were smooth and thick and heavy. He lifted several of the tiles from the heap and revealed the charred remains of a human hand beneath.

Something moved. He whirled, his Springfield rifle raised to mid chest. There stood a strange little man whose clothes were in tatters; his chest and arms had been burned severely; skin from his arms draped over his fingertips. The man was small and stocky. The hair on his head had been singed away. His eyes were almond shaped with heavy drooping lids. His skin was dark and, where unburned, smooth and hairless. He wore a sandal with elevations underneath on his right foot, his left dragging along shoeless. The man pointed a shaky finger at the Private and muttered something in a language the Private had not heard before.

"What do you want?" the Private asked. He got no answer as the man continued his muttering.

"Here," the Private said, offering a drink from his canteen.

The man ignored his offer and moved on.

The Private noticed a burned out streetcar. Streetcar. How did he know it was a streetcar? He had never seen a streetcar before. But not only did he know its name, he also knew its function: a horseless stagecoach powered by electricity. Electricity. . . carried over copper wires suspended from poles with crossbeams. "Like those over there," he said to absolutely no one.

He stepped into the streetcar. The smell overwhelmed him. There, stacked on top of each other, like charcoal in a brazier, were at least a dozen human bodies, perhaps more, all shapes, all ages. People. Like himself. Who had died instantly when the bomb exploded. Which bomb? Their bomb? The tunnel bomb? If he had had anything left in his stomach, he would have upchucked yet again. Indeed he did, causing his throat to ache from the trauma of dry heaves.

Outside the silence of the landscape was broken by the wailing of a small infant, no more than two years old. It lay beside a heap of ashes that vaguely resembled a human being. The child's mother, perhaps? Impossible to tell. He reached a hand toward the baby, but it slapped him away and wailed even louder. "Hey, buddy," he whispered, "it's gonna be all right. Sure thing."

He found a river flowing out of a mountain in the distance. He could smell the stench of decayed flesh rising from the river bed. Somehow the water in the river had drained away, leaving it a third of its original size. And depositing in the mud hundreds upon hundreds of bodies, human and animal, bloating in the sun. He looked up. Better than looking down. Strange. No buzzards. Back home, a dead squirrel attracted twenty or more buzzards that circled above the carrion before swooping in for a free meal. Here, no vultures. Could the bomb have killed the buzzards as well?

To his right, rescue workers were clearing away rubble, pulling more charred bodies from underneath collapsed houses and stacking them in a horse-less cart. "What's going on around here?" the Private asked. "Where am I? Why are so many people dead? And dying?"

The leader of the team turned an angry and scarred face toward him and spat, the cool spray catching him in the left eye and running down the bridge of his nose. He wiped his face clean. He had met the enemy and his enemy was burned to near non-recognition. Should he report this to his Colonel? Instead he moved on.

He found a half burned banner with strange picture-like markings on it, markings made with black paint. An obvious piece of writing, but it was writing he couldn't read.

He heard a noise over his head. He looked up, squinting into the sun. High above the mountains to the west he saw a buzzard. No, wait. No buzzard. A small flying machine which for no explainable reason whatsoever he knew to be an airplane. An airplane? Flown by the enemy, perhaps? He hoped it would land; somehow or other he knew the pilot could explain in his language everything he was seeing. He felt desperate. He needed to know so he could report back to his Colonel. The enemy is defeated, this much he knew, but how and why? And which enemy? These people he saw here were not the enemy behind the earthworks. These people were of a different sort altogether.

He found a building made of concrete. Only half of it had been destroyed by the explosion. The other half was a field hospital. Doctors worked rapidly, treating hundreds upon hundreds of victims, most of them silently waiting, others moaning from an indescribable pain, others not moving or moaning or breathing.

The Head Doctor--he had to be the Head Doctor since he was the only one wearing a white smock--stopped what he was doing and stared at the Private. This man had blondish hair and round inquisitive eyes. He didn't look at all like the injured and dead and dying all around him. And he spoke in a language the Private could understand. "Who are you?" he called from his work station.

"I'm a private in the Union army," the Private called back. "Do you know where I am, sir?" He felt a surge of adrenaline that seemed to urge his arms and legs away from the chaos of the field hospital. Did he really want to know where he was? He was in the crater, that's where he was, and he couldn't find his way out. Which he had to do, soon. He had to report all he was seeing to his Colonel. He felt the urge to share all this, to make his Colonel understand that what had been done here should never be done again, not anywhere.

"You don't know where you are?" the Doctor said with a sadistic laugh that bounced like an echo off the faces of the multitude of injured. "You're here, soldier. That's where you are. You're here. Hiroshima. What's left of it. What more do you need to know?" "I need to know the condition of the enemy, sir," the Private said. "I'm searching for the enemy, sir, and I need to know the enemy's condition so I can report back to my commanding officer." "There is no enemy, you foolish little man," the Doctor said. And again the Doctor laughed. And laughed. And laughed. A laugh filled with the pain of knowing far more than it was safe to know. The Private turned on his heel and marched with determination into the hovering cloud of smoke and mist that had risen behind him. It was so thick he could not see his hand held in front of his face. But he could feel the strange things happening to him as he walked. The hot sun turned to a chilly twilight breeze sending shivers of cold across his sweat-soaked brow, back, and chest. He rushed out of the cloud and stopped. Under his feet was the disturbed earth of the crater. He could see the enemy earthworks with stunned riflemen beginning to gather, and across the open field he saw his Colonel urging him forward, saying something like, "Don't stop, you fool idjit! Run." The word *run* echoed across the crater as it was picked up and repeated by the thousand men waiting for his report. "Run," they screamed. "Don't look back, just run, you damn sumbitch!"

He didn't need to look back. He knew what was there. The enemy. With muskets. Loaded. And cocked. And aimed. . . He ran as fast as the broken field would allow. He didn't hear the rifle's report. But he felt the bullet enter his back just below his right shoulder, spinning him around in a full circle. Still he staggered on as twenty or more of his comrades raced into the crater to help him. They grabbed him as the second minnie ball shattered his left knee. He crumbled into their grasp, dragged like a fallen kite, crashing and breaking into a hundred little pieces. The mad dash of his comrades into the crater was the impetus the army had been waiting for. They charged, all of them, hundreds and hundreds of blue coats, entering the crater and hurling themselves into a barrage of lead like none they had seen before. And men fell like saplings in a tornado, ripped open and torn apart by an enfilade of enemy fire that spoke more of desperation than of anything else.

The engagement lasted less than ten minutes as darkness came on quickly and forced the men to retreat, bloodied but not broken, to the safety of their lines. They brought their dead and wounded with them, leaving them as if on display under the trees for either the medic or the coroner to do his thing.

The Colonel leaned over the Private's tattered body and whispered, "Tell me, son, about the enemy. What did you see over there?"

The Private hissed the only word he knew to describe what he had experienced. "Hell," he said. And laughed.

The Private could hear the Doctor's laughter coming out of his throat. He tried to stop it but he didn't know how. "There is no enemy, you foolish little man," he wanted to say, but the laugh prevented it.

Across the way now that night had settled, the Colonel could hear the enemy scurrying about like ants, repairing the crater to keep their defenses intact.

The Private's strange and inexplicable laughter stopped as suddenly as it had begun.

The Colonel leaned over the young man's body and closed its eyes. "Hell," he repeated, not knowing what the word meant.

About the Author

Kenneth Robbins is the author of BUTTERMILK BOTTOMS, recipient of the Toni Morrison Prize and the Associated Writing Programs Novel Award and publication by the University of Iowa Press. He is a published and produced playwright, author of various essays, numerous stories, and several memoirs. He lives in Ruston, LA where he teaches within the Honors Program of Louisiana Tech University.

GALILEO'S DOG

BY KAREN GEMMA BREWER

PERHAPS THE WIDE canvasses of elephants can detect it, or the highly tuned receptors of bats, but it is our blessing that the plaintive cries ringing out across the universe are beyond human ears.

It's all too easy to blame NASA and their adherence to mechanical science in an emotional vacuum. But they just did not comprehend the perpetual loneliness their systems would impose. A loneliness beyond the understanding of its victim. It is, perhaps, a combination of complete ignorance with steadfast loyalty and innocent faith in the face of continual disappointment that makes the reality of my story so painfully sad.

We begin with a journey, a launch into the unknown, with many miles travelled and numerous hazards successfully negotiated. The trials encountered over many months and 35 million miles would probably make an exciting adventure tale in themselves, but my story begins at the journey's end. Although, how much the participants knew it was a one-way-ticket is open to speculation.

From the window, picturesque canals could be seen as they came in to land, bathed, as everything, in a soft red light. The sun shone brightly in the sky, turning the dust into a heavy mist of graffiti red that painted alien slogans on boulders as it settled.

Galileo, a fine figure in silver and grey, buried his feet in the dust, absorbing the impact in the joints of his legs as he jumped to the ground. It was good to feel something solid underfoot and to stretch his limbs, to level off after such a long flight.

The light, cool breeze was also a comfort after the intense heat of atmospheric friction. He raised a finger to the wind, pointed to the sky, and whistled.

Rover was sound asleep, anesthetized over the many months they sped through the heavens, but at the unmistakable sound of his master's voice, he burst immediately to life like a desert flower after rain.

It was as if joy was emanating in waves from his wagging tail as he poked his nose into the dusty air and ran down the ramp to sit in loyal preparedness at his master's feet. Snuggled against Galileo's legs, Rover was fulfilling the destiny he was created for and appeared enthusiastically content.

His role, the role he was designed for, the role that seemingly made him so happy, energetic, and full of love, was to follow his master's command wherever it might lead him, even to the ends of the universe. To stand at his side, yelp when yelping was appropriate, accompany him in silence when it was not. To respond to every request, every signal, with total, unquestioning obedience. To come when called. To go when sent. To stay when stayed and just to be there, there with Galileo, when there was no need for orders.

If Rover's love for Galileo could be measured, it would add up to a preparedness to die for him. Not that he had ever reasoned this out, Rover was not capable of such thought, but just to see them together, you could tell he would. Without question.

So close the bond between master and dog, you could not imagine Galileo making such a long and difficult journey without Rover. His loyal friend, his protector, his sanity, his joy!

Galileo whistled again. There was work to be done and Rover padded obediently into the dust, feeling his way around the many large and angular rocks strewn across his path. Pausing to sniff carefully at those he was directed to by Galileo's whistled commands, tasting their minerals, memorizing their structure.

They worked hard all day, until the sun set on Rover's fatigue and he drifted into a deep and untroubled sleep as the night froze around him. Galileo worked on, sending the information back to earth, to the scientists at NASA, as the irregular contortions of Phoebus crossed the sky for the third time that day.

Communications completed, Galileo turned off the lights and prepared to rest, wondering what might fill his dreams as he slept for the first time on Mars. As he closed down, Deimos crept slowly above the horizon and kept a watchful eye.

Galileo was stirred from his slumber by an impatient companion. The sun had been up for hours and Rover was re-energized and raring to be sent back to work. The old explorer clicked on his switches, then whistled his ever appreciative sidekick into action.

Rover trundled this way and that, nuzzled the red pebble, then the blue stone, the yellow dust and the orange boulder. He punished his tired frame until it could move no longer and fell abruptly into slumber as the sun set on their second day on the red planet.

As Rover rested, Galileo again worked on, transmitting their discoveries to the blue sphere that seemed so far away. He congratulated the scientists on their foresight in fitting him with batteries, rather than leaving him at the mercy of the stars like his solar powered friend.

Phoebus, perhaps intrigued by their long hours of toil, became a regular visitor, calling by at least three times each day, sometimes four, to check on their progress. But fellow moon, tiny Deimos, kept a more suspicious distance, though it loitered in their sky for hours before moving slowly on his way.

Indifferent to the moons, Galileo and Rover continued about their task day after day, like man and dog. Rover reacted to every whistled command during daylight, then slumbered in the darkness while Galileo continued into the night, sending the information back to NASA. They had been doing well, a great team, but the long hours were beginning to take their toll on Galileo. He was growing old, the cold was getting to him, and every day seemed longer that the last as tiredness welled up inside.

These days, Rover had to bark for hours before Galileo awakened and he went back to sleep before dark, leaving his partner waiting in the late afternoon sun for the next whistle. Rover did not complain, he continued to rise with the sun, bark until Galileo responded, work for as long as commands were issued and continue waiting when they ceased, just in case there was one last requirement before sundown. "I'm getting too old for this, boy," Galileo whispered one afternoon. "My batteries are running down." Rover did not understand, just barked a response that said: 'I love you.'

Next morning, Rover barked and barked but Galileo did not respond. Rover barked all afternoon, but there was no comforting whistle. Rover barked until the darkness blacked him out. Up with the sun, Rover barked all the next day. He did not know that Galileo was dead. He would not understand if he did.

Rover knows that Galileo would never abandon him. He does not understand why he does not answer, but knows he will. Until then he barks on, day after day, waiting for the echo of his master's voice. He asks no questions, seeks no explanations, just expresses how he feels every day, from sunrise to sunset.

"I love you," he barks. "I am here and I love you."

About the Author

Karen Gemma Brewer is an award winning poet, story-teller and performer from west Wales, where she lives on an isolated farm in the Grannell Valley, between Lampeter and Aberaeron. Born of coal-mining and farm-working stock, her writing combines emotion and mundanity with a strong sense of the absurd. Her stories have been published in magazines and anthologies in the UK and Ireland and her first collection of poetry, 'Seeds From A Dandelion' was published in June 2017.

EXHIBIT D

BY MICHAEL K. SCHAEFER

A DULL, distant pain throbbed inside Dale's head, its intensity rising and ebbing with cruel regularity. He struggled against waking up, but it was no use: his dreamless sleep was already slipping away and, little by little, he became aware of the reality surrounding him.

It was cold and damp. His legs and his arms were stiff and he was lying on his side, his face resting on something rough.

He groaned. Apparently, they didn't bother heating the cells at night, and the bed's mattress was so uncomfortable that it seemed like just another form of torture. But at least they had let him sleep.

His eyes still closed, Dale rolled onto his back and yawned. He felt like shit. Every bone in his body was aching, and an unpleasant metallic taste lingered in his mouth. Did his cell have a sink where he could get some water? He couldn't remember. Maybe they expected him to rap against the steel door whenever he needed something. Well, no matter how bad the taste was, he wasn't going to do that--they would come for him sooner or later, but he would prefer to keep it later.

Where was that damn blanket? Shivering made the headache worse. The thin woolen blanket that had lain on the bed when he arrived looked and smelled as though it had never actually been washed, but right now, he didn't care. He was cold and tired and wanted to go back to sleep and forget what had happened.

Dale stretched out his left arm and started to grope about, but rather than feeling the blanket or the hard mattress of his bed, his fingers discovered only sand and rock.

What the--

He opened his eyes. There were no concrete walls and no steel door, and the light wasn't coming from a neon tube attached to the ceiling. In fact, there was no ceiling.

He wasn't in his cell.

Dale was wide awake in an instant, and sat up with a jolt.

All around him lay a thick fog that made it impossible to see further than two feet. Looking down, he saw that he wasn't sitting on a bed, but on dusty red sandstone.

He rubbed his eyes. He *had* to be dreaming.

But the cold rock underneath him, and the moist fog that made his clothes clammy and dank, all of it was as real as the cell had been the evening before.

Thoroughly confused, Dale tried to recall everything he could about last night.

After arresting him, they had thrown him into the back of a black van, and driven around for what felt like hours before they stopped and opened the doors in an underground garage. Then they led him through a maze of corridors and past security checkpoints, and finally they shoved him into a cell and locked it without a word. He expected somebody to come and tell him what would happen next, but nobody had--and eventually he had stopped pacing and lain down on the narrow bed. He must have fallen asleep pretty much immediately.

And then?

He didn't remember. They must have brought him here in his sleep--wherever *here* was. Maybe he was in a prison camp. Or maybe they had decided he wasn't worth the bother and just dumped him at the side of a road outside the city.

Well, sitting here and speculating wouldn't get him anywhere.

Feeling slightly dizzy, he stood up and started walking, but before he had taken so much as three steps, he reached an edge. And beyond that edge was...nothing. The impenetrable fog hid whatever lay underneath. There was no way to tell how far down it went--it could be a few feet or a few miles.

He turned around and walked in the opposite direction. After six or seven steps, he found another edge.

Cursing, he turned left and walked along the rim, but it took him only a few seconds before he realized that he was walking in circles. Whatever this place was, it was more or less round and just a couple of feet across.

Where *was* he?

Lying on the ground, Dale reached his arm down the side of the stone edge. His fingers didn't touch ground. He moved a few feet along the edge and once more stretched his arm as far down as he could, but again found nothing but empty air. It took less than three minutes to confirm that it was the same the whole way around.

He would have to wait until the fog lifted before deciding what to do next. Hopefully he'd be able to see more of his surroundings once the sun rose.

Dale paced nervously as he waited. Without any point of reference, it was impossible to say how much time passed. All the while, he expected to hear shouts and the sound of running footsteps, and to see the contours of guards in black combat gear appearing from the fog, intent on dragging him back to the cell. As much as he wanted it to be true, he still couldn't believe they would let him go just like that. But nothing happened, and he didn't hear anything. If there were sounds, they were muffled by the dense fog.

After what felt like an eternity, the sun finally came up, tinting the fog a warm orange. It dissipated rapidly, like a curtain opening, revealing what lay beyond.

And then Dale saw where he was.

H<small>E WAS STANDING</small> on an impossibly high stone pillar. Looking down over the edge of the platform, he estimated that it had to be at least a six-hundred-foot drop. The pillar itself was so slender that, by all rights, it shouldn't be able to stay upright. And it wasn't the only one.

Countless similar pillars were scattered across a long, barren valley. All of them were about the same height, and so thin that a light breeze should have been enough to make them come tumbling down in thundering chaos. They were composed of red sandstone shot through with layers of beige, brown and black. It must have taken millions of years for the wind and rain to grind out such a curiosity of nature.

But it wasn't the strange valley that made Dale question once more whether he was still asleep. It was the people.

There, atop their own pillars, were about fifty others: women and men alike, standing, sitting, lying, or pacing on the platforms. Their placement seemed haphazard, without order, spread all over the valley. They looked tiny atop the gigantic stone columns. Worse, they looked trapped. Like him.

Dale's knees buckled and he slumped to the ground. His hands shook uncontrollably.

What *was* this place? Why had he and all those other people been brought here?

His head spinning, Dale was close to a full-blown panic attack. He closed his eyes and started counting backwards from one hundred. He had once read it was supposed to help.

After a few minutes, he opened his eyes again. The feeling of panic and desperation hadn't gone entirely, but at least he had succeeded in pushing it far enough into the background to be able to think.

He must have been brought here as a form of punishment. It didn't make any sense, but he couldn't come up with any other explanation. And all because he had taken the train instead of walking home as he usually did.

When the squad of bullies dressed in the uniform of the police had pulled him from the train station queue, frisked him and searched his bag, he had been nervous--everybody was nervous these days when the police were around--but not overly concerned. He was, after all, an ordinary person, keeping his head down and trying to lead as normal a life as possible despite the increasingly questionable actions of the government. He didn't agree with their ideology and many of the new laws, but he couldn't do anything about it, so he figured there was no sense in getting himself into trouble. But somehow, he had managed to do exactly that.

When the police searched his bag, they found the book and demanded to know what it was. It was a silly thing, really: a dream journal he started as a teenager. Just for fun. It was no crime to write down dreams, but they had skimmed the book anyway and had chanced upon a particularly surreal dream about a field of pumpkins. In it, Dale had berated a group of scarecrows because the pumpkins were of different sizes and in no order at all, and demanded that the birds hand in their resignation. It was complete nonsense of course, but the police had announced that these were seditious writings attacking the government and posing a threat to the order of society, and they had arrested him on the spot.

People were arrested as enemies of the state all the time, but Dale had always assumed they were thrown into normal prisons.

His knees still shaking, Dale stood up. He walked over to the edge and looked down once more. It was painfully obvious that climbing down would be impossible. Apart from the height of the pillar, and the strength and skill required--both of which he lacked-- the sandstone was so featureless and brittle that not even an experienced climber would be able to find a secure handhold.

The ground far below was bare except for the occasional wiry bush or dry tree. There were no people down there, and nothing man-made as far as he could see.

Moving away from the edge, he stomped the platform in frustration. To his surprise, he heard a metallic sound. In the fog, he hadn't noticed that there was a metal hatch in the ground, directly in the center of the pillar, covered completely with red stone dust.

Dale knelt and swept away the dirt. The hatch was roughly the length of his arm, made of stainless steel, and had been carefully fitted so that there was almost no gap between the metal and the stone. There was no handle of any kind.

He knocked on the hatch. It made a dull, hollow sound, but nothing happened.

Dale stood again and turned his attention to the other people trapped atop the pillars. The closest was a middle-aged woman about five hundred feet to his right, and he waved to get her attention. She looked at him, but didn't seem to be overly interested.

"Where are we?" he shouted at the top of his voice. "What is this place?"

The woman only shrugged. After a moment, and with what appeared to be considerable effort, she pulled herself out of her lethargy and yelled back. "Don't know. None of us knows."

Her voice was just barely intelligible over this distance. If the light wind had been blowing in another direction or were any stronger, he probably wouldn't have been able to understand her.

"Is there a way out of here?" Dale felt a bit stupid asking the question--clearly his fellow inmates weren't standing on the pillars for fun.

The woman stared at him, then she shook her head slowly. "Some try to climb. They fall. Some jump. Others just...stop. But nobody escapes."

The shouted conversation was exhausting and slow-going. Dale and Antonia--the woman's name--had to repeat every other sentence as the words were swallowed by distance and the wind. Several times, Antonia fell silent, and it took dragging minutes before he could get her attention again. But little by little, Dale learned more about this place.

Every last woman and man there had a similar story to his: they had been arrested following real or imagined actions against the government, thrown into a cell, and then taken to the valley in their sleep. None of them knew how or why they had been brought here--though one man had yelled something about alien abduction before throwing himself off his pillar.

Nobody had ever seen a new prisoner arrive, as every night, without fail, the fog came and only lifted again at dawn. There were no guards, as far as anybody could tell, and they had never seen any movement on the ground below. Nobody knew where this strange valley was.

And that was pretty much it.

In a way, it was both better and worse than what Dale had expected. On the one hand, they apparently wouldn't be tortured or executed, but on the other, there was no hope at all. None.

Antonia had turned away once he had run out of questions. Dale found it impossible to keep still, and so he started to walk in circles around the edge of the platform. It was getting warmer in the valley by the minute, and he was starting to sweat.

The sun was high in the sky and burning with a searing intensity when Dale suddenly heard a metallic click. Turning around, he saw that the metal hatch had sprung open. His heart gave a jolt, and an irrational rush of hope flared up that this might be a way out, that maybe there was a staircase or a ladder hidden underneath. But when he walked over, he discovered that there was only a small compartment. Inside was a bottle of water and a box of sandwiches.

So that was how they were fed.

All around, his fellow prisoners were bending down and picking up items. Apparently, they all had a hatch like his, and they had all opened at the same time.

It reminded Dale of feeding time at the zoo.

After a few minutes, the hatch closed again, interrupting Dale's inspection of the compartment. Still pondering the mechanism, he ate. The sandwiches had some kind of meat and a few leaves of lettuce, but were almost tasteless. When he had eaten the last crumb and washed it down with the stale water, Dale resumed his rounds along the edge of the platform.

The hatch opened a second time at dusk, and it once more contained a box of the bland sandwiches and a bottle of water. And with dusk came the fog. It settled on the valley as suddenly as it had lifted in the morning, and the curtain closed around Dale for the night.

With nothing else to do, and emotionally drained from the day, Dale lay down on the sandstone. For a few moments, he tried to find a comfortable position on the hard ground, but it seemed impossible. Despite his tiredness, he was sure he wouldn't be able to sleep; but before he had even finished the thought, he was already snoring.

***

THE DAYS PASSED in a monotone and uneventful rhythm.

Every morning, the fog lifted and Dale would check whether there had been any new arrivals. There didn't seem to be a pattern. Some days, there were two or three new prisoners, and then nobody would arrive for a week or more.

There was absolutely nothing to do, and so Dale spent the hours mostly pacing and observing his fellow prisoners. He was soon able to tell which had been here for a while: they were the ones whiling away the day sleeping, or simply staring into nothingness.

Of course, there also were the ones who had stopped doing anything: on a couple of platforms lay skeletons, the bones bleached and dry. He was glad he couldn't see any recently deceased, but knew where some must be, as they attracted the only other living beings in the valley. Vultures, big and bald and strangely majestic, would turn up to circle a platform for a while before swooping down to feast.

Every night the fog came, hiding the strange valley and its prisoners from Dale, making it seem, for a few hours, as if he were alone in the world.

***

DALE WAS SITTING at the edge of the platform, his feet dangling over the chasm below. The height no longer bothered him.

Antonia had jumped a couple of days ago. He had been looking in her direction when she suddenly sprang to her feet, straightened her clothes, and walked briskly toward and over the edge. She didn't cry out--there was just a silent and incredibly long fall.

He had counted the seconds in his head without even thinking about it. Eight.

Dale broke a small piece of sandstone off the platform's edge and threw it into the chasm.

The rest of the day passed slowly, and when the sun finally set, he found it difficult to sleep. He wondered how Antonia had known it was time.

HE BLINKED into the early morning sun. So, what should he do today?

Maybe a nice walk around the platform. That might be entertaining for a minute or so if he walked *really* slowly. Or he could do some pushups. Who knew, if he worked out he might one day impress a passing vulture with his chiseled biceps. There was, of course, the option of breaking some stones off the edge of the platform. If he really kept at it, he might be able to demolish the pillar in ten thousand years or so. It could even be possible to--

"Ah, good morning. I see you've finally woken up," came a voice from behind him.

Dale fully opened his eyes. This was new.

He rolled over to find a man standing on a pillar that was no more than thirty feet away from his own. The man gave him a cheery wave.

"Beautiful morning, isn't it?" he asked as if they were meeting in front of their houses in suburbia while fetching the newspaper. "And the air is so fresh." He took a deep breath and exhaled with obvious relish. "Wonderful. I tell you, you don't get air like this in the city."

Dale rubbed his eyes. Maybe he had finally gone insane.

"And the view, it's quite lovely. All these pillars, and the lovely colors, that's something you don't see every day."

Without taking his eyes off the man, Dale slowly stood up and moved closer to the edge of his platform. The man was a little smaller than he was, probably in his early fifties, and what little hair he had left on his head was mussed and sticking out in all directions. He wore thick, horn-rimmed glasses and a matching brown sweater vest, which could only have been fashionable in a time well before the invention of mirrors. Smiling happily at Dale as he chattered away, the man seemed to be a normal, everyday kind of guy.

And, of course, a complete looney.

"Sorry," interrupted Dale, his voice hoarse from sleep. "I don't mean to sound rude, but I have to ask: are you mad?"

The man smiled even more broadly.

"Oh no," he replied, "I don't think I am. At least my doctor told me at my last checkup that I'm fit as a fiddle and that I'm--"

"Sorry," interrupted Dale again, "but could you explain to me why all of this," he made a gesture encompassing the platforms, the pillars, and the other prisoners, "doesn't bother you?"

"Oh, I think this is all quite exciting," said the man, looking around. "I like seeing new places, and this is definitely one I can tell my grandkids stories about someday. Well, if I ever get to have grandkids. My daughter Maggie is 22, and just the other day she told me she thinks the traditional concept of family is outdated and misogynistic. She plans to--"

"I don't think you fully grasp the gravity of the situation." He was really getting annoyed that the man didn't react in a sensible way. He should have been freaking out, trembling, maybe crying a little. Like a *sane* person. "We're prisoners here. There's no way to get off these pillars except jumping. You'll never see your daughter again. This is the end of the line."

The man stared at him for a long moment. Then he chuckled.

"Oh no, I don't think that I'll stay here long. A couple of days maybe. Long enough to really get a feeling for the place. And then I'll be off--I've lots to do, you know. Always busy, busy, busy. But anyway, where are my manners, I'm Magnus." He gave a small wave. "Magnus Beckwick. And you are?"

"Dale," replied Dale in a flat voice, still staring at the man. "Oswick."

"Delighted to make your acquaintance." Magnus smiled brightly at him. "Now, can you tell me a bit about this place? You look like you've been here a while, and probably know the ins and outs of this place from which you say there are no outs and only ins."

Dale shook his head incredulously, but then told the man how he had come to the valley and what he knew about it, which admittedly wasn't much. He did his best to stress the fact that they were *prisoners* here, that there was *no escape*, and that they would *die*.

When Dale had finished his account, he gestured at Magnus. "Your turn. What's your story?"

"Oh, it's not very interesting," replied Magnus. "Very similar to yours. Let's see, I had driven into town to do some shopping. My mother has her eightieth birthday next month, and I was planning--" He broke off when he saw Dale's face. "Anyway, I had just arrived in the town center when I found myself in some kind of rally. There was a man on a podium making a speech about how great the state is, how kind our government, etcetera, etcetera. You know the kind of thing. I listened for a minute or two and was finding all the balderdash very amusing when two police officers approached me and enquired why I was laughing. So I told them. Only a nitwit could believe any of the nonsense that was being spouted. They didn't agree--they were quite angry, in fact--but they were, of course, only the brainless servants of a dictatorial regime that rules through brutality rather than political acumen. What can you expect? So they cuffed me, put me into a van, and drove me to some kind of underground prison. I went to sleep and the next morning--that is, today--I woke up here."

Magnus looked around once more at the many prisoners on their platforms. Then he giggled. He actually *giggled*. "It's like an exhibition of all those the government has deemed enemies, isn't it?

We're like living statues in the world's largest art installation. Wonderful."

"You don't get it," snapped Dale, "you're stuck here. You can't really enjoy this. There is no escape."

"Oh yes, there is," Magnus replied casually as he used his foot to nudge a stone over the edge of his platform. Leaning slightly over the chasm, he added, "At least, for me."

The mere thought of finding a way out of this place made Dale's heart pump fast and hard. Did this guy really know how to escape?

"How?" he asked, his voice quavering.

Magnus shrugged. "I'll just walk out of here."

"Walk out of--" Dale threw his arms up in exasperation. "There is nowhere to go!"

But Magnus was no longer listening. Instead, he was crouching down and inspecting the metallic hatch with intent curiosity.

Dale sat down on the edge of his platform and watched. Well, he had company again, which was nice, though the man was definitely crazy. Then again, maybe he would come to his senses in a few days.

He didn't.

Magnus continued to be unbearably cheery, acting as if this place and their situation was nothing more than an interesting adventure. Whenever Dale brought up the topic of how Magnus planned to escape, he just smiled, bemused, and ignored the question. Instead, he would start babbling about some completely unrelated topic, usually revolving around his extensive family, the *hilarious* hijinks of various pets, or the challenges of organic gardening. When Magnus wasn't talking, he was meditating: he would sit in lotus position on the ground, close his eyes, and stay that way for hours on end.

Even though Dale enjoyed not being alone anymore, and being able to talk to somebody without shouting, it was exhausting being constantly exposed to this guy's particular brand of craziness. And the fact that Magnus was so unwaveringly convinced he would escape was gnawing at him.

Did Magnus really have a way out of here?

Dale tried to come up with a possible explanation for how this apparently unremarkable guy would be able to get out of here when nobody else could. Maybe he wanted to climb down the pillar? Unlikely; he didn't look muscular enough. Or maybe he was friends with somebody who could pull strings to get him freed, like a politician of some kind? Possibly, but also unlikely. Someone with his political views wouldn't be friends with somebody in the establishment, that would be highly dangerous for both of them. There had to be something underneath the food compartments, but Dale was sure it was impossible to find out what it was without a decent crowbar.

So what was Magnus' plan?

It was only on the fourth day that Magnus finally relented to Dale's constant badgering to tell him how he planned to escape.

"All right, all right," he said, "I'll tell you. But I must warn you that you'll probably not believe me. And even if you do, it won't be much use to you. My way to leave this place is...special. Keep that in mind, eh?" He waited until Dale nodded. Then he began:

"As you know, our scientists can do many wonderful things nowadays, and our knowledge in many areas is highly advanced. However, there is one fascinating object that still holds secrets: the human brain. Researchers have mapped its functional regions--there are hundreds--and deciphered the purpose of many, but some remain a complete mystery. Nobody knows what they are for. One theory is that they are an evolutionary 'dead-end' and are no longer in use. Another suggests that humans simply haven't yet progressed far enough in the development of their cognitive capabilities, and that we therefore do not yet have access to the advanced abilities these regions hold. Only the thing is, that is not quite correct: there are individuals who have. Like me." He gave Dale the kind of modest smile that communicates with astounding effectiveness how amazing the wearer of said smile actually is. "I have developed a capability that I would describe as quite extraordinary. One that would seem rather implausible to most people." He looked directly at Dale. "I have access to a way of traveling that isn't limited by the restrictions of the physical world. One that can get me out of any place. One that allows me to travel a huge distance in next to no time."

Dale suppressed a groan. Magnus would probably shout *Beam me up, Scotty!* any second now. But the other man didn't seem to notice the look on Dale's face.

"This capability I'm speaking of is what I like to call *dream hiking*. I'm able to walk into a dream I'm having, and use it to travel to the actual location the dream takes place."

He looked at Dale expectantly, and when Dale didn't do or say anything, Magnus added: "Don't confuse it with dream *walking*, which is the capability of entering someone else's dream. I'm entering my own dreams, to use them as a kind of shortcut."

Apparently thinking this clarified things, he gave a satisfied nod and waited.

At long last, Dale cleared his throat and asked, "You can step into your dreams?"

"It's actually more like stepping *through* my dreams, but yes."

"Just like that?"

"Oh no, of course not." Magnus laid a hand on his chest. "It requires that I'm perfectly attuned to the place I'm currently in-- that's why I'm meditating a lot, you know. Then of course I have to dream of a place I actually want to go to. Places I know very well are easiest--that's what I started with a long time ago, places like my house, or my garden, or my friend Miss Roja's restaurant down the road--but it could be a place I've seen on television or in photos. Imaginary places don't work. I theorize that it should be possible for me to leave the planet and go to the Moon, or maybe to Mars, but it wouldn't change the fact that I couldn't survive there without a spacesuit, you know?"

"Yeah. Sure."

Magnus' eyes suddenly lit up, and he let out a delighted laugh. "It's just now occurring to me: you were arrested because of your dreams and I'll escape through mine. Ironic, isn't it?"

Dale chose not to tell him what he thought of that.

"Here's a question," he said instead, doing his best to sound nonchalant. "Why haven't you left already? It can't be that much fun here."

"Oh, I'm working on it," Magnus assured him. "I think I'm almost there with the meditation part, so now all I need is to dream of a place I want to go to, and then I'm off."

"Right. And how did you develop this, ah, unusual capability?"

Magnus picked up the bottle of water from his hatch and took a quick sip. "It started with me having a lot of intense and very realistic dreams. And one day I told myself: Magnus my boy, you seem to have a knack with dreams, perhaps there's more to it than meets the eye. So I practiced influencing my dreams while I was having them--not an easy thing, mind you, and the first step is, of course, to know that you're dreaming while you're having a dream--and that worked quite well after a while. Over time, I tried to do more than just influence, I attempted pushing the boundaries of those dreams, if that makes sense."

It didn't, not even slightly, but Dale didn't interrupt him.

"And one day," continued Magnus, "when I was dreaming of the orchard behind my parents' house, I just felt I could step through the dream if I wanted to. So I did." He nodded to himself. "This capability has taken me to many fascinating places so far, places I would never have been able to visit otherwise. You know how it is, what with movement being restricted nowadays, and leaving the country-- well, we both know that's near impossible. But thanks to my capability, I've been to many countries; I've seen mountains and deserts and rainforests, and I have met many different people from all around the world. And all of it by dream hiking."

He put down his water bottle, straightened his sweater vest, and gave a slight bow.

"So, there you have it. That's my secret and my plan." He grinned. "What do you think?"

Dale started at him and blinked a couple of times. Then he sighed.

"I think you're insane."

Without waiting for a reaction, he turned around, walked to the other side of his platform, and went to sleep.

When Dale awoke the next morning, he was greeted by the sight of a large vulture circling high above his pillar. He sat up and looked sullenly over at the neighboring platform. Magnus was already meditating.

Dale grunted and turned around to check whether any new prisoners had arrived during the night. There hadn't, but a platform in the distance was empty that hadn't been the day before. Another prisoner had jumped, or maybe accidentally fallen off during the night.

"Ah, good morning, neighbor. Beautiful day, isn't it?"

Dale winced and pretended he hadn't heard anything.

"Did you sleep well? I slept like a baby. A bit surprising, really, given we don't even have pillows. But I think the hard ground is actually good for my back. You see, I've had problems with my lower back ever since..."

Magnus continued to chatter as though he didn't notice that Dale hadn't even bothered to turn around, let alone joined the conversation. He didn't seem to be insulted by what Dale had said to him the previous night. In fact, he appeared to find it amusing. He kept making comments like, "This might be the insanity talking, but I believe the sandwiches are even tastier today than they were yesterday." And he whistled a lot.

He was driving Dale crazy, and when it was already beginning to get dark, he couldn't take it anymore.

"Why don't you take a hike, already!" he snapped, and his voice sounded dry and harsh after a day of not speaking a single word.

Magnus gave him one of his cheery smiles. "Oh, I'm trying to, believe me. I would like nothing better. This place is starting to get a trifle boring."

"Then what are you waiting for? Don't have any dreams, do you?"

"Of course I have dreams," replied Magnus, then he shrugged. "Just none about places I feel like going to. For example, last night I dreamed I was standing underneath the Eiffel Tower in Paris. I started to push through the dream, but then I thought, 'Paris? I don't want to go to Paris. I don't speak the language.' So I decided to stay here for another night or two until I dream of somewhere better."

"Yeah, right," spat Dale. "You decided to stay. That's the only reason why you're still here, not the fact that your 'dream hiking' is a load of crap."

Magnus smiled indulgently. "You'll see."

And he did.

The next morning, Magnus was gone.

THE PLATFORM WAS DESERTED. The few square feet of red sandstone on top of the gigantic column were as empty as they could be.

Standing at the edge of his own pillar, Dale leaned over and looked down. He couldn't see a body, but that wasn't surprising: from up here, the ground was so far that he wouldn't be able to tell Magnus' remains from the boulders and the dry vegetation.

Dale shook his head and sighed. The guy had been a pain in the neck, but nobody deserved--

"See anything interesting?"

Dale gave a start and lost his balance. For a moment, he was sure he would fall off the pillar, and he just barely managed to catch himself in time. He took a hasty step back from the edge, then turned around.

Magnus was standing on a different pillar on the other side of Dale's platform, and he was grinning.

"What did I tell you? I dream hiked over here."

This wasn't possible. How could he-- There shouldn't--

"You climbed," stated Dale, but even as he said it he knew that couldn't be the case.

"Do I look like somebody who could free climb all the way down one of these pillars and then climb up a different one?" asked Magnus, looking at Dale pityingly. "And even if I could, why would I be so stupid as to risk my life over it? If I could climb down, I would stay there and get out of this valley."

"Then you had a rope or something."

"Now where would I get a rope hundreds of feet long?"

"Or you somehow managed to get to whatever is underneath the food compartment."

Magnus shook his head. "Afraid not. That's quite out of the question without proper tools, as you told me yourself."

"But--" Dale was getting desperate. "Yes! Somebody helped you. A guard. They came during the night with another captive, and they helped you change pillars."

"Nope." He smiled apologetically. "Come on, honestly, why would they--whoever they are--do that after they've gone to such lengths to ensure that they're never seen and that there's no way off our allotted platforms? I mean, they don't even remove the skeletons."

There was a long silence.

"So it's true," said Dale slowly, though he couldn't believe he was actually saying it. "You really can walk into your dreams?"

Magnus became very earnest all of a sudden. "I certainly do. I'm not crazy, and I didn't lie to you."

Dale made a helpless gesture toward the platform. "But, if that's true, why on earth did you dream hike to another pillar?"

"Simple, really," replied Magnus. "I was dreaming about this place, and I thought changing pillars might help you to overcome your doubts. And," he chuckled, "I really, really wanted to see your face when you discovered what I'd done."

Dale didn't know what to say. This didn't make any sense.

"So what now?" he finally asked.

"Now I go back to meditating," replied Magnus, before sitting down and doing exactly that.

As he had done before, Magnus spent the hours until dusk in lotus position, breathing in and out deeply and regularly. Unlike him, Dale couldn't sit still. He spent the time nervously pacing from one side of the platform to the other, and when he couldn't stand that anymore, he circled around the edge until he was dizzy.

He tried desperately to come up with a logical explanation for what had happened, but each time he came to the same conclusion: there was no way Magnus could have gotten to the other pillar other than--well, by doing exactly what he said he had done.

When the sun was slowly setting, Dale was surprised to see that the hatch on Magnus' new pillar opened, while the one on his old pillar remained shut. So either somebody was watching them, or there were hidden sensors that determined which pillars were occupied. Neither thought was particularly pleasant.

As he walked over to his own hatch, Dale reached a decision.

"Can you teach me?"

Magnus stopped rearranging the lettuce on his sandwich and looked up at Dale.

There was no congeniality or quirkiness in his eyes anymore. They were uncharacteristically sharp and piercing.

Magnus stared at him like that for a long moment, and Dale was certain he would refuse. But then the man blinked and smiled.

"I can certainly give it a go. It might be an interesting experiment. Of course, I have never met anyone else with the same ability, so it might not be possible. But if you have the patience and are willing to put in the effort, then maybe--just maybe--you can learn dream hiking too." Magnus looked down at his sandwich and moved the lettuce a tiny fraction to the left. "Learning to dream hike requires a lot of meditation and a lot of practice influencing your dreams--and you can't learn either by simply watching what I do. There are some techniques that can certainly make it easier, but still, it will be hard work, and you need to fully commit to the undertaking."

For the first time in a very long time, Dale smiled. "It's not like I have a lot else to do. I'm willing to do whatever it takes to get out of here."

"Good, good." Magnus yawned. "Tomorrow, all right? We'll start your training tomorrow."

With another smile and a nod, Dale turned away from the man as he settled down to sleep. It felt good to have something akin to a plan, to have something to work toward. That was worth a lot, even if what he planned on doing was weird and unlikely and defied common sense. Tomorrow he would start learning how to dream hike.

But the next morning, Magnus was gone for good.

TURNING SLOWLY on the spot and inspecting the pillars in the valley one by one, Dale knew that it was hopeless. Magnus was gone. He'd dreamed of a place he wanted to go to, and that was it.

Dale wasn't mad at him. Disappointed, yes, but not mad. He would have done the same thing in Magnus' place.

He shrugged. This didn't change anything. He would learn how to dream hike even without help from Magnus. Short of being released, whether by his captors or by the long fall, it was his only way out. Maybe it would never work, but he had the time and he certainly had the motivation.

So he started to meditate. He imitated what he had seen Magnus doing for hours on end: he sat down in lotus position, breathed deeply and regularly, and tried to empty his mind of any thoughts.

It was at night time, though, that he worked on the really tricky part: attempting to become aware he was dreaming, which Magnus had mentioned was the first step. The only approach he could think of was concentrating on what he wanted to dream about before sleep, recalling every detail of the dreams he'd had after waking up, and trying to go back to an interrupted dream after he woke up in the middle of the night.

To his surprise, he really started to make progress after a while. It happened gradually, in small steps, and it required patience. And he discovered that being aware he was dreaming and being able to think clearly without letting himself be influenced by the inner logic of a dream were separate skills which he had to learn one after the other.

Once he was confident he had sufficiently mastered the basics, Dale moved on to the next stage: trying to influence his dreams. But here he ran into a brick wall. His dreams just wouldn't behave the way he wanted them to. He was just a passive observer.

Weeks and then months passed, and Dale became increasingly frustrated. The harder he tried, the more his dreams seemed to push back and resist his attempts to steer them. Trying to learn dream hiking had distracted him and given him something to concentrate on, but now he once more started to feel how trapped he really was.

As time continued to roll by without even the slightest bit of progress, Dale descended into a depressed state that part of him recognized as similar to that of Antonia when he had arrived in the valley. But he no longer cared. He found himself more and more often standing at the edge of the platform, looking down, thinking it would be so easy. Just shifting his balance slightly, just a single step or hop, then eight seconds of falling and that would be it. So simple. So tempting. Eight seconds.

He didn't do it, but he was running out of reasons not to.

Eventually, he stopped trying to dream hike altogether. He just couldn't get himself to make the effort anymore. Instead, he spent the days staring at the other prisoners on their pillars, wondering which one would be the next to jump.

And it was in that state of resignation and depression that he finally succeeded in influencing a dream.

In the dream, Dale found himself standing at an intersection: there was a road going to the left and another to the right. It was a warm day, and Dale knew he was on his way to meet his family. They would be sitting outside a café at the edge of the town square, underneath the shady leaves of a big oak tree, waiting for him to finally join them. And he knew one more thing: he'd had this dream before. This exact dream. He had chosen the road to his right, and he had walked endlessly along lonely roads, through suburban settlements, and at one point even through a theme park before he had finally found the town square--only to discover that he would have arrived there in mere steps had he taken the road to the left. And somehow, knowing all this helped. Even though he had started to turn right, Dale realized he could make the conscious decision to turn left instead. He didn't try to *steer* his dream-self, he just walked as if he really were there. And after a few steps, he did indeed arrive at the town square, and there was the café and the tree and underneath it his family. Then he woke up.

After this first dream, it got easier. It didn't always work, but more and more often Dale was able to influence the dream he was having. Dream hiking was finally within his reach!

Magnus had told him the truth.

He quickly discovered that consciously walking around in a dream was one thing, but stepping into it--or *through* it, as Magnus had described--was quite another. It didn't work when he dreamed being back at university, writing a test for a subject he couldn't even pronounce; it didn't work when he dreamed about a picnic in the park with his ex-girlfriend; and it didn't work when he dreamed he was a ballerina wearing a pink tutu dancing in the city's ballet.

Dale would have given anything to be able to talk to Magnus and ask for pointers. Unfortunately, that wasn't an option. All he could do was to continue trying and hope for a breakthrough.

When it finally came, he wasn't prepared for it. It happened so effortlessly and so lacking the dramatic Hollywood-like special effects he had been picturing, that it almost felt like a letdown.

Dale was dreaming about the day five years ago when he had

moved into his apartment. It had been a disaster. One of the two moving vans had been in an accident and its contents had been scattered all over the road. The second van held only his books and his TV and a set of mismatched skis for which he didn't really have an explanation. So he found himself looking around a nigh-on empty apartment, with a few boxes full of books, the TV atop one of them, holding the skis. And that was the scene he was now reliving in his dream.

By now, he was used to being aware he was dreaming, but this was special; everything felt so real and so familiar, even the smell of the room was just as he remembered it. And then he simply *knew* he could not only influence the dream but walk through it. It was like the dream in which he had decided to turn left rather than right: he just had to step in the direction he wanted to go.

And with just a single step, he walked through the dream of his empty apartment, left the valley of pillars behind, and emerged in his real, furnished apartment.

THE TRANSITION from his dream to the real world happened so abruptly that he stumbled, nearly falling onto the coffee table.

Speechless, Dale looked around his living room.

He was home.

With a shaking hand, he picked up one of the photos that lay scattered on the coffee table in front of him. He wiped a thick layer of dust off it. It was an old black and white photograph that showed his great-grandfather playing with his sisters in the courtyard of a farm somewhere. Dale had found the photos when cleaning out his aunt's house after she passed away, and he had taken them home, planning to find out when and where they had been taken. He had only started to look through them again the day before he had been arrested.

Dale put the photo down and moved around, touching things just to confirm they were really there and not part of a dream.

Everything was covered in dust, and the air was stale. The plants on his balcony had probably turned into a veritable jungle in his absence, and he didn't even want to think about the moldy horrors awaiting him in the fridge.

Dale closed his eyes. Home at last. He could go wherever he wanted. He could meet other people, hold them, interact with them. Instead of being on display like a statue, he had the privacy of his apartment. And he could sleep in a bed rather than on the bare ground. And food! He would finally be able to eat and drink something other than sandwiches and water. His stomach rumbled at the thought of fresh vegetables, of noodles and potatoes, and of steak and fish. And of chocolate.

He opened his eyes again. Right, he should let some fresh air in. And then he should check the mail and the answering machine; his family and friends had to be worried sick about him. He smiled at the thought of seeing them again and of--

There was a deafening crash in the hallway and the sound of splintering wood. Dale spun around to see men in black combat gear storming into his living room, assault rifles pointed at his head. Before he knew what was happening, the attacker in front tackled him and threw him down onto the ground. The impact was so brutal it knocked the wind out of him, and he thought he felt several ribs snap.

Dazed and in pain, Dale didn't even try to resist as the attacker pinned him down. Somebody else grabbed his hands and put them into cuffs.

"Subject contained, Sir," he heard one of the men say. "We're bringing him in."

A BLACK VAN. A long drive. An underground garage. A maze of corridors and security checkpoints. It was like a horrible déjà vu, a nightmare he'd had before and from which he'd thought he'd finally awoken.

None of his captors spoke so much as a single word to him, and Dale didn't ask any questions. After all, what was the point? He'd escaped, and they had recaptured him. They would once more throw him into a cell, and he would once more wake up in that strange valley without a trial or an explanation.

Dale was scared, of course, but not as much as he had been the first time. He had dream hiked once, and he was sure that he would be able to do it again. And this time he would go someplace they wouldn't be able to find him.

Come to think of it, how *had* they discovered so fast that he had escaped and returned to his apartment?

The two guards leading him through the underground corridors stopped, opened a door on their right, and shoved him through it. He expected it would be another cell like the one they'd held him in last time, but he was wrong.

Instead of a cell, Dale found himself in a brightly lit office. The walls were decorated with paintings and framed photographs of smiling people, and in the middle of the room stood a desk with a computer and mounds of scattered documents. Behind the desk sat a man.

Magnus.

He was smiling brightly and gestured toward a chair in front of his desk.

"So nice to see you again, my friend. Please, have a seat."

Dale felt incapable of moving. He stood frozen, staring at Magnus.

One of the guards gave him a shove forward and then rudely pushed him down onto the chair.

"Based on the expression on your face," said Magnus, "my little surprise has turned out exactly as I had hoped. Wonderful. I would have been very disappointed if I had given myself away at some point. But, apparently, I didn't, so all is well." He indicated a tray with two cups and a porcelain pot. "Can I offer you a cup of coffee?"

Dale shook his head.

"No? Very well. I assume you would like an explanation?"

Dale nodded.

"Quite understandable." Magnus spread his hands. "Where would you like me to start?"

"Who are you?" asked Dale, his voice little more than a whisper.

"Oh, you know who I am," replied the man. "My name really is Magnus Beckwick. Though I'm not some seditious citizen, and never was incarcerated. No, I'm afraid that was all part of this little ruse of mine. I am, in fact, a senior researcher working on highly classified projects for our benevolent government. And you, my friend, had the pleasure of being part of my latest--and apparently highly successful--experiment."

Magnus took a cup from the tray and poured himself a coffee, a self-satisfied smirk on his face. The aroma of freshly brewed coffee wafted through the room. Dale had dreamed of this smell during his time on the pillar, but at that moment couldn't have cared less. His thoughts were racing, trying to understand what Magnus was saying.

"I was a lab rat to you?" he asked. "You brought me to that goddamned valley and put me on that pillar for some experiment?"

Magnus looked up from his coffee. "Yes, that is correct. But mine wasn't the only experiment in the valley, of course. Everyone was part of some experiment or other, many of which are entirely fascinating, I can tell you."

Dale blinked several times, not knowing what to say.

Magnus smiled indulgently. "You're still confused. Allow me to explain." He took a sip of coffee. "Do you remember how I told you that there are regions in the human brain that are still a mystery?"

Dale nodded.

"Good. That is precisely what we are researching in this institution: how to unlock the capabilities hidden in those regions. We can only speculate what those might be, but we believe that there are clues in ancient legends and myths: abilities like mind reading, telekinesis, clairvoyance, or teleportation can be found in stories from all over the world and in all cultures. This can't be a coincidence.

"My colleagues and I are convinced that these capabilities are real and innate to all of us, although only few humans in history have been able to access them. Why? Well, because people need to make the effort to learn how to use them. So we decided to put our test subjects--like yourself--in a situation that is so completely without hope, that is entirely without a way out except death, that the test subjects have the necessary motivation." He chuckled. "A situation that is do or die, really. The valley is perfect for that, don't you think?"

Dale felt a strong urge to leap forward, grab the man by the throat, and strangle him. Instead, he asked, "How come I've never heard of that place?"

Magnus actually laughed out loud. "My dear friend, our government is quite effective when it comes to suppressing information the public doesn't need to know about. Anyway, the valley allows us to place test subjects in an environment over which we have total control, and which doesn't provide any means of escape or distractions. Each test subject is provided with 'seed information'-- desperate people will believe pretty much anything after a certain point. In your case, I joined you for a few days to plant the idea of dream hiking in your head, and convince you that it was possible. And then I just waited to see whether you could activate your innate capabilities."

Dale felt numb.

"Results vary," Magnus continued, "but that's normal in research. We do have quite a bit of, ah, *fluctuation* in the number of our test subjects. Not many can stand the isolation, you see. Still, there have been very promising results in a couple of our experiments. And you," he pointed at Dale with pride, "are by far our most successful experiment. You've been the first to dream hike, and the first to escape the valley. Wonderful feat, quite wonderful. And the potential of this discovery, my friend, I can't even begin to describe it."

A sharp, throbbing pain set in just above Dale's right temple.

"Why me?"

Magnus raised his eyebrows in surprise. "Isn't it obvious? Your dream journal. It makes a very interesting read. Traitorous, of course, but that's beside the point. What's important is that you've already spent years thinking about your dreams, and that's why I chose you. You were really quite lucky. Most people arrested on charges like yours are simply executed. And what a pity that would have been in your case. Naturally, we were holding out for your success, and we had the most likely places you would go to under constant surveillance, but in this kind of groundbreaking research there just aren't any guarantees. You can imagine how impressed and happy for you we were when you finally managed to dream hike tonight."

Magnus' eyes were glinting with unbridled joy and satisfaction, with possibilities and anticipation.

"And what happens now?" asked Dale.

Magnus looked at him, puzzled. "Oh, I'm sorry, I thought that was clear: now we need to study your dream hiking capability further. We need to understand how it works, what its limits are, and how we can activate it in other people. We have so much work to do--I can't wait to get started. It goes without saying that you'll stay here with us. This is your new home; we've prepared a lovely lab room for you. We," he made a sweeping gesture that included himself and the guards behind Dale, "are your new family, and you'll help us to make *so many* new breakthroughs. Of course, for your own good, we cannot allow you to leave, so we have made provisions that will ensure you can't use your new-found capabilities without our guidance."

He took something from a desk drawer and held it so that Dale could see it. It was a small glass phial containing a milky liquid.

"This is a concoction of rather wonderful chemistry. It suppresses REM sleep, so you won't be able to attempt to dream hike unless we want you to. There are a few unfortunate side effects, mind you. I hear there might be some permanent brain damage, but that is a small price to pay for progress, as I'm sure you agree."

Instead of answering, Dale glanced around. It looked in so many ways like his own office: the desk with the computer and the heaps of paper, the filing cabinets, the pictures on the wall, even the calendar with the inspirational quotes. Just an ordinary office.

He felt endlessly tired. For the few short minutes in his apartment, he had actually thought he had gotten away, that he would be able to get back to his life. For those precious moments, he'd had hope. Now he had nothing. He had stepped over the pillar's edge, and all that existed now was the chasm below.

"So this is how it ends?" he asked. "You'll keep me here as a brain-damaged guinea pig?"

"Oh, no," replied the man called Magnus Beckwick cheerfully as Dale felt a pair of strong hands grip his shoulders. "No, this isn't the end. Quite the contrary. It's the beginning of a wonderful research collaboration. You'll see."

His smile widened and he leaned forward.

"In fact, I'd say it's a dream come true."

About the Author

Michael is a software developer from Germany who has a fondness for books that has gotten slightly out of hand. He spends his free time writing stories, adding books to the ever-growing piles beside the sofa, and gradually converting his living room into a traditional bookbinding workshop. His story 'Ackerley's Genuine Earth Antiques' was published in the anthology 'In Memory--A Tribute to Sir Terry Pratchett'.

ECUMENICAL OUTPOST 732

BY P.K. TYLER

T'SE STARED out her window at the red planet as Station Cassiopeia rotated in orbit. She made sure to be there, ready to watch for each pass. Nothing filled her young heart quite like the idea of real ground beneath her feet. Her teachers said she would weigh more on Peritha than on the station, but that didn't make sense to her. How could her body become heavier without growing larger?

For just a moment, the red haze of Peritha's atmosphere completely covered the window and T'se squinted, imagining living within the dust. Below she would feel wind and have something other than metal beneath her feet. The dirt of the planet would fill in the spaces between her toes and she'd be able to look out into an infinite horizon. The universe wouldn't be just on the other side of a port window. A life where her father came home each day instead of going to the surface for months at a time.

The planet moved, or perhaps the station did, T'se wasn't sure, and a halo effect gleamed behind its silhouette. Did the sun look different to the guards and Jakkattu living on Peritha? Looking up at the star through the red dusty atmosphere of the planet must change its appearance. Would it be brighter? Larger? Would it be warm?

"T'se." Her mother stood in the bunk door cradling her infant sister in a shoulder sling. Her bright blue eyes and close-cropped hair gave her a tough appearance despite the sweetness she bestowed upon her daughters. "Close that and get back into bed."

The young girl latched the heavy metal port window closed and crawled beneath her sheets. "Sorry, Mama, I just wanted to see the planet."

"I know." Her mother smiled, her eyes crinkling in the corners, and sat on the edge of T'se's small mattress. "But soon Mei will sleep in here with you instead of in my room and you can't open the window and wake her when she's sleeping. Besides, it's past your bedtime, too, and you have school tomorrow."

"But this is the only window I can see from!"

"And somehow the rest of the family manages to keep from coming in your room every rotation. I think you can resist when your sister is sleeping. There will be other passings."

T'se frowned and rolled toward the hard metal wall next to her bed.

Her mother sighed and sat on the edge of the small cot, laying her hand on her daughter's back. "No good can come from wishing for something that'll never happen."

"But why? Why can't girls go down?"

"You know all this."

T'se huffed and lay back on her pillow.

Her mother stroked her hair. "There are other planets and other stations you can apply to when you grow up if you're still determined to be land-bound. But Peritha is not safe for women, the Jakkattu prisoners are far too violent. Even if you got someone to agree, would you go and make your mother worry all the time for your safety?" She playfully poked T'se in the rib. "You have plenty of time before you have to think about where you'll live, though."

"I know."

Her mother's fingers tugged at a knot in her long hair. They were stained gray, soot trapped deep within the layers of her skin.

T'se wondered what her mother looked like as a child, before she had to shave her head and began working on the line, sorting the minerals mined on the planet below.

After a few minutes, she shifted position to accommodate Mei's wiggling in her sleep.

"Mama, tell me about Earth."

"Now you're just being silly." Her mother poked T'se in the ribs again.

"Just a little? Please."

"Earth is a fairy tale. A children's story about ancestors who never really lived. All you need to know is that the Mezna rescued our people from self-destruction. Our culture was too primitive to survive long and they wrapped us into their holy fold. You can see the grace in every person on the station." Her mother tapped her finger next to her eye and then ran her thumb over T'se's own impossibly blue eyes; the gift the Mezna had given all their human children. "Besides, you're getting too old for these things, T'se. Maybe your teachers aren't keeping your mind busy enough with lessons."

Mei whimpered. Her mother stood and began the soft rocking that T'se associated with comfort. Even when her mother wasn't holding Mei, she always seemed to be rocking as if a silent rhythm drove her every movement. She leaned down kissed T'se on the forehead before turning off the halo-light overhead. "Sleep, darling. And no more peeking out the window."

The door shut with a metal clang and T'se closed her eyes, counting in her mind until she reached 250. She could go higher, but that should be enough time for her mother to have moved out of the general living space and into her room with Mei. No one else would be up, her father still serving his rotation on the planet and the rest of the family asleep. Except for her aunt who worked the night line. The line never stopped. It wouldn't ever stop, and one day, T'se would be just another human, sorting, covered in soot.

T'se knelt on her bed and reopened the window.

The planet outside had moved almost out of sight, but she could see a sliver of red and the hazy atmosphere hanging above. She pushed her face against the window, straining to see further, to not lose sight of the possibilities below. It drifted away, further out of sight, leaving her orbiting above.

Outside, darkness filled her vision. The sun and planet were on the other side of the station and she wished she could move around freely, open all the windows, and follow the red dust forever. The black void beyond filled her vision until she lost herself in it, face still pressed against the port. Her eyes manifested lights which were not there, attempting to fill the nothingness, but she stared out, welcoming the dark inside her heart.

Her future loomed before her, as bleak and unfulfilled as the space beyond. She would finish school next year and begin her training in metallurgy. When she turned twelve, she would shave her hair off, the only way to stop the mineral dust from spreading through the ship and clogging the air filtration system, and join her mother on the line.

She wanted to apply to other outposts, even to the hydrofarm here at home, but in her young heart she knew she'd never leave this station or the line. Once her skin became stained and her hair was gone, the remainder of her life would be set. The realization landed in her chest like an electroshock.

She'd never leave.

She'd live in this room with her sister and share a pod with her parents and grandparents and aunt until she married one of the few boys raised here, or one of the men who applied for a new position and drew poorly enough in the lottery to be granted reassignment at the end of the universe. He'd be a guard below, missing for months at a time while she worked the line beside her mother until one day her own children joined her.

The inevitability of it bore down on her as the darkness seeped further into her cells, emptying her of hope.

She closed the port window and her eyes adjusted to the dim light of her room. The small pinpoint halos embedded in the walls were always on. As a younger child, she'd thought of them as night-lights, to help her sleep. Now she understood. Without them, her room would fall into the same emptiness as outside, and no one could bear to live in that. Left too long in nothing, a person will go insane.

She slipped out of bed and pulled boots over her feet before sneaking out her door and into the main living space.

Inside her mother's room, Mei cried, masking the sound of T'se opening the latch of the pod's door. The hall was brighter than the pod, but the lights had been dimmed to simulate night. Her teacher said their bodies had natural biorhythms from when they were land-bound. But she never told them where they lived on the ground. Only that the Mezna freed humanity from their limitations when they blended their DNA together to create the people T'se called her own. The lack of answers only made T'se ask more questions. What about Earth? Where had it been? Could they return?

T'se wandered through the dark corridors, ducking out of the way of the few people working the night shift. Keeping the station running was a 24 hour job, no matter what the body's biorhythms may want. Constant maintenance and repairs were required on a ship this size, and on the line that never stopped. She snuck into the landing dock where dock workers were unloading a shipment of minerals from a transport trip. The morning would bring a larger haul. This must have been a late arrival for the day's shipment. A small crew worked silently, grunting as they hauled containers from the ship to the conveyor belt that wound through Station Cassiopeia. Even after flying through the eternal nothing, a film of red dust clung to the hull.

T'se wanted to run her fingers through the dust. Would it feel soft or gritty like the soot that covered her mother's skin? She crouched behind an empty workstation and watched as the orange dust drifted to the ground from the containers. Temptation to crawl out and take a handful filled her: to feel the ground, even if it was just dust. It had been on Peritha only hours ago. It might still be warm from the sun, from feeling the actual sun.

A small figure dashed across the dock to a shadowed corner.

T'se crept closer, running from one obstruction to the next, jogging across the dark expanse, careful to time her movements for when the crew labored. What had she seen? A small animal who'd been trapped on the ship? She had to follow and find out.

The number of containers stored inside the transport seemed endless. They'd be busy for a while. She ducked behind a maintenance station and scanned the room, looking for the movement she'd spotted. While she waited, she questioned if it was just her mind playing tricks on her. Being out in the station so late made her nervous and excited, an easy state for imagining things.

Then she saw it again.

The vast landing dock was also dimly lit for the night shift, making it difficult to discern exactly what she'd seen. The usually bustling work spaces were shut down, utilizing as little energy as possible during the skeleton crew's shift.

In the corner, a small body curled in on itself as T'se approached. It wore dirty pants, and a thin shirt hung from sharp, huddled shoulders. Not an animal, but a person.

"Hey," she whispered below the grunts of those unloading the ship.

A young face peeked up, eyes covered in shadows. Its body shook.

"Come with me." She held out a hand and waited for the next loud drop of the loading crew. "It's okay, I won't tell anyone."

The stowaway unfolded and stood in the corner. It was a boy, much taller than her, with dark eyes like the black of space beyond.

She stared. She'd never seen anyone without blue eyes before, blue eyes that indicated her dual human and Mezna biology.

His face was streaked with tears and reddish-brown dirt.

A loud thunk from the ship's mechanics behind her brought her attention back to how exposed they were. She thrust her hand forward, the boy extended his long arm and slipped his hand into hers. She squeezed his thin fingers and pulled him further into the light. His long light-colored hair had been pulled back at the nape of his neck and the bones on his face and body jutted out from his thin frame.

"Let's go." She pulled him forward to the next work station

where they crouched close together. He smelled alien, like nothing she'd encountered before, but it didn't smell bad. Huddled close together, their breathing synchronized. When it was time to break for the next hiding spot, they moved in unison without speaking or signaling that it was time. His long legs moved quickly as he followed after her.

When the crew finished and began closing up the ship, the two ran for the door and down a side corridor. They hustled down grate stairs, through the winding back access corridors, and past the water processing room until they were hidden deep within the station's interior workings.

In a dark stairway leading toward the waste processing level, T'se finally slowed and leaned against the rusted metallic wall. Her bare feet hurt from running over the grates. The station creaked and the shifting noises of metal on metal echoed in the dark.

The boy towered above her, but his slight frame and round face made her think he wasn't much older than her. She dropped his hand and took a moment to catch her breath.

"I'm T'se. Are you Jakkattu? Are you from the planet? Do you speak English?"

"Rishek. My name is Rishek." His name sounded clipped and strange to her ears. "Thank you."

They stared at each other for a moment and T'se wondered what she'd done, bringing him here. She wasn't supposed to have any contact with the Jakkattu prisoners. Their crimes were unimaginable, so grotesque the entire race had been brought here to work off the misdeeds of their ancestors. Her teachers had taught her all of this and more, but never revealed what they had actually done. Looking at this boy, her already questioning mind was thrown into turmoil. "Are you in trouble?"

"No. Not yet."

"You were on that ship."

"Yes."

"Was anyone with you?"

"No."

"You came alone?"

"Yes."

His one-word answers annoyed her. She needed to understand. "Why did you come?"

He tilted his head and the hair tucked behind his ear fell loose down the side of his face. "I don't understand."

"Why did you come here? You know you'll get in trouble. How were you going to get food or water? You know Jakkattu aren't allowed on the Station, don't you?"

He snorted and his face hardened, dark shadows heightened the sudden feral look on his face. "I don't care if I have food or water. I'm out of the mines. I'm off that planet. I'm somewhere else. I would be happy if I died now. I'm free. I will die free."

T'se recoiled, fearing the venom in his words. "You won't die."

"If they find me I will. But I don't care." His lips pressed together in a hard line, but his hands shook and she knew he had to be afraid.

She looked him over, noticing the way his bones stuck out and his shoulders hunched. "Are you hungry?"

"I haven't eaten since this morning."

"Then we should get you food, and then we'll figure out the rest." She reached out for his hand again and after contemplating her for a moment, he took it and let her lead him further down the stairs and through the labyrinth of corridors that wove through the Station.

Upper decks were laid out in grid patterns with wide corridors and open spaces between sections which kept people from focusing too much on how tight the Station really was, how the walls and air pushed inward, tightening around each citizen's throat. In the darkness, they left a small light on and the people sighed with relief for the minuscule kindness.

Below, away from the living quarters, in the entertainment sectors and workstations, down where few venture and none really understand, the walls are tight and the ceilings low. Priest delegations came once a year to hold services, check the station, and perform any maintenance needed. The residents were simply worker bees buzzing within the greater hive.

Rishek ducked his head as he ran, keeping his eyes pointed to the ground, and hurried to keep up.

They crossed a high bridge spanning between two sections of the Station, a deep well of subzero storage filled the space below. The room filled with bright blue light from far beneath them, giving the bridge an eerie glow. At the other end, T'se opened a hatch door and climbed through, reaching back for her new friend.

"What is down here?" He asked when the door sealed shut and the pair returned to darkness.

"I don't know. They don't really tell kids stuff like that. Storage? Come on, the protein is grown down here."

They slowed and opened a final door. Shelves of troughs filled with organic growth compound sprouted protein at various stages of development.

T'se climbed a ladder at the end of a shelf and plucked a fully grown protein pod. "Here, it's not warm, but it tastes okay when it's fresh from the farm."

"What is it?"

"Protein." She held it out for him to take, growth compound dripping through her fingers. "It's fine, see?" She bit the pod like an apple and chewed the protein. It tasted bland but edible.

With a nod and closed lipped smile she passed it over to Rishek, who bit in with a grimace. He took another bite, wiping growth compound from his chin as he devoured the entire pod.

"It tastes like meat, but like the flavor's been drained out of it."

"What's meat?"

"From an animal—one you hunt and kill and cook."

T'se covered her mouth as she gasped and stepped away from Rishek. "That's horrible, why would you do that?"

"For food. For protein. You grow meat." He looked around the large room and walked down an aisle between the shelves of protein pods. It extended so far, the rows of shelves began to curve like a distant horizon. "How much is here?"

"I don't know. Enough to feed the Station for a while I guess."

"We don't have this on Peritha. If we did, so many would finally have enough to eat. The Jakkattu are always hungry, there's never enough for all of us." He dipped his hand into one of the troughs filled with growth compound and lifted it up to look at, letting the goo run down his hand and arm. "We have to hunt but there aren't many animals left and the larger ones with the best meat and skins are dangerous."

"Do you want more?" She asked, pulling his attention back. She didn't like to talk about killing and eating any living thing. "We should take some with us and find you somewhere to hide."

"Where?"

T'se climbed back up the stairs and plucked five more protein pods. She handed them down and he piled them into the front of his shirt, the goo saturating the thin fabric.

"I don't know."

"What about here? There's no one here."

"For a little while, but someone will be here in the morning for day shift."

"Can I stay with you?" he asked, eyes so dark they reflected her face.

She shook her head. "I would be happy for you to stay with me, but my mother and the rest of my family would never understand. They'd tell."

"I don't want to be alone," he admitted.

As they talked their eyes adjusted to the dim light and the differences between them drifted away, leaving two children to solve the problems of an entire universe. Rishek ate another pod and T'se crossed her arms over her chest, mimicking the stance her mother took when scolding her.

After some time, they sat on the floor and shared the rest of the protein and soon fell asleep, curled together.

The station continued to rotate until the time came for the early morning crew to begin their shift. T'se's mother worked the day shift on the line, but there was no way to know how much time had passed in the dim farm room. And as the children slept, the shift manager arrived early.

The door opened and the dim lights flickered for a moment before pulsing to full strength.

"What are you... Mother God!" The shift manager lunged toward the communication panel on the wall.

"Wait!" T'se cried out, jerked out of her dreamless sleep. She tried to disentangle herself from Rishek's gangly limbs wrapped around her, but the manager had already set the emergency alarm. The holo-lights turned blue and pulsed while a high, almost unperceivable sound pierced the air. Rishek awoke with a scream, curling tight into himself and clutching his ears.

T'se fell to his side and wrapped an arm around his shoulders, holding him close against her as his body shook and he whimpered in pain. She rocked him the way her mother rocked Mei when she cried, trying to calm him so they could figure out what to do.

"What are you doing? Stop hurting him!"

Guards dressed in white uniforms, not yet stained orange from the grit of the planet, rushed in and grabbed Rishek from T'se's embrace.

"No!" she screamed, clutching his thin shirt so tightly it ripped away from his body. "What are you going to do?"

A guard picked her up around the middle and held her while they dragged Rishek out of the room. The alarm ended, but his screams continued to reach out to her from the hall like arms stretched out with a pleading cry.

"He's my friend!" T'se struggled away from the guard holding her, kicking any part of him she could make contact with. "Please."

By the time her mother arrived, tears had worn her out and she hung in the tireless guard's arms like a blanket.

"T'se," she said, pulling her into her arms. "What did you do?"

The girl could only hiccup into her mother's shoulders, exhausted and desperate.

Her mother carried T'se back to her room and settled her on the bed. It was the first time since Mae had been born that she'd been held like that and as much as she wanted to grow up and change her fate, she was relieved for the moment of comfort.

"What are they going to do to Rishek?" she asked once she had been tucked into her cot.

"Is that its name? Where did you meet it?" Her mother's voice was hard and cold when she spoke of Rishek, like the metal walls of their home. The change from loving mother to hardline anti-Jakkattu officer jarred T'se's sense of right and wrong.

"I found him, he ran away from Peritha."

"Did he hurt you?"

"No!" T'se pulled away from her mother. "He was nice!"

"Honey, he was a stowaway Jakkattu. Who knows what kind of diseases he could have brought up from the surface. You know, your father works with these people and he has to go through a complete decontamination before coming home. They're dangerous, impulsive. We're so lucky you didn't get hurt." She pulled T'se to her again and let out a deep sigh. "I don't know what I'd do without you."

"He wasn't going to hurt me. He just wanted to see the Station."

She tightly gripped T'se's shoulders and pulled away. "Those people are animals. They aren't like us. You can't think of them as human. I know most of them speak English, but the things your father has told me... It's time for you to sleep now. I'm so relieved you're okay, but tomorrow we're going to have a conversation about sneaking out after bed and slinking through the Station like a criminal. You're very lucky you weren't hurt or sanctioned."

"I'm sorry, Mama."

"Okay, T'se," another kiss on the head and her mother left.

T'se curled under her sheets and wished for tears. Maybe if she could cry more it would let some of her pain out. She didn't know where they had taken Rishek or if she would see him again. Would they let him stay? Maybe go to her school. Her mother would understand if she could just meet him. She was sure of it.

She relaxed, thinking of seeing him again, but still couldn't fall asleep, her mind too full of worries and possibilities. She sat up and pulled open the hatch covering her window, seeking out the nothingness. The moon had rotated into view and stars filled her vision. They floated in and out of focus, some bright and some so dim she couldn't quite believe they were there. As she stared into a universe filled with impossibilities, a dark figure floated through the void, a silhouette against the stars.

About the Author

P.K. Tyler is the Award-Winning author of Speculative Fiction and other Genre Bending novels. She's also published works as Pavarti K. Tyler and had projects appear on the USA TODAY Bestseller's List. *Ecumenical Outpost 732* is a part of her greater Jakkattu world. *The Jakkattu Vector* is available at all book vendors now.

Like Genre-Bending Literary Fiction? Signup at
smarturl.it/PavNews

THE PILLARS OF THEONASA

BY ROSLYN CAY

"How DARE you!" The proud and arrogant Samyaza pointed his pale face and angular chin heavenward to rage. "Theonasa will not die!"

Samyaza folded his crippled wings uncomfortably. Since his fall they had never healed properly, but instead molted and withered to nubs and useless flaps. The fragile bones rubbed each other and the new dampness in the weather caused teeth-gritting aches.

Once again the morning above his city was overcast by dark clouds. The sunlight that often softened the stern king's face and disposition had failed to appear.

One hundred eighty days and still no sun. He vexed.

It disturbed him. The city was disturbed. All night he heard the creaks and groans of Theonasa's deteriorating infrastructure.

How much longer before I see another perfect day?

On a perfect day, the community of Fallen had combined their strength and created a massive wind vortex and lifted their gleaming township into the immeasurable air, fastening it with only two massive pillars of ground support.

The memory stirred pride.

The vast assembly of buildings extended over more than one

hundred acres. Each ornately carved building had long rectangular windows, allowing air currents to flow freely throughout the city.

A city in the winds. A home for the new Gods of Wind. He and his brothers who had fallen from Paradise had built their own.

A Paradise that had begun to slip its eroding ground supports.

"We beg your forgiveness, Dapo! It's the falling water. It weakens the stone you showed us to build with."

They showed him the pavers and blocks taken from the Pillars. They crumbled in his hand. "Fix it!"

They couldn't and although he had only executed five of the ground workers, it had inspired them to begin deserting the city. Deserting their king.

On the ground below, the city, mountains, and caves had become filled with flooding waters and many of the humans who served him attempted to flee for higher ground. The bridges and city gates leading out of the Theonasa were teeming with humans who believed Theonasa would soon fall.

The first daily downpour began but Samyaza defied the threat to his city. The king strode out onto his palace's air terrace, a magnificent mosaic tiled mobile dais. The air terrace, his favorite place to revel and seduce. The wet and slippery surface nearly caused him to fall.

He noticed some sort of green and black growth covering the elaborately painted peacock feathers and pomegranates, clan symbols on the wooden railing and floors of the platform.

He gritted his teeth in disgust. Casting a wind, he used the pressure of it to strip the growth from his royal transport.

"What is this sky water?" He bit his tongue, holding back fury at the phenomenon.

Six months ago, large globs of water had unceasingly plunged from the atmosphere. It was unlike the morning dew. These fattened drops had the thickened viscosity of honey and burst when they hit the ground. The wet bursts didn't just make small splashing puddles but divided like cells multiplying. The volume of water increased exponentially like a virus.

He lifted his face to the sky to investigate. If Theonasa was to remain airborne, he had to know how to stop it. Still soaking, he cast a command, finding his servant, the wind.

"Everything is on the wind." The winds would tell him what was going on.

The southern wind that flowed through his city in the air was laden with tainted water.

As designed the high winds of the stratosphere continuously struck the resonant walls, creating rhythmic chimes that could be heard for miles to the emptying human settlements below.

The great halls were decorated and paneled with cypress and everything was coated with a fine gold veneer: the rafters, the doorframes, the walls, and the doors. Even the mosaic reliefs that adorned the upper parts of the hall that told their story in friezes.

"Tell me what is happening." Samyaza solicited the southerly airborne servant.

The corrupt south wind came on command.

"I grieve that I have not seen you play in Theonasa's echoing spires for months."

There is woe coming, the wind whispered in his mind. *The water springs have bred into monstrous rivers with waters that swallow humans. The small ponds where animals drank and children played are bloated with their bodies. An unfathomable body of water with destructive tides comes this way.*

"How has this happened?"

Men like you. No, not like you. They flow over the entire continent, changing my brother winds' direction. They are at the bidding of these men. Now my brother winds of the North, East and West come here, grabbing up the falling water to use as a weapon against you. They destroy with torrents and have gradually overspread the Pangaea. A wall of water is pushing toward Theonasa. It cannot withstand this great deluge. It is only a matter of days.

Just then the sonorous, slapping water drowned the resounding beauty of South Wind's voice. In the distance, Samyaza heard

Theonasa stutter under the extra burden of clearing the falling water and debris from the city in addition to holding it aloft.

Theonasa is not dying. She is being murdered.

"You are going to end it all, aren't you?" the King of the Wind Demons demanded of Heaven. "Rather than let me be free, you'll destroy everything?"

"Yaza?" a worried woman's voice called to him from behind.

Raca, the woman who shared his bed this last year, had not waited to be summoned. She called to him from his bedroom.

The woman was not beguiling or beautiful as some of the daughters of men. But when he first saw her he thought she carried herself proudly. He had chosen her above others and demanded her as tribute from her father, the local chieftain.

"She will be the woman who will bear my sons. The sons of a god."

He'd taken her that night in a lavish room of purple linen and crimson textiles. In a warm ember's glow, he'd sheathed himself inside her and conceived a creation of his own.

"The son of a god!" he'd exclaimed to all when the child was born. *"The first of his kind, he is named Danak."*

Raca stood in his bedroom dressed in only a purple dyed robe from head to foot: mourning clothes. Most of the humans wore them now, hoping to appease the sky and stop the falling water.

Despite this, when the others began to lack faith in his godhood, to desert, she had stayed.

Raca received him now as he floated down to her on the parapet. Her elongated head bowed, unusual for her. Her face was weary and pained and she bundled their infant tightly to her body.

Her body language said she was unsure of her status. Though there was no need. She carried his pride. He reached out to see his son.

"Danak, I am not going anywhere." He crooned to the swaddled form he took from her.

He meant every word.

"The priest said he had to make a sacrifice." Raca gasped in despair, her voice breaking. "He says water will stop now."

Sorrow showed on her primitive face.

Samyaza detected the bloody stained wrapping around his son. Alarmed he tore open the flap.

A great noise came from his gut and throat. The only precious thing that had come from his tragic descent from Paradise was now dead.

At first he cursed the sky. "He was a god!" His dead legacy fell to the ground.

Then he cursed her. He reached for the neck of his last human subject. "Faithless! Treacherous!"

Theonasa. It means, in our language, City of the Gods of the Winds, Raca had told him once.

Now his blind wrath snapped her neck so easily.

Welcomed by Raca's father, the Chief of the largest of human settlements, he and his people had bowed low before him. He liked the way the name flowed around his lips and he adopted it immediately.

All his brothers were gone now, gone off to follow the former Garden Cherub. He would have no help.

"We could be Gods ourselves. Rule this place." He tried to reason with them all. But they went off not willing to cross that line.

"Breeding with them? To follow you is a fool's game!" Lucifer spat.

The idea of breeding with the humans to make a race of gods disgusted and horrified most of the Fallen.

Samyaza felt something inside him harden and resolved to survive.

He detached the air terrace from the exterior of his bedroom and, in flowing motions with his hands, guided a few wind currents into a small spiral tornado, using them as an engine of power. In moments, he was escaping into the air, floating higher than the palace itself. He could now look further into the sky.

He floated out of the city, watching water run from the uppermost places; very high walks, supported by the great stone pillars; they allowed the flow to run straight downhill to the galleries and forums beneath him and into the planted gardens.

His eyes followed brackish water in the vast system of aqueducts from the nearby mountain caves invade his floating city. The plants, trees and gardens that he adorned Theonasa with were brown and rotting. All life was dying.

This can't end. I must do something.

This would be his last battle with Heaven.

As he reached the two huge Pillars, each fifty-two feet tall and crowned with an elaborate filigree of chains, like necklaces, from which hung a hundred golden pomegranates. The crude stone phalluses stabbed the firmament of his city.

"I gave them knowledge!" he shouted as the black clouds gathered.

"You gave them death, Samyaza." A part in the black storm opened and admitted two Watchers. "Soon it will all be finished."

Samyaza had been expecting Gabriel or Michael, God's greatest angels.

"Are you my accuser?" he challenged the low-level Archai. "Two whipped pups who dared not leave their master's side when revolution came to the Throne."

"My name is Hastens to Prayer With God and this is Constantly Striving For Their Reconcile."

The first one, Hastens to Prayer moved closer while the second stayed silent and watched with rapt curiosity. Together they repeated their memorized lines.

"Hear your crimes. You who by deception learned the sacred knowledge. You who used it to empower yourself and build this forbidden city. You gave evil counsel to the sons of Adam. You who induced them to corrupt their bodies with demons. You metered out to them every secret wisdom."

"Building a city? A home for myself?" Samyaza sputtered in outrage. "I taught them reading and writing. How is that a crime? "

"They didn't need it." Constantly Striving blurted from

further in the heights. "They were created with a perfect connection to their creator and each other, soul to soul, mind to mind. You taught them ambition and now insatiable yearning consumes them."

"This is a center for all knowledge. Knowledge he held back from them!" the Wind God justified.

"Experiential knowledge is not free. Their knowledge could have come without pain, when they were ready," Hastens exclaimed. "You had no right."

"Hear your sentence." Constantly agreed with grimness altering his angelic face. "Until the appointed time, you will be taken and shall disappear and perish from the face of the earth."

Samyaza made an attempt to harness the wind around him, but his physical movements were too slow for the ethereal telekinesis of the angels.

Constantly produced five great chains of black fire able to pierce the impenetrable demon and wrap the limbs and heart of Samyaza. The spectral chains held him like tar in their power and Samyaza struggled mightily.

"This day you will be taken away into the lowest depths, and in confinement shall you be shut up."

Then a crashing rumble coming from a distance. Screams of terror pierced and surpassed even the noise of the rushing wall of water.

The humans were trapped on the bridges that stretched between the city and the mountain below. The wall of water tore through forests and mountains toward them.

Their panic incited them to tread on each other to get through the seven wide gates leading out of the city when once they had clamored to get in.

Still thousands more he knew were huddled in homes in the mountain cliff-side village at the other side. Now alerted to the danger, they climbed in vain, fleeing to escape the terrible tsunami.

"The water is here. You'd let them die?" Samyaza flailed helplessly and shouted his impotence.

Hastens shook his head. "You don't actually care for them. Only the corruption you bred and fostered."

"Yes, and you're here to wipe them out. To destroy my legacy. Tell me! How can you reconcile them if they're dead?" Samyaza mocked them as his eyes were riveted on the water barreling toward thousands, eager to erase them from creation.

Hastens yanked one of the chains piercing his heart.

It was unfathomably agonizing. Samyaza tried to calm his rising panic.

"There will be survivors," Constantly comforted his prisoner.

The wall of water ate them all, filling the entire valley. In only a few minutes, there was no sound except the scavenging winds.

"King of the Wind Gods!" Hastens pulled the chains again. "Meet your fate!"

The winds that Samyaza once commanded swirled in a destructive pool of air above Theonasa. His city was rising to embrace them.

Theonasa screamed when ripped from its great stone appendages by great invisibilities. Now pulled from its foundations, it danced violently above the sunken valley. Finally, judgment ripped it apart and devoured it whole.

"He is holy." Both angels gave whispered benediction at the awesome power.

This isn't over. The King of Wind Demons, in his last proclamation of defiance to God, said, "They will remember me. My legacy will live on."

But Samyaza had no time to relish his counting coup moment. He followed his city into nothingness.

FROM THE SHADOWS of the new age, Hastens and Constantly watched. Waters receded and still they stayed, poised on either side of the newly blossoming valley.

They watched when the first humans came back to the valley to dig out building stones from the ground. Stones left behind.

Untouched, unblemished. The Pillars of Theonasa still stood, planted into the earth.

They laughed at the Watchers.

He is gone, but I, Theonasa, live on.

About the Author

Roslyn Cay is a native South Floridian. She loves fiction involving adventure, history and the future of humanity. She loves the English language and classical literature and in her free time, she roots for literature's underdogs and righteous causes. She has a deep connection with her native Florida including its rich culture and cuisine. She is also mesmerized by the ocean and believes per John 21 breakfast on the beach is a sacred thing!

THE RITE

BY CHRISTOPHER GODSOE

Even as a freshly minted 18-year-old, Nyla understood that love consisted of a million little things rather than the occasional grand gesture. She understood that because her parents had nothing to give her *but* little things, and over the years she had grown to see that it meant more to give what little you had than to give a lot when you had an abundance.

Of course, in 2134, nobody had an abundance of anything, at least not anyone Nyla knew. The stores had fresh fruit and vegetables, meat, even canned goods, but they could not be purchased with the food vouchers provided by the government, and that was all Nyla's family, along with roughly three quarters of the population, had ever known.

Those attempting to grow their own food met with potentially lethal results. Heavy metals in the soil absorbed into whatever plants people managed to sprout, and anyone who tried to eat them traded a few days of lavish, fresh produce consumption for their life. It was a popular way to end it all for those regretting their choices during The Rite.

Once or twice, her mother had no other choice but to bring Nyla with her to exchange their vouchers for their monthly food rations, which consisted mostly of flavored gruel, labelled differently but all still managing to taste mostly the same.

The packages were careful to print all of the vitamins and minerals that were folded into the batter during production, but Nyla was under no illusion that what she choked down with glass after glass of water everyday was healthy. The water was filtered, but the filters never managed to get the alkali taste out.

This morning was different, though. This was the morning of her 18th birthday, the day she would undergo The Rite. As she trudged down the stairs with her typical sleepy gait, the smell of spice and sweetness hit her, like a life preserver in an otherwise ocean of blue.

On the morning of every child's 18th birthday, it was tradition for their parents to serve them special 12-hour gruel in a cup they decorated themselves. Poverty had wrenched most traditions from society, but this one held firm because it was mandated by the government. The government didn't want hunger, and its requisite mental deficiencies, interfering with the process.

The decorative cup was not, of course, but the gruel was a carefully balanced blend of amino acids and carbohydrates meant to carry the new initiate through The Rite since there was no way to gain sustenance while unconscious.

The Rite, named so by society as a literal rite of passage, required every citizen on their 18th birthday to spend 12 hours of real time inside of a simulated reality. Time dilation stretched that 12 hours to an experiential 24, an entire virtual day designed to allow the citizen to properly evaluate the simulation, after which they were required to choose whether to remain there forever, or to return to the real world to live out their lives.

Nyla picked up the cup, tracing the intricate designs on the rim with her thumb as she inhaled the sweet aroma of the gruel. It smelled how she imagined a cinnamon bun might. She had never had one, of course, but as the fumes curled up her nasal passages, her mind filled in the gaps of the illusion. She had seen videos online of them, torturing herself because she would probably never have a real one, and imagined the texture like......well, she had nothing to truly compare it to, but her mind crafted a well-designed fantasy, and since she would never have a chance to prove it wrong, she reveled in her own ignorance.

It was an unspoken understanding that the government needed a majority of the population to accept the simulation if they stood any chance at preserving the planet. Reality was a dystopia, but generation after generation saw the tide turn back little by little. The Artificially Intelligent mainframe computers that were tasked with the turnaround were calculating and cold, but they were accomplishing a task that millennia of human rule had failed at: managing resources while they convinced everyone to work together to clean up the planet.

The Rite was seen as the most humane way to deal with the problems brought on by the population boom: inability to produce enough clean energy to sustain society, along with enough food, space, and potable water. Every year, more communities saw their archaic fossil fuel heating, energy, and transportation systems replaced by clean, renewable options, but even with the AI's stratospheric genius pulling the strings, the damage proved slow to repair.

All manner of imposed birth control had been implemented, up to and including mandatory sterilization for all children deemed genetically impure, a decision made without the parents' knowledge at the time. Only when large swathes of the population were found infertile was the practice discovered. This caused an understandably brisk and violent response against the government, and other options were considered by the AI's.

One thing the AI's understood more than anything was order, efficiency. They reversed the policy immediately, and made anyone still wishing to undermine them disappear. Their mistake was one of not understanding human emotions properly, of not knowing how to love.

Thinking of that, how the AI's inability to love mirrored the reality that surrounded her, Nyla removed the small, fraying picture from her pocket. The boy's eyes were a startling shade of ice blue, his hair a brown so dark it approached black. The picture, and the emotions it brought out in Nyla, were the antithesis of everything the AIs had fostered. Everything that could be made antiseptic was made so. Clean. Efficient, yet only sufficiently so.

There was never an abundance, never the soft margin or cushion that human beings seemed to need to feel safe. Everything necessary to sustain life, yet never a soft surface when a hard one can be made more pragmatic. In other words, none of the million little things that let a person know they are loved. Love wasn't part of their programming. Their programming was to fix the problems in the world, the hard problems, and to spare no resources to coddle emotions or hurt feelings.

Surrounded by all that, the muted sweetness in her cup, as small as it was, felt like a lifeline to a better place, a more human existence. That was exactly what it was intended to be. The AI's may not have had a great grasp on human emotion, but they were masters in leveraging human motivations. Causality was the machines' stock and trade, and they covered all of the angles.

Every person who chose to remain inside the simulation was one less mouth to feed, one less ant in the anthill that they had to account for. Secretly, Nyla wondered if they wouldn't prefer everyone to choose the simulation. She herself even wondered sometimes if humanity wouldn't be better off there.

The simulation knew no suffering. No loss, no goodbyes. Not a single digitized human consciousness maintained on its vast servers would ever be hungry again, and their reality could be anything that they wanted. There, Nyla could be with Will again, just like they had planned.

She flipped the picture over, and lightly ran her finger over his name written on the back of the photograph, not much larger than a postage stamp. He had saved for weeks to have it printed for her, knowing that he had no need for food once he went through The Rite. Once he chose to remain in the simulation, his body would have been immediately incinerated.

It turned her stomach to think about him that way, to see those handsome cheekbones she had fallen in love with blackened and turned to ash. She quickly drank the rest of her gruel to quiet her stomach, and slid the image back into her pocket.

The plan was for them both to spend eternity together, but Will had passed on over a year ago while Nyla waited to turn 18. She still missed him badly, but she loved her parents just as much as she loved Will.

A year's distance between them had altered her perspective a great deal. Not helping matters, her mother's cough got worse every week, and they had lost her father the year before due to an aggressive form of cancer. A large part of her couldn't wait to see Will. An equally large part of her hoped he had moved on, easing her decision to stay and help her mother.

As per tradition, her mother was to leave the house and not return until she had left for The Rite, as the AI's did not wish to have anyone influence her decision any more than it would already have been. Guilt is a powerful motivating factor, and while the machines did not understand the feelings of loss from having a family member choose nirvana over them, they well understood how much those emotions motivated the actions of other human beings.

With her mother out of the house for the next 24 hours, her gruel finished, and an appointment with a potential new life approaching, Nyla made her way outside and locked the door behind her.

She placed the key under their welcome mat, having not made up her mind yet if she would need it or not. Had she decided to stay, she could have kept it in her pocket. Had she expected to remain in the simulation, it could have gone through the mail slot. Today, she would either leave her mother, or leave the love of her life. There was no way to have it all in this world anymore.

Standing up, she took a deep breath, filling her lungs with air that just a decade earlier would have sent her coughing. The AI's had done a remarkable job at cleaning the environment, at reducing pollution and waste, yet the changes required to make that happen had removed much of the humanity from the world.

Nyla looked around at all of the blinding white buildings with their solar tile roof, and wondered if pollution and waste were humanity's defining characteristics. The human body itself was a shambling mass of sloughing cells and fluids. Dead skin cells fell off at every touch. Every breath, every voiding of bowels and sneeze cast fluids and bacteria into the world. Not for the first time, Nyla thought that maybe it was the destiny of the species to all leave their flesh behind and transcend into the simulated reality of The Rite.

She had no idea what to expect from The Rite, yet duty and tradition nudged her to turn on her heel and make her way to the center of the city. As her time drew near, Nyla took a more pronounced interest in the way the world used to be.

Her mother, always wary of the pending choice Nyla would have to make when she reached her 18th birthday, had dutifully handed down stories of how their ancestors had lived like relative royalty. Color had been everywhere. Tastes, scents, a proliferation of life and inefficient splendor that Nyla had never known except through her mother. The stories would always end with how, once the damage had been repaired, they could return to their lives of abundance. Certainly not this year, but another 10, 20 years down the line...who knew?

Nyla loved these stories in her youth, but as she grew older she began to recognize them for what they were--the only hope her mother had of keeping her daughter after The Rite. She loved Nyla, and Nyla loved her, but the guilt Nyla felt of potentially leaving her alone in the world was almost more than she could bear. If her father were still alive, Nyla might not have worried as much. If Nyla followed through on her promise to join Will in the simulation, her mother would be left to live out her remaining days alone.

At the city center, Nyla stepped into the shadow of the large monolithic building that housed the AI's node for the entire surrounding area. There were no windows, because the AI's had no need for sunlight. Set into its base, a single door, flat and without an external handle. The building was seamlessly constructed of the same non-white that the AI's seemed to like so much, and the door was a dull gunmetal that gave off a cold, ominous vibe as Nyla approached it. With no door handle to grasp, all she could think to do was to stand a few feet away from it.

She assumed that the AI was scanning her, verifying her identity, but she could make out no sensors or cameras. After about twenty seconds, the door clicked open and a sliver of light, warmer than the morning sun, spilled out. It was the tiny bit of reassurance that she needed before brushing the door open and stepping through.

Inside, the floor was made out of some fabric that looked like thousands of soft rope ends glued to the floor. It gave under her feet as she walked, an unstable feeling she didn't care for. A pair of well cushioned armchairs sat against perpendicular walls, each a deep burgundy color. Color was everywhere, just like in the videos she had watched from long ago. The entire room was around twenty feet square, and art hung at regular intervals on each wall. An ornate wooden door bisected the wall immediately opposite her, 180 degrees from the metal door she had just passed through.

The psychology was subtle, but undeniable, just as the majority of mandated traditions had been that day. The sweet gruel, the colorful cup, the extravagant waiting room, all of it meant to contrast the daily drabness she had grown to accept in the outside world. It was designed to make her want to stay.

All she could hear was the simulated fire in the fireplace crackling. The building had no chimney that she could see from the outside, but even a simulated fireplace was considered an inefficient luxury that the world could no longer bear.

Nyla made her way around the room, taking in all of the minor marvels it contained. Crystal lampshades, decorative plants, a bowl of fruit...even a vase of fresh cut flowers. It felt like someone's home. The fruit beckoned to her silently, an imaginary calling that made her mouth water. She wanted nothing more than to sink her teeth into the red flesh of the apple, to rip open the orange and drop one of the juicy segments into her mouth.

She held her ground, not able to shake the feeling of betrayal that hung over the glass bowl of fruit. Her mother was out, most likely walking in the park, or sitting down on one of its many benches, waiting to find out if her daughter would return to her. That she had been forced from her home, with so much uncertainty laid out before her, shamed Nyla. Here she was, contemplating whether or not to eat the wealth of fresh fruit before her when her mother would probably never again taste anything so amazing. What right did she have to it?

She shook the images out of her head and discovered that, quite subconsciously, she had made her way to the edge of the table where the bowl of fruit lay. She was in the middle of backing away from the bowl like a particularly poisonous form of insect when a voice spoke from behind her. Her normal proximity sense told her that the wall was close, making anyone between her and the wall uncomfortably so. She wheeled around, only to find a three-foot-tall painting of a plain looking man hanging there on the wall.

Nearly a life-sized likeness, it still caused her to take an involuntary step back. The backs of her thighs made contact with the table, and one of the apples tumbled from the bowl. It was one of the longer varieties, not especially round, and it only made a revolution or two before tottering still atop the table. Nyla was about to reach out and replace it atop the stack when the painting cracked a smile that struck Nyla as perhaps the most forced expression she had ever seen. The smile hung there, draped over the face like it was being made by someone whose features were being operated remotely, but there was no malice in it.

"We are sorry to have startled you. Please, feel free to help yourself to any of the fruit on the table. It was placed there for you."

Nyla realized it was one of the AI's speaking to her. The painting was not a painting at all, but another video screen like the wall mounted infotainment deck in her apartment. The infotainment deck was what she had gone to school on and watched old video footage on.

"I'm...I'm sorry. I didn't realize you were there."

"It's quite all right, Nyla."

It knew who she was. Of course it did. The door had unlocked for her, hadn't it?

"I can really have some?"

"Absolutely. Once we have finished explaining the process you are about to undergo, you may have as much as you'd like."

Nyla smiled, and the AI took that as a sign to continue.

"You are here to undergo your 18-year Rite. You are no doubt aware of this."

The AI's voice was smooth, light on inflection, and nearly devoid of emotion. It wasn't unpleasant at all to listen to, but Nyla couldn't quite shake the underlying realization that she was talking to a machine.

She nodded.

"And you are also no doubt aware of the decision that you will have to make. All citizens are given 24 hours to acclimate to the simulated nirvana that we have created, to get as full a sense of what it is like as possible in that time, and asked to decide if they would like to remain there for eternity, or return to this plane of existence to live out their remaining years. The current average life expectancy for those choosing to return is 97.8 years."

Nyla's mother was 64, having given birth to Nyla later in her life than most. The AI's had done little to advance average life expectancies, due to their desire to reduce population densities, but they had done a great deal of work in adding vitality to the years of life between birth and death. No attempts had been made to further reduce cancer mortality rates, a thought that brought a tear to her eye as she remembered her father's passing.

She took a deep breath and mastered her anger.

The machine had not stopped talking.

"...In a few moments, you will pass through the wooden door behind you to the antechamber beyond. You will lay down on the metal bench inside, and a device will lower from the ceiling to inject your body with communicative nanoparticles. These particles are otherwise harmless, but will facilitate a wireless connection between your nervous system and our simulation mainframe. You will fall asleep, and the machine will retrieve your consciousness and insert it into the simulation. We have selected a starting point for induction, a town the locals call Haven. Once you awaken, you will have 24 hours to explore the simulation, to craft a new branch within it of your own design, whatever you feel best gives you an understanding of what life is like there. When that time is over, I will reappear to you inside of that simulation, and we will require your answer."

Nyla nodded again. Aside from the bit about the town, all of the information relayed had been more or less common knowledge.

"Do you understand?"

Again, Nyla nodded. Her throat had dried up, and she didn't trust it to not crack if she tried to speak.

"Good. Please, help yourself to as much food as you would like. Once you are ready, continue on through the wooden door to begin The Rite."

With that, the man in the painting fell still once more.

Nyla's hands were shaking. Not uncontrollably so, but when she finally mustered the courage to retrieve the apple that had rolled free of the bowl earlier, she had to concentrate in order to avoid dropping it.

Feeling alone in the room again, she took the first bite of an actual piece of fruit in her life. Her teeth punched through the deep red skin of the apple, the waxed exterior pushing back against her gums in a way that was part tingle, part pain. Her teeth had never eaten anything that actually needed to be chewed before, and had the sublime sweetness of the fruit not swept in to carry her senses away, the awkward sensation might have made her put it back down on the table.

The acidity of that first bite lashed at her tongue, but it carried more sucrose than she had ever enjoyed before, and in the presence of such overpowering decadence, all negativity fell away. She chewed greedily, quickly overcoming any roughness against her gums, and went back for another bite. She swallowed, took another bite, swallowed again, and stopped for a moment. In the center of the fruit, peeking out from a few subtle red streaks where her irritated gums had stained the white flesh of the apple, were black things that she knew had to be seeds.

Part of her wanted to secret them away in her pocket in case she decided to return to see her mother in the hopes that they might find a place to try growing them into actual trees. Had she not been almost entirely certain she was still being watched, she would have made the attempt. Not wanting to risk it, she finished the majority of the apple and picked up a handful of what she thought were grapes.

She pulled one free and tossed it into her mouth, feeling it pop as she bit down. It was an explosion of flavor, even more sweet than the apple. Had she died right then and there, she would have been hard pressed to summon a complaint. That people used to eat like this every day made her want to cry. She had never known such sweetness, at least beyond the conceptual level. Reading all she had about how great apples and grapes tasted, then actually tasting them made her question whether those writers had ever even had the pleasure she was now experiencing herself.

She ate a few more of the grapes before moving on to one of the oranges, wanting to sample all three of the fruits on the table but growing more and more aware of how poorly they were settling in her stomach. The skin of the orange was much harder to breach, and she ended up destroying a large portion of it before she gained access to the segments inside. The acidity of it stung her gums as she popped the segment in her mouth in a fashion not unlike the grape, and the aroma of it ran up her nostrils from the inside in a way that stung.

Not wanting to press her luck any more, and feeling more blessed than deserving, she placed the remnants of the fruit on an adjacent serving plate and wiped her hands and face on the provided towel. She took several, deep, sated breaths, and spoke for the first time in what felt like hours.

"I think I'm ready."

As soon as the last syllable had left her mouth, a pronounced click came from the wooden door with the intricate carvings. She slowly made her way over to the opening, and nudged the door aside.

A faint odor of smoke wafted in, but it was so slight that it wasn't hard for her to fool her mind into thinking it from the fireplace. The room had a dusty gray to the walls, darkening in the corners like an old vignette. The floor was entirely comprised of a dull metal grating, of a color not all that dissimilar from the walls.

Understanding the unspoken reason for its appearance, her heart rate picked up. Behind her, the door clicked shut, and as she turned to look at it, she discovered that the interior of the door was not made of intricately carved wood, but of the same flame retardant material as the walls.

A numbness from the fruit spread from her mouth to her throat, then radiated out to her extremities.

Did fruit always do this? Was it an effect that you had to build up a resistance to, and she simply hadn't had enough of it? Unlikely, she thought. The fruit was most likely either laced or bred to include a numbing agent, some chemical that eased the citizen's nervous system to keep them from panicking.

But how did they know that everyone would eat the fruit?

She knew the answer almost as soon as her mind had asked the question. In a world devoid of such luxuries for 90% of the population, the fruit would be irresistible. For the rest? Well, the machines were nothing if not patient, and even with the 12-hour gruel, eventually they would get hungry enough to pick up an apple and take a bite.

An overwhelming sensation of calm fell over her, and it was all Nyla could do to make it to the metal bench in the center of the room before her legs weakened and she eased herself down. A fine dust came away from the bench when she touched it, and she squeezed her hand distractedly to brush most of it off. Superficially she understood what that dust was, but in her current state she had trouble mustering up much horror over it.

She leaned back, her attention entirely consumed with finding the most comfortable position possible before the chemicals rendered her unconscious. A light grating sound rose from the floor to her right, a panel sliding open from somewhere out of sight. The metal arm snaked up from the floor, a cybernetic scorpion tail punctuated in a four-inch-long needle, and when it slid the needle into her flesh, she felt it only distantly, as though it was happening to someone else.

As everything faded to black, she fumbled the picture of Will out of her pocket in time to take one last look at it before it slipped through her fingers to the grated floor below.

"Baby."

It sounded like the word came from a million miles away, yet in its journey lost none of its sweetness.

Kyla's eyes slid open, expecting to see...what? Will sitting on the side of the bed? Laying behind her, whispering in her ear with his arms around her?

She was alone, with no clue as to where the voice came from. Realizing she probably imagined it, she sat up and looked around the room.

It was *her* room.

No, she thought. *I'm in the simulation,* and it's drawing this out of my memories. Still, there were subtle differences. The blanket on her bed, while appearing exactly like the one she had slept under countless nights, was so much softer. Nyla ran her hand across it, almost sighing at the texture as it gave under her hand. Whereas her own blanket had only softened with age and wear, this one had been made with softness in mind and not just longevity.

There was another difference, as well. The sunlight that came through the window was an almost impossible shade of gold. In reality, the slowly retreating levels of pollution in the world had rendered most days the non-color of clouds that couldn't decide if they wanted to rain or just blanket the sky.

Through the window, she saw a busy street. Much of what she saw made absolutely no sense to her, but the colorful displays and smells wafting up to her made her not want to spend another moment inside of the drab facsimile of her real bedroom.

Outside her door, the similarities to her world ended. The landing outside of her room had an elevator with no buttons. It still somehow knew to take her to the ground floor, and when the doors opened, her mind had a hard time acclimating to the sudden influx of...everything.

There was no lobby, no bulletproof glass to create a buffered, HEPA-filtered space before reaching the outside world. The elevator door opened onto a busy cobblestone street, lined with shops, children playing, food carts and trucks, as well as impromptu concerts that never seemed to talk over one another as she passed from one to another.

There was a transition point, where the concert began to fade out with what Nyla thought to be an unnatural abruptness, and a couple of steps closer to the next performance, it began to fade in just as quickly.

She approached one of the food carts, a brightly colored block of aluminum on wheels with the words NATES HOT DOGS and SAUSAGE stenciled on the side.

"How much for a hot dog?"

The attendant smiled at her.

"You must be new here," he said and handed her a steaming hotdog.

Confused, Nyla thanked him and walked around to the side where the condiments were set out in self-serve containers. Even the food was brightly colored here. In her research about the past, she had learned about hot dogs, which were, to her great surprise, not made out of dog. She took turns squirting small dabs of each condiment onto her finger and tasting it. It all tasted great, but the yellow mustard was a little strong for her newly discovered taste buds, so she ran lines of ketchup and relish down alternate sides of the hot dog, and took a bite. Three bites later, the hot dog was gone and the cart attendant seemed to get a great amount of amusement out of her statements of, "This is amazing," and, "Mmmm," after each bite.

The food was all free, she only had to ask for what she wanted and the attendants handed it over. Having been raised on flavorless gruel, she discovered, in the space of a half an hour, that she had a taste for Beef Chimichangas, Caesar Salad, Cuban Sandwiches, and Bacon double cheeseburgers. She inhaled each in a manner that should have made her stomach upset, but her digestive system seemed to have lost its bottom. The simulation had rendered food a limitless luxury rather than biological necessity. She accidentally dropped one of the wrappers, and when it hit the ground, it disintegrated into a pile of quickly evaporating dust. She quickly understood how this place could have so much abundance, yet remain pristine.

Having carved a wide swath through the culinary heritage of several nations, she set off in search of Will. She had no idea where he might be, and it was beginning to worry her more and more that he hadn't been there to greet her.

She climbed the low topped mountain range that backed the city, weaving her way through the dense forest without knowing why. Nyla had always trusted her urges, so she did again here while taking in the small rivulets of water carving meandering paths down the mountain through the mossy ground. Since the ground had never once stung her feet, it hadn't been until the damp floor of the forest made them feel cool and damp that she realized she'd left her room without wearing any shoes.

Birds chirped in the trees, and furry animals of assorted varieties took breaks from their resource gathering to stop and gawk at her. She had never seen so much life. In her reality, the remaining flora and fauna of the earth had only managed to survive out of adaptation to the new climate of dry heat and pollution. This had killed off most of the animals that lived in trees, as it had killed off most of the trees. Most of what was left were rodents, amphibians, and lizards that easily found shelter, and birds that could migrate more easily to chase whatever liquid water was left on the surface.

This forest, with its shadowy green canopy and lack of undergrowth, felt like it was straight out of one of the children's stories her mother had read to her. Something Cinderella or Red Riding Hood might have lived near.

She reached a clearing near the top and was shocked to see the perfectly mowed grass dotted with small octagon shaped shacks. Some of them served alcohol, some of them played music, and some of them did both. People were seated around bar tops that comprised half of the octagonal width of the buildings, covered entirely with green reed roofs of a tropical variety that looked slightly out of place in a deciduous forest.

She didn't feel tired or thirsty, but not knowing what else to do, she sat down at one of the huts and asked for a drink. The bartender asked her what she would like, and Nyla asked her to recommend something.

"You look like a fruity drink kind of girl," the bartender suggested.

Remembering the plate of fruit at The Rite Center, she nodded back at the bartender with a smile. The bartender handed her a pink colored drink with an umbrella sticking out of the top at a slanted angle, and Nyla took a sip as the bartender tried to spark up a conversation.

"How long have you been InSim?"

"Excuse me?"

The bartender smiled knowingly.

"InSim. Here. Since you don't recognize the term I'm assuming you are here on your last Rite."

Last Rite. Nyla had heard it called that, but it always sounded so final to her, so much about death and not about the hope she needed it to be.

"Yeah, I guess I'm...new."

The bartender extended her hand.

"I'm Nairobi. It's nice to meet you Nyla."

Nyla hadn't remembered giving her name, and her confusion must have showed.

"Apologies. Secrets are strictly opt-in here, nothing is a secret unless you choose to make it so. So everyone will know things you don't consider to be especially private."

"Oh.." Nyla took another sip from her drink, enjoying the cold sweetness as it went into her stomach.

She thought of something.

"Hey, Nairobi?"

Nairobi had already turned around to tidy up, but glanced over her shoulder with a smile.

"Yes?"

"I'm...looking for someone. They were supposed to meet me, but I haven't seen them. Any idea how I might go about finding them?"

Nairobi's smile never faltered, but her eyes took on a glint of sadness.

"How long have they been here? In real time?"

Nyla saw the look and her stomach dropped slightly.

"About a year. Real Time. So, I guess two years here."

Nairobi put down the glass she had been cleaning, and came back to the bar.

"Well, finding people here is easy, you just follow your intuition. Your mind will subconsciously locate someone you want to find and lead you to them."

"Great! So he must be nearby then."

Nairobi frowned.

"He?"

Nyla nodded.

"Yeah, my boyfriend Will passed over about a year ago, and he's supposed to be waiting here for me."

Nairobi sighed.

"Might I give you a bit of advice?"

Nyla, sensing that she might not like this advice, nodded slowly.

"You seem like a sweet girl. I just want you to know that this place changes people. The person you knew in the real world might not be who they are now. I really hope you find your Will, but I'd ask you to keep your expectations in check."

Nyla didn't much care for the implication that Will would have moved on so easily, but she understood that the advice was coming from the right place.

"I understand. Thank you. I will try."

Nairobi nodded, then turned to her left to welcome a new arrival to her hut, and Nyla went back to her drink.

"Yes, hello. Could I get two Manhattan Iced Teas, three Captain and Cokes, and...what did you want, baby?"

Nyla looked over as the man turned around to speak to a woman behind him. The hair was a shade of brown that, even in the diffused glow of gold under the hut's canopy, looked almost black. The voice had been recognizable too, as well as the way he tapped his fingertips on the bartop. She knew who the man was before he turned his startlingly blue eyes on her.

"Will?"

Will looked at her, his eyes going wide.

"Nyla?"

The woman behind Will, sensing that he knew this woman in a way she did not, stepped up to his side.

"Uhh, babe? You did you hear me? I want a Vodka Cranberry."

Will, pulled back to reality, turned to her.

"Yeah. Nairobi? And a Vodka Cranberry, please."

The woman turned to Nyla, extending her hand.

"Hi, I'm Megan. How do you two know each other?"

Nyla wanted to run. In the span of ten seconds, she had pieced everything together. Megan was Will's new girlfriend. He had moved on and had no intention of waiting for her, or had abandoned that intention sometime between entering the simulation and now.

While she was working through those realizations, Will kissed Megan on the cheek and said something to her. Megan took a look at Nyla, frowned sympathetically, and returned to the rest of their group, dancing to music and laughing amongst themselves a few dozen feet away on the edge of the clearing.

"Nyla...I'm sorry."

Nyla was still looking after Megan. Megan didn't seem like a bad person, and didn't seem to get any enjoyment out of Nyla's pain. Maybe that was the small kindness that Nyla needed to keep from breaking down into tears as she sat on that stool. Her dam of self-control was shaking, but she managed to push the pain deep inside her and exhaled slowly. The breath felt like fire, like a forge in her chest had been vented.

"I know you are, Will. I'm sorry, too."

"I want to explain."

"I don't need you to. It was naive of us to think this would work out. It's been two years for you, and one year for me. People...." she looked at Nairobi, "people change."

For the first time since entering the sim, she wanted to leave. She might have, had it been possible, but the AI's wanted to encourage people to give it a shot, so they made it impossible to leave prior to the 24-hour window.

Nyla knew this, so her mind never made it very far down that road.

Will, sensing that there was really nothing left to say, diverted his gaze to the grass.

"It's good to see you."

Nyla's temper flared.

"Really? You're going there?"

Will met her stare.

"I don't know what to say. I tried to wait. I did."

Nyla took a deeper pull of her drink before responding.

"It's fine. Really. Go find Megan. In about twelve hours, I'm going home."

For some reason, this horrified Will.

"What? Are you serious?"

Nyla didn't respond, just took another drink. It was getting low, but Nairobi placed another right next to it when she set it down on the bar. Nyla transferred the straw and umbrella.

"Nyla...I'm sorry that I let you down. I really am, but don't give up on this world just because you are pissed at me. I still care about you."

Nyla took another drink and turned to face the bar, effectively turning her back on Will. She heard him sigh from behind her.

"I really hope you reconsider staying. Not for me, but for you. This place is amazing, and I still think it's a place you can be really happy."

More silence from Nyla.

"I'm sorry, Nyla. I really am."

And with that, he picked up his drinks and left her.

It took about ten seconds for the tears to make their way through her clamped eyelids, but when they did, it was like a dam breaking. The sobs wracked her body, and she placed her head against the bar, arms wrapped around herself in an effort to muffle her cries. After about a minute, she felt someone reach down and take her hand. The touch was gentle, but firm, and Nyla didn't fight it.

When she lifted her head, she saw that it was Nairobi. Her smile was kind, her manner patient. She waited for Nyla to compose herself, only letting go of her hand to reach back and pass her a cloth for Nyla to dab her eyes with.

"Nyla, do you know what my mother told me when I lost my first love?"

"No. What did she say?"

"She told me that the best way to move on is to live well. She said that the hole someone leaves when they leave your life is real, so find something you want to be a part of, whether it's another person, a hobby, a calling, and use that to get by."

Even in her anguish, what Nairobi proposed made a lot of sense. *Yeah*, she thought, *forget Will, I shouldn't rely on anyone for my happiness. I need to get happy and then, if I find someone down the line, it will be a much healthier relationship.*

The thought of an emotional escape hatch for her pain gave Nyla strength, and she was able to regain control. She still had no idea what to do next, but in reality, whenever she needed time to think, she would find the highest point she could, some place with a view, and work things out. She wasn't sure if it was the marginally thinner air, the draw of the distance of far-off landmarks reminding her of how small her problems could be if she just let them, but it always seemed to work.

"Nairobi, is there a scenic view anywhere near here?"

Nairobi looked at her, puzzled.

"You can be anywhere you want to be in an instant, there's no need to make it a long journey."

Nyla sighed.

"Yeah, but I'm assuming that only works if you know where you want to go."

Nairobi smiled.

"That isn't how this place works. You don't need to know where a place is, just where you need to be."

It was now Nyla's turn to look puzzled.

Nairobi continued.

"Just imagine where you want to be, what the place looks like, who or what is there, and you will be."

Nyla closed her eyes.

"All right, I guess this is goodbye then. Thank you, Nairobi."

"You are very welcome, Nyla."

When Nyla opened her eyes, the first thing she noticed was the crispness of the breeze, the way it turned all of the trees into undulating waveforms of green. It gave off the sound of a billion tiny hands clapping in support, and her heart swelled. She took in a deep breath, and the cold air nipped at the back of her throat. It was perfect, more than she could have asked for.

To the left of the grove she stood in, a path led towards what she assumed to be a cliff. The only thing she could see was the tops of far off mountains and the endless blue and white of a pristine summer sky dotted with the sort of cumulus clouds she had only ever seen in old coming of age movies set in the summer of a care-free adolescence.

There were no birds, no animals of any kind, but it felt more a courtesy than a worry. Something inside of her made her believe that they were simply giving her the solitude that she needed right now. How did she know that? She just did, like the contrived way that we all know things we shouldn't in our dreams.

She made her way up to the cliff, and looked down upon what she took to be an enormous lake. The body of water was around five miles across, but as far as she could see, enclosed on all sides. The mountains all around her blocked any further vantage, but the almost magically turquoise water of the lake was something she had only ever seen in photos of old tropical vacation brochures. Nyla looked down and estimated that she must be around a thousand feet above the water's surface, but she had never been scared of heights and hung her legs over the edge and sat down.

At the center of the lake, far enough off in the distance that she couldn't see it clearly enough to be sure, looked to be a city of three concentric circles. Small specs strolled around each ring, which were the hunter green of well-manicured gardens and forests.

With the sun high above her, Nyla sat there on the edge of the cliff and thought. She thought about Will, though she tried not to. She thought about her mother. How much she missed her. How it would be good to see her again. Lastly, she thought about herself, her future. Looking at the situation as coldly as she knew how, her mother's on again, off again cough could be any number of things, some of them even life threatening. It hurt Nyla's heart to think in such a way, but she needed to be honest to make the choice that would be best for her.

On the flipside, she had made the deal with herself to stay with Will, and now that Will was gone, she was effectively alone InSim. She wasn't sure what that would be like, either. Yes, she could have an eternity in paradise, but if she never ended up meeting someone, she would be trading potentially decades with her mother for an eternity of being alone.

She wished that there was a way for her to see the future, to know how much longer she would have with her mother, or if she would find friends or more here inside of the simulation. Sure, Nairobi was incredibly sweet and kind, but Nyla had no way of even knowing if she was a real person or simply a manifestation of the all-powerful computers that ran creation.

She took a deep breath and brought herself back to the simulated reality. The sky had changed, leading Nyla to think that she had been silently contemplating her life for quite some time. What was a majestic ceiling of blue and white had transformed into pinks and oranges. The texture of the clouds reminded Nyla of something that she had read about, Cotton Candy, a spun form of sugar and coloring that had always been one of the things she'd meant to try during her time InSim.

She smiled at the memory, promising herself that she would do so before she left. *If* she left.

A squeak from deep in the trees behind her interrupted her thoughts. Realizing that she wasn't in a great position should the woodland creatures of this world decide to reclaim their homes, she crawled away from the edge of the cliff and stood up. The squeak had been happening at semi-regular intervals, but something about it made Nyla think that whatever was making it meant her no harm.

She stepped down the irregular placement of stones that served as stairs up to the cliff and saw a small animal in the clearing, holding a cone of cotton candy in her mouth. She blinked, not sure if the image before her was an incredibly complex piece of dust that had been trapped in her eye, yet the vision persisted. As she looked closer, she ran through her extensive research on the animals of the preceding century, and what sat before seemed to only match up to a creature that was considered mythological, even then. It appeared to be a unicorn, but more a toy made to look like one, created out of the plush material reserved for things she had read about called teddy bears.

The creature followed her with its head as its eyes only displayed one fixed gaze. When Nyla had closed to a distance of around 15 feet, the one-and-a-half-foot tall plush unicorn stood up. It made no attempt to approach, only patiently waited for Nyla. After another moment or two, Nyla closed the remaining paces and kneeled next to the unicorn.

It stepped forward slowly, and offered the cotton candy to Nyla. She took it, and after a prodding head nod from the unicorn, pulled off a billowy morsel of spun sugar and popped it into her mouth.

The taste was like nothing she had ever experienced before, sweetness that made everything before feel like a trial run.

A few more bites, and she looked up to see that the unicorn had taken a couple of steps away from her. It turned around slowly, reared back on its soft rear hooves, and slowly began to morph into something larger. There was no popping or tearing, the transition was elegant, as were the limbs that grew out as the body took on a humanoid shape.

The fur pulled back into the skin, and over the span of five seconds the plush little unicorn had taken on the shape of a beautiful woman. The woman was completely nude, but Nyla barely noticed. The woman looked almost exactly like her mother. She had the same eyes, the same nose, only the hair and jawline were slightly different. Nyla felt that she should know this woman from somewhere, but couldn't place her.

"Nyla."

The woman spoke her name as though they were long lost friends, and the disconnect between what Nyla felt she should know and what she knew caused her to take an involuntary step back.

"Who...who are you?"

The woman drew her hand across her body, and green semi-opaque netting wrapped around her at chest and hip, giving her a modicum of privacy.

"I am your aunt Mikele. Your mother's sister."

Nyla narrowed her eyes. She had of course heard stories of her aunt Mikele from her mother, but her mother had simply told her that she had "moved away."

"My aunt Mikele?"

The woman nodded.

"And my mother's name would be..."

Nyla was of course testing this strange woman. It was still

entirely possible that the simulation had created this woman for her benefit. Had she not just been thinking about how she had no tie here to this world, no person to connect with? If the machines had access to her thoughts, and it had to in order to make everything work, then the AI's might be playing her loneliness off as a sales tactic meant to keep her InSim.

"Celeste."

Nyla quirked her mouth to the side, still not convinced. With nothing to lose, she decided to play along, though she made a mental note that this might all be a trick. The machines had designed the simulation as a humane means of population control, and in order for the plan to work they needed to persuade every new visitor they could to stay, by whatever means possible. The laws would not allow forcible restraint, meaning the choice would remain with the human in question, but the machines weren't above a game or two of dirty pool in order to meet their goals. Machines don't understand morality or ethics, only cold, hard laws and rules. In the real world, what she saw was almost always the truth, but InSim, anything could be faked. She couldn't trust anything.

"Okay...Assuming you are who you say you are, why are you reaching out to me now?"

Nyla had let a little of her anger from Will leak into her voice, and as soon as the words left her mouth, she understood why. If this was her aunt, then it meant she had left her mother alone in the real world to stay here, and her mother had made excuses for her all of Nyla's life. Propping up that anger was the fear that, if Nyla made the same choice, her mother might hate her for it, even if she made excuses for her publicly.

She didn't want her mother to make excuses for her.

"I came to spend time with my niece before you...well...before you make your decision, whichever way you decide to go."

Nyla looked around the grove. Deciding that she had gleaned whatever insights she could from her time there, she made the call to humor this woman claiming to be her aunt.

"All right, what did you have in mind?"

Mikele smirked.

"Well, I thought I might show you where I live. By my estimate, you have around six hours left before you have to make your decision. Is there anyone else you were planning to spend time with before then, or anything else you wanted to do?"

"No."

Nyla hadn't even had to think about it.

"You understand that it is impossible to hurt yourself here if you don't want to be hurt, right?"

Nyla expression was pure skepticism.

"In theory, yes. In practice? I haven't tested that."

Mikele took that as answer enough.

"Follow me, I know a shortcut."

She strode gracefully up the uneven rocks to the cliff, took three running steps, and launched herself off of the cliff. Nyla had not followed her over, but arrived at the edge of the cliff just in time to see her vertical form create a small round explosion atop the water as she dove through it. The water looked plenty deep enough, but Nyla wasn't sure.

She thought about the risk, and decided that if, halfway through the fall, she changed her mind, she would just close her eyes and deposit herself back here in the grove to wait out the rest of her time.

With every nerve ending in her body screaming at her to stay put, she followed her would-be aunt over the edge. The wind swept her hair back as she accelerated downward, and Nyla had never felt so free. Distantly, she could hear the sound of the wind rushing past her body, but the overwhelming feeling was of peace. The dark turquoise water rushed up to meet her, a spot only about ten feet short of where her aunt bobbed.

Nyla expected the force of the water hitting her face to be crushing, but it felt more like diving into a pile of the softest, most perfectly constructed pillows in the world. Her hands cleaved cleanly through the surface, and she shot down around ten feet before rising. When she broke the surface, Mikele held her hands high into the air, fists clenched and vocal cords straining against a triumphant yell.

Nyla smiled despite herself. It always felt good to have someone be proud of you, even if the reason for that pride was ill-advised. That feeling of elation was short lived, as she realized something that she should have thought of before jumping.

"Aunt Mikele, I can't swim!"

Mikele raised her hands to Nyla, palms out.

"Relax Nyla, just watch me and try to do as I do."

Nyla expected her to try to show her how to paddle in the water to stay afloat, and was ready to scream at her for being incredibly unhelpful, when she began to rise out of the water, lifting clean free of it until she was standing on top of the mirror-like surface.

Nyla, trying desperately not to panic, did as Mikele had instructed. She closed her eyes and tried to imagine herself lifting out of the water. A moment later, standing atop the glassy surface of the lake, she opened her eyes to meet Mikele's.

Nyla raised her hands over her head in an approximation of her aunt's, and screamed the happiest scream of her life. She could walk on water here. Nothing could hurt her if she didn't let it. Only, she knew that wasn't true, not entirely.

Her mother could hurt her, simply by being disappointed in her deciding to stay. That thought took the edge off of her elation, but the smile remained. Her aunt took a few steps across the water and lifted higher, flying through no means of propulsion, her toes trailing minor wakes behind her.

Nyla followed, understanding that the only limits here were of imagination, only she trailed her fingertips through the pristine water as she floated perpendicular to it. They flew to the city at the center of the lake, barrel rolling, breaking into impromptu sessions of tag, and flying by to give each other high-fives as they made their way. When they reached the edge of the outermost ring, Mikele rose into the air and dove down beneath it, into the water, and Nyla followed.

Stretching from the underside of the city, which she had at first assumed was floating, was a spire of coral that reached all the way to the lakebed. As it descended, the spire narrowed from the full width of the city, then widened, regaining that same width as it reached the bottom of the lake. The entire height of the spire was dotted with openings that Nyla assumed were rooms, maybe even homes.

Mikele had said that she lived there, and Nyla finally understood how that might be possible. About halfway down, she slowly came to the realization that she hadn't run out of air in her lungs. Involuntarily, she had breathed several times underwater already, and that knowledge was the only thing that kept her from panicking. She took in another breath, and realized that the water did not fill her lungs like a liquid, choking her and causing her to drown. It flowed into her like air, yet her arms and legs moved through it like the denser form of matter. She understood this to be impossible, or at least not possible within the physics she knew, and another smile spread across her face.

In this place, physics would no longer dictate what could be real, only her imagination held that power.

The rest of the evening progressed like a blur. Her Aunt, for Nyla had accepted she was telling the truth, seemed to be well liked. They danced, they ate food which also seemed to be unaffected by the laws of fluid dynamics, and when Nyla decided she wanted to go for a walk amongst the sandy bottom of the lake, her aunt made no attempt to warn her of any danger, because, as Nyla understood, there was none.

She found a place where the stone ledge beneath the sand was exposed, and sat down with her thoughts. She wished more than anything that her mother could be here. Reality weighed on her mother in ways that it had yet to weigh on Nyla. Gravity had been winning a battle with her shoulders for years, and most days, it seemed to be overwhelming the rest of her, too. She ran out of energy pretty early on in the afternoon, and Nyla would normally take over the work of tidying up or finishing whatever chores her mother had been unable to complete.

She wanted more than anything for her mother to know the

freedom that she now felt, the ease at which she could have or do whatever she thought of. How much easier and better her mother's life could be.

But her mother would never come here again. Had she known all that was possible here? Had she simply not considered it real enough? So many questions, and Nyla wouldn't get the answers without giving up her chance here. Her mother had straight up refused to talk about her time InSim, always saying that she wanted Nyla to make her decision for herself.

"Nyla?"

It was Mikele, approaching out from the dark like a phantom, lit from overhead by the dancing moonlight, product of water that was impossibly clear.

"Over here."

Mikele strode over to her, though it wasn't the self-assured gait she had employed in the forest. Her steps seemed almost tentative, and Nyla understood that she wanted to talk.

"Ah, there you are."

She sat down a few feet away from Nyla, and after sparing the surface an upward glance, turned to her niece.

"I know you have a huge decision to make soon, and I'm not going to try to tell you what to decide, but I did want to ask if you had any questions you wanted to ask me before you had to decide."

Nyla thought for what felt like a solid minute before answering.

"Why did my mother choose to leave this place? Why would she go back to reality?"

Mikele nodded, as though she had been expecting this question.

"You."

Nyla's eyes widened. Realizing she had been taken out of context, Mikele hurried on.

"Well, not you at the time, no. She left because she wanted a chance to have a family. It was important to her."

Nyla thought about that for a moment before responding.

"So, she wanted a family so bad that she left all of this behind?"

Mikele nodded.

"Yes. See, it's the one thing she couldn't have here. Well, she could certainly conjure a child here, raise it, all of that, but it wasn't real enough for her. She decided that her desire to be a mother was enough to sacrifice an eternity here."

Nyla shook her head slightly. The sheer amount of will it must have taken to give all of this up for a chance at having what they had, at least up until her father had passed, floored Nyla. Nyla had barely thought about becoming a mother with Will, the plan had always been to spend eternity together InSim, so becoming a parent had never been an option.

Now that her and Will were through, Nyla had to decide if that was what she wanted, too, or if she wanted to spend the rest of her foreseeable future here in this magical dream, where the food was free and you could fly and breathe under water. Outside of her own heart, Nyla supposed there was no contest. But inside of it, saying goodbye to her mother wasn't something she thought she could do.

"Mikele?"

Mikele lowered her gaze from the dancing reflections of the lake's surface, which had been steadily brightening with the rising sun.

"Yeah?"

"Why does every human being I speak to go out of their way to not push me in one direction or another, while the machines seem to go out of their way to lean on everyone to choose to remain InSim?"

Mikele smiled at her niece, and in that smile Nyla saw the last strands of doubt about who this woman was slide away.

"Because the machines make and follow rules. They have no heart, they have no concept of loss or mortality, and by extension, they don't see how this choice would be a difficult one. They simply have a quota to meet, a goal. They never have to say goodbye. They also never get to feel joy, they never love, and they never get angry. All that is ours, a part of being human. It's the one unspoken, unbreakable rule among human beings; we are not to interfere with The Rite. Each person must make their own choice, and live with it. We respect that choice because we all have had to make it once. The machines, who have created this utopia for us, have never had to struggle with anything approaching that level. It's always 2+2=4 with them. No, I will not try to tell you what to decide, just as I didn't try to interfere with your mother when she made her decision. All I will tell you is that you should make the decision for you. You are the one that will have to live with it."

Nyla said nothing. She still had no idea which regrets she could bear, and which would allow her to still find happiness.

Mikele stood up, kissed her on the forehead, and looked into Nyla's eyes.

"Whatever way you choose, please know that I love you very much, and will continue to do so for all time."

She had made it another five or six steps away when the gong sounded, cutting clearly through the water.

Nyla closed her eyes, and made her decision.

About the Author

Christopher Godsoe is a science fiction author in Central Maine. A single father, he spends his time enjoying video games with his son, cooking, and is an unrepentant film buff. To learn more about his work, please visit www.christophergodsoe.com.

SILICON OAR

BY SHEBAT LEGION

"Can you open your eyes for me?"

Eyes?

The soft voice intruded and then there was light.

"Follow my finger. Left. Now, right."

"Good." The voice sounded satisfied, and that made me happy. I tried to smile but failed.

"Slowly," the voice cautioned.

"Where..."

"Shush now," the voice said. "Let's try blinking."

?

"Try."

I tried.

I heard a cluck of approval. I blinked again and she (she?) laughed.

"Slow down. It will come to you."

I nodded, or tried to nod, but nothing happened.

"Don't try to move," she (it was a she) said. "Let's not get ahead of ourselves."

"Okay," I wanted to say. "I will be okay."

"You'll be okay."

I HAD A TAIL. I moved it back and forth, and it made a swishing sound as if moving through water, except I know that isn't true. I was on a table. Or in one.

"That's a pretty tail."

Her name was Ruth.

I swished it because yes, it was a pretty tail. It had blue and green iridescent scales that glittered beneath the light. I would have liked to feel it move and I wanted to tell Ruth, but I couldn't.

"You will," Ruth said absently, "don't you worry."

So, I didn't worry, not then. But later, I did.

"Shush," Ruth soothed as I screamed without sound, making my mouth, if I had one, wide and gaping. I didn't scream forever, despite Ruth. Or maybe, now that I think of it, in spite of Ruth.

Where am I? I wanted to ask. *What has happened to me?*

Something happened to me.

"Everything is different," Ruth explained, "but you will be okay. You need to trust me."

I did try, but this was different. She wasn't telling me something, and I couldn't tell her I knew. But I *did* know! I knew it in my bones, if I had bones. I may not *have had* bones! Did I have bones?

"I know you're frightened. You need to let yourself drift and understand, no one is trying to hurt you. The pain is behind you."

What did she mean? Behind me? Was I somewhere before? A location, behind of where I was in front? In front of what? And, where was I now? Why didn't she tell me?

"We're helping you. I'm helping you. Me. Ruth."

"Ruth," I tried to say without a mouth to say it, "I will not drift."

"Move your pretty tail."

I swished it angrily, splashing water that wasn't there into the light, making Ruth laugh.

"You are a naughty girl."

Was I a girl?

I didn't like Ruth.

Later...

The light was gone, but I knew it was later. I heard a door open because I could hear things then.

"Sorcha?" It was a soft-sounding voice.

Sorcha? Was that my name or was she asking me something?

"I am Selena," she said.

Hello, I wanted to say. *Who are you and who am I?*

"I'll be your night friend," she said. Another she.

"I'm sitting beside you, and I have a book. I am going to read you a story from the book."

I tried to nod.

"I know you like stories."

I nodded again and then, with surprise, I *realized* I had nodded. Something. I had moved something. Did I nod my tail? Maybe it was that. Maybe it moved, and I felt it move!

"Once upon a time there lived a princess."

A princess. I nodded my tail.

"She lived in a castle that overlooked a sparkling, blue lake."

Yes, it was real. I could feel my tail.

"Good." Selina sounded happy, and I felt my tail as I slapped it around, smacking it up and down, over and over.

"Okay, stop now," Selina laughed, and I would have laughed, too, if I knew how. I think she knew that.

"Now, do you want to hear some more about the princess or do you want to smack your tail around some more? Just a little bit more, mind," she added. "Don't want to overdo."

I wanted to smack my tail around, and my face widened where my mouth was, and I screamed without sound, but I was laughing.

"That is lovely," Selina said, and it was. It was lovely, this sound of my tail slapping. I laughed and laughed.

But it was later, and I stopped because my tail hurt and I wasn't laughing anymore. My mouth widened even further, and I screamed. I knew she could hear me.

"Do you want to hear more about the princess?"

If I wanted to hear more about her, I had to stop screaming, so I did.

"The princess had a mother and a father who loved her very much. They loved her so much they wanted to keep her safe forever, and they warned her about the pretty lake."

Tell me about the lake. I swished my tail, nodding. *The lake.*

"The lake was the prettiest lake in all the kingdom, but it was very deep. A little princess could sink beneath the water and not be able to breathe, and then she would die."

This isn't a nice story. I don't like it. I don't like it at all.

"The princess loved her mother and father with all of her heart and swore she would never go into the lake."

But one day she did. The princess went into the lake. The princess always goes into the lake.

"Yes," Selina says in a sad voice. "The princess always goes into the lake."

Did she hear me?

Do you hear me, Selina?

"Yes. I can hear you."

I slapped my tail. Why can't I hear me?

"You will."

Am I in the lake?

"One day, the princess went into the lake."

Am I the lake?

"No. Listen. Sorcha went into the lake."

But she loved her mother and father. I widened my mouth. *She did!*

"She did. And they loved her forever."

Am I Sorcha?

I reached out with my tail and felt the sound of the box around me.

"You are Sorcha."

Did I go into the lake?

"You are Sorcha, and you are in the lake."

I am in the lake now? No. I am in a box.

"There is a lake in the box, and you are Sorcha."

Am I a princess?

"Yes. And you went into the lake."

Did I die?

"You did."

Am I dead?

"Not anymore, not ever again." Selina sooths but my mouth opened wide, and so did my eyes.

I had eyes!

"Shush now, baby," Selina croons. "Safe forever. A little princess."

In a box!

"In a lake," Selina corrected.

Forever?

"Sorcha is forever."

About the Author

Shebat Legion's quirky works of fiction include, "Dree, On Wednesday, first published in the Halloween anthology, Hoblin Goblin."I Am Anastasia's Bracelet", written in collaboration with Michael H. Hanson and published in the shared universe anthology, Sha'Daa and, "Ophie and The Undertaker," for Dreamers in Hell, in the award-winning Heroes in Hell series. She is the creator of Vampire Therapy: Chronicles of The Cat's Ass Boutique, which includes "A Cat's Ass Christmas," "A Cat's Ass Valentine," and "Lilly Brings Home A Leprechaun." She is the producer of the anthology Klarissa Dreams: The Art of Klarissa Kocsis, and, "The Fork Tree", a book for young children, both for charity. Legion is the author of Vampire Therapy: Jackson and Eva and is presently at work on book two of the Vampire Therapy series called "Elizabetta." Recent stories in anthologies include The Cast Iron skillet for "Rise of the Goddess", Saltwater, A Bird in Hand, both for "The Tale of the Fairy", Sasha Brook for "Darklight Four", Father's Day for Slice Girls, "Pop, Goes the Zombie", for Twisted, "The Apple," for UnCommon Orgins, "Whatever Lola Wants," for UnCommonOrigins, "The Cookie Lottery", and many more.

CARCEREM

BY DANIEL ARTHUR SMITH

THE MORNING BLITZ arrived in Carcerem, he was immediately taken to the two hundredth floor of what, back in the Alpha Plane, was called the Cronington Building. Three men waited in the penthouse office suite, all in suits. A thick set man with bug eyes was sitting behind the desk, a brillo-haired man wearing a pinstriped vest was leaning against the frame of one of the tall windows, and another of the meaty thugs, like those whom had brought him here, was waiting by the door, all age modded like Blitz himself—forever young. Brillo-top appeared not to notice his entrance, as if long hairs in prison jumpsuits strolled in every five minutes. He was busy manicuring his long, black painted fingernails with the tip of a steel stiletto knife. But the bug-eyed man, he noticed Blitz. His face lit up with a crooked smile as exaggerated as his eyes were plump, giving him the greedy expression of a wolf that just had a goat walk into his lair.

Blitz scowled. He was no goat.

The man—his escorts had called him Fromer—shook a finger at Blitz then gestured for him to stop before he reached the desk.

Blitz had little patience for formality, so little that a wee bit of acid flowed down his throat. But he swallowed back the bitter, threw his arms up to the sides, and with a subtle shrug rolled his hands palm upward. He kept a stern eye on Fromer as the meaty thug who'd been waiting by the door patted down his trunk and limbs.

Fromer's bulbous orbs furthered the inspection, scanning Blitz toe to top. When the thug was finished, Blitz kept his arms suspended in the air. He narrowed his eyes and gave Fromer a tight-lipped smile slightly raised to the side. Satisfied, Fromer gestured for Blitz to lower his hands and take a seat in one of the small chairs at the edge of the desk, then sunk back into his throne sized wooden chair, filling the room with a hollow creak.

Blitz noted the gilded chair–and the wood paneling walls surrounding him–were washed over with the gray that absorbed everything here.

"Yeah," Fromer said in a rough gravelly voice that betrayed his age. "You get used to it."

It was as if he was reading Blitz's mind.

Blitz wasn't sure if he was supposed to answer or not. His escorts told him to 'shut up and listen', but Fromer's eyes seemed to bulge as he waited, so in a rapid breath he spat out a, "Used to it?"

Fromer opened his desk drawer and from it he drew a bottle and two glasses. "Would you like a scotch?" he asked.

"Sure," said Blitz.

Fromer poured a finger into each glass and then slid one to Blitz. They each raised and then sipped from their glass. The acid in the back of Blitz' throat was replaced with the near gasoline bite of the whiskey.

"You get used to it," continued Fromer. "The gray. There's not much saturation of color here. The sky is gray, the city is gray, and the ocean is gray." He held up the bottle and swished it around. "Even the whiskey is gray. You get used to it. It's not that bad really. For the first twenty-five years of my life, back in the Meg, the only thing I saw above my head was concrete, but on my last day in the Homeland I saw a cerulean sky, edged by the fuchsia and apricot hues of the morning sun. It was a thing of beauty." He glanced in the direction of Brillo-top. "Timur here says it was a way for them to add one last cruelty." Fromer paused again, this time to rap his finger-tips in a determined drum patter across his desk, "but I disagree. You know what I think?"

"What's that?"

As if sharing some great wisdom, Fromer said, "I believe it was a parting gift. Because I don't remember ever seeing anything as spectacular—before or since. Of course, I didn't get as sick as Timur did. I don't know if it was the DMT they pumped into us for the crossover or simply because they tossed us into such a big open space, but more than half of us were bent over losing our breakfast." His finger-tips struck another double beat onto the desktop. "Not me. My insides were knotted all right. Whose wouldn't be knowing where we were going? But my head was cocked upright the whole time."

Fromer had stopped smiling, but his cheeks maintained the exaggerated deep creases.

"How we ended up queued beneath that forest of indigo banners varies depending on who you ask, but let me tell you, unlike many of the others who were herded off the train with me that morning, I did what they said I did. I don't mind admitting it. I never hurt no one, but the law is the law—when they see fit. They sent us here as a punishment, but that too is a matter of perspective I guess."

"How so?" asked Blitz.

"I'm sure the MidHi and Uppers think this place a step down, but they've never lived in the underbelly of a Meg. Given a choice I'll take the monochrome of Carcerem any day of the week. Of course, no one gets a choice." His smile returned. "The trip to the Prison Plane is a one-way ticket."

"You brought me here to tell me that?"

"No, Mister Blitz. I brought you here to save your life. Had my men not picked you up, you would've been eaten alive by the waiting party as soon as you stepped out of the portal."

"Says you. How did you know I was coming?" Blitz leaned forward and jabbed his finger into the desk. "Or a better question: how do you even know who I am? I thought you guys were cut off over here."

"Relax. So many questions. Where to begin? First. Says me, yes. They would have literally feasted on you as I'm sure they are feasting on any of those that were sent over with you. Uncivilized bunch, really. Ha. They don't even bother to remove any of the implants. A waste. Good implants are rare here." He tapped his desktop yet again. "And what else?"

"How'd you know—"

"Yes. How'd we know about you yada yada? Well. We aren't as cut off as you think. You know, we're rather close to the Homeland. Imagine, up and down the spectrum there are others sharing this—"

"I know how it works."

"But of course you do. Anyway. We don't have any of the food–most organic matter as you know is not interplanar–but we have the ghost architecture. This building, this office. Random objects, cars, clothes. The Library's Archive signal. We even get the big games. Timur tells me the SoEuro Meg is looking good this year, if you care to place a bet. No?"

"No," said Blitz.

"Suit yourself. Truth is, I don't intend you to be around when it's time to collect."

"What's that supposed to mean?"

"What that means, Mister Blitz, is that not only did I save your life, I'm offering you something most every man in here would kill for, mortal or beast: I'm offering you a golden ticket out."

"How's that?"

"How's that? Ha. So quaint. It's simple. I have a job for you. It's a job that's going to get you out of this plane and back to the Homeland. From there, anywhere in the known 'verse you care to go."

"You're kidding me."

"No. Not at all. You see, I've worked out a deal."

"What kind of deal?"

"You're going to help the Reds."

"The Reds? That's just plain crazy. What makes you think I'll get into bed with the Maro?"

"Oh. You see this is a special one-time offer. The simple fact is that you're worth more carved up. So if you don't comply with the terms, Timur here will run his blade into your skull and dig out that precious agent tech. Those blue eyes of yours may have lost their color in this plane, but they haven't lost their value—they're worth quite a bit. Without you."

"I see."

"Good. Because you're going to help them, they're going to help me, and as a side benefit, you get your freedom back. Or at least access to it. You'll have to change your image composition once you're out. But we have friends for that."

"What's so special about me?"

"I said it. You're an agent."

"That was a long time ago. Decades. I'm happy to hear you have a ticket out of here for me. But I don't see how my past can help."

"You're too modest. Timur, the Butcher of Bangkok doesn't know how he can help."

Blitz dropped his arms into his lap.

"How'd you get the name?" Fromer asked.

"The Butcher? I don't think it's a very fair or nice—"

"No. No, not that one. Blitz. How'd you get the name Blitz? I'm sure that's a brilliant story."

"Something tells me you already know."

"Ha ha. See Timur? I told you this one was sharp. Hmmm. Yes, Mister Blitz. I do know how Captain Robin Edgewater came to be forever known as Blitz. It was because of a tactic you made famous in the Spectral Wars."

"Yeah. That's right. So what? We were at war."

"Exactly. So what? But it's that tactic that will save you now. You modified a quantum device so that your team, on your command, could quant to coordinates in the enemy planes, right into the enemy strongholds, taking them by surprise. Over the course of the war your team slaughtered hundreds, thousands even."

"Those numbers are exaggerated."

"Well. I'd go with that story if I were you. The Reds respect a warrior. Not so much an apologist."

"You're forgetting one thing. I only modified the device, I didn't build it. Unless you happen to have a remote quant handy. They're not going anywhere."

"They have one."

Blitz leaned forward in his seat. "How'd they get their claws on one of those?"

"Does it really matter? Let's just say it fell off a truck."

"All right," said Blitz, raising his glass to Fromer. "Get me some new clothes, and I'm in."

"I thought you'd see it our way. We've taken the courtesy of putting together everything we thought you'd need. You can use my private bath. When you're ready, Timur here will take you across town to the Maro lair. Understand, Timur has instructions to keep you safe. But if you step out of line..."

Fromer flashed his eyes to Timur. When Blitz followed into that direction, Timur slowly pulled his blade across his own neck.

TIMUR ESCORTED Blitz back down the two-hundred floors to Carcerem's shadow of the Low—the streets beneath the towering man made chasms of buildings and infrastructure. But as dismal as the overcrowded Low of the Alpha Plane was, it was somehow worse here. The sunlight barely leaked down to the Low of the Homeland, but the bustling crowds amidst the tapestry of neon warmed the permanent night. The trains from the Homeland didn't run here, but the tracks still criss-crossed the layers above. The fog that lingered in the streets of the Homeland didn't manifest here, yet somehow its acrid odor seeped through. The same with the neon. The recognizable signs of the cafés and billboard adverts were turned off, yet were translucently painted with faint white hot outlines where the blues, greens, and pinks of the neighboring plane should have been. Even the subliminal words *buy, spend,* and *relax,* usually hidden beneath the bright imagery of advertisements of the Homeland, were clearly displayed, albeit in a chalky dullness.

Lacking the masses and electric light, the prison plane's mono-chrome shadow of the Low resembled abandoned canyons—canyons of the damned.

Timur hadn't spoken in the penthouse office or on the way down to the street, so when he finally did speak Blitz was surprised to hear an Australian accent, particularly since there were so few left. "We wait here," said Timur. "Our ride will be along shortly."

Blitz gave Timur a closer inspection. It was hard judging color in a monochrome plane. Up in the penthouse Blitz thought that tight curled Brillo-top could be brown; in the light of the street, as dim as it was, Timur's hair looked auburn. Timur could be a ginger. Blitz also decided the bright stripes of the suit–Timur had donned a pinstriped jacket to match his vest—were actually red. But in the gray, that was a guess, too.

Over Timur's shoulder Blitz saw himself, or at least his reflection, on the side of what in the Homeland could have been a news-stand. His age mods had maintained his twenty-four-year-old face for over a century, yet the young man on the grimy steel wall was hardened. His cheeks and jaw were still smooth, but his flesh was pale, inauthentic. His shoulder length dirty blond hair appeared white with black lowlights and the too blue irises of his ocular implants were a steely chrome. His suit and tie were black, not his first preference but much better than the orange–gray in here–jumpsuit.

Blitz pulled himself away from the reflection to face the street. Timur reached beneath his jacket, drew a pistol, and dropped his arm down by his side.

"You see something?" asked Blitz.

"Nope. All the more reason to have it handy. I suggest you do the same."

Blitz shrugged and freed his pistol from his shoulder holster. These firearms weren't the sabre type Blitz was used to. They didn't emit a beam blade or shoot particles. These were old school; they actually shot bullets. Which meant if he had to fire, his hit count would be limited.

"They're almost here," said Timur.

On cue, the air filled with the echo of a light buzz. Blitz couldn't initially determine where the sound was coming from. His chin-chip, the tiny gem of tech implanted into his mandible, was less efficient here. The buzzing increased to a high pitch whir focusing to his right. From around the corner, three armored vehicles, huge wildly painted rectangular beasts, rolled up to where they waited.

"What's with the paint job?" Blitz asked as they boarded the middle vehicle.

"Lets everyone know these are Fromer's. That way we don't get shot at."

"If we're worried about getting shot, why didn't we just hover off the roof?"

"The birds own the skies," said Timur. He pulled the heavy slab of steel shut and the small convoy began to move.

"There're birds here?"

"Oh yeah, the Valkyrie are here, all right. Locked in like everybody else. There are as many planar species in Carcerem as you can throw a hat at."

"I only saw mortals coming in. Are the others hiding?"

"No. You see, things are divvied up a bit different here than in the Homeland. In the Homeland, the Megs are split into the stratums of the towers—between the Upper, the Midhi, the Lows. Regardless of race. Here, the Umbra have downtown, the Maro uptown, and the Mortals, we have the middle of the Meg. It works out better. Gives everyone a chance to spread their legs."

Blitz said nothing to this. The Alpha Plane wasn't exactly as mixed as Timur described it. Money and power separated the Uppers from the Lows. Here it was just power. But the same could be said of Arcadia, the plane of the elites, or of Paradiso, where the over-crowded of the Homeland's Low emigrated each day.

The vehicles sped down the near empty alley ways, far faster than any ever could in the Alpha Plane. The carrier rocked to the left and to the right as the drivers negotiated sudden turns. Timur picked up two helmets and handed one to Blitz. "You'd better put this on."

"I thought you said no one would shoot at us?"

"You can't stop the crazies."

With that, a series of clanks rattled the armor of the transport. Through the wedge of a side window, Blitz saw a sofa slam into the street and explode beside them. He pulled on his helmet. "They're throwing things," he said.

"It's the birds. I told you. You can't stop the crazies."

There was another thunderous crash behind them followed by additional clanks on the armor.

"They always do this?" asked Blitz.

"They're just having fun. The Low opens wide in this stretch. They like to fly down. See what we're up to. Have you run into them before?"

Blitz nodded. "During the Plane Wars we were followed by a flock."

"How lucky they chose your dead to transcend to Valhalla."

"I suppose. But watching them pick the eyes out of the fallen wasn't so peachy."

"Well," said Timur. "They like shiny things."

"That they do...They shift spectrum at will, how'd they end up in here?"

Something hit the roof with a loud thunk.

"Why don't you get out and ask them?" said Timur, gesturing toward the thin side window.

Blitz peeked out and saw three dark-haired winged maidens hovering above the far side of the wide avenue. They wore the same skin tight utilitarian armor he was familiar with: form-fitting bustier breastplates, short skirts composed of scaled metal straps and feather adorned plumes of leather, head pieces more tiara then helmet, and long wrist gauntlets. The scant armor was designed for freedom of movement and to maintain the obvious light weight they needed for flight, but there was no doubt the shimmering outfits accentuated their magnificent physiques. Each held a basket of small stones, and they laughed as they threw them toward the convoy, each trying to outdo the other with every toss. A cascade of stones, from the Valkyries seen and unseen, rattled across the surface of his transport. It was his carrier's turn to be targeted. They seemed to be at home in the monochrome world, as beautiful in black and white as they would have been anywhere else. One of them seemed familiar. Her jeweled eyes glistened white amongst the gray. Eyes that were looking at him. She winked and Blitz threw himself back into his seat. He did recognize her, and the last time he'd seen her he nearly died.

<hr />

AFTER AN HOUR OF TRAVEL, the carriers abruptly stopped.

"We're here," said Timur. He removed his helmet, raked his fingers across his scalp, and then opened the hatch. "It's all right that we're carrying, but I'd keep the piece tucked away." He met eyes with Blitz. "We don't want any misunderstandings."

"Right," said Blitz.

They exited the carriers to the doors of a high arcade. Behind the tall glass façade were grand staircases, rows of escalators, and chandeliers hung stories above. At the door, two large men were waiting. But they weren't men. The Maro had the ability to hide their horns and red flesh, to blend in with mortals. This was common in the Homeland. Some, the Kasmine, went so far as to assume mortal identities. In the Homeland, Blitz could easily spot their kind. His ocular implants would send a fireworks display of augments into his vision and, with a flip of his optic photons, he could see their true form. But even without peering up-spectrum, he could see their crimson ember eyes. But here, there was no crimson, only white fluttering balls of fire where their eyes should be.

The two said nothing, nor did they move, until Timur reached the entrance. One of the two opened his side of the double doors. Blitz followed Timur through, into the atrium. Inside, other suited thugs stood in strategic locations. He followed Timur forward, to an escalator that led to a tunnel in the high ceiling. Behind him, the engines of the transports whirred into action. He spun his head back to see the three armored carriers leave.

"We don't need them," said Timur. He kept his focus forward. "We'll be leaving a different way."

Blitz didn't know which building he was in with relation to the NorEast Meg of his home plane, but it was safe to guess it was one of the four towering ziggurats near the East River. The escalator rose past the ceiling of the five-story atrium, up into the bowels of the structure. White eyes pierced the shadows as they moved floor to floor, the temperature increasing as they rose ever higher, until they reached another grand hall, as hot as a Maro Plane lair.

Here, the Maro weren't disguised as men. A legion of short horns of all shapes crowded the hall. They wore only scant loin cloths or codpieces made of metal or bone, revealing their thick muscled bodies that appeared dark gray rather than red. A variety of horns meant a variety of clans and there were many represented. Those not moving about sat in like-horned groups around open white flame pits, all serious in expression and not one missing the entrance of two mortal men.

Timur seemed to know where he was going. Blitz followed. Not one of the Maro bothered them, but some let their stare rest upon them longer than others. Uncomfortably longer.

When they reached the middle of the room, two suited Maro, in the guise of men, abruptly stepped into their path.

One of them smiled.

"Our welcome party," whispered Blitz.

"The smiling one's Acore," Timur whispered back. "The other Artok. We won't acknowledge him though."

"I know the drill," said Blitz.

When they reached the two Maro, Timur initiated contact. "Acore," said Timur. "Good to see you. May I introduce you to—"

"Captain Edgewater." The deep voiced Maro extended his hand. "We met years ago. In the Maro Plane."

The hall seemed to be sucked of air as every surrounding Maro laid eyes on Blitz.

Blitz grabbed Acore's hand tightly and smiled. "Have we?"

"Yes. At the Battle of Bon Riviera," said Acore, returning the tight squeeze. "Of course, I looked different then. Different times."

"Different times," said Blitz.

The air returned to the room as the hundred eyes fell away.

"Well," said Acore. "As they say, we're on the same point of the spear now."

Blitz smiled tightly and nodded.

"Yes," said Timur. "Yes, we are. So kind of you to meet us."

"My pleasure," said Acore. "I was notified when you arrived. If you would follow me please. I see no reason to delay."

Without waiting for an answer, Acore and Artok led Timur and Blitz to the elevator bays at the side of the hall. When they entered the lift, Blitz stole a quick glance at Acore. Every mortal Bureau agent had the diatomic nanotech and gene therapy, which allowed them to choose which part of the spectrum to perceive. He allowed his photons to shift his view up spectrum. A bull horned beast with dark markings and tattoos where his hair had been replaced Acore's mortal face. Yes, he knew the monster. Yesterday's war clans were today's soldiers for hire, and Acore was a member of a war clan that now operated as an arm of the mob, the notorious Arden Mortuus—the Living Dead.

THE ELEVATOR OPENED TO A LONG, door lined corridor. Acore and Artok led Blitz and Timur past several doors, then stopped and inserted a key into one. They entered a small workshop. Tools lined a bench in the back and on a cart in the center of the room, beneath a single hanging lamp, was the device.

The sphere was an antique by every standard. It was large, low tech, one side severely dented, but it was a remote quantum device.

It made a hollow thud when Blitz rapped it with his knuckles. "Where'd you find this thing?" he asked.

No one answered.

"Listen," he said. "It could give me a better idea of what I'm looking at if I know where it's from."

Acore's eyes shifted to Artok then to Timur.

Timur shrugged.

"We dug it up," said Acore. "In the ruins of the WestCo Meg. Near the Alcatraz Bubble."

"The Omni sunk half the WestCo Meg into the Pacific. San Francisco is under the sea," said Blitz.

"Not here in Carcerem," said Timur. "Here, it's rubble. The Re —" he corrected himself, "they have mining operations there."

Blitz nodded. The Maro were excellent miners. The blistering surface of the Maro Plane was uninhabitable, the lairs tunneled deep, and if the WestCo Meg of this world was different in Carcerem, so be it. But that gave him little to go with other than the quant was old.

"Okay. Hand me that screwdriver. I'll see if I can pry the lid off."

Timur handed Blitz a long screwdriver from the bench. The two Maro watched as he tried to force the tip into the dented crease.

"Here," said Timur. He handed him a mallet.

Blitz raised it to thwack the screwdriver.

Acore stuck out his hand. "Be careful," he said.

"Don't worry," said Blitz. "It's just the lid."

"All the same," said Acore.

He struck the handle of the screwdriver. Nothing happened. He swung the hammer again. The top of the sphere popped up. Blitz moved it aside and peered into the ball.

"It's certainly low tech. That's a good thing."

"Why?" asked Acore.

"Because it's easy to work with. I can teach you to target this quant to most any plane you like. That's the good news."

"And the bad?"

"Well. It's not just low tech. It's old tech. It can get you there. But too many hands on this when it shifts, and not everybody's going to make it. Somebody is going to come through in pieces and parts or be lost in the void with the ancients. No guarantees."

"I see," said Acore. 'That's all right. My mission doesn't require many. Can you do it? Fix it, I mean. Transport us out of here."

"Us?"

"The four of us," said Timur.

"Sure. Four. As long as you have an extra modulator around here somewhere."

"Modulator?"

"Come here. Have a look see."

The two Maro and Timur leaned over the opening of the sphere. Blitz poked the tip of the screwdriver inside. "The diamond batteries in this will last a millennium," he said as a bed of crystals came to life—and in color.

"Amazing," said Timur.

"How did you do that?" asked Acore.

"Ah. It's the resonance. It allows the color to saturate so, as you can see, these old models are crystal driven."

"Yeah," said Timur. "What's wrong with that? I thought all quant tech was driven by crystal resonance."

"It is. Most everything is, but the newer compact models simulate the resonance frequencies of old raw crystals like these. Each of these crystals is its own resonator. Each crystal has as many resonant frequencies as it has degrees of freedom, each degree of freedom can vibrate as a harmonic oscillator. It's like a choir-but this choir's without a leader. We can still tune this quant, but we need this here." Blitz reached in and pulled out a purple crystal the size of his thumb. A light gray luster replaced the purple as it left the sphere.

"What's that?" asked Acore.

"The tip of your modulator. The modulator calibrates the resonance of the other crystals. Together they trigger a quantum reaction in the diatomic heart of the sphere. It was broken off, most likely when this was dented. We need a new one."

"Can't we just fix that tip back to where it came from?"

"No. You don't want to do that."

Timur added, "Because a fractured crystal is untunable."

"Right. You could still trigger the quant, but it would be a wild ride. With no target. You could end up in one of the gas planes or in the void. Even for one passenger, it's too dangerous. But hey, no big deal. You guys are pretty lucky, really. Some of these other crystals are quite rare. If it was one of them, I probably couldn't repair it, but in this case, I can plainly see the single damaged crystal, an amethyst."

Timur smirked.

"It's quartz," said Blitz. "It's quite common. There's a ton of them in the size we need over at the university."

"That's a problem," said Timur.

"How so? They're not in the Carcerem?"

"They are," said Acore. "It's valkyries you see..."

Timur added, "They like shiny things."

THE SPEAKERS BLASTED heavy bass drums and the engine whined loudly as the transport raced through the Meg. The vehicle was nearly the same as the carrier that brought him to the Maro, but rather than navigate the streets of the Low, this one made use of the suspended train trestles that ran through the MidHi. The ride was much smoother than the street. Occasionally, there would be a slight bump. Blitz didn't dwell on what'd caused it. The transport had a huge plow on the front for clearing odd debris. When Blitz boarded the transport he noticed dried blood spatter across the blade.

Timur had stayed behind with Artok, smoothing the dent out of the sphere. The quant didn't have to be perfectly round but Blitz didn't want to take a chance that the harmonics would be distorted. Acore wasn't with him either. He had *some final business to attend to before leaving the Plane*. That left Blitz to find a new modulation crystal. Him and a military team of a half dozen tusked Maro of the boar warrior clan.

The Maro swine were musclebound beasts, easily twice the size of Blitz, and regardless of his reputation–or because of it–they didn't hesitate to add the mortal to their own. They fed him, something that they would only call protein, gave him a set of fatigues, a phase rifle, and then put him in the carrier. They sat across from him and on either side, his head at their shoulders, a toy soldier among the tattooed task force. Their commander, Targa, even offered Blitz a stick of khat, the amphetamine plant the Reds often devoured before a mission. He declined.

They were nearing their destination and the drug was already kicking in. The interior of the carrier was filled with sounds of meaty jowls flapping as the Maro chewed. Remnants of plant matter covered their chins and the bottoms of their snouts.

"When we arrive," Targa yelled over the booming drums. "We'll head straight up to the aviary. The Valkyrie are battle maidens, not warriors. They won't challenge us. We'll acquire the gem, and we'll leave. In and out. That's it."

The team began to snort, working themselves to a frenzy.

Blitz, tussled between the elbows of the mammoth Maro on either side, snorted too, encouraging the Reds to yelp and holler. Their thin porcine tongues lashed and their eyes burned white.

"HUT-HUT-HUT!" yelled Targa. In unison, the team repeated him. "HUT-HUT-HUT!" they all yelled. The hatch flew open, "HUT-HUT-HUT!", the team poured out onto the platform, "HUT-HUT-HUT!", into formation, "HUT-HUT-HUT!", rifles pointed in every direction. Blitz ran out too. He scanned the perimeter, his ocular implants in battle mode.

His augments blinked green.

There was nothing out there.

That didn't stop the Maro team from going full force. Targa swung his arm toward the closest doors and again yelled, "HUT-HUT-HUT!" and again the team repeated, "HUT-HUT-HUT!", as they jogged in a queue through the door.

Blitz followed. His brothers-in-arms made him uneasy. "HUT-HUT-HUT!" They certainly weren't going for a stealth approach. Still, even with all of the racket the squad made, the way was clear.

The path had been laid out before they left the Maro stronghold. They'd enter the Meg's tallest structure from the MidHi station and then take the elevators to the Upper garden atriums—the location of the Aviary. There they would find the hedge maze and the treasures of the Valkyrie, what Targa had called trinkets and rocks.

The lifts were too small for the whole squad to fit. They called two and boarded. Blitz shared a cabin with Targa and two others. When the doors slid shut and the elevator began to rise, smooth jazz poured through the speakers. It was a sharp contrast to the bombastic bass drums of the carrier. Blitz glanced at Targa to his side. The commander had a sedate, almost peaceful smile, his lower jaw gently chewing whatever plant he had saved in his gums

The lift stopped. The door dinged, then opened to either side.

"HUT-HUT-HUT!" yelled Targa.

The mission was back on.

As Targa's team assembled, the second elevator opened to an additional "HUT-HUT-HUT!" from within.

The elevators had opened onto the balcony that circled a huge open air atrium. Across from where they stood were level upon level of cascading gardens. Gray trees, gray flowers, gray vines. Even gray waterfalls.

Targa pointed up. Above the highest level of the gardens, beneath the huge panes of the glass ceiling, were a half dozen winged beings—the Valkyrie.

"That's the Aviary," yelled Targa. He pointed to an escalator on the next level that bridged the outer balconies with the center garden.

"HUT-HUT-HUT!" yelled Targa. "HUT-HUT-HUT!" yelled the squad.

"HUT-HUT-HUT!" they jogged to the bridge, "HUT-HUT-

HUT!" they crossed the chasm, "HUT-HUT-HUT!" they entered a plaza, "HUT-HUT-HUT!" Umbra appeared everywhere.

The Maro in front of him became separated from his head and, diving for cover behind a tall urn, Blitz remembered that Timur had said the downtown belonged to the Umbra.

The Umbra, the black-eyed shadow people, were peaceful in the Homeland. But Carcerem was a prison. These were the bad guys.

Hiding was what Shadows were best at. The squad had jogged into a trap. Blitz peeked around the side of the planter. Of all he had seen in Carcerem, the Umbra looked most at home. Their black hair, the black orbs of their eyes, the pale of their skin, all appeared made ready for monochrome.

Phase pulses flew near and he ducked back.

Targa rounded the urn, his rifle unloading in the direction he came.

"Let's go!" he yelled and grabbed Blitz by the collar.

He dragged Blitz to the next escalator, while Blitz, facing backwards, unleashed his weapon. The augments in his eyes targeted red where Umbra stood. Rapidly squeezing the trigger, he cleared as many as he could from the board. Another Maro had maneuvered with them. He too shot into the plaza, but his size made him a fairer target than Blitz so he was sliced to bits before reaching the stairs.

Midway up the escalator, the plaza fell silent. Another of Targa's team was fighting two tall Shadows at the bottom of the stairs. As he tore their limbs away, the Valkyrie swooped down. Their wings ruffled loudly, sheets unfurled in an indoor sea of air as they searched for those worthy of Valhalla.

Targa was no longer yelling "Hut." He was huffing as he ran, carrying Blitz the way a mother would carry a child. They ascended the garden tiers, finally reaching the Aviary summit.

Targa let loose of Blitz. "Get to the maze," he said, "before the reinforcements come."

"Right," said Blitz. He spun around and searched for the birds's-tockpile.

The grasses and trees grew high. He ran down one path, then

another, and into a hedge maze, blindly rounding corners and doubling back until he became lost. Still he continued running through the maze until he was confronted by her, the maiden from the Low.

She was the same maiden he'd seen that morning, and she was as stunning up close as she had been across the avenue.

"Where are you going?" she asked.

He hadn't seen her lips move, yet her soft voice was clear.

"Excuse me," he said aloud. "I know you."

"Yes, captain." The words came to him, without her speaking. "We've met."

An image flooded his mind of a café and a woman, a century before. A woman who'd went back to his room, who'd left before he'd awaken. And then there was her face above him, on the battlefield, when he fell.

"It's you," he said. "How can that be?"

"We met in my mortal form. I stayed near you for years after."

"How'd you end up here?"

"My sisters and I were caught here, and have been unable to escape."

For a moment, Blitz was the boy fresh out of the academy. A euphoria washed over him. "I can help you. That's why I'm here. The Maro have a device. They need a gem from your garden. I can take you with me...Then you can find a way to help the others."

The maiden's head tilted to the side, then straightened, but she did not answer.

"Your name," he said. "I remember. It's Farah."

The maiden smiled. Her voice came warm and gentle. "Yes," she said. "I am Farah."

"Help me...Please."

"Okay," she said aloud. "This way." She held out her hand for him to take and led him through the maze. After a few short turns,

Blitz found himself in front of a small lot, filled with a collection of gems.

"Oh no," he said.

"What's wrong," she asked.

"They're all gray."

"Does it matter?"

"Yes. Yes it does. I need an amethyst. A purple one."

"Is there no way to see?"

"Maybe," he said. Blitz tensed the muscles around his eyes to manually trigger his ocular implants. With his full focus, he searched the spectrum. He pushed harder, but they still looked gray. The area beneath his skull began to ache, but he saw no difference.

"You're bleeding," said Farah, but she was further down the spectrum and her words were muffled. A sharp pain lanced his forehead, the garden blurred, and then, faintly, color began to appear, the greens of the emerald, the blues of the sapphires and then, a pile of rocks near the center glowed lavender—the amethysts.

Blitz grabbed three that measured appropriate against his augments, and then let himself shift back to the neutral of the spectrum. The pressure in his skull let up immediately.

His upper lip was wet. He wiped his wrist across his face, coloring his sleeve black with his blood.

"Lead me from the maze," he said. "We need to meet the others."

Farah nodded and grabbed his hand.

Targa and his sole surviving soldier were still waiting at the entrance to the hedge. He spun his head back to see Blitz and Farah, but didn't appear surprised. "Do you have it?" he asked.

"Yes."

"Okay," said Targa. "Then we go." The commander nodded at his soldier, who then launched himself toward the top of the stairs—and into a barrage of fire. Chunks of Maro warrior flew away from where the giant stood.

"Hmmf," said Targa. "It's been nice." He smiled at Blitz and Farah and then he too ran to his doom.

As he had when Targa dragged him from the plaza, Blitz began to fire at the augmented targets, while the beautiful dark haired Valkyrie lifted him up and away from the Aviary garden.

FROM THE FRIGID NIGHT SKY, high above Carcerem, Blitz could see beyond the NorEast Meg, and what he saw, in the dark of the Prison Plane, were countless fires burning white. There were few other lights. Of the million windows, few shone brightly. One that was lit was the Maro lair. A small torch upon the roof, a beacon in the night.

Two warriors met them when they landed.

"Take us to Acore," was all Blitz said. But it was enough.

His augments had not failed him. Of the three crystals Blitz had brought back, one was a near perfect fit. He fastened the crystal in place and the quant began to hum.

"So this is it?" asked Acore.

"We don't have labels, per se. But if we jump to a neutral point —say the Homeland—we can gauge from there. Do you have the coordinates for where you plan to go?"

"Not yet. I'll receive the Arcadian points when I meet my master," said Acore.

"Arcadia?" asked Blitz.

Timur nodded.

"I think I understand now," said Blitz. "Arcadia is as hard to get in and out of as Carcerem. You'd need an older, unregistered quant."

Artok, having been quiet, spoke up. "You ask too many questions. Just get us there."

"Us?" said Blitz.

"Acore and I, and you and Timur. As was agreed."

"I don't think there's room for everybody," said Blitz.

Artok drew his phase pistol. "What game are you playing?"

"I'm not playing. I promised this lady here a ride out. And if you want my help, she's going. But I told you before, that only leaves room for two others. Unless you feel like a game of roulette as to whether your head will join your body."

"Hold on," said Timur. "If you want Fromer's connections to do their part, I'm along for the ride, too."

"This is ridiculous," said Artok. "Acore. Solve this. Before I kill this mortal scum."

Acore nodded and drew his phase pistol.

"A deal is a deal," said Acore.

He pointed the pistol toward Blitz and then swung the barrel over toward Artok and fired twice. Artok fell.

Acore slipped his pistol back into its holster. "What now?" he asked.

Blitz smiled at Farah, took her hand into his own, and placed their palms onto the stop of the sphere. "I programmed it to get us there," he said. "All you have to do is place your hand near mine and say good-bye to this place."

Acore and Timur did as Blitz said so that each of the four had a hand on the sphere. The humming resonance from inside the ball increased. "Hold on," said Blitz—and then, there was a flash.

About the Author

Daniel Arthur Smith is the author of the international bestsellers Spectral Shift, Hugh Howey Lives, The Cathari Treasure, The Somali Deception, and a few other novels and short stories. He also curates the phenomenal short fiction series Tales from the Canyons of the Damned.

He was raised in Michigan and graduated from Western Michigan University where he studied philosophy, with focus on cognitive science, meta-physics, and comparative religion. He began his career as a bartender, barista, poetry house proprietor, teacher, and then became a technologist and futurist for the Fortune 100 across the Americas and Europe.

Daniel has traveled to over 300 cities in 22 countries, residing in Los Angeles, Kalamazoo, Prague, Crete, and now writes in Manhattan where he lives with his wife and young sons.

For more information, visit danielarthursmith.com.

SOMEWHERE I BELONG

BY JEREMY RODDEN

As Jessica Rabbit once famously said, "I'm not bad; I'm just drawn that way."

My entrance into the Tooniverse was not an easy one. Of the few people in other realms who have heard of the Tooniverse, even fewer have heard of the section of the Tooniverse to which I was first introduced. Toonopolis has been home to many tales and adventures, but few ever make it out of Ao. I am one of them. My name is Angel. This is my story.

As a creation toon, I had an innate understanding of the Tooniverse at my birth. It was simple to comprehend. Creations were born as the thoughts and imaginations of sentient beings in the 'real' world. The thing the stories from Toonopolis don't tell you, though, is not all thoughts of sentient beings are fun, light-hearted, and pure. Some are violent. Some are evil. Some are sexually deviant. Those creations don't go to Toonopolis. They go to Ao. I discovered very quickly Ao was not a particularly friendly place at all.

I ENTERED the Tooniverse in the middle of a field of scorched earth.

I straightened my halo and ruffled my wings to test them out. Standing up, I raised my nose to the air and smelled an acrid, sulfuric odor emanating from the ground itself. I looked down at myself and saw the tight, white leather jumpsuit pushing my cleavage almost up to my chin and adjusted the zipper so I could breath effectively.

My eyes squinted as I looked for signs of life in any direction from my origination point. I could see fire in one direction. I peered up and an angry-looking sun scowled, quite literally, down at me. I heard a slight popping sound behind me and turned to see a disfigured demon standing there.

The small red creature was stark naked and his face was half-melted. I vomited in my mouth just looking at the disgusting beast. Gathering my strength and steeling my stomach, I found my voice and asked, "Do you know where we go to get sorted?"

The creature looked up at me. I felt sorry for the poor demon and wondered at the human mind that created such a pitiful looking creation. I almost wanted to give him a hug. I looked again at his hideously disfigured face. Almost.

"Screw you, lady. You're on your own!" he replied. Then he gave me the finger and ran off toward the fire I saw on the horizon. I saw a faint sign with an arrow on it pointing the same direction. The sign said, "New Jersey."

After a few stunned seconds, I sighed and extended my wings. A swathe of my hair fell in front of my eyes as I slowly lifted from the ground, testing the wind stream just above the spoiled surface of wherever it was I entered the Tooniverse. I blew the golden strands from my vision and opted to fly in the opposite direction of the fire, towards an unknown horizon that seemed a better choice than where the foul-mouthed demon went.

After a short flight where I heard nothing but the faint crackling of the earth below and the fluttering of my own wings, I finally saw a town on the edge of my vision. I couldn't make out many of the buildings but they were oddly shaped and appeared to be moving around. As I flew closer, I realized many of the buildings were shaped like male genitals. Apparently, the architects of this town were obsessed with all things phallic.

I simultaneously felt a tug on my essence drawing me towards the town and a sense of being appalled at myself for it. What was wrong with me? Did my creator give me desire and guilt at the same time? What was wrong with him/her?

Internal conflict aside, I flew towards the city in front of me and stopped once I was close enough to read the large sign identifying it. In giant, white, and bold lettering on a black billboard was written: "Welcome to Penisville. Population: You." I groaned, landed on a walkway next to the sign, and walked through an arched entranceway to the town that looked suspiciously like vulva. I paused and walked back out to look at the entranceway again. Yes, it was a vulva. I entered again.

"Are you in yet?" a female voice asked from atop the archway.

I looked up and saw a tiny face on what I supposed was meant to be the clitoris. She looked displeased. I turned my attention instead to the town itself.

Penisville's entrance square looked like a university quad. Every building overlooking the open grass field had balconies strewn with all manner of people, creatures, and animals. The overall smell of the town was a mixture of lubricant and shame. I wanted to be disgusted by it, but I actually felt a little aroused by it. This incongruent mixture annoyed me. What dichotomy of emotions had my creator instilled in me that would conflict with each other like this?

I didn't have much time to reflect on my internal dialogue as I felt a hand firmly grab my right breast over the leather jumpsuit. I immediately flew into the air and looked down at my assailant. "What are you doing?!"

A large male rodent in a brown overcoat looked up at me. A weasel, maybe? "Coppin' a feel," he responded incredulously.

"And why would you think that was okay?"

"Because you're hot and your boobs are out." The ferret shrugged his shoulders. "And I wanted to see if they were real."

I instinctively tried to zip up my jumpsuit tighter. The size of my breasts proved to be an occlusion to this strategy and I had to give up. I shook my head annoyingly at my creator for dressing me in such impractical clothing. "I'm a toon. They're as real as the rest of me."

"Why dontcha come down here and show me?" the ferret asked.

I flew down and landed in front of him. I stood about a head taller and realized quickly this created the unfortunate situation where his face was directly in front of my chest. He clearly misread my intentions and shoved his furry face into my cleavage, making *plbplbplbplb* sounds into my sternum. I shoved him backwards and he fell onto his rump.

"What are you, some kind of cocktease?" he asked as he pulled himself to his feet.

"Listen, weasel–"

"Ferret."

"What?"

"I'm a ferret. Not a weasel."

"There's a difference?"

"Of course there is!" he cried. "It's so insensitive of you to not care that there's a difference."

My mouth dropped open in shock, but I quickly closed it. "Says the rat that groped me and then motorboated me? I'm the insensitive one?"

"Yeah. Look." He lifted the back of his overcoat and showed off his brown-black tail. "Weasels have much longer tails."

"Fine, ferret–"

"Chad."

I stared at him. If I were able to shoot lasers from my eyes, I would have. I tried, just in case. It didn't work.

He seemed to finally realize I was not pleased. His voice got quieter. "My name is Chad. But hey, how would you like it if I just called you Angel because you're an angel?"

"That *is* my name."

Chad blinked. "You're an angel named Angel? Is your creator as blond as you sugarbreasts? Because that's not very original."

"Can we get back to the problem of you groping me without my permission and not discuss our names for a moment?"

Chad shrugged again. "Just tryin' ta be polite."

I couldn't control my anger anymore and punched Chad in his little rodent face. I could hear hooting and hollering from the balconies around the quad and became instantly aware that most of the eyes surrounding us had fallen on Chad and I. I saw two pigs dressed as police officers approaching us through the grass. I sighed in relief.

"Oh, I'm glad you're here officers," I said when they reached us.

The two anthropomorphic pigs brushed right past me and approached Chad, who was wiping blood from the corner of his mouth with the back of his hand. "Are you okay, son?" asked one of the officers.

"Excuse me?" I asked.

"We'll get to you in a moment, girl. This man has clearly been injured. We need to make sure he's okay."

"Of course he's injured," I cried. "I just punched him in the face!"

The slightly larger pig turned to me and finally paid attention. "So you're admitting you punched him?"

"Of course I did. He assaulted me! All these people saw it." I waved my hand to the people and creatures on the balconies around the quad.

The officer ran his eyes up and down my body. "Well, what do you expect dressed like that?"

I tried to use my non-existent laser eyes again. They still did not work. "Why does that give him the right to grab me? Why does it matter what I'm wearing?" *Not that I had any say in it anyway*, I thought to myself.

"Don't you know where you are?" the other officer asked.

"I saw the sign. I'm in Penisville."

Chad the ferret spoke up, "In Soviet Russia, Penisville is in you."

The three men laughed. I did not. "Look, I'm just trying to find out where I get sorted so I can go to where I belong. I've barely been in Toonopolis for like, I don't know, not very long. Clearly I don't belong here."

The larger pig cop had a look of realization on his face. "Oh, you think you're in Toonopolis. Now I get the problem."

I felt like I got punched in the stomach when I realized what that meant. "No. I can't be. I don't belong in–"

"Ao?" the cop asked.

"I am not one of *those* toons. I don't curse. I'm not naked."

The cop stared at my chest and raised a fat pink eyebrow.

"Not completely anyway. And I'm not killing and maiming and bloodying the place." Chad squeaked and pointed to his lip. I ignored him. "Why am I in Ao?!"

The more portly of the porkers placed an arm around my shoulder. "I'm not sure, but how do you feel about being the bread inside a ham sandwich?" He pointed a fat finger back and forth between himself and the other cop.

I vomited in my mouth for the second time since entering the Tooniverse. Brushing his arm off my shoulder, I said, "Aren't you supposed to be cops? Why would you be just as bad as that ferret over there?" I pointed to Chad.

The smaller cop laughed. "There is only one rule in Penisville."

"You do not talk about Penisville!" Chad exclaimed.

The pig next to him smacked him on the back of the head. "No. The only rule in Penisville is 'Boys will be boys.'"

"And what about girls?" I asked.

"Playthings," the cop closer to me whispered in my ear.

I knew it was time for me to leave when I felt the pig's hand on my butt. I leapt into the air and let out a huge downward gust with my wings before the disgusting animals of Penisville could lay their hands on me again. I wasn't sure where I was going to go, but I knew I had to get away from Penisville.

I could hear the hooting and hollering of the ferret and pigs as I ascended. I picked a random direction and flew until I was well away from the horrid town. Once I felt I was safe enough, I slowed my flight and considered my predicament. If I was sent to Ao instead of Toonopolis, there had to be a reason. As far as I could fathom, I wasn't the type of toon that belonged in Ao. It couldn't be just based on the way I look, could it? Plenty of sexy-looking toons have made it to Toonopolis and even into TM status. Could the mixture of feelings I had in Penisville have something to do with it? Maybe my creator intended me to be more adult in nature but ended up making me some sort of hybrid, sexual but ashamed of it at the same time?

CLANG!!

I clearly wasn't watching where I was flying and was stunned into the reality of the moment by crashing headfirst into a large metal sign. I landed on my back and could feel one of my wings twist underneath me. It was not a pleasant feeling.

I gathered my senses and looked at the sign that snuck up on me. It was written in large calligraphic Asian-style letters. "Hentaitown," the sign read. A pleasant pond with large orange fish in it sat under the sign. After my experience in Penisville, I was leery about entering another section of Ao unprepared.

"I'll be ready this time," I mumbled to myself as I reached behind my back and pulled a sword from C-space. I touched it to my halo and watched it envelop in flames. I smiled. *Eat your heart out, Archangel Michael*, I thought to myself. I quenched my sword in the pond and pulled a white sheath from C-space to place it in. I winced as I saw my sword-quenching seemed to have killed the fish in the pond.

After attaching the sheath to my white leather belt, I entered Hentaitown with my head held high. The village I saw when I entered was drastically different from the quad that was the entrance to Penisville. Hentaitown had a tall bamboo forest in the center of the town and small, paper-door lined huts surrounding it. I saw a figure sitting on the porch of the hut closest to the entrance and approached with a hand on the hilt of my sword.

"Hello, sir?" I called, trying not to sound meek.

A small Asian man stood from the shadows and came to the edge of his porch to look at me. "Eh? *Gaijin?*"

Seeing how small and old the man was, I felt the tension in my hand ease up on my sword. "I don't know what that means."

The old man laughed. It was quite comforting to hear a laughter that was not mocking for the first time in Ao. Hentaitown was already light years better than Penisville. "*Gaijin,*" he repeated. "Not from around here."

Oh good, he speaks English, I thought. "No. I'm not. I don't know where I belong. You see I just got to the Tooniverse not too long ago and I didn't realize I was in Ao so I was expecting to get sorted and I'm just trying to find out where I should be and all I know so far is Penisville is *not* my home." I took a deep breath. I could see the old man staring at my chest as I heaved and covered myself with my arms.

"What is your name, *kawaii onna?*"

"My name is Angel. I'm sorry for rambling. What's your name, kind sir?"

"Around here they call me Kaiju." He smiled again. I felt calmer. "There is a place you might belong just down the street over there. Many pretty girls with," he gestured at my halo and wings, "unique attributes."

"Thank you," I said, bowing.

"The word here is *arigato,* Angel-chan."

I smiled. I liked the sound of Angel-chan. Maybe this was a good place for me. "*Arigato,*" I parroted.

"*Ieie,*" he said and bowed back to me.

I felt much more relaxed as I turned away from Kaiju's hut and walked in the direction he indicated to a place that was clearly far better for me. Ao couldn't be all bad. I turned back to wave to Kaiju but he was gone. Must have gone to bed.

The town smelled like fresh grass and the tips of the bamboo bent under a slight breeze. It was a beautiful town in all ways. I reached a larger building at the end of the street. A matronly Asian woman sat on the porch with two young school girls. The woman was dressed in a pretty red kimono and the schoolgirls had matching red skirts with white blouses.

"Hello," I said pleasantly.

"What you want, *gaijin?*" the woman asked with a gruff voice.

"I know I'm not from around here, ma'am," I began, "but I am new to Ao and trying to find a place to call home. I was told there were other women here who were . . . like me." I turned to show off my wings.

The two schoolgirls giggled and whispered to each other. I felt self-conscious and pulled my wings closer to my back—not that I could make them any smaller, but I tried. My good feelings from my conversation with Kaiju were starting to fade.

"Why are they laughing at me, ma'am?"

"My name is Oiran," she corrected.

"I am sorry, Oiran. I am Angel." I pointed to the schoolgirls. "Why are they laughing?"

"They are laughing because you think your wings are something special that make you different. That is nothing compared to those here."

I could feel my eyebrows crease together on my forehead. "But you three look perfectly normal," I protested.

Oiran laughed this time. Her voice was harsh, like that of an eighty-year smoker. "Futa. Nari," she called to the two schoolgirls. "Show this *gaijin* what makes you . . . unique."

"Yes, Oiran-sama," the two girls said in unison. They moved to a spot on the porch where I could see them. They twirled and produced beautiful spirals and stars in the air around them as they spun. I couldn't see them through the light show but I could hear them speaking some incantation in Japanese. When they stopped and the pyrotechnics cleared, they were standing in front of me completely nude.

They still seemed perfectly normal to me, albeit naked, until my eyes arrived at their crotch. In place of their girly bits, each had a large, erect, and veiny penis. They had to be over a foot long each and I wasn't sure whether I should be aroused or appalled. My own girly bits battled with my stomach for control of my senses and neither one could find winning ground.

Girlish giggling broke my concentration. "I think she likes us," one of the girls said to Oiran.

"Should we give her a taste?" the other one asked.

"Maybe later, Nari. And I think you're right, Futa. She looks to be a little squishy in that leather jumpsuit." Oiran laughed her smoker laugh again. She addressed me next. "And you think a pair of wings is unique?"

I tried again to make my wings shrink. "But Kaiju said–"

"What?!" Oiran interrupted. "What did you just say?"

The two girls immediately ceased their giggling and re-dressed. I tried to understand where they hid their giant penises underneath those short skirts but I didn't have time to ponder it long. Oiran ran down the stairs and grabbed me by my shoulders.

"I said Kaiju said I'd fit well here."

"Where did you see Kaiju? When?!"

The frantic tone in her voice made me scared. I reached my hand to my sword hilt again. "The little old man that lives at the hut next to the entrance? He was very nice. He called me *kawaii*."

"Of course he would," Oiran said. "He loves new toys. And, Angel, he is no little old man. He is whatever he chooses to appear to be. His true form is not what you saw."

From behind me, slow laughter built. It sounded like the old man I met at the entrance to Hentaitown. The laughter twisted into a more maniacal cackle and I turned to look at the source. Kaiju, as I met him, stood on the path I had just travelled from the entrance to Oiran's house. His eyes were wild and his laughter became crazier and crazier. Black smoke swirled around his feet.

"Do you know what Kaiju means?" Oiran asked. I shook my head no. "It means 'monster,'" she said gravely.

The black smoke covered the old man entirely now. The only things I could see through the smoke were two red, glaring eyes. Futa and Nari were crying behind me on the porch and I could feel Oiran backing up onto the porch herself. The smoke dissipated and standing in place of the old man whom I knew as Kaiju was a large, green, amorphous creature with two giant red eyes.

"That's it?" I asked Oiran over my shoulder. "That's the monster?" I felt a surge of confidence as I pulled my sword from its sheath.

"This isn't even my final form," Kaiju said, his voice sounding deeper and more menacing.

Seeing no reason to wait for his final form, I ignited my sword from my halo as I practiced before. Determined not to allow myself to be a victim like in Penisville, I gathered my courage to charge at the monster and defend myself and the women behind me.

I didn't even see the tentacles coming before I felt them on my wrists.

In less than the time it took for me to decide to attack and take my first step, Kaiju sprouted what looked like hundreds of tentacles. Two of them had a firm grip on my wrists and lifted me into the air. My flaming sword fell uselessly to the ground and sputtered out. I turned my head to look at the other women and Kaiju's tentacles had a hold of them as well.

Oiran screamed up at me. "It is useless to fight him, Angel. Best just to give in and let him have his way. He is too strong. He is too fast."

Sounds of pleasure and pain came Futa and Nari. Some of Kaiju's tentacles were already having their way with them.

I bit into the tentacle on one of my wrists.

It released its hold and pulled back briefly.

I reached with my free hand to grab my halo from above my head and slash at the other tentacle with it. I could smell singed flesh as the tentacle was severed and immediately cauterized by the holy fire of my halo. Once free, I flew up into the air and out of range of Kaiju's tentacles.

I could have just flown away at that point, with the monster distracted by the schoolgirls and the matron, but something inside me compelled me to fight for them. I reached behind me in mid-air to the C-space at my back and pulled out a large white shield with a red cross on it. Gathering my strength again, I dove towards Kaiju's back with the shield in front of me and screamed, "Die, you beast!"

A flurry of tentacles struck my shield and grazed to either side of me. I was able to deflect them all as I came to a crashing roll on the ground in front of the monster. I kept the shield raised as I retrieved my sword.

Kaiju's tentacles seemed to be getting slower. Or maybe I was getting faster. I couldn't tell.

"Leave them alone," I commanded.

"Do you not know who I am, girl? I am the master of Hentaitown. I take what I want and do what I want. No *gaijin* whore will tell me otherwise!"

I leapt off my feet into a roll and slashed wildly at the tentacles that were still holding the other women. I heard the schoolgirls moan as they hit the ground. They actually sounded disappointed their assault was over.

"What is wrong with them?" I called to Oiran.

"Kaiju's venom is addictive," Oiran said from the ground. "They crave it as much as they fear it. I will look after them, *eiyuu*. Go. Fight."

I nodded back to Oiran while continuing to evade and slice at tentacles. Kaiju seemed to barely feel any pain from losing the tentacles and simply grew new ones to replace them. This fight would last forever at this rate. Or at least until I grew weary enough to succumb to him. I had to try something new.

I re-ignited my sword for the third time, slashed more ferociously at the tentacles, and flew into the air. I dropped the shield to the ground and willed my sword to grow larger, wielding it in two hands. I built up tension in my wings, stuck the sword straight out in front of me, and spun in a tight barrel roll towards the monster, creating a vortex of wind and fire and steel and cutting through any tentacles that shot out at me.

I did not stop until I felt myself barrel through Kaiju to the other side of the beast. I could smell even more burning flesh and heard a bubbling of boiling liquid behind me. I turned to look at the monster.

I had bored a giant hole directly through his body. He was literally melting from the inside out.

Kaiju emitted a gurgling scream as he melted into a puddle of green goo on the ground in front of me. Oiran, having safely placed Futa and Nari in the house, came to me and gave me a deep bow. "You saved us," she cried. "You could have left but you came back for us."

"That was stupid of me, wasn't it?" I quipped. Then I fell to one knee in exhaustion, dropping my sword to the ground.

"Are you okay, Angel?"

"I'm fine. Just tired. I am not sure I was meant to be a fighter. Or a plaything for men." I glanced at the still bubbling pile of goo. "Or monsters."

"I'm not sure what you were meant to be, dear, but today you were a hero."

I smiled. "Maybe, but I still don't think this is where I belong." I grabbed my sword and got to my feet slowly. "This doesn't feel like me."

"You truly are unique and special, Angel-san. Maybe I know of a place that can help you figure out where you belong in Ao."

I felt a small spark of hope light in my chest. "Or if I even belong in Ao?"

"I have been here a long time. I have never heard of a toon leaving Ao and existing somewhere else in the Tooniverse."

The light fizzled. "Oh," I muttered. "So I guess I'll never be able to go to Toonopolis, where I think I belong?"

"I don't know. But maybe Madame Rogue in the Black Light District can help you. I know that is the place where the two realms connect. Maybe you can find a way through there?"

"Thank you, Oiran. Please tell me how to get to the Black Light District."

"With pleasure," she said through a huge grin.

It did not take me long to fly to the Black Light District on the edge of Ao. I was surprised to find it was not a very populous area of this part of the Tooniverse. Apparently, this was where the softcore, as Oiran from Hentaitown put it, toons ended up. These were the ones that were too adult-themed for Toonopolis but not really so mature they went to places like Penisville and Hentaitown.

It was for this reason she felt it was the best place for me to find information or, if all else failed, find a home. I knocked on a green door in the Black Light District and found myself standing in front of a pretty fox lady in a green dress when it opened.

"Can I help you?" she said.

"Yes, ma'am. I am looking for Madame Rogue."

"I'm her. And you are?"

"My name is Angel."

She scoffed. "Of course it is. Come in, blondie." She twirled and her green hair flew beautifully in a swirl as she did. I followed her inside and she directed me to a pale green sofa. I sat on the edge so my wings had room to breathe behind me. "What can I do for you?" she asked politely but firmly.

"I don't know where I belong," I began. I recounted my story so far. I told her of the ferret and pigs in Penisville and the women I defended from the tentacle monster in Hentaitown. She listened intently at my story but made no move to interrupt me or ask any questions. When I finished, I could see in her eyes she could help me.

"It sounds to me like you'd fit in perfectly well here, toots," she finally said. "If you wanted. BLD isn't too different on this side than it is on the other."

"I guess–"

"But I can tell that isn't good enough for you," she interrupted with a laugh. "Gods, you remind me of her so much." Her eyes glazed over. She wasn't look at me anymore. She was looking through me.

"Of who?" I asked, breaking her hazy vision.

"My sister, Rouge. We both came into this world together. She said she always felt like something was wrong. That we didn't belong in this world and we should have been in Toonopolis. I didn't agree with her. I feel like you should stay where you belong, but . . ."

She let the pause hang in the air. It felt like a minute but was probably only a few seconds. "But what?" I asked impatiently.

"But I helped her figure out a way past the morality police, the ones that guard the path between Ao and Toonopolis. They are called the Forever Code Commanders. And they cannot be fooled."

The spark of hope that had fizzled when Oiran told me she knew someone who could help me reignited into a flame. Oiran was wrong. Someone had found a way from Ao to Toonopolis and I was talking to the one who helped her do it. I could get there and start a new life for myself, away from all the perverts and monsters and melty-face demons.

"But the technique ain't easy," Madame Rogue said. "And it could kill you."

"But toons can't die, right?"

"You can if your creator does. You know that much from the knowledge built into us all. No creator equals no toon. The process I developed for my sister to cross could have killed us both, since we share a creator."

I thought about my time in Ao since I came into existence and felt that non-existence was a better future than living out my time dealing with the things I faced. "Teach me."

Now, I don't want to tell all the secrets about how I followed the thread back from myself into my creator's actual mind in order to force him to change what I was, because anyone hearing this story might think it's a great idea to copy it. It's not my place to suggest anyone else follow the path I followed.

What I did is not considered a noble thing. In Ao, there are no rules so no one cares what you do. I experienced that. In Toonopolis, though, there are certain expectations of remaining who you were meant to be. The technique, which I learned later was actually dubbed Rogueing, is frowned upon. I felt a life of potential solitude in Toonopolis was better than staying in Ao, so I did it. As I stood in front of the FCC guards, who I learned were unmoving suits of armor, I was confident in myself and my choice.

The creations in Toonopolis may look at me as some kind of abomination, a Rogue toon who changed herself to be who she wanted to be instead of what her creator made her out to be. To those creations I say, "Forget the haters. My name is Angel. And this is *my* story!" And I walked past the guards with my head held high and into the Toonopolis side of the Black Light District.

About the Author

Jeremy Rodden considers himself a dad first and an author second. He is the author of the middle grade/young adult *Toonopolis* series of books which take place in his cartoon universe. He also edited, contributed to, and published *The Myth of Mr. Mom*, a non-fiction series of essays by stay-at-home dads. He can be found at his author blog (www.toonopolis.com) or on Twitter @toonopolis.

A TRAP IN ESHWAR

BY E.E. GIORGI

GENERAL FEDRUS WEBER clasped his hands behind his back and watched the third fleet of Stingrays enter Sarai's mesosphere. Third and *last*, as the attack had been so successful he'd already sent orders to withdraw the fourth squadron. As commander in chief of the Sarai Task Force, he couldn't have been more satisfied with the way operations had rolled out.

His whole career depended on this mission. Not a single separatist base was to be left standing, no matter how high the price his fleets were going to pay. Sarai had been a long-awaited jewel to add to the Imperial Kraal's crown of conquered planets, and his success was sure to grant him a higher spot in the Kraal's long string of favorites.

Weber thought of his long-time rival, General Zika, now struggling to find Quarium—their fleets' and weapons' primary source of energy—on the dead planet Yulia. His smile grew wider, knowing that Zika was out of sight and out of the Kraal's mind. Even if Zika's efforts turned out an ounce of Quarium—which now seemed unlikely—it was still a dull slog that would earn no recognition for his rival.

Weber watched with cold eyes as smoke rose over Sarai's two

major continents, bleeding into the surrounding storm clouds. Warships were no longer taking off from Sunan, the planet's most populated city.

No victory came cheap, that lesson he'd learned many years ago.

Today was no different. He'd already lost half of his Stingray fleet and countless starfighter jets. But the reports popping up on his computer screens were clear: Sarai was mortally wounded. One more strike and the planet would fall.

The locals had defended themselves fiercely. *A useless show of pride on their part,* Weber thought, tapping his fingers together. The Saraiians' rudimentary military could do very little to overpower the Stingray's pulse propulsion bombs with Quarium warheads. Space debris from the battle now drifted in the outer layers of Sarai's atmosphere. The last fleet of Stingrays plowed through the debris, leaving a trail of red smoke behind.

The last of the second element of the Stingray fleet—now a cluster of dots over Sarai's sea of orange clouds—broke through the atmosphere and vanished under Sarai's smoky clouds. Weber turned to the hologram floating above the navigation console.

"Zoom in," he ordered his first navigator.

"Aye, General."

An electronic bell chimed through the navigation room.

The chief engineer ogled over his screen. "Incoming communication, General."

Weber shot a murderous glare at the ship's captain. The man—a lanky officer in his first extra-planetary assignment—leaned over the chief engineer's shoulder and barked, "Kill the damn channel. What the hell are you doing keeping outside comms open during an attack? That's a potential vulnerability."

"It's an inside comm, Sir," the engineer protested. "It appears to have been quantum encrypted by one of our secured channels."

The captain clicked his jaw. "I said—"

"Enough," Weber interjected. He couldn't stand this kind of bickering in his own ship. He'd lost his faithful captain of five years in a tragic mission two months prior and now he was stuck with the spoiled son of a senator who'd gained his favors with the Kraal through cheating.

First thing on Weber's list once he was free to return to Aplaya was to get rid of this guy. *He should be on desk duty, not on a military ship supervising major operations.*

The comm bell chimed again.

Weber inhaled. Through the window screens, he saw a puff of smoke rise up and break the even layer of clouds on Sarai. There. He'd just missed the first launch from the last element. Who could possibly interfere with such delicate operations?

"Shall I put it through, General?" the chief engineer asked.

Weber nodded. If this turned out to be a breach he was sure to have the captain's head on a silver plate.

"Imperial Kraal code SCD 456X," the engineer read from her screen.

The captain leaned a little closer and squinted at the screen. "That's General Zika's key."

Zika? Weber had to laugh at that. Zika had his hands full finding nonexistent Quarium on planet Yulia.

"Nonsense," he said. Another pulse propulsion bomb was about to be launched and in the meantime he was wasting his time with a ridiculous infiltration.

The message started playing despite his skepticism. "Greetings, General Weber."

Icy silence fell in the room. The three engineers and navigator tapped at their screens. The captain sulked. The bomb dropped and a new plume broke through Sarai's atmosphere, the final wound on a planet already bleeding to death.

Weber watched the scene and clenched his jaw.

"General Zika," he said at last, recognizing his rival's voice. "It must be something urgent that's prompted your comm request today. We're just completing the last operation on Sarai and, frankly, this call is a breach of protocol—"

"Urgent indeed," Zika interjected. "In fact, I would much rather discuss in person."

Weber snorted. "Of course. We will return to Aplaya as soon as—"

"No. I need to see you *now*, General."

Weber resented the tone. Zika was his equal, he had no business treating him like his subordinate. He took few, calculated steps to the computer screen displaying the comm.

"What's the matter, General?" he demanded.

Zika's voice came after a moment of static. "The matter is of extreme urgency and can only be discussed in person. I've launched a shuttle to pick you up. See you in thirty minutes."

A click, more static.

"Comm channel closed," the engineer confirmed.

Thirty minutes, Weber thought. That put Zika within two hundred thousand miles from Sarai, certainly away from Yulia as he'd originally thought. Why?

"Sir?" the captain said.

"What?" Weber snapped.

"The shuttle has just entered our radar space."

"Great way to anticipate a breach in space," Weber snapped, striding off to the bridge.

"It was a friendly line," the first engineer protested, but his voice trailed off disregarded.

AFTER THIRTY-SIX HOURS of non-stop travel, Egon had arrived at his destination feeling queasy and light-headed. He hated traveling through wormholes. It damaged his circulation and depleted his energy. To make matters worse, now he barely had the time to deliver his message before returning to his ship and crossing the wormhole all over again.

Egon rushed down the long corridor of the Electra—the Imperial Mothership—at a brisk pace. The Imperial guards struggled to keep up with him, but he didn't care. The message he was carrying was of great urgency. That was why General Zika had demanded he delivered it personally. No hologram, no radio freqs, no light waves.

Go, deliver, and bring back the Kraal's response.

Those had been Egon's instructions.

"You do understand that this is the Kraal's personal time, yes?" one of the guards asked. His breathing was quick and strained by the hurried pace.

Free of all the weapons and paraphernalia these guys had to carry with them at all times, Egon had a much easier time rushing down the ship's labyrinthine walkways.

"General Zika has already announced my immediate arrival to the Kraal."

The guard shrugged. Those were his orders, too. Soldiers didn't question orders.

They reached the Kraal's living quarters, submitted their fingerprints and retinal scans to the readers by the gateway, then stepped through the parting doors. A brightly lit hallway with lavish gold floors welcomed them. Along the sides, screen windows simulated the views of white, endless beaches. Soft music played on the speakers.

Good. The Kraal is in a playful mood.

The Kraal's personal assistant rushed to meet them at the end of the hallway. Straight white hair parted in the middle framed his long face and draped his tunic—a vibrant turquoise with elaborate gold and ruby embroidery.

Quite elegant, Egon noted.

Definitely a good day to deliver his message to the Kraal.

The assistant waved his ringed hands and once again asserted in a high-pitched voice how this was the Kraal's personal time.

Egon licked his thin lips, anticipation prickling at his fingertips. He steepled his hands together and bowed his head.

"I respectfully request to override your instructions. The Kraal knows me very well and knows my orders come directly from General Zika himself. As such, I have access to the Kraal's own intimate circles. My message is of utter urgency and needs to be delivered immediately. Our imperial and military security is at stake."

The assistant nodded and waved the guards away.

"This way," he said, his voice softer this time.

The next door led them to a dimly lit corridor at the end of which awaited red velvet curtains. The notes from a loud, almost grating electric guitar spilled through. Projections on the ceiling simulated the wavering lights of torches.

The assistant shouldered through the curtains and snapped his fingers.

The music stopped immediately.

The stench of human sweat laced with sweet balm oils filled the room. Naked bodies lay entangled over an expanse of red cushions and equally red sheets.

The Kraal had a weakness for the color of blood.

The moaning and rocking trailed off a little longer than the music.

Egon bit hard on his lower lip and held his breath. He craned his neck trying to get a glimpse of flesh. No, not the white, milky breasts and feminine curves sprawled over the bed. He had no interest in those.

The Kraal rolled over, his fair locks spilled over the pillows. "What the fuck?" he growled. "And I don't mean the one I just had," he added with a sly grin, pointing at the ladies around him.

Egon counted at least three Zhai women—Imperial sex slaves—entangled in the red sheets. Again, he licked his lips, eager for them to part.

The women slid off the Kraal's bare chest and his finely rippled pectoral muscles finally came into view. Egon admired the tight tendons of his taurine neck and the full curve of his shoulder as it dipped down and then rose again into bulging biceps. The Kraal's face was flushed, sweat pearled his forehead. His masculinity bulged through the sheets, still hard and high.

There never had been a finer view. Egon swallowed and crossed his hands over his crotch, trying to keep a check on his libido. This view alone was worth all the lightspeed trips in the world.

"A message of utter urgency, your Imperial Greatness," the assistant said. He flicked his fingers and undimmed the lights. The Kraal propped himself up on his elbow and gave the two men a hard stare, sneering.

"Egon, my good man, you have some steel guts to walk into my playroom like this."

Egon bowed. "It's a very serious matter, your Imperial Greatness."

The Kraal rolled his eyes and snapped his fingers. The three naked Zhai women keeping him company immediately crawled out of the bed and made to leave.

"No, not you," the Kraal said to the one he'd been riding until moments earlier. He grabbed her by the thigh, pulled her back on the sheets, and squeezed her breast. He grinned. "She's got some fine stuff here for me. Wanna share some, Egon?"

Egon felt his face blush to the root of his hair. No, not the woman. There was something else he would've loved to share, but that would've cost his life. For the time being, he still cared for his life.

So he watched the Kraal caress the Zhai's milky curves and wondered what it would be like to have those hands on his own skin, to have the Kraal's body for *his* personal pleasure.

He swallowed, trained his thoughts back to his task.

"We had a very serious security breach," he said, bowing his head again.

The statement seemed to perk the Kraal's interest. He squeezed harder on the breast, making the Zhai woman yelp.

"Speak up, then!" he ordered.

"A very prominent figure of our military defected. He's still on the loose and we are actively on his trail. But we couldn't afford taking any chances. His entire troop—about two hundred men—has been eliminated."

"The name," the Kraal demanded.

"His immediate kinship had to go, too," Egon continued, ignoring the Kraal's request.

The Kraal pushed the Zhai woman away and sat up, rolling the sheets around his waist. "The name!"

Egon treaded his ground carefully. The Kraal was not going to like this. He had to make sure he understood.

"The defector left us no choice, Imperial Greatness," he said, speaking softly. "We had to eradicate this cancer at its roots, destroy it before it metastasized. My immediate superior, whom you know well, pluri-medaled General Zika, your faithful servant, had to take the matter into his own hands."

The Kraal was getting impatient. "I know who you work for, you filthy slut. Now quit playing games with me and spit out the name or I'll make sure Zika will have to reassemble you piece by piece in order to see your face again."

The comment upset Egon. It made him lose his train of thought. The fantasy of his own hands navigating the flawless body of the Kraal shattered. Rage took its place, a rage he had to swallow hard to keep under control. Lust could so easily give into anger.

"The defector is Captain Weber, Your Greatness," Egon said at last. "There was no way to know whether his father, General Weber, had been compromised too. We had to intervene before it was too late."

The Kraal's face fell. His clear eyes glazed over. Then a fit of fury took over him. He roared, lifted his arm, and spanked hard the woman's buttocks. The slave gave out a cry of pain.

"Get out," the Kraal yelled. "Get out now!"

The Zhai scrambled to her feet and ran out of the room, her large breasts wobbling and her nakedness completely exposed.

The Kraal balled the sheets in front of him and squeezed them. His biceps bulged, the muscles in his neck strained. He was beautiful, and Egon couldn't help but feel his lust surge again.

"You eliminated ... General ... Weber?"

Egon swallowed. "We had to. It was a very clean operation, Sir. We immediately sent out an official report stating that the general was lost in a bloody battle over Sarai. No other losses were suffered. General Zika immediately took possession of the conquered planet. The transition of power was completely smooth."

The Kraal looked down at the sheets. He squeezed them in his fists, his knuckles white with anger.

"Where's Captain Weber now? And what do we know about the information he has?"

Egon had to get out of this quickly. He'd delivered the good news, but the bad ones he wasn't so keen on speculating over.

"He was last seen on planet Yulia," Egon blurted out. "A hot pursue was ensured and we believe he died in the aftermath.

The Kraal tossed sheets and rose to his feet. The view of his cock, swollen and hard, sent blood pulsing to Egon's head. It was a marvelous view—too bad the fear of the Kraal's reprimand dampened the pleasure.

"You *believe* he died?' the Kraal yelled.

Egon stepped back toward the red curtains. "A body was never found. Nor was his ship. We are canvassing all nearby planets. We have leads. Our men are on it."

The Kraal extended a hand. On cue his assistant, who'd been quietly standing by the wall the entire time, stepped closer and handed him his weapon.

"Leave," the Kraal hissed wrapping his fingers around the gun. "Leave before I take your life. Go back to General Zika and tell him I lost an entire troop and one of my best generals because of this stupid incident. I hope the executions came quickly before the information was leaked."

Egon lingered one moment longer between the red curtains. "They were, Sir. I can assure you. We acted quickly, General Weber didn't even realize what was going on. No word has come out."

The Kraal squeezed the butt of his gun. "Find. Captain. Weber."

Egon lowered his head down to his knees. "We're on it. We will not fail."

He took one last step backwards, closed the red curtains before him, and ran.

Totally worth the view, was his last thought as he left the antechamber and once again joined the Imperial guards waiting to escort him back to his ship.

———

HYLEESH STARED into the ionization chamber of the auxiliary cruiser—an E-Beta X5 model, as far as he could tell, though the fuselage was badly battered and half buried into the ground. He rapped the wrench against the chamber's edge and let the sound waves echo across the inner rings.

Moving through the thick fog of Eshwar felt like walking underwater. Even the sound waves were distorted. The clanging of his wrench rippled through the swooshing and became a gentle ding as the mic of his space helmet registered the sound.

The chamber seemed solid enough.

He adjusted the flashlight on top of his visor and crawled inside. Lying on his back, he located the gasket around the lithium rings and started working the bolts. Harvesting all four rings was going to take a while. Luckily, he had four hours' worth of oxygen in his tank and no need to hurry.

The deep valleys of planet Eshwar, filled with dense, toxic fogs, were the best hiding spot for his ship. The fact that the place was riddled with fallen warships and battlefield relics was an added perk, providing an endless source of replacement parts for his ship, the Orion. The spacecraft needed a makeover before she could ever leave Eshwar again.

He would need to fly the Orion out of Eshwar, eventually, especially after the latest news he'd intercepted through an encrypted line from his home planet, Aplaya.

General Weber dead in the aftermath of the battle over Sarai.

Bullshit, he thought, twisting the wrench against the rusted surface of the ionization chamber.

Soldiers die in battlefields. Corporals, pilots, navigators. Fighter jets explode, warships shred under the enemy's fire. And all along, generals watch from the safety of their mothership.

Generals don't die in battlefields.

It didn't matter that the general in question was his father. He'd long stopped thinking of him as kinship. His father was an abuser, a rapist, and a mass murderer. He deserved to die. But any death among the inner circles of the Kraal meant a shift in power in the highest spheres.

No, General Weber didn't just die.

Somebody murdered him.

Hyleesh knew exactly who was going to benefit the most from this sudden vacancy: General Zika, whom Hyleesh had narrowly escaped after a brief confrontation on planet Yulia. Without his father around, Zika rose as the Kraal's closest adviser and confidant, and the second most powerful man in the Yaxee-dominated sectors of the Old System. The fact that Zika hadn't found a single molecule of Quarium after wasting three tons of pulse propulsion bombs on Yulia was now a forgivable sin.

Hyleesh removed the first lithium ring and checked the oxygen level on his WristComp. He was down to forty-five percent—plenty for retrieving a second ring, but somehow he felt too tired to even bother. He could always come back tomorrow.

He slid out of the chamber, strapped the oxygen tank to his back, and hauled the ring around his shoulders. He relied on his WristComp compass to hike back to his ship. This low into the ghost city the thick toxic fog reduced visibility to just a couple of feet. It was nothing like he'd ever experienced before. He'd done space-walks to fix exterior panels of his ship; he'd used robotic legs on extreme gravity planets, where one step would leave a five-inch deep hole in the ground; and ballasts on planets where he could somersault in the air like a ballerina.

But the fog of Eshwar—composed of 60% water and 40% propane—was so dense it felt like walking through liquid, his body constantly swayed by the currents. As soon as he stepped inside the

Orion's airlock, Hyleesh collapsed on the bench, heaving. He waited the customary three minutes for the chamber to depressurize and fill with oxygen, then he yanked off his helmet and ran a hand through his sweat-drenched hair.

The door blades to the ship opened and Argos came rushing through. It had only taken a few days for the mutt to get confident on his new robotic hind legs, and now he was already running all over the place—especially when Hyleesh came back after long hours away from the ship.

In the midst of dog kisses, Hyleesh peeled off his spacesuit and hauled into his workshop the oxygen tank and the precious finds he'd scavenged out of the ghost city. He made a quick stop into the navigation room to check his computer screen before heading over to the shower stall.

A red dot was blinking on his computer screen. Hyleesh tapped it.

The electronic voice of the navigator drawled, "You have one new message."

"Decrypt," he ordered.

"One moment, please."

He had maintained sparse yet careful communications with his home planet Aplaya. All his official accounts had been destroyed once he'd defected, yet he still possessed classified information that allowed him to navigate privileged channels under strictly encrypted firewalls.

He ruffled up Argos's neck while waiting. "You hungry, huh? How about reconstituted bacon for dinner tonight? I got one last batch from Aplaya—that's a very special treat—"

"Message decrypted. Source: ZA41."

ZA41. Two letters, one number. Yet so much more than just a code.

Bittersweet memories flooded of his mind like unleashed ghosts.

You're not dancing.

She played with a scarf around her neck.

I never do.

Why?

They don't let the bad ones dance.

She pulled the scarf down. A row of circular bruises marked her neck from just below her jawline all the way down to her throat.

He'd forgotten many things of his previous life as a Yaxee captain, yet that one row of bruises remained impressed in his memory as though he'd seen it yesterday. He kept thinking about those bruises as he made love to her, as he peeled off her clothes and discovered the scars on her thighs and nipples, and after that he thought of his own scars—*the scars of victory*, as the Kraal had called them.

Hyleesh—Captain Weber as he was called in his previous life— had won a battle but lost a fleet. Lost himself, his life, his beliefs.

That night, as he stared at the bruises and scars on ZA41—*the bad one*, as she'd called herself—he knew he could no longer be Captain Weber.

No longer be a Yaxee, no longer be his father's son.

I'll come back, he'd told her.

She'd laughed. A rugged, throaty laugh.

No you won't. Nobody ever does. You're no different.

Her words stung.

Hyleesh stared at the code on his computer screen—ZA41—and swallowed, chasing the memories away.

"Read," he told the navigator.

"Confirmed. Jaya heard."

He waited for more, another word, something he could've possibly missed, but none came. That was the entire message. Confirmed—Zika had indeed killed his father. Jaya—the source— was as reliable as ZA41 herself. Zhai women—sex slaves at the service of the Imperial Kraal—were often privy to the most intimate and confidential secrets floating around the Imperial courts.

Argos barked, begging for attention. Hyleesh absent-mindedly patted his head, his eyes still glued to the screen.

The computer bleeped again. "New message."

"Same source?"

"Negative. Retrieving... unable to retrieve new source."

Hyleesh exhaled, too tired to worry about it. "Just read the message."

"I want to meet you," the navigator read, the words clashing with the computerized metallic voice.

Hyleesh swiped a finger over the screen and tapped. The navigator reread the message, "I want to meet you," yet no matter what decryption pathway Hyleesh tried, it always came back empty.

He couldn't break that firewall.

Who the hell...

No, this wasn't from Aplaya. This was somebody who'd intercepted his presence on Eshwar and had been smart enough to cover up their trail. He launched a whole system scan, wondering if the brief communication with ZA41 had been compromised. Quantum encryption was virtually impossible to break or hijack. Whoever the mysterious sender was, they had found him via something else.

The system scan came back clean. His question remained. He peeled off the chair and shuffled to the shower stall, his thoughts reeling. General Zika had murdered his father. His next move was a no brainer: deploy all his undercover men to find Hyleesh and bring him to the Kraal. Nothing appeases a narcissistic ego like the bloody head of a traitor.

If the message was an indication that he'd already been breached, then he'd better fire up the ship and leave. But the message could also be a trap, smoke to get him out of his hiding spot. He lathered his hair while steam filled the shower stall. Eshwar was fairly unknown to the Yaxees and off their major war routes. Because of its toxic fogs periodically rising to higher altitudes, it was known as an outlandish world, a favorite for scavengers and pirates whose main goal was to smuggle loot and relics from abandoned battlefields.

He rinsed, shut off the water, and stood in the stall, dripping.

By the time he came back to the kitchenette, all dried and dressed, he felt re-energized. The last of the freeze-dried bacon sizzled inside the reconstituting oven while two yeast packets grew into dinner biscuits as he poured water onto them—not fresh out of the oven, but close enough. He ate hastily, sharing morsels with Argos, knowing it was the last of the bacon he'd brought from home and from now on it was going to be porridge and vitamin pills both for breakfast and dinner.

But he was a free man, now, and nothing else mattered anymore.

When the meal was over, he walked back to the navigation room, sat at his computer, and tapped the screen.

You're out to get me? he thought. *Well, here I come.*

"Where?" he typed and then hit send.

No man of honor hides when challenged.

No man.

HYLEESH EMERGED FROM THE FOREST, removed his space helmet, and looked down into the valley. After two weeks of hiding inside the ghost city, it felt good to be above the toxic level and breathing fresh air again. Below, confined within the high mountain range, the propane fog looked like a tamed beast, its purple hues shimmering under the rising sun.

Hyleesh peeled off his space suit and hid it behind a rock. He rubbed dirt on his hands and smeared his face and hair. He'd grown a five-day stubble and was wearing a long shirt and pajama pants. His ash blonde hair and pale complexion were never going to pass him for a Golowan, let alone a dark skinned Silighen. The best he could hope for was some sort of extradited runaway.

Which wasn't too far from truth, to be honest.

So long as you keep your mouth shut.

The Black Mesa was a lip of land that rose high above the forest and stretched over the sea of propane fog like a forlorn finger. It was home to one of the largest war junkyard on Eshwar, a favorite destination for scavengers, smugglers, and pirates looting the nearby moons and planets.

Today must have been a special day for Ghoros, the old

Golowan running the place. The sun was barely out, and the place was already packed with crowds of dubious geopolitical origin. Many were Ghoros's shady associates—scavengers, dealers, and a few keepers the old man paid a pittance just to keep an eye on his stuff. Hyleesh tucked his HPN gun into his waistline, well hidden under the long shirt, and joined the party.

Whether it was his disguise or simply the fact that his pale skin was still showing *despite* the disguise, the moment he crossed the ranch-style gates to the junkyard, all eyes were on him. A group of tanned space riders—heads shaved and tattooed with open shark jaws—turned away from the SF-93 fuselage they'd been staring at and stepped closer to size him up.

Their alpha man strode right in front of Hyleesh, blocking his way. Metal studs replaced his shaved eyebrows, and concentric tattoos decorated his cheekbones and jawline. *A real piece of art*, Hyleesh thought.

The guy planted his heavy boots on the ground and crossed his arms. "Are you missing a handle for your tricycle, baby?" he said, roaring in laughter.

Don't say a word.

Even a simple greeting could've betrayed his accent. So he shrugged and touched his chin with the tip of his fingers. The space biker frowned and cocked his head. One of his lady friends snapped her fingers.

"He's deaf! Can't you see? He can't talk!"

The biker made a disgusted face. "A retard?"

The woman propped a hand on her hip and sneered. "I don't know, he's kind of cute for a retard."

Clearly her pal didn't share her view. He slapped Hyleesh on the shoulder, pushing him backward. "Get out of my way, moron!"

Hyleesh stumbled backwards and clenched his jaw. Every fiber in his body wanted to plant a well-assessed fist in those tattooed eyes, but he knew better than to get in trouble on a hostile planet. His old allies were his new enemies, and his old enemies had yet to become friends. So he flashed a tight-lipped smile and moved on, letting the bikers' guffaws trail behind him.

Past a pile of mosquito parts—small one-man vehicles that walked on robotic legs and flew with copter blades—the view opened up to the biggest attraction of Ghoros's business: bordered by fringes of fog lapping up the walls of the mesa, an entire field scattered with spacecrafts, warships, and starfighters extended beyond the ranch-style gates, some vessels so old and battered all there was left was a hollow fuselage.

The variety of humanity scattered around these fallen beauties was almost as fascinating: there were mercenaries in their military gear and fancy HPN rifles—men and women who preyed on war to make a living. Smugglers came in small groups, two or three at most, no two alike in their stance or clothes, except for one thing: they never made eye contact, their gazes as slippery as eels underwater. No visible weapons on them either, yet the bulges on their thighs and waist betrayed electronic knives and automatic firearms.

He strode down a row of battered SATVs—special armored tactical vehicles used in ground battles. Hyleesh counted at least two-dozen models spanning fifty years of interplanetary wars. The oldest ones were reduced to few rusted body parts, but the more modern ones could've been brought back to life with a little work.

Hyleesh hopped inside the doorless body of a T-510 minitank and played with the manual levers. A knock on the hood startled him. Ghoros—the junkyard owner—stood by the vehicle, bushy eyebrows knitted together in a scowl. He wore a shaggy tunic and his wispy hair looked like it hadn't seen a shower in a full rotation around the sun, yet that didn't prevent him from crassly challenging, "You got money to pay, *bryhak?*"

Bryhak—peasant. At least Hyleesh's disguise was working.

Hyleesh dipped a hand in his pocket and fished out a gold yhat. Interplanetary quick-money codes read on WristComps weren't good enough for the stingy Golowan, but the sight of old fashioned gold seemed to appease his senses. He leaned forward, snatched the piece of gold, and held it up to the light.

"It's authentic," he said, pocketing it. "Good for one entry. Hope you find what you're looking for, stranger."

He licked his lips, grinned, and moved on to his next client.

A long line of bidders snaked around the fuselage of an old S-Kys 42 fighter, the first model of starfighters used by the separatist forces. These older models had faulty deflector shield generators and were soon discontinued, making this particular specimen a rare find. It had caught the attention of the space riders too, who were making a show of how much they knew about the aircraft and its history. Ghoros's paid cronies swarmed around them, ready to fend off any bickering over the biddings.

Hyleesh wearily eyed their concealed—and less concealed—weapons, and decided it wasn't worth sticking around to see who was going to win the S-Kys 42 fuselage. He turned away and meandered in less popular sections of the junkyard, feigning an interest in refueling cells and vector magnets.

A tall woman scavenger came by, long legs of a runner and fine cornbraids that covered her shoulders all the way down to her narrow waist. Chained *shavah* fighting sticks clinked from her belt and a compact firearm bulged from the small of her back. She started what looked like a heated altercation with one of the armed cronies over some unpaid deal. Ghoros finally showed up, his old face a mask of unhappiness.

"You always bring me junk and demand a fortune for it," he said to the woman. "I paid you a fair price, now leave."

"You sell *your* junk for a fortune," she replied.

She stretched out her open palm, demanding her payment.

Ghoros sneered and pointed to the S-Kys aircraft. "Tell you what. Get me another one of those and I'll pay you twice as much this time."

The woman opened her mouth in disdain and cocked her head. "You're a filthy son of a bitch, Ghoros," she spat and walked away. She didn't walk back toward the gates, though. She strode right past Hyleesh instead and casually dropped a coin by his feet.

Ghoros shook his head and returned to his clients. The guards ringed around the animated bidders.

Hyleesh stooped down and picked up the coin.

It was a copper Gal'han from Sarai—the signal they'd agreed on.

The woman rounded the corner of the standing hull of a Yaxee mothership. Hyleesh looked over his shoulder, made sure Ghoros and his cronies were happily distracted, then followed her.

A good portion of the mothership's main deck and bridge were still attached to the hull and extended past the rim of the mesa, like an arm reaching over the wavering sea of fog. None of Ghoros's clients seemed interested in this vintage relic, and the way it stood by the cliff and away from the rest of the junkyard made it a perfect shield from indiscreet eyes.

Silhouetted by the sharp light, the scavenger woman was waiting for him behind the hull, her arm crossed and her head tilted in a challenging stance. She made a point of leaning in a way that showed off the fighting sticks hanging from her hip.

Liberty Bennet, Hyleesh thought, walking toward her. *Wanted on five different planets on an interplanetary extradition warrant for war crimes and cyber espionage.*

Hyleesh walked past her to the rim and stared down at the shimmering fog. Laced with toxic levels of propane, the low clouds moved restlessly over the basin. They'd already risen at least twenty feet since the morning, yet Ghoros and his cronies didn't seem too worried for now. Tides that reached over Black Mesa had been rare, and usually there was enough of a forewarning in the winds to reach for higher and safer altitudes.

"Nice *shavah* sticks," he said.

She gave him a half smile. "I'm a panther fighter—highest rank out there. You don't want to get into a fight with me."

"I've heard a little about that."

The response sparked a twinkle in her dark eyes. She swept her long cornbraids off her shoulder and raised her chin. "What else have you heard?"

"I've heard that your mother was a Golowan ambassador who firmly opposed any kind of alliance with the Kraal," Hyleesh said.

Liberty sighed. "When you guys—" she started, then paused, sending him a sideways glance. "When the Yaxees first attacked the Quarium-rich planet of Xawhan, they did so based on a false promise of freeing the people from a cruel dictatorship. The Golowans—my people—jumped on the opportunity and sided with the invading Yaxees, ignoring decades of diplomacy and interplanetary treaties. Then the Kraal showed his true colors and turned out to be an even worse dictator, yet the Golowans didn't turn away from their sworn alliance."

"Of course they didn't," Hyleesh interjected. "The Yaxees go where there's Quarium, and Quarium means power."

She clenched her jaw. "My mother opposed siding with the Yaxees from the beginning. She called the Xawahan War for what it was, a violation of planetary laws and an abuse of power. She was murdered on the last day of the third decagon of the galactic year. The next day, the underground opposition bombed the Golowan parliament on planet Uhrwen, and the SFA—the separatist force alliance—was born." She turned to him. "But of course, you already know all this."

Hyleesh nodded. "You took on your mother's legacy and became one of the driving forces for the SFA."

Her eyes glimmered. "I'm very proud of that."

"Why did you want to meet?"

She gave the question a little thought before replying. "You're a Yaxee, a high member of their military. Yet you gave us Yaxee intel claiming that you defected your own troops. Why should I trust you?"

Hyleesh chuckled. "I gave you a terabyte worth of stolen data. War intel, Stingray prototypes, and clearance codes. I'm sure you've already verified the authenticity of every encrypted byte. And you're still not sure you can trust me?"

Liberty hooked her hands on the loops of her belt and walked up to him. She was tall, but still not as tall as him. Her bronze complexion almost glistened under the high sun. She held his gaze for a long time, then said, "I trust no one unless I can look them in the eyes."

The zap of HPN beams reverberated in the distance. Shouts followed.

They both acted on instinct, slid out their weapons, and sought cover behind the hull. Hyleesh craned his neck, looking for the cause of the sudden commotion.

"Did the bikers put up a fight over the S-Kys?" Liberty asked.

"No," Hyleesh replied. "It's worse than that."

The line of bidders had spread thin. Bodies lay sprawled on the ground. The crowd parted and soldiers marched through. Not Ghoros's paid cronies.

Yaxee soldiers.

They advanced in formation, rifles poised, paving the way for the SATV wheeling behind them. Even from a distance, Hyleesh recognized General Zika's personal armored vehicle.

Zika himself had come to Eshwar to find him.

Had he been too naïve in trusting this woman...

"Stop!"

Ghoros came running to the soldiers. "Stop killing my men!" he shouted, and then pointed to the mothership hull where Hyleesh and Liberty were hiding.

"Fucking son of a bitch," Liberty muttered. She leaned out of a crack in the hull and fired one single shot. Ghoros flopped to the ground like the useless rag he was.

The soldiers fired back almost instantly.

"Get down!" Hyleesh shouted, pulling her back behind the cover.

The guards' beamfire zapped into the metal shell of the ship but didn't break through. Hyleesh and Liberty ducked, ran to the opposite side of the deck, closest to the rim, and climbed along the inner scaffolding of the bridge.

They shifted their position barely in time. The blast from the SATV's cannons blew away the first portion of hull and the recoil caused the whole structure to pivot. The segment of bridge they'd been perched on spun and came to rest hanging over the cliff. A second blast rocked the bridge once more. Liberty lost her grip, slipped, then caught one of the bottom runners, her legs dangling in the void. Hyleesh reached down to help her but she refused his hand and pulled herself up, cussing.

"Fucking traitor gave us up," she muttered.

"How did he know?"

She stared back at him, eyes narrowed. "I didn't spill the beans, if that's what you're insinuating," she spat.

Below them, the toxic fog lapped angrily at the lower portion of the bridge. A harsh wind rose from the basin and blew in their faces.

"Damn it, the fog's rising," Hyleesh said.

A familiar voice crackled through the megaphone. "We meet again, Weber."

Hyleesh climbed up the rungs lining the inside of the hull and peeked over the top edge. He cocked his gun even though he was fully aware there was nothing his beamfire could do against Zika's fully armored vehicle.

The SATV advanced, its cannons aimed at the mothership bridge. One blast of those weapons and they'd be flying in pieces.

"I'm in a good mood, Weber," Zika went on through the static of his megaphone. "Thanks to you I just found this beautiful little planet with what appears a nearly bottomless source of propane. Not Quarium, but still. Good enough to power a few construction plants and freighters. So, you see, I'm feeling magnanimous today and you, on the other hand, have nowhere to go right now." A cold chuckle crackled through the mic. "Poor Captain Weber. I bet it feels very lonely to be a traitor."

"Want me to reply to that?" Liberty whispered behind him. She had her small firearm cocked and ready.

Hyleesh shook his head. "Stay down. This one's mine." He slid the muzzle of his gun forward along the edge of the hull, fired twice and then ducked. Through a crack in the hull, he saw he'd taken down one soldier and injured another one.

The cannon on the SATV spun and took aim. The megaphone crackled one last time. "My patience has expired, Weber," Zika said. "I gave you a chance to explain yourself to the Kraal and you just refused it. The Kraal will have to content himself with your dead body, then."

The engine of the SATV roared and the vehicle approached, its cannons poised.

Hyleesh climbed down the scaffolding and motioned Liberty to do the same. He pointed to the fog below. It was still swelling, and the far edge of the hull was now dipping into the low clouds.

"How long can one survive down there?"

Liberty scowled. "What? Without a suit? It's so deep you can never get out alive." She made to climb back toward the mesa, but Hyleesh stopped her.

"We don't have a choice!"

The roar of the engine came closer, getting the cannons into firing range. It was a matter of seconds.

Liberty gripped her weapon. "You're nuts. I'm not jumping. I'm gonna fight Zika to the last drop of juice in my gun." She reached for the scaffolding to the left, but Hyleesh grabbed her ankle and pulled her back down. Hanging onto the beams with one hand only, she kicked and punched him with her free hand. The engine roar came to a stop. Hyleesh climbed up, grabbed Liberty by the waist, and slammed the butt of his gun on her fist, making her let go of the beam.

He jumped one instant before the cannons fired. The mothership hull exploded into a million pieces and then silence fell as he plummeted backward into the fog.

SHE WANTED to kill the bloody bastard. Too bad she lost the grip on her firearm the minute she fell into the fog and now she could no longer find it.

Her skin prickled. Her eyes and lips burned. She plunged

silently into a sea of gray, her fall cushioned by the waving currents, and yet no matter how hard she fought to swim back up, gravity kept pulling her down. She spotted Hyleesh's shadow not too far down from her. The last thing she'd do before dying would be to kill him with her bare hands.

Libbie touched the ground and fell forward, the currents pushing her. She saw Hyleesh vanish in the fog, something bouncing off his chest.

She got up, tried to jog after him. Her energy was quickly dropping, her lungs starved for air. The propane was getting on her skin, cutting off sensation in her hands and face.

Where the hell is the bastard going?

Her vision started spotting, her head spinning.

Even the drive to kill him could no longer keep her going.

She stumbled on her knees and dug her fingers into the dirt.

Fuck you, she cussed. *Fuck me for trusting you, fuck ...*

A beam of light emerged through the fog and grew larger. She wanted to run into it, find shelter in it, but she just didn't have the energy anymore, did not...

A hand came around her waist and lifted her, dragging her into the light and through a door.

She fell on the floor, eyes burning. Yet she had to see, had to grasp what was happening. The door closed behind them, a sprinkler went off somewhere above her. Water. Cool. Relief.

Hyleesh shoved an oxygen mask in her hands while pressing a second one to his mouth. Libbie sunk her face into it and drew in the longest breath she could ever remember before rolling onto her back and closing her eyes, exhausted.

No telling how much time had passed when she could finally breathe again without wheezing. She opened her eyes and slowly took in the surroundings.

They were in a small room, sealed in on both sides by airtight doors.

Libbie dropped the oxygen mask and sat up. Airlock. She was inside an airlock. Did this mean ...

Hyleesh was gone. He must've left while she was semi-unconscious and breathing into the mask. She was sure he'd been the one to get her inside the airlock and pass her the oxygen. Her hair and clothes were wet, but the dampness felt cool over her skin, still numb from the exposure to the propane.

One of the airtight doors slid open with a soft hiss.

Libbie got up, fought a wave of dizziness, and then stumbled through the door. She followed the lit-up corridor onto the ship's main bridge, where floor-to-ceiling window screens showed a surreal view of the fog swirling outside.

A holographic projection played above the navigation console. It was the same clip playing over and over again in fast forward: Libbie recognized the far stretch of the Black Mesa, where Ghoros's junkyard was, being gradually submerged under a tide of fog. She pinched the projection with the tip of her fingers, zoomed in to the cliff where the mothership hull was, and started it over.

This time she saw herself walk behind the hull, soon followed by Hyleesh. Zika's SATV had already arrived, but it wasn't until roughly ten minutes later that the soldiers pressed through the crowds without any second thoughts of killing anyone who tried to stop them. Libbie watched the SATV blast the first portion of the hull, and then, still in fast forward, blow up the rest of the bridge right as Hyleesh, holding her by the waist—jumped off it and plunged into the fog. In the minutes that followed, the SATV drove to the rim of the mesa, and Zika came out looking out onto the valley.

Making sure we're both cooked in propane, you son of a bitch.

The last frames of the hologram showed the fog rising over the rim of the mesa and Zika running back inside his vehicle and fleeing.

"Glad you saw the holo projection."

Libbie turned around, startled. Hyleesh stood in the door, holding a towel to his wet hair and a mug in his other hand. A dog leaped from behind him and came running to Libbie, licking her boots and hands. As she crouched to hug the dog, Hyleesh walked over and offered her the mug.

"It's just water for now." He smirked. "Ran out of alcohol."

He'd looked like a peasant when she first spotted him on the mesa. But now, the sprinkler had washed the dirt off his face and the sudden charm of his blue eyes caught Libbie off guard.

Beware of their beauty, her mother used to say. *Even the devil can be handsome.*

She took the mug from his hands and drained the water in three thirsty gulps.

Was that why after receiving his leaked data, she'd obsessed in meeting with Hyleesh? *You wanted to stare into the devil's eyes, see if it's true that they're as handsome as your mother used to say.*

"What's up with the shoes?" she asked, noticing how he'd taken off his boots, laced them together, and hung them around his neck. That's what she'd spotted bobbing over his chest when following him through the fog.

"These?" he laughed, took them off his neck and showed her the right boot. "This is how I call my ship, by pressing the remote embedded inside the sole. Not very convenient, but safe." He winked and pointed to the hologram. "Did you take a good look? The mesa's under the fog right now."

Libbie turned to the console. "How did you get that footage?"

"Kid named Jahnu gave me access to Ghoros's external cameras. I believe you met him, yes?"

Libbie smiled. It was a rhetorical question. Jahnu was the intermediary Hyleesh had used to deliver the data to her. The kid had been stuck on Eshwar after his mother's death, and thanks to his proficiency with droids, Libbie's commander had decided to offer him a job on the Asyla trading post.

She watched the hologram loop over once more, then clonked the mug down on the console and inhaled. The dog grabbed the hem of Hyleesh's towel and pulled, starting a game of tug of war.

"Bad boy, Argos," Hyleesh said, laughing.

It was as though the tension of one hour ago had completely melted away.

Yet she knew it wasn't true. The war was real, the enemy slowly eroding every post, every freedom, every right of the people in the Old System. And the man in front of her had once been that enemy.

The thought triggered a new sense of urgency. The data Hyleesh had given her outlined plans for new battles—battles the separatists could hope to turn advantageously if they could use the leaked data to overcome the Yaxees's surprise factor. Libbie needed to communicate with Petros, the second lieutenant in her SFA squadron. Her people were supposed to send a quadcopter disguised as a scavenger vehicle to pick her up, but now that Ghoros was dead, there was no way to know if his cronies would still allow scavengers into the junkyard.

Even worse, Zika now knew about Eshwar and its richness in propane.

The fog swirled and swooshed against the window screens. The ship was moving, probably gliding deeper into the valley.

"I need to catch a ride as soon as it's safe to get back out there," she said.

"Sure thing."

She watched him get on his knees, wrestling the towel off Argos's teeth. The dog was missing his hind legs, replaced by robotic prosthetics, yet he was extremely nimble despite his handicap.

"What are *you* going to do?" she asked.

Argos yanked the towel off his owner's hands and scuttled off with his trophy. Hyleesh got back up and shrugged.

"What am I going to do?" he asked. "Leave as soon as possible. You've heard the bastard. He'll come back for the propane and turn the whole planet inside out for my body."

"You'd make the heck of a separatist, Captain Weber," she said. "We desperately need an insider like yourself."

There was a melancholy stroke to his smile. "I'm no captain. I'm just a lone soldier and I go by Hyleesh. Name's pretty much all I got left."

Argos came back and pushed the towel into Hyleesh's hands.

"Same here," she said. "I go by Libbie and I've got nothing else left but this fight."

Hyleesh walked to the console and killed the hologram. "Make yourself at home, Libbie. Dinner's reconstituted beans and porridge —that's all the house has to offer. Tomorrow this ship will take sail and I can drop you off wherever you wish."

He never replied to her question, nor did she expect an answer. She noticed how he eyed the computer monitor for a brief moment —maybe checking for a message, a word, a memory.

What kind of baggage did you leave behind, Captain Weber?

The next day, back on the mesa, Libbie watched the Orion skim the sea of low clouds and then skirt off the mountain peaks until it vanished in the distance. The sky was a metallic blue and the air pregnant with the sweet scent of new leaves.

So long, soldier, she thought, squinting in the sun. *Until next time.*

About the Author

E.E. Giorgi is a scientist, and an award winning author and photographer. She spends her days analyzing genetic data, her evenings chasing sunsets, and her nights pretending she's somebody else. She writes sci-fi thrillers and mysteries with a scientific premise. To find out more about her books, please visit her website www.eegiorgi.com and sign up for her newsletter to be notified of her future book releases and receive two free stories to download on your Kindle.

A Trap in Eshwar is part of the Quarium Wars series, which first appeared in the anthology BEYOND THE STARS: At Galaxy's Edge. The next story set in this world, *Escaping Eshwar,* appeared in the following volume, BEYOND THE STARS: New Worlds, New Suns, and the third story, *Octant VI,* will appear in *Tails of the Apocalypse* in November 2017. The first novel-length book in the series, *Anarchy,* will be released this fall, and the following two books, *Liberty* and *Destiny,* later in 2018.

DREAM SOLUTION

BY MICHAEL J.P. WHITMER

Jesse exited a dark sub-corner of the internet where posters were convinced their nightmares were visions of parallel lives in alternate dimensions. Across the room, his fiancé Heather defiantly muttered, "No," rolling violently onto her back beneath the strewn bed covers. He waited for a scream to follow. When it didn't, he settled into the desk chair and turned back to the computer.

His mind was exhausted and crammed with fringe devices and folksy testimonies for ridding someone of nightmares. None seemed feasible. He'd seen instructions for crafting a tinfoil and wire hanger sleep prevention hat and visited sketchy subscriptions to poorly made websites with blinking dream-catcher and pentagram animations, promising bullshit for a paid subscription. The last few months had rendered identical results.

An unchecked, blinking tab at the top of his browser snared his interest. He couldn't recall opening the link. The webpage had a gray background and was void of ads. The name of the site spread across the top of the page like an insignia. A motto accompanied the title in matching but smaller font.

Dreamsolution: The door to resolving dream ailments.

Jesse found a rectangular button with the words *I Accept*

inscribed in the center. Scrolling the page, there were no other details. He hovered the cursor over the icon, toying with the idea.

"Honey?" Heather's voice came from behind him.

He snapped up, spinning in his chair toward her. Under the dim, gray-blue glow of the monitor, he saw Heather staring back at him with the same hue gaze.

"I miss you," she whispered.

"You okay?"

"Yes." She always answered the same, though it was not always true. "Come get some sleep."

"I'm just finishing up." He turned to the website. His eyes locked onto the button before clicking it. *I Accept* blanked out, then —nothing. No pop-up screens, no hourglass.

Nothing.

Slightly disappointed, and surprised his anti-virus software didn't detect any malware, he closed the browser and made his way across the room. Crawling into bed, Jesse cuddled with Heather beneath the covers. He held her close, and she settled into his embrace as they drifted away.

JESSE BURST AWAKE, rolling down the slope of a massive dune. Reaching the bottom, he shook off gray sand. Before him, a waste-land expanded as far as he could see. A gray static-energy lingering in the air like a miasma and settling on the land like an unnatural sheet of grainy rot blotted out the sky. Where there might have been life, the pulsating dullness smothered the terrain and distorted it gray. A broken post lay protruding up out of the ground near a beaten path. Jesse kicked sand from a detached and buried arrow-shaped sign.

"Dream Doors," he read before the static covered the words again. Jesse became lucid, aware he was dreaming. He was there for Heather. That was the only explanation.

The path vanished in the foggy expanse. Reaching like a giant's claw from hell, mountains capped with the gray decay lined the horizon. He took a step onto the trail, pressing through the static, strangling the color from everything but him.

Further Jesse pushed into the gray. Ghostly shapes, masked by the static and looming along the trail in the forms of broken doors and empty archways, littered the landscape. Amid the hollowed frames, static-festered tree trunks leaned like tombstones, pointing him back to the dunes of sleep. When day and night should have come and gone there was only gray. His legs and lungs worked without wearing, as the path meandered and ascended into the shadowy mountain foot.

The quest for Heather's dream door had brought him into a narrow pass between the mountains. There he discovered the first intact door. It opened on its own, revealing a window with a bird's eye view of his father's funeral.

Jesse watched from above. As the casket lowered into the ground, his mother cried on the shoulder of a black suited dream version of himself. Heather stood nearby, crying too. When the first scoop of dirt was shoveled, his father's corpse sprung from the coffin and lunged at Jesse.

"You weren't there. You didn't care!" His father moaned, wrapping his cold digits around his son's throat.

"No!" Jesse slammed the door on the scene. "I'm not here for me!" He fled, turning back onto the path and climbing further into the mountains of static. The feeling of the nightmare's frigid touch at his neck remained.

Jesse followed the trail upwards into the fading, endless gray sky. He clung to the rock face to keep from going over the ledge. The static vibrated at his touch, prickling his skin like electricity. More doors materialized in the air beyond the edge. The doors swung open as he hiked by. In fear of what they might reveal, he only permitted himself glimpses. Through their apertures, he could see into worlds where his darkest dreams were realized. Each glance fueled him hurtling higher until the trail turned into the entrance of a cavern.

Heather's voice echoed throughout the enclosure from behind a dream door.

GRAYNESS STRETCHED FOREVER at his back before fading into a colorful field of wildflowers in front of him. Jesse watched a little girl dance in the meadow. Her brunette hair glistened in the bright blue sky overhead. Crossing the threshold, the door and the gray behind him vanished.

"Heather?"

The girl turned. "Jesse!" She rushed to him, hugging his leg.

Jesse let her lead him further into her dreamworld, through the field of flowers and onto a dirt road that ran up to a house buried at the boundary of a dark forest. Bent and decrepit, the house was half consumed by the wilderness surrounding it. Where not covered with growth, the paint was faded and cracked, and the windows were busted and boarded up. Behind the house, a little deeper into the wood but in view from the road, a leaning shed was nestled amid the twisted treeline.

"Come on. We have to hurry before they come back," she stressed.

Heather led him up the bare path and onto a lopsided porch where a screen door clung to its frame. The front door creaked as Heather eased it open.

The place looked abandoned. A fireplace in shambles and trash littered the floor. Roaches scurried out of sight under a torn, stained sofa where a deranged woman oddly proportioned to the rest of the surroundings lay. Bulbous and bizarre, she was unconscious with a syringe sticking from her slack spider leg like arm.

"Shh, don't wake momma." Little Heather implored, as she ushered Jesse further into the house. The door closed on its own.

They moved toward the staircase away from the caricature of her mother.

"You little bitch... What are you doing out!"

Jesse and Heather stopped.

"Answer me!" She screeched.

They turned to see her towering over them. The creature's bulging bloodshot eyes and red matted hair were crazed. In her long, bony arm, she wielded the syringe like an insect's stinger.

"Get to the shed! Your father 'n brothers 're waitin'!" She slurred through a pox infested mouth.

"No, I'm not going!" Heather hid behind Jesse. "They're not my family!" She clung to his pant leg as if finding strength from doing so.

The nightmare reached out for Heather but Jesse intervened.

"Don't touch her!" He pushed the creature away.

The woman recoiled and then lunged at him with the syringe, as if anticipating such an action. Jesse shoved Heather aside before grappling her mother's armed hand by the wrist. The nightmare had uncanny strength, forcing Jesse backward to keep the point from his neck. He winced as they collapsed to the ground, with the syringe stabbing him in the gut.

"Get off him!" Heather screamed as she rushed to Jesse's aid. Beating her little fists against the woman's side was of no avail. Heather picked up a rock from the crumbling fireplace and threw it, striking her mother's head, causing a lapse in her onslaught.

Jesse kicked the nightmare from atop him, prying the syringe from her in the process. He scrambled to his feet. As Heather's mother spun back around at him, he pierced the tip through the nightmare's heart. The creature clutched the syringe protruding from her chest. She hissed and flailed madly away. Black muck formed at the wound, filling the tube until busting black stink everywhere. The beast gave a final shriek, falling out, sprawled and oozing, on the sofa.

His hands, now stained black, trembled. He looked to Heather whose eyes had pooled with tears. Jesse rushed to her and hugged her.

"I'm sorry. It's all right... It's only a..."

The front door flew open. In a blur, three berserkers burst

through, knocking Jesse unconscious. The last image in his mind was of Heather, screaming while being torn from his arms by a nightmarish beast.

Darkness. Not gray.

Jesse awoke on the floor among the trash and rubble. His head ached, and a small pool of blood had formed beneath him where he had been impaled by the syringe. His mind forced the pain aside, as he remembered the shed.

THE BLUE SKY gave way to dark clouds. Jesse stood before the shack, gathering his wits before braving the unknown.

The interior was narrow and leaning with shelves of assorted tools and oddities. There was no back wall, just an opening to the forest that wasn't visible from the outside. A trail snaked between the trees into the darkness.

Jesse found a bladeless axe handle he could use as a makeshift club. Armed and with Heather in mind, he left the shack and followed the path. A flickering of lights came through the shadows and gaps in the trees. Voices followed as the trail widened into a larger clearing illuminated by several torches.

Young Heather cried at the center of the clearing, her body cloaked in a bloody fur and bound at the legs and wrists to a wooden post. A mask covering her head muffled the sounds of her sobbing. The face was a patchwork of fawn skin with its antlers as a crown. The stepfather and his twin sons were giant and grotesque cross forms of pig and man. They snuffed and snarled from tusked boar snouts, standing at a stone altar where the baby deer lay butchered.

His mind went red. In a mad fury, Jesse rushed into the clearing. "She's not an animal!"

Jesse raised the club and swung with all his might. The blow connected with the first twin's head, dropping the beast. The stepfather and other twin tackled Jesse to the ground, as he lifted the club for a second attack. They disarmed him, then tied Jesse with rope.

From the altar, the stepfather drew a machete dripping with blood. The nightmare raised the blade, readying to slice into Jesse's chest.

"Heather! You have the control here! You're dreaming!"

"Leave. Us. Alone!" Heather screamed from behind her mask.

The stepfather froze, stuck inches from finishing the fatal blow. The machete flew from his hands and buried into the last twin's skull. The monster stiffened and fell limp. The stepfather lifted into the air. His arms and legs drew apart until they tore off. The rest of his body ripped in every direction in an explosion of bloody mist and chunks.

The ropes at Jesse's wrists and legs unlaced as if invisible hands had undone them. He was staggered at what he had just seen. Heather stood over him, freed of her mask and bonds. She was no longer a child but had transformed into her adult self.

Heather helped him to his feet. They cried, holding one another. She guided Jesse to a torch, grabbing it. Heather proceeded to light the clearing ablaze. The two followed the trail, leaving a wake of flames behind them. The shed was next then, finally, the house.

Heather and Jesse watched from where the wildflowers grew as the fire ate away at the nightmare.

"It's beautiful. I've dreamed of this." The firelight danced in her eyes.

"I already told you, you are dreaming."

The flames reached the sky, tearing it asunder. They kissed, as the nightmare burned and rained ash around them. Heather faded until Jesse was standing alone. When the fire died and the ash had settled, the gray dreamworld and the mountains of static were revealed. Heather's door unhinged and fell to the path, leaving a hollow archway.

His stomach throbbed at the stab wound. Blood ran gray. The static buzzed and crawled from every direction. He went to move but the decay had rooted him in place, devouring his color from the feet up. He collapsed to his knees as the gray swarmed around his throat. His last thought was the realization that the static-festered silhouettes were not trees but the husks of previous dreamers, fated like him along the road of broken dreams. Jesse's scream of madness was silenced by the gray enveloping his face. His mind and senses voided but for an endless white-noise.

About the Author

Michael J.P. Whitmer is a father, husband, and published speculative fiction writer, casting a shadow in his sunny hometown of Jacksonville Beach, Florida. His writing has appeared electronically and in print. Follow his ramblings at @MJPWhit on Twitter.

CONSEQUENT

BY BRENT MESKE

THE SHIP DESCENDED out of the sky to the echoing sound of drum-beats and the familiar hum of ringing metal. Far, far above, the magtree roots ensnared another huge chunk of rock, but it was too high to detect any traces of human civilization.

A team of four men jumped up to catch the lead ropes, and the first to grab one shouted, laughing, to the others to get their acts together. With all of them pulling, they heaved the ship towards the dock, really not much more than a thick earthen trench dug out and cleared of trees for fifty feet in all directions.

The hollow gong of drumbeats had fallen to four per minute, and then the berthers called for two. The skyship shuddered a few seconds later and rose a few feet. The berthers used the time to swing the ship's prow and settle it over the center of the dock. While the ship nestled quietly, folks came from all round the village to get a glance at the skysailors. Some hefted baskets of produce, others pulled carts led by donkeys to the market just beside the island's only dock.

The Watcher followed all this passively: the townsfolk wheeled in the scaffolds with the help of their cows and oxen, skysailors dropped down lines fore and aft at the first chance to get some land under their legs, the pulley and cranes were lashed into place, and up on deck the hold was being opened. The dockmaster was on hand with his ledger and pen, with a table set up at the base of the scaffolding where the inspectors would count and ensure inventory matched the logs before loading up onto carts or strong backs. Soon crates, barrels and goods passed from hold to storehouse.

Children were laughing and chasing one another underfoot, despite the shouted pleas of the old school marm, and playfully enduring the gruff orders of men to clear the way. The Watcher considered interfering, but held back. He'd be nothing but a hindrance.

"Folk of the Vall!" the skycaptain called, from fifteen feet above them, up on deck. "Grave news, and all would hear it before midday turns to supper."

A hush fell over the assembled folk, and then a flurry of whispers followed. The elders dispatched runners to the fringes of their island to collect woodcutters and farmers still tending to their flocks.

In short order, all assembled, somewhere short of a thousand men, women and children. With the elders satisfied all would hear, they signaled the skycaptain.

A woman came forward, this time, a Magestrix. "I bring fell news, but it must be told. Our rule of law was undone not two weeks past. Folk of the Vall were attacked. Their goods were unlawfully seized, and their lives were threatened. Those responsible had taken a skyship and descended from the sky, and set the homes of the peaceful Vallfolk ablaze."

A collective gasp of terror passed over the Vallfolk. They looked to the roots, some ways distant, snaring their chunk of dirt in its clutches. If it should ever catch fire... shudders stopped them from fully pursuing an unimaginably horrific line of thought.

"Even now, we are working diligently to replace the homes and property lost to this scourge. Before we leave, we will ask a donation from right-minded Vallfolk to help in the rebuilding."

Now the collected villagers shook their heads and muttered to friends and relatives. Before sunset, cords of wood, tools, and hammered iron would stand fast at the foot of the skyship, and many men would utter their 'least I could do' while rubbing their necks in delighted embarrassment.

"We were forced to task several of our own right-minded skycaptains with apprehending these...these evildoers. Along with the blue hats, they were tracked, they were discovered, and now I bring one of them to you, that you might witness justice done. The laws are simple, as are the punishments."

"To take is to die," the vallfolk muttered as one. "To hurt is to die. To lie is to die. To defy is to die."

The captain reappeared, dragging a bound and gagged man. She shoved him forward and he nearly fell to his death right there. Were it not for him catching himself on the ship's figurehead, appropriately Justice, blind with scales in hand, he surely would have fallen fifteen feet and brained himself.

He couldn't have been more than sixteen or seventeen years old, and was sobbing pathetically. Some of the children watching also began to cry. One side of his face spoke a story of beating and abuse at least a week old. Grimy rags hung from his shrunken body.

"The magtree tolerates no wildfire," the Magestrix shouted. "Without it, we would plummet to our deaths. Never the Magtree be harmed!"

"Never!" the rest of them shouted. "To hurt is to die! To defy is to die!"

The theft and the fire were far worse than putting a boy to death. The Watcher turned and left to think on this. He hadn't been doing his own duty well enough. Without a word or sound, he vanished.

"Aunt Letzey, Aunt Letzey!" chanted the little ones, before the boldest child went, "Tell us where the stories come from."

Aunt Letzey was neither their aunt nor was she born and named Letzey. Still she favored the pack of gleaming eyes and hopeful faces with a warm, ancient smile and stood. She put a new kettle on to boil, and hefted the old off the potbelly stove to pour herself some roble tea. She dipped the bag into the water and cast a glance over her shoulder at the rapt interest she was working up.

"Well," she said, "I suppose you mean the Scaredywog and Jack the Clipper."

They nodded fervently.

"And the story of the Mad King and the Clone." More nods. "And who could forget Clemilla and the Cloud Catchers. You mean those stories?"

"Yes, Auntie!"

Letzey dunked the fragrant bag again and savored: first the expectation, second the robleberries with hint of magtree blossom steeping, staining her steaming water a musky pink.

"Well," she began, just as she always did. "Let's see..."

The lot of them, every pink-cheeked lass and every mischievous boy, giggled.

"Out beyond the stars—" she started, but froze. A shadow had fallen over the school's entryway, and the assembled young people turned to find the Watcher leaning against the doorway.

He said nothing, but instead held up a hand. Then he flipped his hand palm up and swept it to the side, the clear sign to continue.

"Well, out beyond the stars, an age beyond an age ago, people made these skyships, only bigger than the ones you see, o'course, big enough to go from one star to the next. And the time it took to make such a voyage... it's unthinkable. The ships carried only the teensiest wee babies, smaller'n you can see with your wee peepers."

"You mean cells?" the sharp one asked, and then her hand shot up.

"Precise-olutely," Letzey said, and a fresh round of giggles erupted.

She rapped her knuckle on the tea kettle, which rang sweetly in the afternoon stillness and began to rise off its woolen hot pad. It levitated for several moments until it slowly drifted back down. The assembled children quieted.

"And they came to this here world," Letzey said. "Course, y'all know that."

The stories came along with them, Letzey told them, from beyond the stars. "Farther away than you or I could imagine. Some of these, like Clemilla and the Cloud Catchers, were products of this world. Others survived the population of this place, while people were watching this world for safety's sake, before the great ships were shaken apart by their new home."

"All of you know Clemilla and the Cloud Catchers?" the Watcher asked quietly.

Quiet as he was, they all turned to regard him. The boldest one nodded, and then the rest followed.

"I hadn't heard it, I'm sad to say," the Watcher said.

"Well, I think we ought to have a telling," Letzey said. "Let's see... who can begin?"

They giggled and snickered again, and hands shot up.

Letzey pointed out one.

"Clemilla was very poor!" the boldest child began. "They din't have any food left!"

"And her mother sent her to the market with their last piece of the Great Ship, to sell for some wogs, for their farm."

"But then the sky pirates got her!" another one shouted.

"They had a secret island in the clouds!"

"One at a time, children," Letzey said. "You'll give the poor man an achin' head."

"They was gonna kill her!"

"They *were*, you dummy."

"I'm not a dummy! You're a big ole wog!"

"Only she said she was a great cook. She cooked for 'em for a year an' a day."

"Until one day," Letzey said, "she put some of the black roble into their stew. While they was... while they *were* thrashin' around holdin' their bellies, she stole their ship."

"And when the blue hats heard about it, they laughed fit to

burst, and had Clemilla take 'em up there, and catched those nasty pirates."

"Caught, dear," Letzey said.

"Right!"

"And the blue hats gave her and her mama a big old herd of wogs and fifty barter shells, and they lived happily ever after!"

Silence fell as they stared at the Watcher. He digested this for a while, and then raised his hand once more.

"What's the lesson we learn from our story?" he asked.

Suddenly they seemed bashful again. Only one boy, after a time, timidly raised his hand.

"Don't take what isn't yours?"

"That's one very important lesson, to be sure. Strange, though... did you notice that Clemilla also took what didn't belong to her? She took the skyship."

He watched minds explode in realization and coping mechanisms stir and shift into low gear. Even Letzey seemed uncomfortable.

"She lied as well... and hurt the skypirates."

"But—"

He held up a hand and they immediately fell silent. "One time, and one time only, will you be allowed to lie or steal or hurt, and that is when your life is in danger."

"To take is to die," they called out. "To hurt is to die. To lie is to die. To defy is to die."

"Unless..." the Watcher said. "Unless peace means death. Unless the truth means death. I thank you, Aunt Letzey. I am sorry to have taken up your time. Pray, grant me leave."

Now Letzey went smiley and bright red. "Not at all. Not at all."

He left the same way he had entered, silently. A few seconds later, he vanished.

For now, she smiled and checked the position of the sun before returning to the lessons. In under an hour, she would be murdered.

DEVLIN PACED BACK and forth in his office, turning the problem over in his mind. A few minutes of frantic to and fro and the decision was made. He raced out the door, forgot to lock it in his haste, grabbed his coat, and bolted for the car. After maybe thirty seconds of patting himself down, he realized he no longer needed his keys, what with all the voice authenticated entry. With a laugh at himself, he jumped in the car and made for the university.

It was a bit of a jaunt, and he spent that time logging notes on the various factors and interactions that most closely aligned with his hypothesis. Other conveyances whipped by, all blurs of shape, size, color and speed. In minutes the car made an automatic turnoff toward his destination, while he hurriedly dictated notes into his tablet.

THE WATCHER STROLLED SLOWLY through the town. All eyes turned to watch him go. Now that the sun was dipping below the horizon, he appeared more of a ghost than a man, for he made not a sound.

He beheld everything the town had to offer: its weak, flickering electric light bulbs, sooty black with thick glass, the wooden houses and general store and smithy, the dying light of sunset glinting off warped, imperfect glass.

And the Isles. High above, they floated soundlessly. Magtree roots thick as houses creaked and swayed and held the Isles high, with buildings clustered round until they practically climbed up the roots themselves. Far, far above, fifty foot leaves showed black against the deepening indigo.

And though hardly a soul stirred, the Watcher detected the scents of baking pies and mog stew.

If he closed his eyes and held his breath, he could make out the low murmur of dinner conversation, plus the clop and thwok of wooden cutlery on wooden stew bowls.

Suddenly, a pack of children burst out of the nearest one room shack, and holding the door was an ancient hag of a woman whose face had crags and valleys in place of wrinkles.

"Whew," the Watcher said, "Would you look at that? That is hideous!"

As one, all the children froze and did an abrupt about face to behold Aunt Letzey. Then folks from nearby houses appeared to stare at the old woman. They looked on in silence.

DEVLIN TOOK the stairs at a sprint rather than wait for the elevator. On the third floor he rapped on the office door and let himself in before Dr. Wenz could answer.

It took him time before he got his breathing under control. Devlin wasn't twenty-two years old anymore. Finally he managed, "We've got originality and spontaneity."

"Already?"

Dr. Wenz was a sharp, matronly woman in holographic lenses and a simple but formal black suit. Her office was decorated similarly: only a few volumes on tastefully arranged shelves, along with a handful of awards and framed photos of her meeting with senators, the president, and other famous scientists. A keyboard was all that sat on her desk.

"Well, you had better settle down and tell me everything."

He did. It took some doing, but he laid out the broad strokes of his assignment, stammering in his excitement like a child gabbing about a new video game.

"I kept everything simple... although, I guess, not really. I don't know what I'm saying. Let me start over. I found a way to alter the gravitational constant by interfering with the magnetic fields surrounding a planet. The first thing it did was keep all other space-craft well away, or else they'd have broken up on approach."

The doctor brought up a holographic map of the parameters, and began puzzling through a huge bluish sphere while Devlin talked.

"Otherwise it was all hands off. I had a total non-interference policy."

THEY HAD STOOD THERE for a good five minutes in silence, staring at the old woman, and then the children slowly turned and made their slow way toward their homes. Folks in the doorways of their homes, meals interrupted, began to back up and shut those doors.

"Wait!" the Watcher called.

Everyone in hearing range froze.

"Come back here," the Watcher said.

They turned and regarded him for a moment before approaching him. It was eerie how they did, too, in complete obedient silence. Many others peeked out of their houses further off. All eyes were on him.

"INTERESTING CHOICES, I MUST SAY," Dr. Wenz said. "You've spent a great deal of time on the landscape."

Devlin laughed, but couldn't keep the nervousness out of his voice. "I wanted to enhance the sense of wonder and keep communities somewhat constrained. Also, we're completely dependent on a structure for life... this magtree, if it's destroyed, all their lives are over, possibly for everyone on the entire planet. I thought it would help impose order: if one person does something terrible, all of them would die."

"You weren't worried about stifling choice or limiting expansion? These Isles are awfully small. You're looking at village sizes of less than a thousand.

"On second thought, perhaps it is for the best. I see that you've had only one instance of interference from outside groups. Remarkable, actually. Similar to the beginning of my own doctoral thesis, with obvious differences."

She arched an eyebrow at him.

"I... hadn't read it."

"Of course you hadn't," Wenz laughed. "The Aeronautics and Space Exploration division of the ISC bought it and classified it."

He made a respectful, low whistle.

"I have a number of trials where the candidates encouraged complete anarchy. We've bogged down into a series of life or death squabbles. No progress whatsoever, which is a bit sad. You'd expect more creativity in those sorts of situations, but it's really the opposite. Only in the movies does everyone come up with the perfect solution out of nothing, and just in time. I see you've also restricted technology by destroying the colonial ships. The breadth and range of technological competence has also been detrimental in a number of situations. Once the drive engineer or the life support systems analyst dies or decides to stop working, we see an unbelievable waste of time and resources just getting basic function back underway."

"Far too complicated for my little project," he said.

"I am impressed, though."

"Thank you, doctor."

They lapsed into an uncomfortable silence, while Dr. Wenz looked at Devlin's hypothesis and summary write-ups. Devlin, meanwhile, tried not to drum on his knees or bounce his feet too much from the anxiousness.

Finally, he said, "Actually, I've been meaning to ask you something... I hope it's not too much of an imposition. It's... personal in nature."

She laughed. "Devlin, don't you worry yourself about that. We've been colleagues for quite long enough for me to call you friend."

"It's... I suppose it's about your age. It's a conscious choice you make to look it. You clearly have the money to roll back to your younger self."

The wrinkles appeared, the crow's feet, when she grinned at him. "I don't believe I detected a question. But the answer is, I rather like this age. There's enough pain here to remind me I won't be around forever, but I still move around well enough. My bones and joints ache from time to time. Perfection bores me. Besides, I believe you're a father... it's merely my opinion, of course, but I believe a father ought to look older than his son."

As Devlin pondered this, she turned back to the holo display before her.

"Let's talk about the future. If the trial is successful, we can put your work before a board and perhaps get you a symposium presentation. I'll discuss a timeline with you as well. But what we'll need to do next is—"

She froze.

"What is it?" he asked.

"I'm showing that you're logged in."

The Watcher considered these filthy, primitive townsfolk, with their homespun clothes and their dead gazes resting expectantly on him.

"Turn in a circle?" he tried.

Every single one of them executed a perfect pirouette simultaneously.

Distantly, an alarm blared.

The Watcher was having far too much fun to be interrupted now. He pointed at a number of them.

"You're chickens."

The townsfolk began to jerk their necks back and forth, flicking their gazes about. They crooked arms back into their armpits and stamped around the soil. The others watched only briefly, before turning back toward the Watcher in utter silence.

"What? That's not funny?"

The entire assembly began to laugh riotously. It was fake and annoying, so he waved them to silence.

"The old hag. I want her killed."

Instantly everyone began to move toward Aunt Letzey.

"Wait! Wait!" They stopped. "Only the children can do it. The rest of you have to watch."

And they did it. He was hoping for some tears and pleas. A little bit of 'no, don't, why would you do this!' But the old woman stood there as they came, and they knocked her down. Some of them began stomping on the old schoolteacher, others beat at her with their fists, and a few children ran to their parents for wooden cutlery, which did it. Letzey made not a sound as she died.

"Boring," the Watcher said. "Everyone, fight to the death!"

Far off, the alarm continued blaring. Now a voice cut in, all around him.

"Quent Donagel Rixen!"

The Watcher looked to the sky. "What?" Around him, the vallfolk moved towards one another, raising fists and shoes and rocks.

"I told you never to enter my office, didn't I? How many times have I told you?"

"And?"

The Watcher sneered at the rage in his father's voice.

"What have you done to my simulation?" his father whispered.

"It's not a big deal," Quent said. "They're not even real. I can't believe you're playing this game anyway. It's like ten years old."

"Order them to stop and return to their lives."

The Watcher laughed. "Why should I do that?"

"Go back to your 3D protein printing, okay? Make whatever monsters you like, have them fight to the death. Not here."

It was already too late. People were rolling around on the dirt and grunting with the effort of ending one another. One woman slammed her husband's head into a rock again and again. A young man threw his sister off the edge of the island and she disappeared into the night mists swirling below.

"What are you gonna do about it?"

The alarms blasted Quent out of his reverie. He staggered back from the sudden, blinding darkness, ripped off the VR goggles and turned. The office door shut itself, and beeped as the lock engaged.

A calm female voice began to announce 'Intruder Alert' over and over again.

"What are you doing?" he asked, but knew. His father had remote access over the house.

"This was going to be big, Quent, important. They were going to load my code, my sims, into the broadcast to the Colonization ships. I could've been responsible for peaceful human civilization thousands of years from now, light years away, but no. You ruined it." Truth or not, all Devlin's expectations had just solidified into hard-boiled rage.

"Whatever."

Lights died. The room went red. The female voice called out. "Warning! Lifeforms present. Atmospheric purge will result in death."

A sheet of ice froze Quent from scalp to balls to toes. He whispered, "Dad?"

"Override password accepted," the female voice said.

"Dad!"

In the car, away from Dr. Wenz, it was easy to let loose a scream into the screen. "You think you're irreplaceable? I can have a test tube growing a new Quent as we speak."

"Dad, please! I'm sorry!"

"That's what you said last time," Devlin said quietly. "To lie is to die. To defy is to die."

About the Author

Brent Meske is a dad, husband, professor, author, and sometimes artist living and working near Seoul, South Korea. He wishes you'd search out his name on Amazon or Smashwords and give some of his free or paid books a read, or head over to brentmeske.com, where moldering blog posts await.

Thanks so much for reading!

DRAGOMIR

BY TAUSHA JOHNSON

DRAGOMIR LIVED in a cottage at the edge of a wild wood. He lived with his two elder brothers, Micrea and Radu, who taught him everything he needed to know about the forest and about sheep herding—how to drove and gather the flock, where to take them to feed, where not to take them, and what to do if one or more strayed. They also taught him how to deal with the creatures of the forest.

"What do you do if you encounter a bear?" Micrea pointed the bread knife at him during their breakfast of bread and cheese.

"I know how to deal with a bear. But what should I do if I meet Muma Pădurii?"

"You're too old to believe in fairy stories."

"But what about Silviu? The people are saying—"

"People believe too much in nonsense superstition. Now, what will you do if a bear crosses your path," Micrea, irritated, asked again.

"Back away slowly. Try to retreat unnoticed," Dragomir responded, but wondered if that's what he'd do if he met Muma Pădurii.

"What if it's aggressive?" Radu asked.

His reaction would depend on the type of bear and the situation. It was rare for a bear to attack a shepherd unless it was with cubs and felt threatened. Usually, they detected human scent and shied away. "I'll climb a tree higher than it can or play dead, depending."

Dragomir understood his brothers' obsession with bears. When Dragomir was only a wee babe, their father fell victim to an attack. Micrea still blamed himself for snaring a cub and forcing his father to protect him from the enraged mother bear. Micrea also carried the blame of their mother's passing. Days after the bear attack, their mother went to sleep one evening and never woke up. The villagers had said all their tragedy was surely a witch's curse put on the family.

"There's no such thing as witches and curses," Micrea had once told Dragomir. *"Mother died because her heart was broken. That was my doing, not a witch's. We must take responsibility for our actions."*

Even after what had happened with their father and with all the warnings and teachings, it wasn't the bears that worried Dragomir. There were far more dangerous beasts in the forest that might harm him, such as wolves that killed sheep. Wolves that could tear him to shreds with their razor-sharp teeth and scythe-like claws.

And then there were monsters.

Like the Pricolici. For centuries, these undead creatures appeared as giant wolves seeking to harm and kill humans. They detected human scent from miles away and became ravenous. An attack would be silent and unexpected. There'd be no running up a tree. No playing dead. No chance of escaping. And, of course, there were the strigoi, undead blood-hungry creatures who could shape-shift into any animal. They would steal his soul, or spawn him into one of their own.

But the being Dragomir most feared was Muma Pădurii, an old crone with petrified wooden teeth who kidnapped children and eventually ate them. Muma Pădurii, The Mother of the Forest, protected the forest and all its creatures. Those who took from it or harmed it were expected to pay. Over the years, several village children disappeared in the forest and never returned. And now, his friend Silviu had recently vanished. Rumors spread through the surrounding villages that Muma Pădurii had the boy enslaved and was eating him piece by piece.

The village mothers cast spells and used brooms, scissors and pokers to form the shape of the cross to protect their children. Dragomir and his brothers made no such cross. Micrea wouldn't allow it. "A cross in the ground won't save you from a bear," he'd said.

Part of Dragomir wondered if these tales of shape-shifting creatures were only that—tales to terrify children and prevent them from wandering into the forest and getting lost or stolen by a bad person. Radu had told him such stories when he was very young, but now that Dragomir was older, nothing more was said of them. His brothers did, however, warn of places in and near the forest to avoid.

The field around old Dalca's abandoned barn attracted lightning. The path going left at the end of the main road was crawling with poisonous plants. The pond beyond that road, swimming with plague. While many believed these places were haunted or hexed, his brothers explained they simply weren't good feeding grounds.

"Stay on the right path. The giant hog-weed on the left will make you ill if you cross it," Micrea warned as Dragomir finished his bread and cheese.

Micrea and Radu would stay to scythe the fields. The scything usually took a full cycle of the moon to complete, so it was their ritual to start in summer before any chance of frost. Dragomir still wasn't fast enough. Not like Micrea and Radu whose scythes, like sinister smiles, sliced greedily through the grass.

The day before, Dragomir complained of wrist pains only minutes into cutting and often stopped for breaks. The constant stopping infuriated Micrea and frustrated Radu, making Dragomir feel as useless as a tree stump.

Micrea exploded, "If the grass isn't cut in time, the sheep will starve and then we too will either starve or freeze to death."

Dragomir understood that losing one sheep would mean less wool, and less wool meant less food for exchange. How would they make it through the long winter with less food? Especially now that he was growing and, as his brothers teased, ate like a horse. It was decided Micrea and Radu would do the scything, and it was up to Dragomir to take the flock out for feeding.

Tending the sheep was a great responsibility, and Dragomir felt elated the job was his. Finally, a chance to prove to his brothers he wasn't a little boy any longer. He was, after all, almost thirteen and on the verge of becoming a man.

"Have you said your prayers?" Radu asked.

"Twice," Dragomir proudly replied.

"Have you got the purse I gave you?"

"Yes." He held up the leather pouch full of frankincense, salt and garlic. He also carried their father's silver coin in his waist pocket belt. If Micrea knew, he would have rolled his eyes and called them sheepheaded.

"Pin it on the inside of your shirt, close to your heart," Radu instructed.

Dragomir did as he was told, though he didn't like all the fuss Radu made. He was a bit nervous as it was, and all Radu's fretting didn't help. He told himself, *Nothing will go wrong. Just another day with the sheep. What could go wrong?* As well, he had Max, their trusty Raven shepherd, and the two younger mountain dogs to help him. *Nothing will go wrong.*

As Dragomir opened the pen, the flock, braying and running, almost in a state of confusion, flooded out. He counted them—forty-four to be exact. He'd count again every so often to make sure one hadn't wandered off.

He followed the main road, then took them higher up the mountain and into the woods. A grassy meadow on the other side of a small stream looked perfect for grazing. His brothers had warned him to be careful of the circular clearing as wolves could easily surround the flock. Even so, it was excellent feeding land, and Dragomir felt secure he'd be able to keep a good eye on them.

They crossed the stream and, as Dragomir expected, the sheep were naturally drawn to the meadow. Among all the lush grass, the field was dotted with an array of wildflowers—bellflowers and dandelions, ox-eye daisies, clovers and cowslips. Paradise on Earth.

In the middle of the meadow stood a singular Juniper tree. Dragomir found a comfortable spot under the leafy tree to shade himself from the heat of the afternoon sun and still allow him a full view of the flock. While the two pups ran around the clearing, investigating, Max sat by his side, silently sniffing the air.

"Ah, it doesn't get much better than this, eh Max?" Dragomir leaned against the Juniper. "This is the life."

The birds chirping their melodious songs soothed him like a lullaby. He lifted his face to the sky, closed his eyes and took in the fresh summer air. Wildflowers mingled with the warm, earthy scent of fir and balsam. Suddenly, behind the pleasant mountain fragrance, far far behind it, he detected a strange odor. Something rotten. A stench. Overpowered by the other smells, he only got a hint of it; but the dogs, he knew, could pick up on so much more. The scent of other animals. Traces of what had passed through before. Dead things.

Can you smell if Silviu has passed this way? Can you smell what has taken him? He patted the purse of frankincense Radu had given him, and it struck him that all around were old wives and witches' plants for potions and disease. Daisy fleabane to cure one from a frenzy, saxifrage for head wounds and convulsions, columbine for love charms or fever, and nettle to purify the blood or take the poison out of it's own sting.

Dragomir remembered Silviu's mother had fleabane and John's wart hanging on the lintel of their door to protect them from evil spirits and devils. What good had it done them? *And what good will garlic and salt do if Muma Pădurii finds me? She'll lure me to her hut and use them in the roast she'll make of me.*

The more he thought of Muma Pădurii, the more anxious he became. He stood and counted the sheep. Forty-three. One missing. He quickly counted again. Forty-four. He counted again. Forty-four. He must've miscounted the first time. Oh, what simple animals they were, but at least they were safe.

"You're too old to believe in fairy stories," Micrea had said.

Yes, Dragomir told himself, *Micrea's right. It's only a story. But what power a story has— the power to make one believe in the unbelievable!*

Relieved all was well, he rested against the tree trunk again and laughed at his foolishness. How silly to believe, even for a moment, what people were saying about Silviu's disappearance. Ghosts, monsters, witches. They were nothing more than old wives' tales.

There was a chance, Micrea had told him, that the boy had gotten lost in the forest, but more likely he'd run away to the city. More and more young people were abandoning their roots in search of fortune in the city, ditching the old for the new. They were tired of scythes and sheep and bears. They wanted big houses filled with useless trinkets, devices that told them their lives were passing, and shiny, impractical shoes.

Dragomir couldn't understand their obsession with wealth. In fact, he'd heard most ended up living in squalid conditions, working day after day in some dark factory where an ambitious and heartless supervisor decided when, or even whether, they could take a break. Evil bosses that controlled their lives. No, thank you. Dragomir would rather get lost in the forest than in a city any day. Cities had their monsters, too.

"Yep, this is the life." He looked across the meadow and smiled.

Later in the afternoon, after eating the sausage and bread he'd packed, the sky turned granite gray. Radu had warned him he'd seen the neighbor's cows' tails up that morning, so there was a good chance of rain. A summer shower didn't worry Dragomir. The sheep were accustomed to it, even though he knew they'd try to search for shelter if it started beating down. They'd want to crowd with him under the Juniper tree.

What worried him was thunder. It was difficult to know how the flock might react. They got spooked at the sound of a tree branch snapping. Sometimes one would run off in a panic and then he or Micrea would have to track it down. Since he was alone, Dragomir thought it best to start home just in case they were in for a downpour.

But before he could gather them, something went wrong. Something in the woods had gotten Max's attention. The sheep dog growled, and his hackles stood on end.

"What is it, boy? Whatcha smell?" Dragomir looked in the direction Max was growling, a part of the forest Dragomir had never entered. Although he couldn't see anything, he knew that didn't mean there was nothing there.

Max's growling escalated until he finally erupted into rabid barking. The two pups also barked. Then suddenly, as if being called, the three of them bolted into the woods.

"Max! Come boy! Max!" Dragomir shouted numerous times, but the dogs had obviously caught the scent of some animal and weren't letting up. Dragomir hoped it was only a hare or rabbit, and they'd soon bring it back to him. Radu could make up a nice stew for their supper.

The barking soon died down, but then turned into full-blown howling. Dragomir thought it was eerie the way the howling echoed across the forest. Right through his skin, cold and prickling. It was as if the dogs were calling to their wolf ancestors. As if they were communicating with another time or world.

It was the silence that frightened Dragomir more than the howling. There was no telling what was happening. Thoughts of a bear or wild boar attack raced through his mind. He knew there was little he could do but wait and hope the dogs would return unscathed. He couldn't imagine having to put one out of its misery. Not today. Not his first day alone with the flock. Micrea and Radu would be furious and blame him for not keeping better control of the situation. They were already disappointed with him about the scything; and, now, if he didn't return home with all the dogs, it would take ages before they'd trust him again.

Several minutes passed when the two pups came running back, tails tucked under as if they'd been whipped. Otherwise, not a scratch on them. But where was Max?

"Max, here boy!" he called again, but the dog still didn't return.

Not long after, Dragomir heard Max whining in the distance. Part of him was relieved, but another part of him knew something was wrong. "Max, here boy. Here!" Dragomir called and whistled, but the dog still wouldn't come. Only the whining continued.

I can't leave him, Max thought. *No good shepherd leaves his best dog to die in the forest.* His mind was made up; he'd have to find Max, even if that meant leaving the flock alone. He figured it would only take a few minutes. The flock would be safe. What could possibly happen in two minutes?

He ordered the two pups to stay, and, rubbing his father's silver coin for protection, entered the wooded area where Max had disappeared.

The denseness of the forest made it difficult to know where to search, so he continued to call out, encouraging the dog to bark now and again so he knew which direction to take. Luckily, there was a narrow well-trodden path. So long as he stayed on or near it, he wouldn't get lost.

He was deep in the forest when he finally found Max trapped between thick bramble and thorns the length of bear claws. "What a mess you've gotten yourself into. How did you get in there?"

Dragomir was relieved the situation wasn't as serious as it could have been. There was no real, present danger. In fact, Max wasn't injured at all. The dog was only uncertain of how to escape. Dragomir only had to cut through the shrub, and they'd be on their way. He took his bone-handled pocket knife from the leather satchel he wore tied to his belt and cut away the bramble.

After Dragomir freed him, the old mountain dog doused him with wet, slobbery kisses. "All right," Dragomir patted Max on the head. "We better get back before a storm comes."

As he turned to follow the path, Dragomir was surprised to discover there wasn't one path, but several. When he entered the wooded area, there had only been one, he was sure of it. Otherwise, he would've set down sticks or stones as markers to make sure he'd find his way back to the flock. Even more confounding was that none of the paths looked familiar. They all branched off into various directions. Normally, Dragomir could smell his way out of the woods, but here his senses defied him.

He searched for any object he might've noticed coming in—a specific tree, an odd branch, or a peculiar formation of sticks on the forest floor. The sun would be setting in the west now, but with all the trees, he couldn't see the sun. In fact, there was no sky to be seen; it was as though the forest had swallowed it whole. He listened for sounds from his flock, the ram's bell or ewe's braying, but there was nothing to help him.

"Max, what do you think boy, which way should we go?"

Max sniffed, and Dragomir finally settled on a path he prayed would lead him back to the grassy meadow. This time, he wouldn't make the same mistake. He used his knife to strike at trees and left large sticks in the form of arrows. He'd be able retrace his steps if it came to that, though he hoped it wouldn't.

After walking for some time, Dragomir became even more nervous. He still had no idea if he was going in the right direction. Everywhere, the forest looked the same. Row after row of tall, slender pine trees, all identical. Other than the trees he'd marked, there were no natural landmarks. No unique tree species. No water source. No discernible vegetation. Even the path had somehow disappeared, and the forest floor was covered in a blanket of dead needles.

He raised his head towards the sky and thought if only he could see the sun, he'd know the direction and how much time he had before dark. But there was no sky and, for a moment, he felt as if the world had disappeared.

The crack of a branch breaking behind him brought him back to the moment. Something or someone was not far behind him. Dragomir immediately thought it was a wild animal, though he prayed it was someone who knew the forest to help lead him out. He stood still and listened. *Strange*, he thought. He'd definitely heard it —the snapping of a branch—but now there was only a chilling silence.

He moved in the opposite direction from where he'd heard the branch breaking and said as calmly as he could, "Come on, Max. We better keep moving." It was advice Micrea had given him about dealing with bears: *"Speak in a calm voice to let them know you're human but not a threat."* If it was a bear or any non-predatory beast that heard his voice, it would run off to avoid him.

But whatever it was never ran off. As they continued, something not far, perhaps a few leaps behind, was watching him. *Watching,* he told himself, praying it wasn't stalking them.

The direction he'd chosen took them to a part of the forest where the trees grew in a bizarre formation. They were strangely curved, shaped like soup ladles that appeared as if they hadn't grown from the ground, but had fallen from nowhere or were placed there by giants. There was also a peculiar charring on several of the stumps and branches. *Lightening,* Dragomir concluded, but it still didn't put his mind at ease.

Max, too, had become agitated. He was wildly barking at what Dragomir thought to be a large stone. Upon closer inspection, he discovered it wasn't a stone at all, but some sort of human-made device. Though it looked like nothing he'd ever seen before in his young life, he thought, *How could it be anything other than human-made?*

The triangular-shaped object was nearly as tall as Dragomir, the top point forming a pinnacle just below his nose. He didn't recognize the material. At first he thought it might be iron, but it struck him that it was far heavier. With his brothers' help, they might be able to shift it, but he doubted it could be moved from its place. He wondered if it was a farming machine someone had made then abandoned in the forest when it failed to work. But, because of it's weight, he doubted any one person could transport it so far without a horse and cart. Even then, the narrow path leading into the woods and the topography made it impossible to enter with a cart.

Then he noticed small drawings engraved on one side of the triangular object. He recognized a few images—a bird like an eagle, crosses, an eye, geometric shapes. As well there were peculiar symbols he'd never seen. Dragomir decided it was a code and became excited. *It must be something used for battle,* he thought. *A weapon for war.*

He traced his fingers over the images and wondered what they could mean. Was it a message explaining its purpose and where the object originated? Perhaps it came from an ancient empire and was a secret invading machine. But why had it been left in the middle of nowhere?

Then the buzzing started. Thousands of drones filled every pocket of silence. Not from an insect. Nor from any bird he recognized. Not even from the strange object. It was a buzzing, it seemed, created by the air spreading around him. Spreading... spreading... until the ground below him started vibrating. It hummed in his ears, and Dragomir suddenly felt dizzy and nauseous. He held onto the object to keep his balance, but the buzzing only intensified. *"Come, come here,"* he thought he heard a boy's voice.

"Silviu, is that you?"

"Come, Dragomir. Come here." His vision became blurred as strange orbs of light surrounded him. White orbs the size of giant stones of hail. At first they were translucent until they grew as bright as the sun shining on a stone, blinding him.

Everything went white.

IT WAS dusk when he found his way back to the meadow where he'd left the sheep. A blood red sky affirming he was too late. The flock was gone. At first he thought it might be a different clearing; but, no, the solitary Juniper tree which he'd sat under earlier that day told him it was the same place. His heart sank. He searched the ground for tracks or droppings, but, curiously, there were none.

Dragomir evaluated the situation. There were two possibilities: the flock was in another part of the forest, or the pups were leading them home. They couldn't have gotten too far. Surely he wasn't gone all that long. He'd gotten dizzy and sat a moment to rest and then found the path he'd taken in.

"I guess it's time we head back," he decided, knowing if he didn't encounter the flock on the way, or if they weren't at home when he arrived, his brothers would wring his neck for sure. "Let's go, boy."

The old dog wagged his tail and stuck by Dragomir's side as they crossed the stream and found their way to the main road leading to the cottage.

It was dark when he finally returned home. He had never noticed before, but in the moonlight, the little wooden house looked tired. It appeared to have a lean to it, as if it was yearning for the ground to rest upon. The roof sagged like an old hag, and many stones from the chimney were gone, like a mouth with missing teeth. Dragomir figured it was probably the moonlight playing tricks on him. He'd have to get a better look in the morning and repair anything that needed fixing.

As he approached, he was surprised to see a broom hanging upside down beside the door. He knew Radu believed in the super-stitions of the old ones, but Dragomir had never known him to leave a broom outside to keep away witches. *He must put it out when I'm sleeping, so as not to scare me*, Dragomir thought.

At the entrance, Dragomir ordered Max to go to his place in the barn. The dog whined and refused. "Max, go to your bed," he insisted, but the old dog moaned and lay down in defiance beside the cottage door. "Okay, if that's the way you want it," Dragomir said. "But you'd be much more comfortable in the barn."

"It's me. I'm home," Dragomir said timidly as he entered the cottage, certain he'd be met with a scolding.

Micrea, looking tired and worn in the candlelight, sat at the table alone, a bottle of plum brandy in front of him. Dragomir stood behind him, waiting for permission to sit.

"Brother," Dragomir said. "The sheep..."

"The sheep? What about the sheep?" Micrea's voice was shaky and thin.

"I...I'm sorry..."

Micrea turned and peered at him, and Dragomir felt the heaviness of the stare. It was a look of distrust, as if he was a stranger Micrea no longer recognized. His expression caught Dragomir off guard. Micrea could get angry—and there was no doubt he was livid about the sheep—but in the light of the flame, his face appeared transfigured. His color drained, he looked broken down, almost decrepit. Obviously, his eldest brother had been worrying himself sick.

"Brother, I'm okay. I can explain. I didn't mean to lose them."

"Lose them?"

The confusion in Micrea's voice made Dragomir hopeful. Perhaps the flock had returned home. Perhaps they were in the pen this very moment and Dragomir hadn't realized. But if they had come home, why was Micrea staring at him so crossly, as if he was disappointed with him, as if he was suspicious of him.

"Brother, I—"

"Are you a ghost?" Micrea interrupted.

"A ghost? Why no, Brother." *What a strange thing to say.*

"Have you have risen from the dead?"

Now it was Dragomir who was confused. What was Micrea going on about? "No, Brother, I am alive."

"Then you're a devil."

"No, it's me. I am Dragomir." He took a step closer to Micrea. What kind of joke was he playing? Was this his brothers' way of punishing him for losing the sheep?

"But that's not possible." Micrea's glassy red eyes bored into Dragomir.

Those red eyes—it was the pálinka. Micrea had too much to drink. Dragomir knew full well that too much pálinka could make a man go mad and say irrational things.

No longer waiting for permission, Dragomir sat in the chair directly opposite his brother.

Micrea leaned in closer, never taking his eyes off Dragomir. "You... you look exactly the same. You haven't changed."

Was it a question or a comment? Dragomir felt he was under interrogation.

"Of course I haven't changed." What a curious thing to say, even though Micrea himself looked like an old man in the candlelight. Darkness could deceive the eyes. Still, he'd heard about people who suddenly grew old overnight. He remembered how the innkeeper's young wife's hair suddenly turned white after her second-born son got ill and died. One day it was black as a crow, and the next day, bone white. And then there was old man Bălan who looked twenty years older after his heart stopped for a full three minutes before starting again. He claimed he'd seen his mother come back from the grave, but refused to go with her even though she begged. Sometimes it was life's hardships that made them turn old, but there were those who believed it was a witch's hex. Had Micrea been hexed? Was that the reason for the upside down broom?

"Where's Radu?" Dragomir asked, searching the room as if expecting his brother to appear out of thin air. Even in the low glow of the candlelight, he could make out the room was in complete disarray. Cobwebs in the corners. Dirt as thick and greasy as butter.

"Ra... Radu?" Micrea stuttered. "But... but don't you know?"

"Know what?"

Micrea reached for the bottle of pálinka, his hands as shaky as his voice. He brought it to his lips, took a swig, then looked long and hard again at Dragomir. "Radu is dead," he said.

"Dead?" Dragomir's eyes grew wide. "But how? Was there an accident?" He expected his brother to explain there was incident while Radu scythed that morning. Or perhaps Radu had gone looking for him and was attacked by a bear. Radu had been in perfect health, so there was no other explanation. Not unless a witch had indeed hexed them.

This time, when Micrea's bloodshot eyes looked into his own, it struck Dragomir he was searching for an answer, as if Dragomir himself was the only one who knew the truth about Radu's passing.

"Where did you take him? Where did you take Radu?" Micrea demanded as he clutched the bottle.

244 | UNCOMMON LANDS

"Brother, I have taken him nowhere. How could I? I was lost in the forest. Brother, please tell me what has happened to our dear Radu."

"But you must know."

"Brother, I know nothing."

Dragomir remained silent as his brother stared at him, sour-eyed and full of distrust. Micrea sucked in his lips and when he opened his mouth to speak again, Dragomir thought he saw his brother was toothless. *But how can that be?* he thought. *Did he lose his teeth in the accident?*

"If you are only a ghost, you may not know. But if you are the devil, you have fooled me. You look so much like Dragomir. So, whether you know or not, I believe it wouldn't matter now if I tell you how Radu died.

"It happened one winter night. It was the worst winter we've ever had. The cold and the snow. So much snow. He was sitting right there," Micrea pointed to a wooden stool in the corner of the room, the stool Dragomir had once watched Radu make with his own hands. "He said, 'I think I'll go and meet Dragomir.' Then he walked out the door and into the cold winter night."

None of Micrea's words made any sense. Whatever game his brothers were playing had gone on long enough. "Brother, you are full of too much brandy, or are punishing me for leaving the flock. I have not been gone a winter's time. I know I only left this warm summer morning, so what you say I know cannot be the truth."

Micrea's expression became stern once again, but this time with a beastly wildness that appears in a man cursed with madness. "Dragomir, if it *is* you, you must know the sheep were not the ones who were lost. They returned before nightfall with the two shepherd pups. It was you who had gone missing. And now you return. Nearly forty years later, unchanged and wearing the same clothes. How is that possible if you've not risen from the dead or are the devil himself? What is an old man to think?"

Dragomir shook his head. "I don't believe you! Look here, I am alive. I am flesh and blood. I only left this morning. I am Dragomir. I am Dragomir!" he insisted although he couldn't hear the words as he spoke. It was not his voice at all, but a buzzing, like the strange sound he'd heard earlier in the woods.

Micrea, however, seemed to understand and said nothing of the buzzing. In fact, his expression softened, and his tone became warm and gentle. "They said Muma Pădurii took you to the land beyond the forest. At first I didn't believe, but then she called Radu. And now here you are, unchanged. Muma Pădurii, The Mother of the Forest, from her belly we come and to her belly we must one day return."

Dragomir squeezed his eyes shut and tried to remember. The dogs' howling, the strange buzzing, and then the voice luring him—a call to return. "Come, Micrea. Come with me," he heard himself say, and now he understood.

Micrea stood and went to the door. "Yes, I am an old man. It's time. I am ready."

"Radu is also waiting," Dragomir said, but felt his words were drowned by the buzzing. So rather than continue trying to speak, he took his brother by the hand and led him into the night, the soft glow of the moonlight guiding their way.

About the Author

Tausha Johnson is a writer of dark speculative fiction and poetry. Her works have appeared in various magazines and anthologies, including Apex's *Undead: A Poetry Anthology of Ghouls, Ghosts and More, UnCommon Minds, The Horror Zine, Folk Horror Revival: Corpse Roads, HWA Poetry Showcase 2 & 3, Danse Macabre* and *The Best of Vine Leaves Literary Journal*, among others. She currently lives in the countryside of Spain, but sometimes surfaces as the program director for The Horror Writers Workshop in Transylvania.

THE LAST IMMACULATE

BY LEVI JACOBS

ANOTHER DELETION. Mei gritted her teeth, wiping black hair stuck to her scalp in the heat. The path across the island was rugged, a day's hike, but she was glad for the exertion. Another deletion, and the boy wasn't even sick. She'd known the mother for years, since she started her fieldwork, a bawdy old woman with keen eyes and the best fighting cocks in her village. When the woman had gotten pregnant five years after her husband's death, no one doubted it was an immaculate. And though immaculates could disappear at any time, you couldn't blame a woman for loving her child. Could not fault a child as bright as hers had been, weaving intricate baskets on their front porch. Could not help but be angry when he vanished from his bed one night. Deleted.

In the old days, in the time of the admin cult, immaculates had been seen as divine gifts, visitors sent from another world for a brief time. It was harder to believe now that the administrators were known to be common men.

So Mei had done precious little fieldwork this trip, spending her time instead sitting with the bereaved, arguing with the village elders, trying to reassure the other immaculate mothers they would not wake up to find their children gone. If she did not calm them, if someone didn't, they might start resisting—start giving moon herbs to immaculations still in the womb, or refusing to give data to their fieldworkers. Then they would be deleted too, one by one, 'til the village cooperated. Like her own parents had been.

Which was why Mei chose fieldwork over laboratory or analysis, though she had passed all the tests. Because she couldn't sit inside and let more children lose their parents, or vice versa. Still, it was hard to be a voice for peace, for acceptance of administrative action, when all she wanted to do was scream with them, to curse the admins, to attack the Academy with spears and arrows drawn. She knew it would accomplish nothing—the admins weren't *in* the Academy, they were on Earth, appearing only in projection—but that didn't stop her anger. It only focused it.

There were other ways to resist.

The case of blood samples rattled under her arm, and Mei realized she was clutching it with white knuckles. She took a deep breath, trying to calm down. The jungle air smelled of soil and chrysanthemum, flowering vines crawling up the long trunks of kapok trees. In the canopy, birds sang and monkeys chattered. Shifting spackles of light on the beaten path reminded her of the ocean bottom, glimpsed in the moment before the salt made her eyes tear.

Blue words appeared in the air, hovering in front of her face. *Surprise! Look left.*

Mei turned and caught a flash of white a hundred paces into the jungle. There, again: a waving arm. Oliver. An admin.

And her lover, or close enough.

"Oliver!" she cried, running to him, feeling the usual mix of affection and calculation. She didn't love him like he loved her, but she liked him. Admired him. There was no room in her life for a lover, not yet. But Oliver was one of the good ones. The only good one, maybe. And he was sympathetic to her cause, which overshadowed everything else. Still, he was an admin.

"Mei," he breathed, holding arms out to her. She leaned in, fitting her body into his. As ever, he smelled like nothing, and his entire body hummed beneath her, like a cage full of wasps. They had never touched outside of projection.

"Ollie! This is unexpected." He usually came to her bedroom at night, but that was impossible when she was in the field.

He adjusted his necktie. "Well, no one's around the office, so I thought I'd drop by. I missed you. How is the island?"

"It's good! It's good."

"Something wrong?"

He could always tell. She sighed. "Another deletion. In Sha'cove."

He frowned. "You knew her?"

"Him. Ly'eka, son of Ta'moka. I knew him. An Immaculate. He started swelling."

Oliver nodded. "I heard of another round of deletions. I'm sorry, Mei. If I could do something, I would."

He couldn't talk to the admins. Couldn't stop the deletions. They'd established this—he was in charge of keeping the island running, of maintaining whatever systems allowed it to mimic his world. He'd explained it like a giant projection, though it felt real here, mimicking his world on the atomic level. Oliver kept it running, and others were in charge of research.

"I know," she said. "Any progress on our...project?"

His eyes lit up. "There is. I think I may have found something." They'd been talking about a way to get her out after things got serious, about a year ago. Some way to get her mind into his reality, onto Earth. To give her a voice where the admins couldn't ignore her—though what mattered to him was getting her physically with him. "Sleep. I think sleep is the key. I read a study arguing cognitive dissonance is least when the mind is emitting delta-waves..."

"That's wonderful, Ollie." She knew better than to let him talk research. "I can't wait to be there with you."

"Well, you'll be in a machine, but—"

She nodded. Something for crash-victims in his world, he'd said. "Yes, yes. But I'll be there."

He grinned, and pulled her in again. "Yes. And we'll be together."

He was a good man. Better than most of those she knew on the island, who had acquiesced to the injustice, and certainly better than the other admins. At least he acknowledged there was a problem. Supported her in doing something about it.

Something jingled along the path and he tensed. Mei put a finger to her lips and he nodded, crouching down. She listened, waited until whoever it was had passed, then touched his shoulder.

"Ollie, I should go. People might notice if I stay too long." There were already rumors about their relationship. It wasn't forbidden, but the less who knew the better. "Let me know as soon as you have something. Lover."

He smiled. "I will." Then his humming body blinked out of existence, and she was left with jungle again.

OLIVER SHIFTED IN HIS SEAT. Mei's boss Philippe was leaning over the conference room table, pointing to a particular set of numbers on a chart, his projected body humming as it brushed a coffee cup. Phillippe was head researcher on the island's Academy, a confident man with close-set eyes and a carefully-trimmed goatee.

"With the latest results from the fishing villages, then, these numbers indicate the Delphia 18 series gene runs are also failing. We've lost four of the six surviving immaculates."

Mark spoke without leaning forward in his chair. "I don't think these failings are conclusive; we've yet to see second gen tolerances. We'll run another round." He was head researcher for the project, a slim man with gray bags under his eyes. It had been his idea, years back, to train test subjects on the islands in the basics of genetic research, reasoning that if they were as intelligent as physical human beings, why not put them to work? Evzen wasn't the only corporation doing genetic research with atomic-level simulations— they were just the most efficient. Training sim-level research partners had meant a huge upswing in productivity, leaving the team free to focus on design and analysis. The downside to this, for people like Mark, was simulating human relations. They didn't see the beauty in wholly created humans.

"There's no *need* to run another set of trials," Phillippe said in projection, jaw working. "You'll just be cursing another set of our women to deleted children. Two survivals of twenty trials is enough data, this is conclusive—"

"It *isn't* conclusive, researcher," Mark said, not bothering to look at him or use his name, "and we *will* run another set of trials. Now, if there's nothing else?"

Philippe looked offended, about to speak.

"Then good day, gentleman." Mark cut the link and the four sim scientists winked out, along with their chairs, leaving the table half empty.

"Disappointing news," Dean said, steepling his hairy hands. "I had hoped the Delphia 18s would survive."

"It's not conclusive," Mark said again, reaching for his coffee. "Though I am beginning to think this iteration could be erased."

Oliver's heart clenched. Erase Mei? "It's—not much burden on the system," he put in. "The Delphia 18s showed such promise."

Mark cocked his head. "Not much burden? If it stops producing valuable data what use is the iteration? We'll erase back to third or fourth generation and start again."

Dean was nodding his head. "We're what, twenty generations in? Some of our failed strains are likely part of the gene pool now. Finding adequate carriers for new trials may be difficult."

Oliver's heart squeezed tighter. He couldn't let this happen. "But, you can't deny the research partners are producing good work." In addition to doing all the gene isolation and analysis for them, Philippe's team had designed a splicing technique Evzen was currently marketing as patented technology. "Who knows what they'll come up with if we leave them be?"

Mark gave Oliver a considering look. "You're not getting fond of them, are you? Computer programs?" Dean smirked behind him, like he did when he caught Oliver watching anime in the office.

Oliver tightened his necktie. "Fond? No. I just—that splicing technique is practically paying for our lab expenses. Seems premature to stop them now."

"Mm," Mark nodded. "You know personal relationships with the sims are prohibited."

"Of course! I just—none of the other islands have taken to the education as well. But do what you need to."

Mark eyed him a second longer, then stood. "A week. We'll give them one more week. That's three in sim. See how the next round of immaculates hold, take it from there."

A week. The others were generally agreeing, scraping chairs back to return to their desks. Oliver got up too, in a kind of daze. One week to get Mei out. Either that, or convince them to let the island run. But how? He knew Dean was right, that the viability of the gene pool was starting to diminish as past gene trials increased genetic drift from the human population on Earth. Erasures were part of the testing process. Still, it was hard to believe they could erase Mei, erase Philippe and his team, erase the whole island, without even blinking. He knew it was hypocritical, knew he would have done it before Mei, but he hated the thought now. He had to get her out. Which meant one week to solve a problem no one ever had before.

Oliver turned back to his desk. He had work to do.

———

It was an hour before the door opened.

From the sounds of raised voices in the conference room, Mei intuited the meeting had not gone well, and Philippe's thundercloud face was confirmation of that. He let an assistant do the talking, the usual report on gene successes, the progress of ongoing trials, opinions of the admins, etc. She wondered what Oliver had said as they discussed immaculations and deletions like strategies in a chess game. Had he been a voice for reason? Did he secretly agree?

The assistant seemed to be finishing up. "...and, against our better judgment, it looks like we will have another round of immaculates modeling the Delphia 18 sequence. No word on which areas or women will be affected, but just keep an eye on this as you make your next rounds. We'll need to establish conceptions early and keep a close watch on them; last round we lost five mothers of the forty during gestation, and I know some of you thought that could have been avoided with better care. Any questions?"

A north shore fieldworker asked a question, and she watched Philippe's face as he answered—not good. Someone was going to get it today.

"Anyone else?" Philippe waited, then closed the meeting. As they were getting up, he said, "Mei, could we see you for a minute afterwards?"

Her stomach clenched. They must have heard about Oliver. "Sure, Philippe."

He led her back into the conference room. His assistant followed, along with Daigo, a fieldworker from the south shore. That was strange. Mei didn't know the wiry woman well—Daigo kept to herself, and the south shore was remote—but it seemed odd that she'd be included in a meeting like this. Rumor was that most of Daigo's field sites were admin cults, that Daigo was able to work there because she'd grown up in one.

Philippe closed the door. "Mei, let's not waste words. We've known for awhile that you have a special relationship with admin Oliver. How would you describe your relationship?"

Shit. They knew. No good denying it then. But they couldn't find out her plan—it would mean the end of the Academy, and of all their research. They would expose Oliver to his coworkers, maybe get her deleted. Love, then. All about love. "We're dating. As much as that's possible."

The scientists exchanged small nods. It was Philippe who continued. "And how long has this been going on?"

"A year and a half, two years? I swear it doesn't interfere with my work." If they endangered her relationship—kept her from getting out and protesting the deletions—

"We're not worried about your work, Mei," Daigo said, her voice low.

"What?"

Philippe again. "Two years. Has he ever talked about taking you to their world?"

Another twist in her stomach. How much did they know? "We've—talked about it, but it doesn't seem possible..."

"But he's trying?" Daigo was watching her intensely.

"I—yes."

The three exchanged a look, as if they'd been expecting this. They must have been monitoring her meetings with Oliver. They probably knew everything. "And you want to go?"

"Yes."

"Why?"

"Because... because I love him, I guess. I want to be with him."

Philippe spoke now, his voice kind. "Mei, you're an important fieldworker to us. We understand about your love for an administrator. Really, it's okay. We brought you here to let you know that, and to know that this in no way affects your position in the Academy. We just have one request."

She drew in a breath. "You don't want me to go?"

"No," Philippe said. "We want to go too."

"IT'S SIMPLE," Philippe puffed as they hiked. "The more of us out there, the less they can ignore us."

They were climbing the pass into West Cove, Daigo's field site, carrying provisions to camp. "And what would you say, that needs to not be ignored?" This is what she'd been wondering all morning, ever since the meeting, since they said only that there was something in West Cove she needed to see. What did Philippe want?

"I read your fieldnotes from the last trip, Mei," he said instead of answering. "About Ta'moka. I'm very sorry for what's happened. I know you're close to her."

"Yes, I am." But what she felt was anger, not sorrow.

"I guess we should feel lucky the child survived this long. You must see much of the other side of the immaculates, of mothers lost, children getting deleted."

"I do," she said, hope rising in her belly. Was that what this was about? Did they want to stop the immaculations too? "It's awful."

He nodded. "I lost my wife and our second child to immaculation, you know." She hadn't known that. He looked back. "Have you ever wondered why you weren't chosen?"

Hope mixed with confusion. "Few immaculates are."

"Yes, but since you have become involved with Oliver, I don't doubt the chances dropped to zero. And now you have the chance to give that gift to every woman on the island."

She frowned. "What?" What were they going to show her out here?

"If you can bring Philippe and I out, why not others? Why not all of them? Why should we have to stay here, dying and watching our loved ones die for their research, when we have a chance to be free?"

She frowned. "I—of course. We should all be free. No one should have to die for their research. But they would just create others. They'd never agree to stop."

Philippe smiled, and there was something cold to it despite the heat. "That's why we don't give them a choice."

She frowned. "What do you mean?"

He just smiled and waved her on, and they hiked for a time in silence, climbing up the switchbacks between the island's peak and Second Child, one of the smaller calderas. The view from the top of the pass was breathtaking, ocean breaking white on the south shore's rocky shoals, but she could hardly focus on it, thinking over what Philippe had said. What could they do that she couldn't alone? She had ruled out any kind of violence long ago—as one

person, even as an island of people, they would make little difference to the millions of people Oliver said lived on Earth, and
would only be seen as terrorists—as deserving of deletion. She
needed to wow them with intelligence, with compassion, with
stories of life under immaculation and deletion. To prove to them it
was wrong, and that people on the island deserved better, whether
they were projections or not. Oliver was her beacon of hope in this
because he understood it. The question was whether his coworkers
would.

The way down was easier, and they were most of the way to the
ridge that separated them from Na'cov, the largest cultist settlement,
when Philippe spoke again. "We tried reasoning with them, you
know. The admins. When we presented the splicing technique."

Mei's eyes widened—it was like he'd read her mind. Or like they
had been listening in on her for months. "And?"

"Subjects. They said we were test subjects, *humanlike* subjects
yes, but not human, not protected by their laws." He laughed
without mirth. "That was a hard pill to swallow, but we swallowed
it. That's when we realized we needed more than reasoning." He
waved her on.

Mei smelled it before she saw it—a whiff of decay, carried on the
breeze with the tang of salt and jungle. The whiff become a reek as
they topped the west ridge of the inlet and the town of Na'cov came
into view. It wasn't large, and at first nothing appeared out of the
ordinary: boats were drawn up at the shore, the cottages were
orderly in semicircular rows, and a few chickens and pigs were
poking around at the vegetation where the cliff rose up from
the sand.

No one seemed to be around. Then she saw someone, a man,
head and shoulders hanging from one of the boats, covered in open
sores. She thought he was dead at first, then watched in horror as he
lifted a hand slowly from the water, trying to carry water to his
mouth. In the boat behind him were others, clearly dead, and the
water around them was pinkish. She could make out more shapes
along the shore, in the water, leaning in the shadow of buildings.

They were all covered in red sores, some bloated with decay. The entire village had late-stage lymphomic cancer.

Mei gagged, turned, and lost her lunch in the ferns. Daigo watched impassively, and Philippe offered her the waterskin when she was done.

"What, what happened here?" She had a horrible thought. "The administrators? Did they do this?"

"No, Mei," Philippe said, smiling softly. "We did this. It's our own experiment, of sorts."

She stared at him, not understanding.

"The admins are always wanting new genes, better genes, cures for their diseases. That's why they implant us with them, with experimental fetuses altered to try and resist them. They want to find a cure. And they taught us, Mei, taught us how to isolate those genes, analyze them, to report back on our findings, though we've never found their cure. It was only one step further to start altering our own genes, running our own experiments."

"You... did this?"

He nodded like a proud father. "Not all at once. But slowly, we started running our own experiments in South Cove. Making our own subjects. The admins don't monitor the island anymore—they leave that to the fieldworkers—so we had free reign. Daigo came up with the idea of *encouraging* the Red, causing it, making it communicable. What you see is proof that we can. We've hidden a virus that damages telomeres inside a gene we've isolated, one that should otherwise help extend the lives of tissue cells."

Her stomach swam. "How *could* you?"

"It takes a while to work. The residents of Na'cov appeared normal for six or seven months. Then they all started swelling in the neck and arms. You see, the virus spreads through saliva, through a sneeze or shared food, so it didn't take long for the whole village to get it. Long before any of them started noticing the effects."

"You made cancer... communicable?" He was suddenly profoundly ugly to her, his face monstrous. Down below, the man in the boat was trying to drink seawater again. Mei turned and ran, back up the path, blindly, needing to escape, to get back to sanity. Footsteps crunched behind her, closing, then something hit her head and the world went black.

THE MACAQUE SCREECHED. Or rather, the humanoid silicone face screeched like a macaque, because a macaque's mind was inside. Or rather, the simulated consciousness of an island macaque raised by descendants of the original uploaded macaques.

And he'd brought it back to Earth, sort of.

Oliver grinned, hands stroking his necktie in the dark recesses of the office. He planned a few tests, a few basic cognition checks to make sure the macaque had come through unhurt, but this was the first time it seemed normal. He was getting close. He could do this.

"Just hold on, Mei," he whispered to the screeching humanoid macaque. "Hold on."

SHE WOKE WITH A POUNDING HEADACHE. It was night time; on the far side of a fire, Philippe and Daigo were toasting dried fish. She stirred and they turned to her.

"Ah, you're awake," Philippe said, mouth half-full of fish. "Sorry about the head, we were afraid you might hurt yourself."

Daigo said nothing, looking at her.

"We maybe shouldn't have shown you that all at once," he continued. "I'm sure it was overwhelming, and we didn't mean to frighten you."

She stared at them, remembering what she'd seen.

Philippe cleared his throat and continued, "We wanted to assure you that we have no intentions of using the virus on the island. Na'cov was a controlled experiment, done to them because, well, they were admin cultists. It's no worse than when the admins delete an entire village, person by person, for aborting an immaculate. Call it poetic justice, if you will. And we have an antidote—it's been totally effective with Daigo and her helpers."

Mei shook her head. immaculates and deletions were at least controlled, targeted. A virus that spread cancer...

"I want to assure you that Oliver is in no danger, we can administer the antidote to him after we're all out. We hope, actually, to never have to use it on Oliver or his world; the best would be if they agree to stop experimenting on the island, and to bring out those who want to come. But if they don't, we have options. Once they start getting sick, and learn we have the antidote, they'll be in no position to deny us what we want."

It was probably better to stay quiet. Get out of here. But she couldn't. "They'll think we're monsters."

He turned a fish on the fire. "No more monstrous than them."

"But they won't see it that way! Philippe we have to prove we are *better* than them, that we deserve to be treated like humans!"

He chuckled, while Daigo watched with dark eyes. "We tried that. We know what they think. No, now we need to prove we are just as bad as them. That we deserve to be feared as they are." He looked up. "So are you in?"

No. Absolutely not. There was no way this could go down without war, and no way they could win that war when the admins could kill them with the push of button and them getting out depended on a complicated process Oliver hadn't even finished yet. But how would Philippe react if she said that? Or Daigo? "Have you given them the gene yet?"

Philippe and Daigo exchanged looks. "We have. We got confirmation at the last meeting that they've started animal trials. There's no stopping it now. Daigo and I are the only ones who know of the antidote, Mei, and we've erased the files, so we'll need to be in his world to administer it." He looked at her levelly across the fire. "So I ask again, are you in?"

She tried to look at him, but the firelight distorted his face until he looked uncomfortably inhuman. What choice did she have?

"I—"

Something stung her shoulder and Mei tried to slap it away only to find Daigo pushing a syringe into her arm. "You need the antidote now," the dark woman said. "You're in."

HE WAS READY. Two days left and he had mastered the process. Oliver switched on the projectors, then dialed in Mei's parent's house, hoping to find her sleeping. To extract her now and let her wake up in the real world. To finally have her here. He worked his tie in anticipation.

It was not to be: she was waiting for him on the edge of the bed in her parent's house, looking haunted. Had they threatened her parents again? She looked up as his projection appeared. "Oliver!"

He put on a bright tone. "Mei, hi love, I was hoping to find you sleeping."

She said nothing, just held out her arms, and they embraced. There was something tighter to her hug tonight, something deeper. Maybe she knew, somehow. He spoke soft, into her ear. "I'm ready to take you, love. Tonight. You just have to sleep."

She pulled back and looked at him, tears starting in her eyes.

"What's wrong?"

"Ollie, I haven't slept in days. I don't know if I can."

"What happened? Did they threaten your parents again?"

She was crying now. "Worse, worse."

"Look, love, you've got to get to sleep, I—I didn't want to tell you this, but tonight may be our last chance."

She looked up at him. "What?"

"Mark and the others are discussing erasing the island. If we don't do it tonight, and they decide to erase, it will be too late."

The horror of it stopped her tears for a moment. "You mean, they would erase...everyone?"

He nodded, eyes sober. "At least back to the fourth or fifth generation. To clear out the gene pool."

She looked away. "Is everyone a monster?"

"What do you mean? Mei, it's not too late—"

"They killed a whole village, Ollie. Philippe and the others. They made a—"

With a crash, the window next to her shattered, a hooded figure leaping through.

Mei looked behind in sudden fear, and a woman Oliver didn't recognize grabbed her and headed for the door.

The woman turned. "Try anything and we kill her, admin." Then she kicked open the door and dragged a screaming Mei out.

"Mei!" Oliver surged after her, and ran into the wall of his office back on Earth. The projection blinked out and was gone

---

Daigo gagged her and tied her like a goat, then threw her over one shoulder. "Idiot," the woman cursed under her breath. "What were you thinking?"

Mei went limp, trying to make sense of it. Of the fact that Oliver's coworkers could delete the *entire island* at once, for the sake of 'clearing out the gene pool.' They were no better than Philippe and Daigo. She could see that now. Whatever she had wanted to do, whatever pleas she planned to make, the administrators would be deaf to them. No one could erase an island then learn to care about its erased people.

But what to do? If she did nothing, Oliver would likely get her out eventually—and leave Ta'moka and the rest here, to continue getting immaculated and deleted. Or erased entirely, if she couldn't stop the admins. Did she then agree to Philippe's plan, and threaten Oliver's entire world with cancer in order to save the island? But she had no illusions about that—as soon as they had the antidote, the island and everyone on it would be deleted.

Besides that, and more importantly, Philippe's attack made them no better than the admins—using power because they had it, and damn the consequences to anyone in their way. It confirmed that the admins were justified in erasing them, in immaculating and deleting them, because they could. The virus might at least save a few of them, but at what cost? Oliver said there were other islands—what happened to them?

Daigo kicked open the doors to the Academy. As she did, blue letters flashed in front of Mei's eyes. *Are you okay? Should I delete them?*

"Don't delete them," she tried to say, but the gag was in her mouth, so she shook her head, violently.

The letters disappeared, but not before Daigo noticed. "Talking to him? What are you saying? Don't be stupid. You're not so important we can't find another way."

Daigo carried her down the elementary corridor, up the stairs, toward the main laboratory. *Then what can I do? Should I come?*

Oliver coming would do no good. The gene was out. It was in their world. Philippe would have his way, and then the admins would have theirs, and no one would be the better for it. Worse yet, if the admins erased the island before they knew of the virus, knew of the antidote, their whole world might die like Na'cov. And then this one would too.

Philippe was in the lab, his assistant with him. "She was going to tell the Admin the plan," Daigo said. She bent forward and Mei banged to the ground, struggling to sit up with feet and hands tied.

Philippe was angrier than she'd ever seen him. "So, little Mei turns out to be a traitor." His voice was dangerously low. "Well, no matter. This is faster than we planned on, but it will work." He turned to her. "He's monitoring us, yeah? Can hear everything we say?"

Blue letters appeared in the air, backwards to Mei's eyes. *I can. Hurt her in any way and get deleted.*

Philippe smiled a grim smile. "Oh, I have no intention of hurting her. I like little Mei as much as you do. But I guess I should finish telling you what she started. About a virus. Infecting your world."

What?

Mei shook her head as Philippe explained their plan, sick to her stomach at how Oliver would react, how he would think of them now. Would he think she had some part in it? Side with his colleagues, deciding they weren't really human? Would he erase them all as soon as they had the antidote?

"And that's why you will upload not only Mei, but Daigo and I and whoever else wants to come. Understood, administrator?"

There was a pause, then *I want to speak to Mei.*

Philippe chewed at his lip, then nodded to Daigo. "Can't hurt now. The cat's out of the bag."

Daigo pulled the gag from her mouth and Mei coughed, swallowed. "Oliver! I'm sorry, I tried to warn you—"

It's all right. I'd come in projection but I need to be here in case I have to delete someone.

She nodded, heartsick and angry and sad, then something came to her. "Would you do it? Would you have let them erase the island?"

The words came at once. *No. Of course not. I love you.*

"And if I wasn't here? If this was just some other island?"

The words were slower this time. *No. I think...* They erased themselves, reformed. *You are worth more than that. All of you.*

Mei nodded, something deep in her chest releasing. Something she hadn't known she'd held. He understood. He truly did. "Then I need you to do something."

Anything.

"I need you to come here. Not in projection. In flesh. Like the first admins."

There was a pause, maybe two breaths, then, *I'm on my way.*

"What are you doing?" Daigo spat. "Without him we'll never get out!"

"He won't come," Philippe said, waving a hand. "And leave his body for good? It's a bluff." He turned back to the air, to the general place where Oliver's letters had appeared. "Give it up, admin. Upload Philippe, or you'll never get the antidote. Daigo and I will be here with Mei, and if either one of us gets deleted, be sure the other will kill her before you delete the other. And we'll keep doing that 'til everyone who wants to come out is out. You can't deny us anymore."

Empty air greeted him. Silence. "What did you do?" Philippe asked again. "What is this?"

"He didn't go," Daigo said, shaking her head. "He didn't go."

Mei let herself smile then, the deep smile that had been building since Oliver said, *You are worth more than that. All of you.* "I figured it out. How to stop you from killing them, and them from killing us, and stop the immaculations too."

"What?" He shook his head. "What do you mean? The virus—"

There was a clap and the door banged open in a rush of wind. Oliver stood outside, naked. Not humming Oliver, not scentless Oliver, but *Oliver*, truly come to life on the island. She ran to him, threw her arms around him. "Thank you, thank you so much, I—"

The hug he answered her with was stronger, too strong, her ribs creaking under the pressure, but she didn't care. They were safe now.

"Idiots," Philippe spat. "You've ruined everything. Now this admin will have to teach the others how to get us out, and the virus will be spreading—"

"No," Oliver rumbled, not letting go of her. "No one is getting out. But with me here, no one is getting erased either."

"Why? How?"

"Your island is past genetic viability. There have been too many generations of tests, too much genetic drift from Earth's populations. They were planning to stop immaculating, to erase the island back to an early generation. But with me here, they can no longer erase us. It would be murder."

"It was always murder," Philippe spat. "But they'll just erase you too. Claim it was an accident."

"No." Oliver smiled, looking down at her. "When Mei asked me to come, I realized it was to save you all. So I sent a message to all my friends and family, and to my coworkers, explaining what I was doing. Why I was doing it. And how our research ethics need to change."

"So you... did this to save us?"

"To save Mei," he said, "but yes, you, because she proved to me you were worth it. I hope she wasn't wrong."

Philippe looked ashamed then, and Mei knew she'd won. That the immaculations and deletions and erasures would all stop, at least on this island, without killing anyone other than Na'cov. She would never get out, none of them likely would, but it didn't matter. That was never the goal. But Oliver—she turned to him. "Are you okay? Is this really what you wanted?"

He shook his head. "I just wanted to be with you. I never thought—but this is perfect. Yes. I want to be here. I wanted to introduce you to my parents, but—maybe they can come in projection. We'll be getting a lot of attention from Earth, after this. Hope you're ready for it."

"I am." She hugged him close.

"So what do we do now?" Oliver asked. "Do you... have some clothes I could wear?" She realized he was hugging her in a very strategic way.

Mei laughed. She didn't love this man, but for the first time, she thought maybe she could. "We go home," she said. "And yes. Though I kind of like you like this."

About the Author

Levi Jacobs was born in North Dakota and grew up in Japan and Uganda, so he was bound to have a speculative take on modern life. Currently marketing his award-winning novel *ACHE* and at work on three more, he runs a small fruit company to pay the bills.

ANDERSON'S NECESSARIES

BY JON ETTER

MOST FOLKS DON'T BELIEVE in magic because they don't know where to look for it. But if you ask any kid, they'll tell you it hides out in the cracks and crevices of life: under beds and in the backs of closets, amongst tombstones or deep in the woods, down in cellars or high up in attics, tiptoeing in shadows or lurking in the night.

Few places have more cracks and crevices for magic to hide in than the tiny town of Meadowbrook, Illinois. Hell, that town of 2,100 odd souls located out on a rarely-driven state road is so dinky and so out of the way that the whole place is little more than a crack itself.

Of all the places in Meadowbrook—not that there are many— few had more nooks and crannies for magic to hide in than Anderson's Necessaries.

Meadowbrook's first and only variety store, Anderson's Necessaries was established in the 1880s by William Wallace "Old Willy" Anderson, a Scottish immigrant with more money and ambition than storekeeping acumen. Sure, he knew how to purchase goods from wholesalers, but when it came to keeping track of stock or organizing it in any logical manner, he was entirely inept. A more disorganized shop would have been hard to find: one single shelf might very well hold fishing lures, Mason jars, penny whistles, cigars, baby pacifiers, dog collars, adventure magazines, and shoe polish one week and an equally random but completely different assortment of products the next.

Old Willy's customer service was equally helpful. When asked if he might have anything in stock, his reply, usually given from behind a newspaper or magazine, was invariably, "Oh, aye!" Bolder customers who pressed for an exact location of said item could expect an exasperated sigh, a vague wave of his hand, and a grumbled, "Bloody hell if I know—try tha' wee."

Despite Old Willy's ineptitude—or maybe because of it—whatever it was a body was looking for always turned up somewhere in the store. It might not have been "tha' wee" (in fact, it rarely was), but somewhere amongst all the brick-a-brack was that bottle of paste or typewriter ribbon or weather vane or what have you. Granted, it might not be exactly what you were looking for—that gingham cloth might be powder blue instead of navy, you might have to settle for a dime novel about Buffalo Bill Cody rather than Wild Bill Hickok— but Anderson's Necessaries always had more or less what you needed. It was as if the store itself decided it would live up to its name and provide everything necessary to the residents of Meadowbrook.

That actually was the conclusion Old Willy's son, Robert Bruce "Young Bobby" Anderson, came to when he took over the store. Having developed the orderly mind that growing up in the great green grid of corn and soybean fields tended to foster, Young Bobby began his tenure as proprietor with a full reorganization and official cataloging of existing stock, the first in the store's history. At least that's what he tried to do. He began organizing the store shelf by shelf, writing down items and quantities, fully confident that by the end, he would have the tidiest, easiest to shop in store in town.

But as soon as he finished fixing up one shelf of stock, the one he worked on before would be a jumbled mess again. When he wrote down that there were three packages of little plastic army men in the toy section, the next thing he knew there was only one, and then somehow by the end of the day there were five. Eventually he closed the store for a full week in an effort to tame the beast, believing careless, whimsical, and possibly malicious shoppers were to blame. But it made no difference—every morning he found all his previous day's efforts undone.

After that week's closure, he became convinced that the store itself insisted on being disorderly, maybe for the sake of being able to sneak in the various and sundry items that residents needed that he may lack the knowledge or forethought to ever order. Thus he gave up his Sisyphean struggles and quietly allowed the shop to be what it wanted to be and to provide everyone in Meadowbrook with what they needed, which included a comfortable income for himself and his family.

When Young Bobby's son Earl Gardner Anderson was born, Young Bobby and his wife, Edna, had hoped that Earl (or "Andy," as everyone outside the family called him) would someday take over the family business just as Young Bobby had before him. However, a dreamy streak fed by a steady diet of pulp magazines, adventure novels, movie serials, and radio dramas cast a little doubt on that— the boy, they feared, might run off to see the world via boxcar and tramp steamer or seek fame and fortune in the radio or the motion picture industries on the coasts—but he liked working in the store and had a quiet, easy way with the customers that made him seem like a natural. When Pearl Harbor got bombed just days after his eighteenth birthday, Andy, like most of Meadowbrook's young men, signed up to go do their duty for God and country, and, like most of Meadowbrook's young men, he came back four years later, a little wiser and a little more serious, and took his place as the third proprietor of Anderson's Necessaries, quite certain that it was all he would want out of life from then on to the end of his days.

Over the course of his first year home, Andy settled into a quiet, cozy, routine life: breakfasts in his apartment at the Necessaries; lunches at the local diner; dinners at whichever seemed most appealing each night; long days in the shop helping customers, reading during the quiet stretches, and always listening to either the wireless or the phonograph, both additions to the shop made by Andy that proved quite popular with the clientele; long nights spent playing checkers or rummy at the local tavern (where he, being a good Methodist, drank exclusively Coca-Cola), reading at home, or enjoying walks in the stillness of the country. Andy was content.

───────

ONE SULTRY SUMMER DAY, Andy, feeling a bit decadent, decided to enjoy the usual 2 o'clock to 4 o'clock lull in business by tuning the wireless to a music program, slumping down in his chair, propping his feet up on the counter, and burying his nose in a copy of *Weird Tales* magazine while sipping from a bottle of Coke. *How could life possibly get better than this?* Andy wondered as the sound of "Stardust" filled the shop.

"Excuse me?" Someone from the other side of Andy's magazine said.

Suppressing a sigh over having to abandon a Robert Bloch story just as someone was about to get murdered, Andy lowered his magazine slightly to see who it was. Standing in front of him was a young woman, by his reckoning not too far off from his own age, loose brown curls framing a round, tan face that Andy found rather pretty. Suddenly and unexpectedly appalled at his own lack of professionalism, Andy tried to swiftly and elegantly snap to attention from his position of extreme leisure. His efforts, however, fell somewhat short, amounting to a series of flails and stumbles that did end with him standing up ready to serve, but not before spilling Coke on his thigh and sending *Weird Tales* tumbling over the counter to land with a slap on the floor next to his customer. Even hidden behind round, wire-rimmed spectacles, the customer's rich, shoe-leather brown eyes twinkled with amusement.

"Can I, uh, I mean, how can I help you?" Andy managed to choke out, the words uncharacteristically reluctant to leave his mouth, like children headed to school on a warm May morning.

Looking like she wished to giggle, the young woman replied,

"Are you sure you don't want to..." She pointed to the Coke-dampened spot on the side of his pants.

"Oh, that?" Andy waved a hand dismissively, trying to appear nonchalant. "Nothing to...I mean it'll...dry. What with the heat and all."

Andy stood there nodding, as if in agreement with himself. With her eyes twinkling even more and a Mona Lisa-esque smile playing about her lips, the young woman looked at Andy expectantly.

I'm supposed to be saying something, aren't I? What in tarnation am I supposed to be saying?

The young woman leaned forward slightly. "I believe this is the part where you ask me again what you can help me with," she stage-whispered.

"Oh. Yeah. Right," Andy said, embarrassed but relieved by her prompt. "So...what can I help you with?"

"I was hoping to buy some colored chalk. Do you have any?"

"Chalk?"

"*Colored* chalk. I have plenty of the white variety."

"I think I spotted some art supplies in the back of the store the other day," Andy said, stepping out from behind the counter. Standing next to the woman, she was even smaller than he had first thought. At 5' 11" and 190 pounds, he loomed over her short, thin frame. "We'll probably find some back there... I mean, I can probably find some back there. You can wait here—"

"No, I'll come with you," the woman replied. "Maybe I'll see something else I want along the way."

"Yeah, maybe," Andy said. "I mean, we do have a lot of...stuff. Here, follow me."

Andy wasn't sure, but he thought he heard the young woman chuckle as he walked briskly to the back of the store. In a far corner, Andy spied boxes of crayons and drawing paper. "Over this way," he said over his shoulder. "I bet we'll find some here."

"Are you sure you have chalk?" the young woman asked skeptically, as she picked up a canister of goldfish food and a mousetrap from the same shelf as the crayons.

"Definitely," Andy assured her as he scanned the shelves. "If you need it, Anderson's Necessaries has got it."

"Well, I don't know that I exactly *need* colored chalk, but it would be nice to have for the kids when school starts in a couple months."

"I think that's close enough to 'need' to fit the bill," Andy said. He took his eyes off the shelves just long enough to steal another look at the little woman in the blue floral-print dress standing next to him then quickly turned back, his cheeks flushed, upon getting caught. "So you must be the new grade school teacher?"

"Just graduated from Illinois State Normal University." She held out a dainty hand, forcing Andy to turn and face her. "Ruth Thatcher."

Andy self-consciously wiped his sweaty hand on his trousers, making sure to avoid the patch soaked in Coke, before shaking hers. He found her grip to be surprisingly strong. "Andy. Andy Anderson."

"That should be easy enough to remember." Again, she looked extremely amused. "A little redundant though, isn't it?"

"Well, it's really Earl, but everybody just calls me Andy," he said with a shrug.

"Okay, then. Andy it is." She smiled. Andy once again felt like there was something he was supposed to say or do but for the life of him he had no idea what. And once again, Ruth came to his rescue. "You can let go of my hand now."

"Oh, uh, sorry—"

"Any sign of that chalk?"

"Not here, but it'll be somewhere in the store."

"You sound awfully sure of that."

Now it was time for Andy to smile with the confidence that came from years of experience. "Oh, I am. Like I said, we have everything you need here."

"Everything?" Ruth asked. "*Really?*"

"Sure," Andy assured her. "Just ask anyone. We've got anything and everything in this shop. Sometimes it's just a little hard to find. Why don't you check that side of the shop and I'll check this one."

Once there was around thirty feet of cluttered store-space between them, Andy found breathing and thinking much, much easier. *What the heck is wrong with me?* Andy wondered as he scoured shelf after shelf in search of colored chalk. *She's just a customer, for crying out loud! I help customers—it's what I do.*

His self-recriminations were interrupted by a call from the other side of the store. "Any luck over there?"

"Not yet. Nothing over there?"

"No, there's lots of stuff over here, just not my chalk."

"Keep looking. One of us will find some."

"If you say so. Not much for organization, are you?"

"Oh, I try," Andy said, hopefully peeking behind a chemistry set only to be disappointed by a set of shoehorns. "But the shop wants it this way, so it never sticks."

"The *shop* wants it this way?"

"Yeah. It's...kind of hard to explain."

"Sounds like it."

As Andy searched row after row, his frustration grew and grew. *Come on, Necessaries! You always have everything! After shooting my mouth off, if I don't have what she needs, I don't know how I can face her—*

Which is exactly what he did as he rounded the corner into the center aisle of the shop. "Do you really have colored chalk in stock," Ruth asked placing her hands on her hips, "or was all this just an elaborate ruse to get me to spend the afternoon here with you?"

"No! Of course not! I—we—the shop—" Andy stammered, again finding his thinking and breathing oddly constricted, "That is— we've always got what's needed."

"Not this time, it seems," Ruth said, giving him another of her enigmatic little half-smiles.

"I guess not..." Andy muttered as he frowned at the cluttered shelves flanking them. "Tell you what—the supplier who usually brings us art supplies is due to come the end of this week. I'll give him a call and make sure we get some colored chalk. If you leave me your number, I can call you when it comes in."

Ruth arched an eyebrow at this. "Ah... So that's your game, is it?"

"Game?" Earl could feel his face getting hot. "I, uh, no, no game—"

"Mmm-hmm..." Ruth said, as she turned and walked to the front of the store. Earl stood there and dumbly watched her for a moment before it dawned on him to follow her, at which point he jogged to catch up. After closing the distance, he slowed to what he hoped look like a casual, professional gait.

Ruth took a scrap piece of paper from countertop and a pencil. After jotting down her name and phone number, she held it out to Andy with a flourish. "I'm renting a room from Mrs. Detweiler. You'll have to assure her of your moral character and good intentions if you call."

Andy summoned all his willpower to make has hand reach out and take the paper from Ruth. "I'll, uh, give you a call...when the chalk comes in, of course."

"Of course. Well, I should be—oh here," she stooped down and picked up the copy of *Weird Tales* from the floor. After studying the cover illustration of a bat creature drooling over a scantily clad young woman being squeezed to death by a giant snake, she held it out to Andy. "Your magazine."

"Oh, it's, uh, not really mine," Andy said, tossing it behind him onto the counter. "But, you know, some folks 'round here like to read it."

"Really? Well, you should give it a try. This one's got stories by Bradbury, Bloch, *and* Derleth. Well, give me a call when the chalk comes in." With that and a little wave, she turned and left the store. Andy stood and watched her until she finally disappeared from view, at which point he made the most urgent purchase call he had ever made in his life...

"Something gnawing at you, son?" Young Bobby asked Andy at their weekly family dinner the next night.

"Huh?"

"If you were any more lost in thought, we'd have to send out a search party," his mother said.

"Oh, it's nothing," Andy said, shaking his head. After a long pause, he finally asked, "Has the shop ever not had something that someone needs?"

Young Bobby stroked his chin. "Well now, let me think... I don't recall a time when it ever did. Edna?"

"There was that time back in aught-nine, when Pee-Wee Watkins came in looking for rat poison."

"Oh right!"

"Asked me for rat poison—no luck. Straight razor—no luck. Rope—no luck."

"Too bad he owned that gas oven—poor man might still be around today if he didn't. But that's a special case, of course: everything him wanting being exactly what he *didn't* need. This customer you had—was he after anything that could do him or someone else any harm?"

"Colored chalk."

"Colored chalk?" His mother chuckled. "I can't imagine much damage can be done with that."

"Maybe the store's protecting the local school kids from being sentence diagrammed to death," Young Bobby quipped.

Edna's eyes lit up. "Say, was it that pretty young teacher who wanted the chalk? The one staying with Irene Detweiler?"

"I think she mentioned something about teaching," Andy muttered, studying his roast chicken with intense interest.

"Young teacher?" Young Bobby asked. "Why, I think I saw her at the market the other day. Awfully pretty."

"Irene says she's smart as a whip. Big reader, too. I believe she said the first thing the girl did after putting down her bags was to run over to the library and get a card and a stack of books."

"Is that right? You know what I've always liked most about books? Talking with other folks about them once I'm done. 'Course, her being new to town, she probably doesn't know many folks at all, let alone ones of the bookish sort..."

"And Meadowbrook can be a bit standoffish at first with new folks."

Growing more uncomfortable by the second, Andy finally had enough. "Okay, I know what you're both trying to do."

Young Bobby and Edna Anderson both feigned confusion. "Doing? Son, we have no idea—" Edna began.

"Look, Mom, she's just a customer—"

"Mmm-hmm."

Andy's face grew red. "I'm just...trying to do a good job running the shop. That's all."

"Mmm-hmm."

"Glad to hear it, son," his father said. "'Course, being a shop-keeper doesn't require a vow of celibacy last time I checked. Well, maybe the Catholic ones do—I never can keep up with what them papists believe in—but a good Methodist like yourself..."

Andy sighed heavily. "Look, after constantly spending four years around other people and doing and seeing things that nobody should have to, I just want a nice, quiet life alone, okay? Besides, I'm not sure that I'm the marrying sort anyway."

Young Bobby chuckled. "'Course you're not, son. No man's the marrying sort...until he meets his match, that is."

"Dad..."

"All right, all right. Listen to the game this afternoon? Hank Wyse was throwing some fire today."

Appreciating the act of conversational mercy, Andy was happy to spend the rest of their meal talking about the Chicago Cubs, Jack Benny, and other trifles. Ruth Thatcher and the mystery of the shop's failure were not mentioned again, although they were much on his mind that night as he lay in bed waiting unsuccessfully for sleep to come.

———

At the end of the week, Andy was relieved to find a case of colored chalk amongst the goods delivered that Friday afternoon. After shelving a few boxes in an empty space on one of the lower shelves in the middle of the store, he placed a box under the checkout counter, steeled himself, and picked up the phone. He was both relieved and disappointed when Mrs. Detweiler told him that Ruth Thatcher was out, but that she would pass word along when she returned.

The next morning, with the store wireless playing at a much lower volume than usual, Andy sat straight in his chair with a copy of *The Collected Works of William Blake* in his hands, which he was having a great deal of trouble focusing on. Every time his eyes detected the faintest of movements, he looked expectantly toward the door. As the time dragged on to noon, Andy began to despair that he wouldn't see Ruth until sometime the following week. When the snowy-haired little man who was Meadowbrook's mayor came in hoping to find a new thermos, Andy welcomed the distraction.

As he helped the mayor search, a voice sang out from the front, "Hello, shopkeep? I believe I have an order in."

Andy whipped around, knocking a good number of spools of thread to the ground as he did so, and found a smiling Ruth Thatcher waiting at the front of the store, both hands holding the top of her purse and one eyebrow arched. Without turning to look at the mayor, Andy muttered, "Um...Sorry. I need to..."

"I can see that you do," the mayor chuckled, giving him a little shove.

"Hi," Andy said, acting as cool and collected as possible, which was to say not very cool or collected at all. He walked behind the counter. "Your chalk came this morning. In fact, I put a box of it aside for you just down—"

But as he looked at the top shelf under the counter, there was no chalk to be found. Andy's eyes widened and he crouched down, searching all three shelves frantically for the now-missing box. "I—I'm really sorry," he stammered. "I swear I put some aside for you."

"A likely story," Ruth replied as she peered down at him. Catching his reflection in her spectacles, Andy got a good sense of exactly how ridiculous he looked crouched down behind on the floor of the shop, so he stood up quickly, banging his shoulder hard on the countertop as he did so.

Ruth grimaced. "That looked painful."

"It was," Andy agreed as he turned and headed toward the aisle where he had shelved the boxes of chalk just hours ago. "Okay, I don't know what happened to the box I set aside for you, but I did put ten whole boxes of colored chalk right...here?"

There on the shelf where the chalk should have been was an empty space.

Ruth walked up next to him. "So you sold out already? Awfully high demand for colored chalk in this town, it seems."

"I...I have more in the back!" Andy held up a finger. "Wait right here!"

But his dash to the back, like all of his efforts, ended in frustration. No boxes of colored chalk nor even the big shipping box they had all come in were there. Andy groaned, leaned against the wall, and banged his head against it, making his horn-rimmed glasses slide down his nose.

"Stock issues?" a deep voice rumbled. Over the tops of his glasses, Andy could see the thin figure of the mayor standing in the doorway. In his blurry, uncorrected vision, the diminutive man rather resembled a plaid and denim-clad Q-Tip.

"Yeah," Andy sighed, pushing up his glasses. "You know how this shop is, Mayor."

"Oh, I should say I do," the mayor agreed, and he wasn't just being polite. There were few secrets, magical or otherwise, in Meadowbrook that Mayor Jonathan Robinson wasn't aware of.

"So that young lady out there—"

"The pretty one?"

"Yes. The very pretty one. It won't let me sell her what she needs. Not only did it not cough up some chalk for her when she last came in, but now it's hiding the chalk that I ordered specifically for her."

"Excuse me," inquired a round, tan, bespectacled face as it peeked out from behind the mayor, "but did you just say that the shop was hiding my chalk?"

"Um...uh...well...kind of?"

Ruth's brow furrowed. "*Really?* That's—"

"Odd?" The mayor offered. "Far-fetched? Inconceivable? Beyond belief?"

"Yes," Ruth answered. "And you could throw a few more synonyms on the pile if you want."

The mayor laughed. "Don't encourage me—I might just do that. As for things being beyond belief... Well, I think if you stick with us a while, Miss Thatcher, and keep your eyes open, you'll find that beyond belief is kind of a specialty of our little town. Speaking of which, as mayor, I don't believe I've had the chance to officially welcome you to Meadowbrook. To make up for that, I'd like to treat you to lunch at our best and only establishment of fine dining: The Grey Goose."

Ruth looked to Andy. "Well, I don't know—"

The mayor held up his hands to stop her. "I won't take no for an answer, young lady. And Andy, you'll join us, of course."

"I-I will?"

"Naturally. It's noon. That's your usual lunch hour."

Ruth looked up at him. "Well, I suppose if the mayor insists..."

"Oh, I do, which is about as close to a royal decree as you'll find in these parts." The mayor gestured to the front of the store. "As always, age and wisdom will follow youth and beauty. Hoof it, young'uns."

Andy and Ruth walked a block down Main Street to the sleek chrome and white-painted brick town diner whose red awning declared the place to be The Grey Goose, a name that pre-dated its modern makeover by over thirty years. Once inside, the mayor led them across the black and white checkerboard floor to a red vinyl booth. As soon as the two were seated, the mayor glanced at his watch. His eyes widened in faux surprise.

"Aw, hell! I just remembered I've got to meet with Bill Trainor over at the grain elevator about my soybeans. Sorry to abandon you, but I really can't stay."

Andy's heart dropped. "Oh, well then..."

Andy started to get up, but the mayor put a hand on his shoulder and stopped him. "No, you two stay—I'll tell Claire to put it on my tab. Ruth, I'm sure Andy here can sing Meadowbrook's praises just as well as I could."

Ruth looked from Andy to the mayor and back. "I'm sure you're right."

"Well, there we go then. Andy, do us proud." The mayor gave Andy a slap on the shoulder and a sly wink and left.

"So... I guess it's just the two of us then," Ruth said slowly.

There's that Mona Lisa smile again, Andy thought. "Yeah. Sure looks that way."

Ruth reached across the table and patted his big pale hand with her dainty little one. "Doesn't sound that bad, does it?"

Andy looked down at the hand as it lingered on his. He looked up and smiled a smile that held no mystery, no enigma. "I guess not."

For the next hour, the two talked. Well, Ruth mostly talked—about her hometown of Kaskaskia, her time in college, her plans for her first school year—and Andy mostly listened. When asked about his life, Andy didn't feel there was much to say—his life in Meadowbrook seemed rather dull; his time in the war something he wished to leave over the seas and long in the past—and Ruth, mercifully, didn't press him, instead turning the conversation to favorite authors and radio programs and other topics that Andy only half-focused on, the music of Ruth's voice much more interesting than anything it said.

When their meal was done and pangs of responsibility finally forced Andy to admit to himself that he should probably get back to work, both insisted on picking up the check for the other. An animated discussion about courtesy, hospitality, tradition, and gender equality was eventually settled by the revelation that the mayor, on his way out, had already picked up the tab. With the matter taken care of, Ruth insisted on walking Andy back to the shop. "To protect your safety and honor," she explained before shooting him a dirty look for the loud laugh that had followed.

When they made it back to the shop, the two stopped in front of the door. "Well, I suppose I should let you get back to tending your shop," Ruth said, looking slightly disappointed as she did so.

"I suppose," Andy agreed reluctantly.

"So...I should probably stop back in on Monday?"

"Monday?"

"For my chalk."

"Oh...yes. Absolutely." Andy grinned.

Ruth grinned back. "Do you think the store will let you sell me some then?"

"I guess we'll have to wait and see."

"I guess we will."

Andy watched Ruth walk down the street. When she glanced back to see if he was watching, he didn't bother to pretend that he wasn't and lifted his hand. She gave a little wave then disappeared around the corner.

Andy unlocked the shop, stepped in, and exhaled heavily. He scanned the store, appreciating its wonderful, cluttered glory. "Thanks," he said.

Andy put Jack Teagarden's recording of "S'Wonderful" on the phonograph, grabbed a feather duster, and got to cleaning. It was well-earned, he felt, plus Monday wasn't that far away...

THE FOLLOWING MONDAY, Andy and Ruth spent a good fifteen minutes unsuccessfully searching for colored chalk before giving up and discussing the relative merits of the authors most frequently appearing in *Weird Tales, Amazing Stories,* and *Black Mask.* Tuesday it was ten minutes followed by selections from Andy's record collection. Wednesday, five minutes then the Cubs game on the wireless. Thursday, Friday, and Saturday only the most cursory of searches were made before they settled into the pleasure of each other's company. After two weeks, visits to the shop sometimes lasted until closing time and were often followed by dinners at the Grey Goose, trips to the picture show, checkers or rummy at the local tavern, or nighttime walks out in the country, colored chalk rarely mentioned let alone looked for.

At the very end of August, just before the children of Meadowbrook would be trudging reluctantly back to school, Andy unlocked the door to Anderson's Necessaries and flipped the sign in the window to *Open.* Looking forward to Ruth's daily visit, even though she was getting increasingly anxious as the school year loomed, Andy put a record on the phonograph and began straightening up to the sweet sounds of Washington Phillips strumming his manzarene when he spied something that made him stop in his tracks. There on a shelf just inches above the floor a small, square, multi-colored box sat sandwiched between a model airplane kit and canisters of Dr. Milgrom's Petroleum Udder Balm.

"I'll be damned," Andy muttered. "Colored chalk."

It made sense, he figured. School was due to start in a couple days, so Ruth did actually *need* the chalk now. For a fleeting moment, Andy wondered if this meant that Ruth's visits would soon come to an end. But, no, he knew that while the chalk had been why she had originally come into the store, it was not at all why she had kept coming back.

Andy got down on one knee and picked up the chalk, chuckling at his foolishness. That's when he noticed the small, velvet-covered box that had been hidden behind it. He flipped the lid to look at the gold ring with the very small but well-cut diamond in the middle that he had suspected would be inside.

Behind him, Andy could hear the clicking of women's shoes.

"What are you doing there?" a now-very-familiar and welcome voice asked.

"Just getting something I need." Andy smiled to himself and turned to see Ruth standing with the morning sun shining through the doorway behind her. "Now how about you come over here and save me the trouble of standing up?"

About the Author

Jon Etter is a writer and English instructor living in the American Midwest. His fiction has appeared in a number of different publications, including *The London Journal of Fiction*, *The Singularity*, and the anthology *The Great Tome of Forgotten Relics and Artifacts*. For a full list of his work and where it can be found, visit him on the web at www.jonetter.com.

NO SMALL FAVORS

BY ANNE SKINNER

Lucy Jones sat in her beat-to-hell, gray sedan and stared at the small wooden coin lying on the dashboard. Nothing about this felt real. *Damon must have lied*, she thought. She brushed her blonde hair back from her face and turned off the ignition. As she stared at the dusty tan stucco building, the conversation played back through her mind.

"Anything you want, really," Damon said with an easy smile. His *green eyes sparkled in the reflected light from the bar as he brushed his dark hair away from his handsome face. "Give them this."* He *pressed the token into her palm. "And you can have it."*

"Oh sure, anything I want, for a price, I bet," Lucy giggled. But as *she wrapped her fingers around the coin, the whole idea suddenly felt more plausible. This could be just what she needed.*

When she awoke the next day, hungover and bleary, she decided to throw the coin away. What an idiot, to fall for such a fantastic tale, just because they guy was so good-looking! She felt differently as soon as she swept the coin off the table and into her open palm. He'd given her an extraordinary opportunity, if such a thing existed. It couldn't hurt to just check it out, right? So, she'd driven to the address on the coin and found this place.

It did exist, to her surprise.

She glanced around the shadowed storefront. 603 Pine St., Suite 44A. The plain white letters on the glass displayed the name, Attainment, right above the suite number. Stubby, poorly trimmed hedges lined up in front, bits of paper and windblown detritus stuck in their brambles. Hardly what she'd expected.

"Anything?" she asked as she steadied herself with a hand on a nearby barstool. "Anything I want?"

Damon nodded slowly, the grin never fading from his face.

"Why me? How does it work? This kinda feels like I won the lottery."

"Just go there," he replied. "You'll love it." He wrapped his hand around hers, ignoring her chipped manicure. The coin felt warmer in her grip. The background sounds of people chatting, glassware clinking, and the sports broadcast on the TVs over the bar fell away, taking her doubts with them.

"It sounds amazing," she breathed, looking into his eyes.

"You'll have to go see it," he said. "You deserve this, Lucy, you really do. In fact, there's no one in the whole world who deserves this more than you do."

The world shimmered and shifted a little—must have been the booze—and she nodded in agreement.

Sitting in the car, Lucy chewed at the corner of her mouth. She'd know if it was a scam. If they asked her for money or offered her a resort trip if she'd only sit through a timeshare presentation, she'd know it ended up too good to be true. The worst that could happen would be that she got back in her car and drove away with a story to tell the girls the next time they went out for cocktails.

Besides, maybe Damon would be here.

An off-key, electronic chime greeted her as she stepped into the lobby of Attainment. Smooth jazz played quietly overhead and the room smelled of artificial lavender. She walked up to the curved reception desk and noticed the scuff marks on the front and the scratches on the surface. Everything in the room looked worn. Tired.

She frowned.

Before she could ring the bell, a skinny man in a threadbare cardigan stepped into the room.

"Oh!" He jumped, startled. "You're early!"

"I am?"

"You're Miss Jones, right?" The man tilted his head and slightly greasy, combed-over hair fell into his face. His accent reminded her of something, but she couldn't put a finger on it.

"Uh, yeah." Her eyes went wide with surprise. "How did you know my name? Did Damon say I'd come by? I didn't have an appointment or anything." Lucy took a small step back toward the door. "Should I have made one?"

The clerk looked her up and down with muddy hazel eyes like a bird sizing up some new curiosity. "Oh, no, not at all! I heard you'd likely be in around noon. No trouble, though, no trouble." He wrung his gnarled hands and smiled, the expression stretching unnaturally across his weathered features.

"But, I..." She swallowed, confused. "I never told Damon I'd come here." She took another step backward. "This is a mistake. I should just go." Lucy turned and hurried for the door.

And nearly smacked into the man.

She barely halted herself in time.

"Oh!" Lucy gasped, close enough to smell the faint odor that surrounded the small man in an invisible fog. He smelled of vegetation just on the edge of rot, of gradual decay.

How had he—

"Oh no, don't go." His yellowed, watery eyes searched her face, the horrible grin still in place. "This is a very singular opportunity, Miss Jones. What we at Attainment offer is completely unlike anything you'll find anywhere else." He gently rested his gnarled fingers on Lucy's shoulders and turned her, guiding her toward the desk. "Yes, quite unique indeed. Please, won't you join me in the Room? I'm certain you're very curious to see what we have in store for someone as special as yourself."

Lucy did want to see what the Room held, very much. She

found herself relaxing, smiling back at him, and let herself be lead. The way he said its name, she knew the Room must be important. Curiosity gnawed at her.

A small part of her, growing more distant by the moment, screamed she should leave. That tiny part of her wailed and protested and begged her to run, to get in her car and leave. Right. Goddamn. Now!

But she kept walking.

They reached the door he'd come out of, the only other door in the lobby.

A dwindling part of her sobbed for the exit not so far behind her.

The small man opened the door and motioned for Lucy to walk through. She found herself disappointed. She couldn't recall what she'd expected, but the Room, in all its importance and glory, contained the same worn carpet as the lobby, the same unsteady fluorescent lighting, the same beige walls. Only a small wooden table that had seen better days and a dumpy leather recliner awaited her.

Her escort followed her into the Room and closed the door before he held out a hand for her to shake. "Where are my manners? My name is Roger Thornbrook, and I am the Concierge." He pronounced his title with the same emphasis as the Room, with the same satisfaction and pride.

Lucy shook his proffered hand, finding it much warmer than she'd thought. The tiny voice of protest in her head all but disappeared.

"I'm very pleased to meet you, Roger," she replied, the words tasting surprisingly genuine on her tongue. "I'm—"

Roger cut her off. "Oh," he said with a knowing smile, waving his hands, "we know who you are. We know exactly who you are, Miss Jones." He gestured to the table. "Won't you join me for a moment? There's a tiny bit of paperwork we must attend to first."

At the table, Lucy found a large sheet of paper with ornate, scrolling lettering. She brushed it with one finger. Not paper. Something else. Something thicker and far more formal. An actual feather quill pen lay beside the paper.

She smiled again. Such niceties felt so fitting for the Room.

"This is our standard contract, Miss Jones," Roger explained. "If you would, please look it over and then sign at the bottom." He extended a withered digit toward a line across the bottom.

Lucy briefly considered simply signing the sheet without a second glance, but the tiny voice in her head finally screamed loudly enough for her to take notice.

She took the sheet from Roger.

The contents of the page swam before her eyes. Elaborate script spelled out words she'd never seen. Great flourishes of ink marked out terms and conditions, with a line at the bottom for her signature.

"What am I signing?" she asked, taking the quill from Roger and squinting again at the page.

"Oh, nothing too out of the ordinary," he answered with a dismissive wave of one hand. "For the insignificant price of one year of your life, the Room," he paused to gesture around to the four walls surrounding them, "will give you, the undersigned, an entire year of bliss. Whatever you want."

"A year of my life?" She stopped short with the quill above the parchment.

"You won't miss it," he said with what, on another face, could have been a reassuring smile, "A year of your heart's desire should more than compensate you for a year of trouble, struggle, and hardship."

The room swam and shifted, just a tiny bit. It felt a little like being drunk, but only for the barest moment.

"I give the Room a year of problems and difficulties and it gives me a year where I'm happy?" She grinned. The voice in the back of her mind didn't grin; it sobbed and begged her to run out of there as fast as she could. "Am I just gone for a year?"

"No, of course not. People would notice such a thing," he

answered. "Through the generosity of the Room, you'll be back here having only lost a half hour. You'll still be able to go grocery shopping tonight when you get home."

"Sounds like a good deal to me," she said. She felt giddy, and laughter bubbled up from deep within her. She'd finally caught a break. The voice screamed in panic from a faraway place, but every minute she stood in the room made it easier and easier to ignore.

She smiled at Roger and signed her name.

"Excellent," he breathed, a sour odor flowing out of his mouth as his lips stretched back to show more of his yellow teeth. "Please, Miss Jones, have a seat, won't you?"

"So, how does this work?" she asked as she leaned back in the recliner. The leather had split on the armrests, making it uncomfortable to rest her hands.

"Most find they are hideously dehydrated when they return from their year," Roger explained as he handed her a glass of water. "I would advise that you drink half of it before you go and the remainder upon your return. Drink it slowly, and consider carefully your desire."

While she sipped, she thought about what she wanted. She could wish to be beautiful. She thought about all the hours spent trying in vain to live up to the pictures she saw in magazines and online. She hated her figure, her hair, and her skin. Exercise took too much effort, though, and beauty routines took too much time. She thought about all the times she went out with her friends and ended up the only one going home alone. No one asked her to dance or bought her drinks. She even tried online dating a few times. None of the guys looked half as good as their profile pictures, and she guessed they felt the same about her, since they never called for a second date.

She thought about wishing to be extra-smart or extra-talented.

In school, she ranked right in the middle of the pack, always just high enough to move up to the next grade. Her teachers told her she could excel with some effort, if she just studied and applied herself. Studying took a lot of work. She saw her friends pushing themselves to do as well as they could in their classes and extra-curricular activities. They looked so exhausted at the end of each term. She envied their passion, but never found anything that unlocked that much desire within her.

She could have all those things, without breaking a sweat. If she wished for unlimited wealth, she could buy everything she lacked, or at least pay enough to compensate for it. Every beauty product and style guru could be at her beck and call. She could buy a huge company instead of working for one. With one wish, she could fulfill every desire she'd ever had, and then some.

She grinned, giddy with anticipation, and took her last sip. The water was sweet and cooling and tasted better than she thought water could taste. The Room shimmered a little and she assumed she'd needed the hydration more than she realized.

"I know what I want," she said.

He nodded and smiled a too-wide, too-stiff smile, took the glass back from her, and set it on the shabby, wooden table with her contract.

"Very good," he replied. "Lean back in the chair, close your eyes, and concentrate on that desire burning in your heart. Once you've got it firmly in mind, the Room will do the rest. You will know when modifications are complete. It's all very intuitive; I am certain you'll have no trouble, as exceptional a young lady as you are."

Her mind focused and her heart set, she leaned back in the recliner and smiled at Roger. Her eyelids felt suddenly quite heavy and she found them nearly impossible to keep open. She started to say something, but Roger hushed her with a cold, clammy finger pressed to her lips.

"I know, you're wonderfully grateful and this is such a lovely opportunity. It always is. Quiet now. Shhhh, close those eyes, and get to your reward."

The tiny voice of protest disappeared down a black hole in the back of her mind. Nothing about the Room's gift troubled her anymore. Comfortable and confident, Lucy let her eyes fall closed and drifted off quicker than she ever had before.

LUCY'S EYES popped open and swept the Room.

No one. She sat alone.

Silence echoed in the musty, swampy Room. Lucy wrinkled her nose. It smelled like damp wool and rotting wood.

Pulling hard on the lever of the recliner, Lucy sat up. The pronounced cracks in the leather caught at her sleeves. To one side sat the little wooden table, a layer of dust on the top of it. Her contract, the quill, and her water glass were nowhere to be seen.

The lighting fixture over the door flickered disconcertingly in the rather dim Room. When had it gotten so dark?

"Hello?" she called out as she stood. "Roger? Is anyone here?"

No reply.

She stood, swiped up her purse, and stepped cautiously toward the door. The carpet squished wetly under her little black flats. "Ew, gross!" she exclaimed, wrinkling her nose. She hoped the wet wouldn't ruin them. They were cheap but comfortable. With a horrified thought, she checked the bottom of her bag, sighing with relief when her hand found the bottom of it dry.

"Roger? Concierge?" she called again. Still no reply.

She reached for the door handle, but at her slightest touch, the door creaked slowly open. She stepped through into the lobby and glanced around.

Worn carpeting and a few scraps of paper greeted her. The desk and chairs were gone. Someone had taped a note and an envelope on the inside of the front door.

She walked over, peeled it off, and read.

Lock the door behind you and throw the key into the trees. Enjoy yourself; we'll see you in a year.

A key waited for her inside the envelope. Glancing from it to the note, she shrugged.

"Nothing else to do but go. I guess." Lucy dumped the key into her palm and stepped outside. "I must've slept for hours." She rubbed her stiff neck. "Long enough for them to clean the place out, at least." She locked the door and reached for her own keys. "So weird. Well, I guess I'm not out anything except some time."

Unless...

The tiny voice in her head woke up and started shouting all sorts of unsavory possibilities at her.

Oh no.

What if it *was* an elaborate prank? Lucy's mind reeled at the possibilities. She pictured Roger standing over her unconscious form with a sinister grin, camera phone in hand, drool running down the side of her face. He could have made her do all kinds of things without her knowledge or consent. Had he danced her around the room like a puppet? Had he undressed her and posed her doing god-knows-what? She could practically hear the insipid sitcom sound-track and see people all over the world watching and laughing at the latest upload from Roger's feed. They'd tell all their friends to check out the video of the stupid whore who believed some magic Room would grant her a wish. Tears of humiliation stung the corners of her eyes.

Lucy frantically fumbled in her bag for her keys. She had to get home, *right now*. She had to assess what sort of shape she was in, and probably call the cops.

No keys.

"No!" she howled. When she raised her head to bawl to the sky, she discovered she couldn't find her beat-up, gray sedan either.

Oh *GOD*, Roger had raped and robbed her!

All the strength went out of her legs and she dropped to the pavement. Tears poured down her face.

"How could I be so stupid?" She dug around in her handbag for her phone. She could call her sister, Lisa. Lisa would come and pick her up, and not ask too many humiliating questions. Lisa wouldn't judge her and, most importantly, she wouldn't tell their mother.

Finally, her shaking fingers wrapped around a mobile device in the very bottom of her bag.

Pulling it out, she realized it wasn't her phone.

Lucy stared, dumbstruck.

Her phone had a cracked screen that she couldn't quite afford to repair and a tattered case she hadn't bothered to replace. This phone appeared to be the newer model she'd covetously stalked online. The flawless screen shone in the sun. The pretty, pink leather case sparkled with pink glitter; exactly what she'd have gotten if she could.

Her brows furrowed as she stared. It might not have been hers, but it *was* what she'd wanted.

She pressed her thumb onto the button, just to see what would happen.

And nearly dropped the thing when it unlocked at her touch.

"Holy cow," she breathed as she scrolled through its contents. It *had* to be her phone. It held pictures of her with her friends, in places she didn't remember, eating meals she hadn't ever tasted. It featured fancy cocktails from expensive bars and a selfie in a blue convertible with a tan leather interior.

Just like the car parked next to the spot she'd left her sedan in earlier.

She stood up and brushed off her rear end. The tears and worry dissipated quickly.

Lucy wandered over to the shiny midlife crisis and tried the driver's side handle.

It opened.

A giant grin split her face from ear to ear as she slid into the seat, which she found already adjusted to fit her perfectly.

Why wouldn't it be? she thought. *It's my car, after all.*

She reached back into her handbag, and this time pulled out a fancy remote keyfob. Of course. She'd been looking for her giant, clumsy key ring before, not something so sleek as this. She pressed the button next to the steering wheel and the car roared to life.

She couldn't stifle her excited giggles.

The GPS display in the center console lit up and directed her to an unfamiliar address. She consulted her new phone, and discovered that particular address listed as *Home*.

Definitely not the third floor studio apartment she'd rented before now. This place was out in the suburbs. The really nice suburbs.

While the engine rumbled like a happy panther, she went through the contents of her handbag and emerged with a wallet. Instead of the worn-out Louis Vuitton knock-off, she found she'd traded up again.

Lucy hadn't known that real leather smelled so nice.

She opened it and discovered unfamiliar cards from unfamiliar banks. It might be well worth her while to stop by one on the way 'home'. With that, she updated the GPS and headed out, top down and stereo up.

A girl could get used to this.

***

HALF AN HOUR LATER, she drove down the road to her new home with a satchel beside her. The bank clerk hadn't been able to give her exactly what she'd asked for, but he'd given her a solid alternative. How was she supposed to know they wouldn't really have a million dollars in cash in their vault? The clerk had assured her, with an amazingly stoic expression, that she wouldn't know the difference between that and ten thousand dollars if she wanted to roll around in it. He did, however, advise her to shower afterward.

She pulled into a long driveway that arced in front of an enormous, Mediterranean style mansion with particularly and painstakingly groomed shaped shrubs and perfectly green grass in front. Just the sort of house she had pored over lovingly in magazines.

As soon as she shut the car door, she heard a small dog barking inside the house. She knew immediately what that dog would look like. She'd always wanted a little, fancy, fluffy, white dog. One of those that had to get groomed all the time, and that people carried around with them in handbags. She knew it would have a pink rhinestone collar, too.

She took her time climbing the brick steps to the front door. She let her fingers trace along the smooth wooden railing. *This is all mine. Everything. Every bit of it. For an entire year.* She giggled again, giddy with the thought. No more secretarial work. No getting up early to take the bus on the days she couldn't afford the gas. The new possibilities open to her dizzyingly whirled through her mind.

Her hand trembled as she reached for the door knob. The little dog kept barking as she pushed the door open. She stepped through the door and into a new life.

CHAPTER Six

ELEVEN MONTHS, three weeks, and six days later, Lucy sat at a table in a sidewalk cafe in Paris. The tiny, white dog, which did indeed have a pink rhinestone collar, napped in its carrier on the seat beside her. She held her phone in her hand and scrolled through the pictures of the previous year. She saw selfies taken in front of the pyramids in Egypt and the Forbidden City in Beijing. She grinned with pride as she scrolled through the section with the pictures of the house she bought her mother. She blushed a little when she saw the shirtless photos of her boyfriend's perfect abs. She looked up from her phone and gazed at Aiden over her cup as she sipped her perfectly prepared latte. The morning sun glinted off his dark hair and his olive skin radiated a warmth all its own as he bought flowers from a street vendor. Everything fell into place exactly how she had wished. She sighed contentedly.

Aidan walked back to the table, smiling at her as he handed her the bouquet and sat down.

"Oh, they're lovely!" she exclaimed and held them to her face.

"Not nearly as lovely as you," he replied, taking her free hand in his. "Darling, there's something I've wanted to ask..." He gazed earnestly into her eyes. But something he saw there filled his face with horror.

"Wha—" she began, her pulse pounding in her ears drowned out the noise of the Paris streets.

The world suddenly went gray, then black, and she felt herself fall backward. Time abruptly stopped for Lucy Jones.

UNTIL SHE OPENED HER EYES. Instead of Aiden's beautiful gaze of love and concern, however, the world snapped into focus centered on Roger, the Concierge.

Aiden, her dog, the sights and sounds and smells of Paris had all vanished, replaced with Roger's greasy smile, flickering fluorescents, and the stale, artificial scent of lavender.

Lucy's hands gripped the cracked leather of the decrepit recliner as muffled soprano saxophone covers of 80's hits assaulted her ears.

She was back in the Room.

"No! No, it can't be over! My time's not up yet!" she screamed as she fought to get the chair upright. "No, please! Put it all back! Put me back! I swear to god, I will sue the holy hell out of this place if you don't put me back right now!" She kicked her legs and managed to knock the footrest down so the chair ratcheted her forward. She bolted to her feet and grabbed Roger by the lapels of his threadbare cardigan.

"I'm so sorry, Miss Jones." Roger gently pried her fingers loose and took a step back. "I'm afraid that's not how this works. You signed a contract, you see. Did we not fulfill our portion of the bargain?" He blinked watery eyes in what she could only assume was feigned innocence.

"But, I want more! I need more!" She stepped forward to fill the gap where he'd stood. "Give me another contract! I'll sign it right now! I'll give you all the years you want, just put me back there!"

"Miss Jones, please, calm yourself. Why don't you try going back to your old life for a little while? You've only been gone from it for half an hour, after all. Come back in a week, and perhaps we can negotiate something for you." Roger's soothing tones echoed weirdly in her ears and her panic subsided a little.

"A week? Here?" She bit her lip. "But what happens there? How long will they think I'm gone? What happened when I left?"

"That all depends, I suppose," he contemplated. "If we can work something out for you in a week, you'll go back right where you left. If we can't, then that reality will have never existed at all, will it?"

"But I *can't* wait a week!" Tears threatened, but she halted them at a sudden thought. Roger implied she'd have to consider whether or not she wanted to return. Silly man. "I don't have to take that long! I already know I want to go back! Isn't there something I can sign right now? Please!" She choked on the last word as unbidden tears stung the corners of her eyes. Her lip quivered as she whispered, "Anything. I will do *anything*."

If her vision hadn't been clouded by tears and panic, if her heart hadn't been so focused on the fear of that loss, she might have seen the greedy glint in Roger's eye or caught the smirk curling up the edges of his mouth. But her senses were occupied, so all she heard was his laugh, which she mistook for kindness.

"Anything, Miss Jones? Would you truly do anything to return to that life?" Roger's voice sounded deeper and richer than it had before.

Involuntarily, Lucy took a step back. Her eyes widened and she looked him up and down.

Roger's presence felt suddenly different. He straightened to his full height and stopped hunching forward which had masked his broad, strong shoulders. The wateriness left his eyes entirely.

A predatory air hung about him.

Instead of turning and running, instead of backing slowly out the front door, getting in her car, and getting away from there as quickly as she could, Lucy took a deep breath and steeled herself.

"Yes, anything. Get me back there. Now."

The fluorescent lights of the Room flared brighter. The lavender scent that permeated everything grew stronger, more nuanced.

Lucy glanced around in sudden alarm and saw the leather on the recliner had smoothed itself out, the cracks and tears gone, the sagging seat full and factory-new. Roger's grin held entirely too many teeth when she looked back at him.

"Well, if you're that desperate, Miss Jones, I am certain we can arrange *something*." His words curled around her like oily smoke. He gestured to the small table.

Another sheet of parchment and a quill sat there as solidly as if they'd been there all along. A small bottle sat beside the contract.

At first, Lucy thought it must be ink. Maybe Roger would write a new contract right here in front of her. As she approached, she realized that the parchment contained the same legalese she'd seen before.

The bottle glittered in the light, drawing her eye to it again and again. She reached for it.

Roger grabbed her wrist before she could touch it. He moved faster than she thought possible.

"Tsk. Not yet. Not until we finalize the details." The too-stretched smile snapped back on his face, but Lucy didn't remember his teeth looking quite so sharp and white. He handed her the parchment.

"To summarize, Miss Jones, as I am certain you do not want to linger upon the details, the Room will return you to the life that you have experienced for the past year, entirely intact, without any disruption whatsoever to that lifestyle. All that the Room requires of you is a small favor." Roger paused, then confided, "In fact, I am certain you will find it is a trifling thing when compared to the reward you would reap."

Lucy licked her lips. Her mouth had gone dry and her heart beat faster in her chest. *Yes! Just one small favor and she went back. Forever. Easy.* Relief flooded her.

"What's the favor?" she asked, reaching for the quill to sign the new contract. It didn't matter what the Concierge told her she'd have to do, not really. She blew on the fresh ink of her signature and reached again for the glittering bottle.

This time, Roger didn't stop her.

The light played off the glass like an aurora borealis, and the liquid inside swirled on its own. It was one of the most beautiful things she'd ever seen.

"I can keep this, right?"

"That pretty bottle is part of the favor, Miss Jones," Roger said, glancing over the parchment to make sure everything was in order.

She started to pull out the cork.

Roger raised one hand. "Ah, no, Miss Jones, not yet. The liquid inside is extremely rare and exceedingly difficult to procure. The Room requires you to put it to a rather specific purpose." The too-stretched smile grew even wider. "It only requires that you make a simple delivery."

"I don't know if I can give it to anybody else," she breathed. Lucy stared at the bottle, mesmerized by the swirling and shifting colors. It would look so pretty in her living room...

"Oh, but you must, Miss Jones. I can see how much you want to get back to luxury and excess. You want to be back in that sidewalk cafe with your dog and your fiancé."

"He's not my fiancé," she muttered, still staring at the bottle.

"Not yet." Roger clucked his tongue against his teeth. "Don't you know what he planned to ask you right before you returned to the Room? Can't you imagine him now, leaning over your incapacitated form, wondering what's happened to you? Your poor dog must be barking like mad with panic."

Lucy chewed her lip. She did want to get back to her life. Her *real* life. She wanted comfort and ease. And she deserved it, didn't she?

She didn't even know this man, so what harm would it really do? And the bottle was so pretty. The liquid couldn't be anything bad. Attainment had been so very kind to her, hadn't it? It gave her everything she wanted, even more than she'd thought she wanted. It was only fair. And it really was such a small favor.

———

LATER THAT EVENING, Lucy walked into one of the more exclusive downtown clubs. She wasn't back to her life yet, but the Room had provided her with what she'd needed to accomplish her evening's task. She could never have done it with the resources she had in her old life.

The Concierge had given her suitable clothing and a handbag full of money. Just for the evening, he'd said. Sort of like Cinderella, if she didn't accomplish tonight what she had promised the Room, the clothes and cash would disappear and she'd be stuck here, so she better not get any ideas about backing out and just running off with the money.

"Um, no, I don't have a reservation, but I think you can squeeze me in," she said to the enormous, hairy bouncer at the door. She discreetly palmed him a crisp, new one hundred dollar bill. Not her money, after all. Might as well spend it. She gave him her sweetest smile.

He glanced down at the bill in his hand and raised an eyebrow. He grunted something and unclipped the rope for her, quickly waving her through.

She nodded at him, satisfied as she glided past. Living with fabulous wealth for a year had taught her a few things.

The instructions the Room had given her still reverberated in her head, loud enough to drown out the thumping bass emanating from the speakers all around the place. She walked straight to the bar and waved for the bartender's attention. As the man leaned over, she asked him a few questions, yelling to make herself heard.

The bartender grinned and pointed to a table in the far corner, partially concealed by elegant velvet drapes.

Lucy nodded her thanks and headed over.

She wove her way across a crowded dance floor, dodging sweaty, lean bodies. Colored lights pulsed in time to the music, crafted specifically by a young man in a gray hoodie showcased on the stage behind stacks of equipment.

The corner table came into view. Three men in well-tailored suits sat together, watching the pulsing throng of humanity as they sipped short glasses of dark liquor.

Lucy assumed scotch or bourbon. Certainly nothing like her favored fanciful cocktails.

The large blonde man with the crooked nose at the end of the booth made eye contact with her and smiled. He waved her over to their table. Lucy slid into the booth beside him.

"You must be my contact," the man said. His piercing blue eyes roved over her body in a way that made her want to crawl away and vomit.

His friends, all in similar pinstripes, with slicked back brown hair, leered at her, smiling with thin, wet lips.

Lucy suddenly wanted nothing more than to run. Nothing, except to return to her real life. She only had to do this one small favor.

"I am," she replied, swallowing hard and shoving down her fear and loathing. "Roger said you'd expect me." She tightened her grip on her handbag, careful to not crush the pretty little bottle contained within.

"Right. Very good." The words oozed out of his mouth. The men beside him grunted agreement, lecherous smiles never fading from their faces. Her contact reached up and lifted her chin with one ice-cold finger. A ragged fingernail poked at the soft tissue under her jaw. "Such a good, pretty girl," he said, his head turning this way and that, continuing his inspection.

The echo of his words, murmured by his companions, made her think of a flock of scavenger birds cawing and mimicking. She hoped they did not consider her to be the dead or dying creature that would furnish their next meal.

"I... I'm sorry, I didn't catch your name," she said to the man next to her as she shifted a few inches away from him.

"No names, pet," he purred. "Not how we do business. Wouldn't want you running about telling everyone, would we?" He drew out the last two words, his mouth inches from her face with his fetid breath puffing directly into her nostrils with every syllable.

"Oh, I won't say anything to anyone," she assured them, forcing a smile onto her face. "In fact, after this, I'll be so far gone from here, it'll be like I'm in another world completely."

He laughed appreciatively. "That's always the way! It's how this works. Has to be. The Room plans it well. Gives us what we need so we can give it what it needs. Enough palaver, pretty girl. Down to it. Do you have it? Did you bring me the lovely little bottle?" His eyes glittered with unfathomable desire. His tongue flickered over his crooked, yellow teeth.

"What does it do?" she asked, eaten alive with curiosity. "How does me bringing this to you give the Room something it needs? You could just as easily go pick it up from the Concierge yourself."

"Suddenly so curious about the whys and hows." He clucked his tongue and shook his head. "Every question you ask, every moment you hesitate, it's another moment you're not back there, where everything is perfect."

She chewed the inside of her lip. Still. Knowing couldn't hurt, could it? She would be gone in a moment, and this world wouldn't be any of her concern anymore.

She had to know. Lucy's lips parted.

"Don't furrow those pretty brows, girlie," the Brit cooed. "I'll tell you. Not that you can do anything about it. All you have to do is hand me that bottle." The lights inside the club glinted off his too-wide, yellow grin. The other men chuckled beside him.

Lucy clicked open the clasp of her handbag and drew out the opalescent bottle. She gazed at it as its warm weight sat in her palm.

The swirling pulled at her, hypnotized her. She had half a mind to keep it. Lucy moved to put it back in her purse.

But.

Aiden waited for her. That perfect life waited for her. With the resources she had there, she'd surely be able to find a similar trinket.

With a sigh, she handed it over.

He swept it out of her hand and cradled it like a child.

The other men crowded closer to him.

He held it close to his face and gazed at it lovingly.

She thought for a moment that he might kiss it.

"Such a good girl you are, dear," he murmured, eyes locked on the bottle. After several hard blinks and a small shake of the head, he eventually managed to turn his attention back to Lucy. "You want to know what it is, love? What swirls so prettily in this tiny bottle?"

Wordlessly, Lucy nodded.

"This," he said, "is a year. Your year, actually."

"My what?" she asked confused. "What do you mean, it's my year?"

"The first bargain you struck with the Room, remember?"

She stared at the bottle, lips slightly parted.

"You do remember!" he continued with a chortle. "Well, we have a deal of our own with Attainment. The Room gives us the years of the short-sighted folk like yourself who are willing to trade the days you think are so far away for pleasures and delights now. You agree to give a year and the Room gives you everything you desire."

Her eyes widened. Her nose picked up a faint tinge of sulphur in the air.

"Do you have any idea how many hopes and dreams are in that year? How many perfectly good things you'd never remember anyway because the bad things seem to outweigh them so vividly?" He paused to uncork the bottle and swirled the contents under his nose like perfume or a particularly good bottle of wine. "This would have been the year your sister finished her degree." He sniffed again. "And your mother paid off the house. She broke her hip that year, too. But you met her nurse and he was wonderful. You bonded with him while you watched her mend." He sipped at the bottle. He leaned in and whispered to her conspiratorially, "I think he was the one, if you want my opinion. So patient and kind." He shrugged. "That's just the highlight reel. So many small, lovely things, too. It really was an excellent year."

She stared at him in disbelief.

"We'll consume your freely given gift and savor every last second of it. And when we're done, we'll get to work consuming this, your old world."

"*What?* You'll what?"

"Consume this world." Every clipped syllable felt like a punch in the gut.

"Why?" Her heart beat rabbit-fast in her chest. Surely that was a euphemism. "What? How? Wouldn't that would destroy you, too?"

"Never mind the *how*, girl," he said. "Attainment needs material to make new worlds for its customers, doesn't it? And a demon needs to eat, doesn't he? The Room, you insipid mortal, isn't in this world. It isn't in any world. It's between. So it's safe. It's a way to all the many worlds that *could be*. My friends and I need to eat to survive, but how to choose the worlds?" He sighed, overdramatic. "But then we hit on an idea. Why not let the sheep choose the method of their slaughter? One lucky, little duck in each world gets picked to be the Beginning and the End, the Alpha and the Omega."

The other men that Lucy knew weren't really men at all laughed. Not a chuckle like they had before. Full-throated belly laughs came from the other side of the table.

She stared at them, unable to move, barely able to blink and breathe.

"The Room being in between is why we can't go there. But," he grinned and poked her in the center of her chest, "you *can*. All you need is a little motivation and you're handing over years left and right. You silly creatures even bring your discarded years to us without any fuss! It's the perfect arrangement, really."

Her mind reeled. For her perfect life, she sacrificed an entire *world*. "B–but," she stammered, "what happens to everyone here?"

"It will be as though they never existed. This world, this time-line, this strand of reality; all gone. Entirely."

Tears stung the corners of her eyes. "No..." she croaked.

"It's already done. Bargained and paid for." He drew up short and stared into her face. "Come now. None of that." He dabbed at her eyes with a monogrammed silk handkerchief. "You get to go on to your perfect life, your perfect world. Everyone there is safe. They'll never know how many thousands of versions of themselves have been erased from existence as we work our way through the multiverse."

"It's not fair!" she sniffled.

"Nothing is ever fair," he retorted, handing her his glass of dark liquor. "Take a sip of this and be on your way. I tire of explaining the way of the multiverse to lesser beings. Besides, you have a whole lovely new life to get back to. I'm feeling generous, so I will give you a full thirty minutes to get back to the Room and be on your merry. Now, off you pop!"

Automatically. Lucy sipped as directed.

The liquor tasted like sunlight and clean, fresh cotton.

It definitely wasn't scotch or bourbon. It coated the whole of her mouth and throat with a curious, comforting warmth as it went down.

The conversation went a bit fuzzy. She wondered why she got so upset. She had given the bottle to the men, who'd turned out to be so nice, and now she got to go live her life.

Lucy handed back the tumbler of liquor, thanked the men, and made her way out to the car she knew would be waiting to whisk her back to the Room.

The lights of the city passed by the car window in a blur as she watched, contentment swelling within her. The car pulled up in front of the Room exactly twenty five minutes after she'd left the club. She couldn't quite remember why that felt significant, but she was in such a hurry to get back to her new life that she didn't give it further thought.

Roger the Concierge waited for her by the reception desk in the lobby. The too-thin smile spread across his face and he stretched out his arms toward her to greet her.

"That's a good girl, miss," he said as he warmly put one arm around her shoulders. "Let's hurry and get you back to where you should be." He gently but firmly led her toward the door of the Room.

From behind, Lucy heard a faint rumble and many cracks, like distant thunder. The lights flickered a little and she saw ripples in a coffee cup sitting on the desk. She tried to turn around to see what had caused the commotion, but Roger held her fast.

"It's just a little rain," he hissed in her ear. "Nothing you should worry about."

It hadn't looked like rain on her ride back, but she felt like she couldn't argue the point. Thunderstorms popped up. It happened. And anyway, she had somewhere to be.

SHE WOKE with Aiden's beautiful face staring down at her, furrowed brows and concerned eyes taking him from handsome to drop dead gorgeous. When he saw her blink her eyes and wake, his smile returned like the sun coming out from behind a cloud.

"What happened?" she asked as he helped her back into her chair.

The small crowd of onlookers that had gathered began to dissipate.

She recognized Fluff's frantic barks, so she took him out of the carrier to cradle and coo soothingly.

"You fainted," Aiden told her. "I'd just sat down and your eyes rolled up in your head and you passed out. Are you all right? How do you feel?"

"I'm fine," she replied, gazing at him with a smile, stroking the fluffy head of her now-calm dog. "Everything is absolutely perfect."

About the Author

Aided by a tenuous grip on reality and copious amounts of coffee, Anne writes very short fiction about monsters and men. When she's not torturing characters, she's spoiling her dogs, playing video games or reading.

WALKER BETWEEN THE WORLDS

BY ASHLEIGH GAUCH

How DO I describe the sound of wet earth hitting a coffin lid? It's a thudding sound, but soft, like shuffling feet. What matters isn't the sound but the feeling, the way my gut snakes itself around my lungs and stifles my breath. The way I press my arms under my back to keep from clawing at the lid. The way my lungs ache from smothered screams.

I deserve this. I took everything from Aria and must pay by rescuing the piece of her soul my negligence allowed Ta'xit to steal. She lies dormant in a Seattle hospital, with the greatest medical care Western science can offer, but it's for naught unless I act. Even then...

I have to save her from my folly. I owe her that much, for her loyalty and kindness, her long-suffering faith in me.

The sound of burial grows distant.

The scent of varnish and fresh satin mingles with sweat and fear. Whether Rowan digs me up or lets me rot, I'm grateful she allowed me to redeem myself. Old Ones are far less forgiving.

Light from the anemic sunset fades. Darkness smothers me. Lungs work mechanically; thundering heart drowns out sound. The only voices I'll hear from now on are the spirits that visit me, if they show. I pray they, too, will forgive me.

My fingers shake, thoughts race as I reach for the canteen containing the sacred herbs. Mugwort and sage, mixed with the more traditional wavy cap mushroom scavenged from the forest above me. It'll ease my journey into the spirit world; the mugwort will calm me, and sage is cleansing. With many of the traditional Haida sacred plants driven to extinction, it's the best Rowan and I could do. I thank their spirits for this kindness.

This may be my last journey. I fill my lungs with stale air and suck down the foul-tasting mixture.

The mix wastes no time. My body flushes, catching fire. It starts small, as though a salamander is sitting on my fingers and toes with kindling. It creeps inward, pain that isn't quite pain, burning with no destruction of flesh. I wish the pain would stop but finish its work.

My wish granted, inferno consumes body and soul. Distant screaming overwhelms my heartbeat. Concern flashes through my thoughts for Rowan, before it dawns that the screaming is my own and she has done nothing for it. How could she? This is my redemption, my moment.

Thought manifests as a spiked daemon and hovers in the air in front of me, drilling its guilt-laced claws into my chest and sinking its fangs into my shame. I meet its eyes—my eyes—before it bursts ethereal and washes over me in a sea of ice. I shiver, and the world fades to black.

BLOOD THRUMMING in my ears serves as a drum and spins me into blackness and oblivion. I fear I'll fall forever before the landscape of the World Between bursts into full color.

Bile rises in my throat. I freeze away tears. Fine ash rains from a charcoal sky, billowing into dust devils with each painful step.

My path cracks and shatters with obsidian shards, slashing my exposed feet. Rowan's ghostly image strides beside me, words as frail as spider silk.

"The Place Between," she explains to young me, "is your resting ground. It reflects the state of your soul in the moment you visit it. When you are well, the flowers bloom, waves lap against the shore, and your tree stretches to the heaven. Allow temptations to seize you, and the World will let you know..."

I choke back a round of tears. We met on the reservation where I grew up, back on Haida Gwaii. She took me in when I was ten, saw me for the twin spirit I was. Shamanic training ate every piece of my life that wasn't spent beating the Native out of me in school. She made sure I never forgot who I was under the white mask.

Poverty has a way of searing itself into one's skin, however, and soon the lust for more caught up with me. I was accepted to a prestigious American university and went into business. She made me promise I'd never use my powers for personal gain—shamanic training benefits the tribe, never the individual—and with all the brashness of youth I shattered that promise as soon as real challenge came my way.

Too many bad deals. My job at Goldman clung by a thread. So I took the first step down the obsidian road, manipulated the dreams and ambitions of CEO's from companies my clients traded in.

Rowan's image fades. I am alone at the center of a once-familiar path. I fall to my knees; they too sting and bleed. "It wasn't my fault! They forced me! The world forced me!" I scream, but the World doesn't waver. Judgment is absolute. Whatever lies I whisper to allow unfettered sleep change nothing here.

I force myself to my feet. Needle-like shards of obsidian sting my knees; cuts swarm and cry in my feet. I press on, fixed on the willow tree at the end of the path.

It has served as the gate between the worlds for the whole of my training. Skeletal branches crack and groan in a non-existent breeze; once blue-green leaves scatter on the desolate ground. Snake coils around its base, disappointment radiating from every shifting scale.

This time She's taken the form of a gopher snake, with alternating tiger stripes of eggshell white and steely grey.

The tree's roots curl in such a way that one finds it natural to sit there, and I settle into the soft ashes. My connection to Earth, Sea, and Sky is weak, wavering. I twine my own roots with the tree's, strain for it, find emptiness where the force of the Universe once dwelled.

A glimmer of light, of hope, but it shimmers just out of reach.

I seize the connection, squirming and writhing between my fingers, and it escapes. It hovers on the end of my extended fingertips, out of my grasp.

Cold scales around my ankle shock me back to focus. "Gull is always late," Snake intones, with no trace of a dragging S. "Greetings, Shephard."

"You haven't abandoned me."

"You still want to redeem yourself."

"I can wish all I want, but wishing won't make it so. Where's Gull?"

White feathers flash against the inky sky, the black wingtips blending in, red in His beak invisible until He settles and preens. His landing is dignified though not graceful, and he nods in my direction. No verbal acknowledgment this time.

I take a deep breath and ready my declaration. Sullied with sin, my shaman's spirit denies me the joy of connection and focus.

"I Journey to the Lower World to rescue Aria's soul. To..." I take a breath. "To fix my mistakes and atone for my sin." The words sound decisive yet my heart refuses to slow. Lungs cry, voice quivers.

Roots twist and expand into a tunnel leading into the deep places where the spirits dwell.

A jolt rockets down my spine. Ordinary reality seeps through, darkness and damp earth and silence. Suffocating heat and panic flash through me before the trance resumes. Snake's grip cuts off my circulation; my leg tingles and sparks with static. Outstretched hand invites Her to a more comfortable position on my arm, and She accepts.

"You must not forget why you're here." Gull's raspy voice slices through the stillness. "I will aid you only in your declared intent. Any further relationship depends on your actions."

Faith alone leads me underground. If I want any hope of returning to my former life I can't turn back, so blood-caked feet hit soft soil and I descend.

THE LOWER WORLD tunnel's consuming black can't be compared to anything in ordinary reality. The going is treacherous. Jutting roots snag at my robes. My feet slide through damp soil.

Static shifts and moves in my vision, giving form to darkness, bloodshot eyes and sharpened teeth, claws just out of reach. The soft scratchy sounds of thousands of insect legs and mandibles become menacing. A patch of brighter darkness takes sinister shape. Chills wrack my body and my throat closes, lungs freeze. Every muscle tries to stiffen, but my will prevails. It must.

To turn back is failure and death. Enough mistakes already weigh on my soul.

A breeze carries a whiff of fresh air through the tunnel, the slight scent of algae and flowers. "I must be getting close," I whisper, and my feet find firmer, drier purchase.

At last I reach the entrance. Endless dark opens into the landscape of the Lower World, the sky aflame in perpetual sunset and the leaves of the nearby maple and alder forest tinted in orange and gold.

I empty my lungs of stagnant air and revel in the freshness of my new surroundings. Sweetness stings my nostrils. I smile.

Snake stirs on my shoulder. "Follow the path," She whispers.

A worn footpath appears. Such is the nature of the Three Worlds. Even the Middle, closest to our reality, is unpredictable. My

feet smolder and smart, their wounds caked with mud and coagu-
lated blood.

"Do not fall off it," Gull warns, and I nod.

Distantly, a drum beat calls, commanding in its urgency, and I
spot a group of men dancing around a bonfire. My heart warms in
kinship. *My tribe*, my shaman's spirit whispers. Their hair is coal
black like mine, their eyes almond, as dark as hornbeam bark.
Shadows from their central bonfire enhance their tawny skin.

The drum seizes my feet.

Gull sinks his claws into my shoulder, but the pain is distant,
unreal. Distance between my ancestors and me melts away. They
call in a language both foreign and familiar, the drum shouts louder,
and I am drawn into the dance.

Firelight flashes as I writhe with them, drowning in the eternal
music. This is a war dance, celebrating force and will. For the first
time in my life, strength to act flows through me, to take command of
everything my timidity stopped me from defending. Time disappears until the drum ceases and I find myself facing the Chief.

"Ta'xit," Snake hisses. The God of Death in battle.

He's clothed in deer skin, His black hair bound with sinew.
Slung across His back is a spear near the length of His body, the
flint-sharpened bone tip glinting in the wan light. "You joined
the dance."

I nod.

"You came for this." He opens a clenched fist, and a tiny glowing
shard quivers in His palm. *Aria.*

"I came to make right."

He nods. "I require a price. Together, we'll right the wrongs
done to our people. Serve as my vessel, and stop the pale scourge
that has stolen our lands. The West will quake with fear at the sight.
Shamans wielding my godly power!"

His voice shakes the ground. Power flows through me, the
connection to Earth, Sea, and Sky solidifies in a blind fury. My chest
swells with pride, mind and heart alight with bloodlust.

A vision dances in my mind, His soul and mine entwine, leading His army, my ancestors. A merciless tsunami of wrath washing over the West destroys, ending the whitewashing forced upon my ancestors.

I am power. I am retribution. I am war.

Ta'xit's tendrils snake around my heart, binding me to the vision. Our spears and adzes destroy the West's mechanical weapons, lay waste to cities and military bases, slash the government's puppet strings. The furor of the dead restores the birthright of the living. Our people are free.

Gull's claws pierce my skin. Pain shocks me from my reverie; the world snaps back into focus.

"What they did to us is unacceptable," I hiss through gritted teeth. My gaze falls to the ground.

"Once the shamans were great warriors. They led our people to glory. You have the power to carry their legacy."

Rowan's words echo through my mind. Shamans are healers. But what Ta'xit says is also true, we were once warriors. The West took everything from us.

I sigh and shake my head. "Give me time to think" I say, and my chest aches. It hurts to turn from him.

"So be it." Ta'xit seizes the soul shard and transforms into a great black bird, larger even than Raven, and soars past the forest to the hills.

I'll be waiting in my longhouse. Face me there.

SUNSET SHADOWS crisscross into star patterns on the forest floor made ragged by discarded evergreen needles. The path plunges into the thick of them when the stars disappear into endless black. Once, this forest was bright, even in the perpetual sunset, wreathed in red and gold. Now my breath forms clouds before me, the chill piercing through the marrow and into my deepest self.

"Gull? Can you use your wings to guide me?" I glance at the

canopy. There's a hole just large enough for him to pierce, should he agree.

"As you wish." He nods, then takes flight. My shoulder aches despite his lightness. He disappears and I continue with Snake coiled around my right arm, dormant.

"Are you awake?"

She turns, cold eyes soften. "Yes, I am. You were brave."

"I deserve no praise for my past choices."

"True. But bravery can be for foolish or wise reasons. The balance lies in the state of one's soul."

"I'll make sure to choose correctly this time."

"Everyone is."

She lays her head on my shoulder and returns to dormancy. Roots and rocks snag and slip under my feet, and the sparse light-holes in the canopy come less often as I travel. My pulse quickens, my steps uncertain.

Where is Gull?

A flurry of wingbeats above me, not Gull but bats, and I'm plunged back into silence. Footsteps become oppressive, unease sets every nerve alight. Poised to flee, glancing from sky to ground, I slip into the depths with naught but my connection to Earth and Sky to guide me, a silver thread snaking along the path as thin as fishing line.

The ground melts, snares my feet, and swallows my legs to the knees. I claw and gasp for air; Snake doesn't stir. Arms also ensnared, struggling proves pointless. Darkness gains substance and presses me into the mire. My lungs fill with it. I sputter and drown.

Everything fades to white.

I slam into my office high in New York's towers, gearing up for another day of buying and selling securities. *It was one year ago, and yet I'm here again now. Does this mean I have a chance to change?* My body moves without my influence, my lips and throat form words I once said with confidence and wish I could erase. With each forced step, my hopes are crushed beneath the weight of the past.

The bright green leaves on my dwarf palm shimmer in the spring sunlight. The blue pot glistens with beads of fresh water.

I turn my attention back to Aria, who squirms under the weight of the briefcase she's holding. We went to college together, now she's my secretary, and I relish her company. She has a medical degree and is saving up to work with Doctors Without Borders. Why she ever left business school with her sharp wit and intelligence I'll never know.

My eyes glide along her curves, admiring the formfitting black dress she's chosen. It ends just above her knees, and my body suppresses a shudder. I want to stop the gaze, bury myself in shame, but the words come out regardless of my will.

"Sell the Genie options. They've peaked. Lock in the gains."

"Mr. Mercer? Are you sure? They're on the upswing..."

"Call it a gut feeling."

Aria's eyes sparkle admiration. By now, my "gut feelings" had become legendary. Insider trading is illegal, but the kind of "inside" I have is impossible to prove. What court would allow shamanic dream manipulation of CEOs into evidence? The judge would laugh the case right out of court.

"As you wish. I'll put in the order." She gives me her award-winning smile, all glistening teeth and brilliant blue eyes, and heads to the great glass double doors out of the office. I watch the way her hips swing, the way the dress shifts with her weight. We have a date scheduled for later tonight, and no doubt she chose the outfit for just that occasion.

Time drags as it had that day, a whirlwind of boring phone calls and arguments with clients, re-organization, and research for my next target. Playing the market like a mad god was my trademark. I had two penthouses, one in New York and one in Bellevue, Washington.

I watch, frozen, as I move and breathe and speak and suffer with

*no ability to change my choices, until the sun sets and she awaits me
at the door to the ground floor.*

Her gentleness astounds me, even now. There's a reason she
never made it in the cutthroat world of business. Other women in
her class were ruthless, but she cared too much, refused to take the
risks. She watched from afar and lived her dreams through me, and I
soaked up her admiration and kept it for myself. No wonder her soul
was weak.

I want to shake my head or shed a tear, but my alien body just
keeps bantering, pinching her rear to eruptions of surprised laughter, discussing everything and nothing, business, money, emptiness.
The waiter has our reservation when we arrive. Table wreathed in
satin, the waiter lays out the specials in a thick French accent as he
pours us each a glass of Cabernet.

She's dazzled by the diamond necklace I slip around her neck as
the entrees arrive, bloody steak and steamed broccoli and mussels
with garlic butter. The smells nauseate me as my stomach growls; I
fill myself and inwardly retch.

Make it stop, I scream, *don't take her!* Yet we finish our meal. I
wrap my hand around her waist and toss a Benjamin on the table for
the waiter with a wink. We slip into the limousine with the airport
in mind. I'm flush with alcohol induced confidence. I'd dazzle her
again tonight.

For years we've argued about the proper place for healing,
whether modern medicine is the solution for all the world's ills or
whether my practices still have a place in the wake of it. This time,
I'd have proof to back my argument. I thought she'd be mine forever
when I showed her the Place Between. *What a fool.*

We glide through security and head to our private terminal. My
pilot smiles and greets us, and the engines rumble.

The plane is narrow, with only six seats, two taken by private
security. They banter and laugh, likely tipsy themselves, and
propose a toast to "the lady of the evening," much to Aria's embarrassment. She'll adjust soon, I tell myself. I knew it was a lie.

Our pilot issues his standard instructions to snide comments and raucous laughter, and the engines rumble to life. My stomach drops. *Here we go again.*

<hr />

THERE ARE no words to describe the awe and sense of homecoming I feel crossing the Cascades at six in the morning. The sun is a shining orb peeking through a notch in the mountains to the east, the sky a blazing red sore behind them. Puget Sound sparkles as the Emerald City's lights switch off with the dawn.

Aria whimpers and stirs beneath my arm.

I smile.

My pilot lands and security trails behind us. We make our way through the massive airport to our ride. My thoughts center on my penthouse. I shake my head and direct my driver to the wilderness instead. He steps back, surprised, and a brief flash of my wad of bills convinces him. "Wherever you want to go, boss," he says in a thick Indian accent.

"Where are we going?" Aria whispers.

I kiss her nose. "Somewhere special."

One of the amazing things about Washington is its quick transition from endless stretches of pavement to pure wilderness. We're going to Tiger Mountain, ten miles into a hiking trail to a place called Silent Swamp, where a lone willow tree sits amidst a circle of stones. The stones are covered in moss, and the path is unpaved, writhing up and around the mountain and surrounding foothills.

The hike isn't challenging for me, but she huffs and puffs between stomach growls. I know she'll make it, and when we're done with the Journey she can eat. But the mix works best on an empty stomach, so we hike.

After a steep descent into near-black forest, the path opens onto a wooden foot bridge. Dragonflies dance over shallow water. A chorus of frogs sends love-calls into the still morning air. Willow, ancient, world-linking willow, sits where it always has, branches swaying in the breeze.

"It's beautiful," she breathes. "You grew up in this area?"

"No. I grew up in Canada, but my second home is a few hours out. We often visited Washington growing up. I have relatives here."

"I've never seen anything like it."

Stop! I scream, but my legs keep moving. We settle at the base of the tree where the gnarled branches invite a weary traveler to rest and steady our breathing from the hike. I pull my drum from my bag and release excess energy. Two wavy-cap mushrooms grow at the willow's base, I pluck them and hand her one, downing mine with a relaxed grin. Sacred herbs steep in my water bottle.

"Are you sure that's safe?"

I chuckle and hand her the mix. "As safe as it's ever been. I've taken some variation of this mix every time I've journeyed most of my life."

"But if those mushrooms contain psilocybin, in addition to being illegal, they'll also make you hallucinate every experience you have 'there'. How do you know any of it is real?"

"Oh, you'll know it's real when you come back with scars or wounds from the other side."

She purses her lips, but takes a swig anyway.

"I trust you."

I release excess energy one final time, and declare the purpose of my journey aloud. "I am traveling to the Place Between to show Aria its wonder."

The heartbeat rhythm begins, steady, entrancing. She closes her eyes; her breathing slows. I follow, spinning through the willow's roots to the World Between.

THE BLAZING AFTERNOON sun presses its warmth on my skin, tingling without burning. I find Aria standing, mouth agape, in wild-flower fields off the path—the World Between has a plateau and field instead of a swamp here—and we tumble together, giggling. Dragonfly flits over the field to greet us. Aria buries her face in my chest.

"Maybe soon she'll be able to speak to you," I say, and it dips low. A nod.

Winds from the south carry the smell of brine and ozone: a storm approaches. Clouds, black and menacing, solidify from nothing, and lightning strikes the southern hill. The ground trembles. In the distance, the vibration takes the form of thousands of bare feet trampling in unison, the clattering of reinforced bone weapons.

Take her, I scream, *run!* But the past me does not hear, hears no one, not even my inner spirit.

I stand, staring at the encroaching army, the silly grin still plastered on my face with the conceit of misplaced overconfidence.

She clings to my arm. Snake and Gull appear, confronting me.

"What is she doing here," Gull demands.

I shake my head. "That's not my current concern. Why has Ta'xit left the Forest?" *No wonder He was angry when I returned. No wonder He left me in the woods.*

Gull huffs and preens himself, Snake sways from side to side. "You brought someone from Outside here. With no training. Her soul is weak, and so is yours."

"Shephard? What's going on? Why the hell can they talk?" Aria's words fall on deaf ears.

Red blurs my vision, pride swallows me. I'm deaf to their declarations, even as my spirit decries my words. "Weak? I fought Ta'xit twice during my Initiation. I can stop him now."

"Ta'xit is no villain. If he comes, he has a reason." Gull doesn't try to hide His disgust before taking flight. Snake disappears into the grass. Deserted, I stand between Aria and the approaching army.

Ta'xit, in all His glory, grins. "Have you brought me a gift, Shephard?"

I grit my teeth, braced for a fight. His movement is swift. By the time I realize what He's done, Aria is gone and her glimmering spirit writhes in His hand.

"What rights have you?" I bellow, swinging my fist at His sacred face. He dodges me with little effort. Each parry and dodge fuels the coiled beast within me. It grows until my muscles ache with tension. I collapse, spent.

He stands over me and plants His foot on my chest, smirking. "This is a punishment, Shephard. Named by a mother who knew little of you. You abandoned your sacred duty, your tribe, your life. You chased after the West's gold and traded away your soul for it. I could take you just as I took her, but the greater punishment is to lose your prize. Your conquest was for her, was it not? Come get her."

Gods how I wanted to wipe that smirk right off his face! But coiled with that prideful beast lay recognition, and his words cut to the marrow. The clouds devour the sun, the earth roils and shakes.

"I deny you," I growl, and spit in his face. Claws crush my chest to powder, pain chokes out my breath. I disappear from the World Between and sit, alone, next to the body of my love, tears streaming from my face.

Frantic, I call my personal copter for an emergency pickup, and have to hike over two miles with her body slung over my back before I find a suitable landing site. She's whisked away to a hospital.

Concerned doctors tell me she must've collapsed from exhaustion or a stroke, but they find no signs. I know the truth.

Still, I let the theater play out for months, whispering to myself that nothing could've changed. I'd have no success without the manipulation, no job, the market forced me, my boss forced me, Aria forced me. I want to run, scream, hide, throw up, destroy myself, cease to exist.

I seize my breath and face it, shaky fingers typing out the number for my last hope: Rowan.

SHE AWAITS me at the willow in Silent Swamp. After her condemnations over the phone, I expected rage, frustration, even disappointment. When I find the courage to look, pity and pain stare back. Like the shaman she is, she bleeds for me, witnesses the wounds on my soul. Tears roll down her face, drip down her chin as I slip into the coffin. As soon as I find a comfortable position away from where it could impact me, she slams the lid and begins the burial.

I think it's over, and again I awaken in my office. I scream in my mind, shake, try to seize my body. My muscles move as they had in the memory, and once more I'm thrust through the events leading up to my burial.

Let me change it! I'm living the past, I can change the World Between, I can touch the kingdoms of Sea, Sky, and Land. Why can't I change the kingdom of Man?

I want to sob but the tears won't come. My eyes don't even ache. Helpless, I weep within, trapped in a prison of flesh and shame.

Even if I can't change the past, let me fix the present! Send me back to the path so I can pay for my sins!

Time freezes, the memory melts into black. I sink into the swamp, suffocating in blackness, before I awaken on the other side of the forest.

SQUINTING, I emerge from the trees into the now-blinding light of a thousand torches surrounding Ta'xit's great Longhouse of the Dead. Thousands of thunderous war drums cease. My face burns with the heat of my ancestors' collective gaze.

The path, now straight and open, leads to Ta'xit's wooden door. I try to swallow, and my parched throat rubs against itself.

A winged shadow coalesces above me; Gull lands on my shoulder. "You passed," He says. Forgiveness and pride radiate from His gaze.

Snake stirs, yawns, and stares at me. Her smile, though not physical, warms my shaman spirit. "Go," She says, and I do. Thousands of heads turn as I follow the path, the heat now on my back, and I knock.

"You made it." Ta'xit's voice booms. The door swings open and I'm pulled inside. The great log door slams shut behind me, and I am beckoned to the center of the longhouse.

"Have you considered my offer?"

My chest tightens. Pain shoots from my heart through my arms. "Yes, I've considered."

"What is your choice?" His brow furrows, eyes drive themselves into my soul.

My breath catches, and the pain intensifies. It's as though he'd driven that spear through my skull and into my chest. "I cannot accept." I dig my fingernails into my thighs and meet his gaze. "Shamans are healers. What happened is wrong, but violence can't heal our broken lands any more than acquiescence and white-washing have."

"This isn't what you want."

The vision from before flashes through my mind, bloodshed, glee, revenge. I swallow it along with my pride, and sink the violent energy into the earth.

"What I want isn't always what I need."

Snake nods, Gull fluffs his feathers and preens himself.

"Then I owe you nothing." He rises and heads toward the door.

I swallow again. My throat is a desert filled with daggers. "We're not done. I still have something to offer."

He huffs, then settles. Shadows deepen and shift across his chiseled features. "I'm listening."

"A life for a life. I have sinned, my soul is sullied, but I will fight by your side, should you find a suitable shaman to be your vessel in the future. Take me into your Longhouse. I offer you my soul."

Surprise and anger flit across his face. He sighs and shakes his head. "You think a piece of her soul is worth the entirety of yours, a shaman, a warrior?"

I nod. She was always the less selfish of the two of us. This wasn't her mistake.

"I have forsaken my right to either of those titles. All I can do to fix this is end it."

He nods and grins. "As you wish."

THE LONGHOUSE DOOR SWINGS WIDE, and he shoves me onto the path. His dead army rises in unison at the sight, thousands of spear shafts slam into thousands of chests. He beams. This is His purpose, how He was once recognized.

My eyes well with tears, shoulders droop, feet drag. I don't fear my fate. When I exited the Forest, I knew this was the only solution. No, this is something more.

I ache for him. A great God of war, forsaken and alone in times of peace, only able to contact the few trained shamans left in the world after His people disappeared.

Even as he leads me to the bonfire at the center of his eternal camp, my spirit weeps. As I collapse to my knees, His voice rises with the crowd's. He releases Aria's spirit. It takes the shape of a golden dragonfly and flutters into the distance. It will make its way back to her: His protection surrounds it.

I smile through the tears and close my eyes. I open my arms wide and expose my chest as, for the first time in months, the tension drains from my body into the Earth. I have nothing. Aria is safe. My redemption is complete.

His joints crack, beads clack against the end of His spear. I wait for the blow, the bloodlust in his eyes still burns in my mind, but it never comes.

"What?"

BEHIND ME, a great golden eagle lands and transforms.

"Rowan!"

She holds her arms out wide, and I rush to embrace her.

"What are you doing here?" I exclaim.

"He is mine!" Ta'xit's bellow slashes through our joyful reunion.

Rowan's eyes narrow.

"I am here to claim my student, Chief."

"We struck a bargain. His soul is forfeit."

She shakes her head. Raven perches on her shoulder, Eagle lands nearby. Both are focused on Ta'xit.

"He let go of his selfishness," Eagle says. "That was the requirement for his retribution. He humbled himself before You."

"Shephard." Raven's raspy voice pulls me. "If you give up your ill-gotten gains and start over on your true path, your bargain with Ta'xit will be forgiven."

"You have no right!" Ta'xit's face reddens.

"I stand here on the Old Ones' authority," Rowan says. Raven and Eagle nod.

I turn to Gull.

"Did you know?"

He nods. "Rowan followed you. You are her student. When I left, I informed her of the trap Ta'xit left for you in the forest. You made it, so I knew you had a chance."

"I intervened with the Council on your behalf. Tia wants to see you, if you take the bargain."

I gasp. Tia, the god of non-violent death, had Her kingdom grow in recent years with the end of Haida participation in direct warfare. Her alliances throughout the Kingdom of Sky were well known, and had allowed Her to take up the mantle of God of Healing in addition to Her responsibility for the dead.

Ta'xit growls. "Of course my sister stuck her nose in."

"I've never met Her," I mumble. "Why...?"

"Because you're destined for great things. Your talent is clairvoyance, and you are a healer. You embraced your fate. She presides over healing spirits. There are also many totems that wish to meet you, including your House's totem, Dogfish."

I pause. Everything gone—my penthouse, my fortune, perhaps even Aria. Will she still want me?

Eagle shakes his head. "The path of the shaman is often a lonely one. Historically, few on the path took wives. If she loves you, she'll understand."

"I hate when you do that."

Eagle chuckles.

Raven's tail flicks. He fluffs his feathers. "What is your choice?"

Time slows. The vision, my memories, everything flashes before me. The weight drops on me, threatens to crush me into the earth.

"I accept the great responsibility," I whisper, "to my people, to the Forest, Sea, Sky, and Man. Walk the lonely path in service of those who need me. I am the needle that stitches wounded hearts, the thread that seals festering wounds, the healing winds of change." My words intensify until I bellow the last line of my oath, "I am a shaman."

As my connection to the Four Kingdoms returns, my posture straightens, filled with newfound strength.

Snake and Gull beam with pride.

"I accept."

The world around me melts, coalesces into white light.

EVERY MUSCLE CRIES, feet ache, newfound scratches and scars litter my body. I open my swollen eyes and squint. Rowan crouches above me, hand outstretched, the biggest grin I've ever seen on her face.

"You worried me, you know."

I nod and look away.

Rowan tilts my face towards hers and glowers.

"Feel no shame for what has already passed. You have a new life awaiting you. Follow through." She leans back, arms once more outstretched.

"I'll take care of it when I get back."

"You better. Now, let's go see Aria."

About the Author

Ashleigh Gauch is a Haida author currently living just south of her hometown Seattle, Washington. She went to college for nutrition but ultimately found her true passion not in the study of science, but in the genesis of science fiction.

Her work has been featured in the online periodical Bewildering Stories, Starward Tales from Manawaker Press, Uncommon Minds from Fighting Monkey Press, and the magazine Teaching Tolerance.

THANK YOU FOR READING UNCOMMON MINDS

We hope you have enjoyed the stories contained within. Please take a moment to leave a review!

The UnCommon Anthologies Series
UnCommonly Good: at all Retailers!
UnCommon Bodies: Available at all Retailers!
UnCommon Origins: Available at all Retailers!
UnCommon Minds: Available at all Retailers!
UnCommon Lands: Available at Amazon.com

To hear about more projects and writing opportunities from Fighting Monkey Press, check out our website at www.FightingMonkeyPress.com

59736239R10188

Made in the USA
San Bernardino, CA
07 December 2017